Th

The Book of Curses
And Their Remedies

J. Gerold

ISBN : 1-59457-650-5

To order additional copies, please contact us.
BookSurge, LLC
www.booksurge.com
1-866-308-6235
orders@booksurge.com

The Book of Curses

BOOK ONE

I.

The garage door opened and Dan drove inside. He turned off the engine and was immediately consumed with dread. He knew he had to go inside but he really didn't want to. He knew what was waiting for him and he wanted to do nothing more than restart the engine and burn rubber out of there. But he couldn't.

He opened the door that connected the garage to the kitchen and stepped through, very slowly. He couldn't have walked faster if he'd wanted to, for the very air inside the darkened kitchen seemed to be the consistency of heavy syrup mixed with molasses.

The sink faucet dripped. The drip was slow and loud, like cymbals crashing in slow motion. Dan ignored the sounds, however, as he walked across the room to the light switch. Even though he knew what he was going to see, he had to turn on the light. He then stared at the bloody footprints on the floor, his body and mind frozen in terror.

He didn't want to continue, but he had no choice. He entered the living room, his dread mounting.

Muffled voices floated towards him as he stepped onto the plush carpet, the shag soft under his feet. The voices were on the television. The evening news. As he rounded the corner, he saw the television was now off. The voices had ceased.

Billy sat on the floor in front of the couch, his usual spot to watch the tube. Billy usually watched cartoons, sitcoms and game shows, though, never the news. Dan didn't think it odd that his eight-year-old son was watching the news because he was too terrified to even think about it.

Spreading out in an irregular circle around Billy was a dark pool. The circle continued to expand, fueled by the opening in Billy's chest. A butcher knife was wedged between his ribs.

Dan tried to scream, but had no voice. All he could do was turn away, toward the stairs. The dreaded, horrible stairs. He didn't want to, but he had to go up. There was no turning back now.

His foot landed on the first step, the action creating a squishy sound. Dan looked down. The stair carpet was saturated with blood.

This is new, he thought, his mind amazingly calm as his body screamed out to turn and flee and never return. His brain had no control over his body at all. Dan would rather die than continue up the steps, but he had no choice. It wasn't up to his brain or his body whether or not he should continue. Something else was compelling him. And it was going to be very bad this time. He could feel it. It was going to be worse than ever before.

The blood flow increased, becoming a mini-waterfall down the steps. Dan's feet propelled him upward, through the flowing ichor, toward the bedroom. His entire being felt cold, his entire body one huge nerve about to reach aneurysm. He felt the stroke about to happen the very instant the closed bedroom door came into view.

The blood in front of the door was a half-inch thick, seeping out from under it, miring his shoes. His hand fell slowly upon the door handle.

A sudden shriek from downstairs startled him.

"Don't open the door, Daddy!" Billy screamed. Dan became so frightened he thought his nerves would catch fire. Billy was dead, yet the proximity of his son's voice made it sound like Billy had moved to the foot of the stairs. Dan didn't dare turn to look. He didn't want to see what he knew was there.

"You don't want to go in there, Daddy!"

Dan hurried up the steps, now more afraid of Billy than what lie ahead. He knew that what waited for him beyond the bedroom door was going to be the most terrifying, gruesome thing he'd ever seen, but couldn't go back. His hand gripped the knob and he slowly turned it, sensing a presence behind him larger than Billy, a presence wholly unnatural.

Abruptly, the bedroom door buckled outward and burst from its hinges. Dan was thrown backward like a twig caught in a dam burst as blood and pieces of door exploded into him, knocking him into a flood of crimson fluid.

As he was carried by the rapid current, all he could think of was that he hadn't seen Amy this time, hadn't seen her naked mutilated body lying in a wash of blood in their bed, her head between her legs, severed. He was thankful for that. But Billy, or whatever it had been behind him, had been very terrifying. Dan didn't like the fact that the dream was beginning to change. In the past, he had known what to expect. It had become less and less horrifying to have to go through the ritual. He didn't know if he could handle it changing on him now. The unknown, the unexpected made it all the more terrifying.

A familiar sound rang in his ears and he bolted upright in bed. It took him a moment to realize where he was and by the time he was fully awake, the ringing had ceased.

The noise had just been part of the dream, he realized. Thank God.

He settled back down and slept restlessly until dawn.

2.

The springs in the recliner squeaked loudly as Dan's full weight collapsed onto the cushion. "Thanks for helping me move, Sarah. I really appreciate it." He wiped his brow on his sleeve.

Sarah set down the box she was carrying. "Itch!" she cried, urgently scratching her nose. "I'm glad to help. You could be a good brother and reward me with a drink, though."

"All I've got is water." He got back up with a weary groan and walked to the kitchen, Sarah trailing. He grabbed a bottle of water from the fridge and tossed it to her. She caught it deftly and unscrewed the top. Dan retrieved another bottle for himself and leaned against the counter. Half the bottle was gone before he withdrew it from his mouth. He sat the bottle on the counter and surveyed his new kitchen.

"Nice old place, isn't it?"

"It's a great house, Dan." Sarah wandered back to the living room and threw herself into a recliner, her legs hanging over the arm. "I like old houses."

"Since when?" Dan asked, sitting on the arm of the sofa. "You *hate* old things."

"I'm starting to like them now," she decided, jutting out her lower lip. "Well, I guess I really *don't* like old things, but I like this house. I wish *I* could afford to live in an old house. *Any* house, actually."

"Moving in is the easy part," Dan said and looked up at the ceiling. "This place needs some remodeling. Like those stairs. They're treacherous. I think the boards are rotten. I think the upstairs hallway floor needs to be redone, too. I'm kind of anxious to get started, actually. It will help get my mind off things."

"Yeah," Sarah said. "But this house doesn't need *that* much remodeling. Unless, of course, you plan on totally transforming it."

"I don't know. I don't think so. I don't have any plans to totally redo *everything*. I don't know if I could do it if I wanted to. I may end up not doing anything at all." He shrugged.

"Well," Sarah said, looking at the ceiling. "It looks like the molding needs to be replaced."

Dan sighed. "The bathroom tile *and* the kitchen tile need to be replaced. The top of the chimney is a little crumbly. The wallpaper in the bedrooms upstairs needs to be stripped. I need to reshingle the roof—"

"Okay, okay," Sarah said. "Enough."

He grinned. "I'm also thinking of writing a book."

Sarah's brow crinkled. "Really? *You?*"

"Now, why is that so funny?"

"You're not the literary type, Dan," she pointed out with a grin. "Mr. Jock, Mr. Football, Mr. Beer Drinking, Heavy Metal Listening—"

"Okay, okay, I get your point," he said. "You can add Mr. Guitar to that list, too. I'm going to teach myself to play."

"Man, how are you going to find time to remodel the house with all that going on? Sounds like you're overextending yourself."

He shrugged. "Maybe. I've never been alone this long before, Sarah. I want to make sure I have enough to keep myself occupied."

"So you're going to try to do everything you've always wanted to do."

"Right. I'm sick of sitting around, watching television and going to work without ever having fulfilled any of my dreams. I have a chance to do whatever I want now. I have an entirely new life to live. I'm going to make the most of it. I think I need to."

"But you're not giving up football?"

"I might still catch a game here and there," he said then

took a deep breath. "Although, if I hadn't spent so much time watching games, I would have been able to spend more time with Amy and Billy. I want to take up new hobbies, Sarah. Maybe I'll even take up rock climbing or skydiving."

Sarah laughed. "Well, good luck finding time to do all of that." She stood up. "I've got to get going."

"I thought I was buying you lunch," he said. "You know, as a reward for helping me move."

"Oh, that's right, even though it's more like dinner now. It's after four-thirty."

"Really?" Dan looked at his watch. "Okay, dinner. Where do you want to go?"

Two hours later, Dan returned to his new home with a bag of groceries. A brisk wind followed him through the door. He flicked on the light and took the groceries to the kitchen. After they were put away, he realized the house was cold. He went out back to the woodshed. The previous owners had left behind a small supply of firewood, but it wouldn't last him long. He would have to get more wood soon; winter was only two months away.

He loaded as much wood into his arms as he could manage then stepped out into the brisk air. His eyes darted to the old oak tree that dominated the backyard. Standing tall and wide in the middle of the yard, it's stark branches stretched out in all directions, reaching for the night sky. Its leaves cushioned Dan's footsteps as he walked back to the house.

Dan walked through the kitchen, through the small dining area to the living room. He dropped the wood in the metal cradle by the fireplace, withdrew a newspaper from under the cradle and tore it into strips. He threw the crumpled strips into the fireplace then threw some of the smaller, splintery pieces of wood on top of them. He removed a long match from its box and ignited it. He touched the flame to the newspaper and it slowly spread. The flame was blown out by wind howling down the chimney. Dan made two more attempts at lighting before the wood finally caught.

He sat back, gazed at the fire, and then returned to the

kitchen for a beer. Just one, he told himself. He had bought some soda in an attempt to wean himself off alcohol and hoped it would work. If he hadn't been out drinking with his buddies every week, he would have been able to spend more time with Amy and Billy. When he thought about it, though, his buddies weren't really his friends, just a bunch of guys he always drank with. He had always known they weren't friends, but it hadn't mattered at the time. It hadn't made a difference until later. He definitely wouldn't be seeing them again. Besides, he'd moved to another state.

Dan stared at the beer then put it back. He opened a can of soda and took a sip. He coughed once, having tried to swallow with his windpipe. He carried the soda back to the warmth of the living room, still coughing.

He picked up the television remote and clicked the power button. The Patriots were beating the Ravens, 14 to 7. He watched a few minutes, but couldn't concentrate. He kept thinking about what he was going to do with the house. It was exhausting just thinking about it and he was already exhausted from moving. He had a new job to start in the morning, too.

He yawned. It was only eight o'clock, but he was sleepy. He turned the television off and stoked the fire for a few minutes. He stared into the coals, thinking a little about the past and a little about the future.

Finally, deigning it was safe to leave the fire alone for the night, he switched off the light and went upstairs. The steps groaned beneath his feet in the darkness. He switched on the hall light at the top of the stairs and headed across the hall to his bedroom. He yawned again. His head barely hit the pillow before he was sound asleep.

He awoke with a start. Somewhere a shutter was banging. He groggily rolled over while his brain processed what was happening. The source of the annoying noise was a room down the hall. The noise was harsh and grating, vibrating along the outside wall. It wasn't going to let him sleep.

Dan wiped the sleep from his eyes and slid out of bed. He groaned and padded down the darkened hallway to the source of the sound.

The screen of his computer stared dully at him as he entered. He walked past it to the window where the shutter had come loose. He unlatched the window and pulled it open. With both hands, he reached out to restrain the shutters. He pulled and fastened them shut. He was clad only in briefs and the cold night wind whistling through the shutter slats chilled him. He shivered, shut the window and headed back to his warm bed.

The sun was setting in Oahu. Next to Dan walked Amy, her long auburn hair fluttering in the breeze. She was wearing her blue-and-pink-pattern bikini, the one he had helped her pick out. Her eyes reflected the crimson-orange of the sun as she smiled at him.

Dan put his arm around her middle and drew her close. She was warm and soft and his skin tingled where he touched her skin. She slid her arm around his middle and leaned her head on his shoulder.

"I'm so glad we can spend time together like this," she said with a sigh. "I miss times like these."

"Me, too," he said. He turned and kissed the top of her head, her hair tickling his nose. He loved the smell of her hair, the smell of her skin. He loved everything about her. "I'm so happy when I'm with you. We will be happy for a very long time."

"Yesss..." Amy's reply turned into a hiss. She moved her hand from around his waist to take his hand. She slid her long, elegant fingers between his. "Billy sends you his love."

"Billy," he said, confused. Billy was back home with Dan's mother. Wasn't he? Was he even born yet? Wasn't this his honeymoon? He couldn't figure out what time in his life this was supposed to be. He seemed to be experiencing many different time periods at once. When he finally thought he had a grasp on the situation, he asked, "He will be starting first grade soon, won't he?"

Amy looked up at him, but didn't reply. She returned her head to his shoulder. They walked.

"How do you like your new house?"

Dan didn't think it was an unusual question for her to ask. "Oh, I like it fine. It's very nice. It needs some work, but nothing I can't handle. It was built in the 1850s."

"Dan," Amy said. She had stopped walking, her grip on his hand pulling him to a halt. She turned to face him, squeezing his hand with both of hers. "I want to tell you something. Something very important."

"What is it?"

She paused, her eyes cast down. "I want to tell you that it is okay for you to remarry if you want to. Billy and I are perfectly fine with it."

Dan gaped at her. What was she talking about? "But, Amy, *we're* married!"

She looked up and smiled sorrowfully, the wind blowing her hair into her face. "Yes, Dan, we are married." She then turned her head to look at something in the distance. Her brow wrinkled.

"What's wrong?" He turned to watch the ocean. Each wave that lapped across the sand was accompanied by a harsh banging sound. Wood against wood.

"I love you, Dan," Amy said.

He was about to reply in kind, but the scene abruptly faded. He was awake in bed, the sound of the shutter banging loudly, rapidly.

"God*damn*it!" he said.

He returned to the room and closed the shutters again. He noticed this time that the screw holding the hook in place was loose. That explained it. He screwed it in as tightly as he could with his thumbnail then tugged on the shutters to make sure they held. They did.

He returned to his bedroom.

3.

The morning air was crisp, his breath a trail of condensation behind him. He jogged several blocks down the street, getting a good look at his new neighborhood. Many of the houses in the area were survivors of the nineteenth century and he saw two from the Colonial Era. All of them were nicely kept with only a few empty lots among them. He found this sad in a way. Not even something as durable as a house lasted forever.

Six blocks out, he turned and headed back, albeit in a roundabout way. He encountered an old woman walking an Irish setter on the corner of his block.

"Good morning!" she exclaimed when he was close enough to hear.

"Hi," he breathed. He intended to keep going by, but she continued to talk.

"You just moved into the house there, didn't you?" she asked loudly.

"Yeah!" he exhaled, already several feet past her.

"Do you know anything about the place?" she called.

He stopped jogging and turned. "I know it was built in 1851."

"That's it?"

"Uh, yeah," he replied. Then, against his better judgment, asked, "Is there something you want to tell me about it?"

The woman stepped closer, her eyes locked on his. She appeared to be in her late seventies, her hair an unruly cloud that was the hue of barbecue smoke. The dog she held on a leash was currently sniffing the grass. The woman pulled the leash and the dog crouched. Its tail lifted and feces oozed from the animal's anus like a slug emerging from a hole in a tree. Dan looked quickly away, feeling slightly queasy. When the aroma hit, he nearly gagged.

"Someone was murdered in that house," the woman said gleefully.

"What?" Dan asked, his hand over his nose. "When?"

"Oh, it wasn't really *that* house," she clarified. "There was an older one built on the same site. It burned down."

"Really," Dan said, relieved. "That must have been a very long time ago."

"That doesn't mean shit." She let loose an explosive fart then yanked her dog down the sidewalk.

ॐ

A woman in her forties, hair bleached to her jaw-line, met him at the door of his new office. "Good morning, Dan! I'm Ella, your secretary."

"Hi, Ella," he said, clasping her hand. "Nice to meet you."

"Nice to meet *you*," She took her hand back. "All moved in now?"

"Uh, yes I am." Dan thought that his new boss must have told his employees about him. "I've still got a lot of boxes sitting around waiting to be unpacked, but other than that, I'm all settled in. It's a very nice neighborhood."

Ella smiled. "That's nice."

Dan smiled politely then noticed a woman in a short, pink business dress and jacket. She had kinky, dark blonde hair clipped together at the middle of her back. She smiled at Dan and stopped.

"Did you say you just moved?" she asked. "Where to?" Dan told her. "Oh, that *is* a nice area. Actually, I wouldn't mind living there myself. Too bad I can't afford a house." She smiled again. "Well, see ya." She turned and walked away, her bound locks bouncing ebulliently between her shoulder blades.

Dan was unable to tear his gaze from her, finding her astoundingly attractive. He had to force his attention back to Ella.

"That's a temp in accounting," Ella replied with a frown. "I forgot what her name is. Here, let me show you to your office."

He was busy the entire day, learning his new job. This included having a quick introductory meeting with the people he would be supervising. He was disappointed that the blonde-haired woman in pink wasn't one of his employees. Then again, maybe it was better that way. It would be too much of a distraction to have her under his supervision. It could cause problems later down the road. It was never a good thing to be incredibly attracted to a coworker. It always ended badly. At least, according to the stories he'd heard.

He saw the woman in pink again on the way to his car after work. She saw him and waved. He waved back.

"Worked late on your first day, huh?" she asked from twenty feet away, her voice echoey in the parking garage.

Dan glanced at his watch. It was nearly five-thirty. "I guess I did. Did you work late, too?"

"Yeah," she said, tossing her hair. "I'm trying to make a good impression, too. I just started last Thursday." She shrugged.

"That's the way to do it if you want to get on permanently," he replied.

"That's what I'm working for!" she said. Then, "I'm sorry, what is it you do?"

"I'm the Director of Insurance Services," he told her. "Dan."

"I'm Lettice," she said, coming closer. "Accounting temp."

"I knew that," he replied awkwardly. "Well, nice meeting you, Lettice."

She grinned. "Nice meeting you, too, Dan. Have fun in your new house."

"I will, thanks." He gazed back at her and went to unlock his car. He looked back to see that she was now at her car. She waved. He waved back. He felt very self-conscious and anxious as he got into his car.

What am I doing? he asked himself as he started his car. What would Amy think?

Lettice's car was ahead of his as he exited the parking

garage. She flashed her card to the laser that opened the garage gate and saw him in her rear view mirror. She waggled her fingers. He smiled and returned the wave.

Once outside, she turned left and he turned right.

It was sprinkling by the time Dan got home. A chubby woman wearing a large brown T-shirt and black jeans stood in his yard. She looked angry.

He rolled down his window, but before he could speak, she yelled, "I don't appreciate your dog shitting in my yard, Mister. Keep him on a leash or I'm calling Animal Control."

"I don't have a dog," he said calmly, rolling up the window. He turned his car engine off and got out. The woman intercepted him, waggling her finger at him.

"Then how do you explain all the piles of shit in everyone's yard *except* yours? No one *else* has a dog around here."

"Look, lady," he began. She was making him angry and he wasn't in the mood to be angry. "I don't own a pet of any kind and I know for a *fact* that there is an old lady in the neighborhood who has a dog because I met her this morning. Now, if you'll excuse me—"

He moved to walk past her.

"Then why hasn't your yard been crapped on?" she demanded, blocking him. "Can you tell me that, smartass?"

Dan took a moment to calm down and looked at the neighbors' yards on either side. There was one pile of canine feces on each one. The three houses across the street each had a pile of crap on their lawn. Dan's lawn was immaculate.

"How am I supposed to know?" he replied. He was weary of the woman and the drizzle. "Maybe dogs don't like the way my grass smells. I'd love to stand around here chatting, but I have a life outside dog shit."

He walked past her to his porch, glanced at her, waited for her to depart. She didn't move. She looked confused. She turned to look at the other yards and scratched her head.

"This has been going on for weeks," she told him.

"Well, there you go," Dan said. "I didn't start moving in until Thursday."

She glared at him then walked across his driveway to her house.

"Nice meeting you!" he shouted. He unlocked his door and stepped inside.

❧

"Hi, Ma."

"Hello, Dan. I just thought I'd call, see how everything's going."

"Just great, Ma. How's the family tree going?"

Dan found it better to direct the conversation toward her immediately, to preempt any probing questions she might ask about his personal life. He didn't want to discuss his feelings with her, or with anyone, for that matter. Especially the dreams. He'd made the mistake of mentioning them one time and now every time he talked to her, she brought it up.

"Oh, the family tree is going fine," she replied. "I just traced your father's line back to eleventh century France. Normandy, to be exact."

"Really," Dan said. He didn't think his mother sounded as happy as she would have otherwise. She was normally very excited about finding new information regarding the family tree. She had been trying to go farther back on Dan's father's line for a long time and had now finally made the breakthrough. She should have been more excited about it.

"What's wrong, Ma?" he asked.

She sighed. "Oh, your grandmother is in the hospital again. It's another stroke. A bad one this time. Really bad. I'm flying out to Seattle to see her tomorrow."

"Oh, man, that's awful," he told her, experiencing a heaviness in his chest. "I sure hope she's going to be all right."

"This is her fourth," Ma said. "I've heard most people don't survive more than three. The holidays won't be the same without her."

"Ma, don't talk that way. She'll be okay. Besides, she never comes out here for the holidays anyway."

"Yes, but I always talk to her on the phone." Ma sighed

again then paused. "So, how are you doing? All settled into your new house?"

Dan sat down uncomfortably on the couch, feeling the dread that accompanied the conversation floating his way. "Pretty much. Still got a bunch of stuff in boxes that I won't get to until this weekend. It's a big place. I can't wait for you to see it."

"I'll get out there some time," she said. "Still having the dreams?"

"No, Ma," he lied, rolling his eyes. "I haven't had them for a long time now."

"Good, but if you *do* start having them again, you have that number."

"Yes—" She had tried to get him to see a psychoanalyst and he had flatly refused. He felt there was nothing a psychoanalyst could do for him that time couldn't take care of. He just needed time to get over the murders. Time was the only cure, he believed. There was no rushing it.

"Actually, Ma, I had a nice dream the other night," he told her. "One where Amy and I were walking down a sandy beach."

"Well, that's good," she said, "but you need to move on. You need to find someone else. It's been well over a year now—"

"I wasn't aware of a time limit on grief," he replied coolly. "Is it written somewhere that I have to find someone else exactly one year after losing the love of my life to a crazed lunatic?"

"Well, no—"

"I just don't know that I'm ready for someone else right now, Ma," he said. "I don't know if I ever will be." A vision of Lettice came unbidden to him for a second. It was time to redirect the conversation. "So, eleventh century, huh? You must be excited. Any luck with your line?"

She sighed again. "No, it's a lost cause. I still can't find a record of any ancestors existing before my grandmother. It's as if my family line didn't exist before that! I haven't given up yet, though."

"Too bad grandma can't tell you anything about the family."

"Yes, well, I've got to go now, Dan," she said hurriedly. "Your father's home."

4.

"Mind if I join you?"

Dan's gaze traveled up from the paper he was reading. Lettice stood next to him clad in a white blouse and skirt with a short tan vest. He couldn't help but notice that the top two buttons were undone. A heart-shaped opal pendant glittered from its nestling place in the hollow of her throat.

He hastily folded the paper and stood. "Of course, of course! Please! Have a seat."

Lettice smiled. She sat across the table from him, placing her purse beside her in the booth. "Am I too late to order?"

"Uh, yeah, but I haven't gotten my food yet."

Just as Dan finished speaking, the waiter arrived to take Lettice's order. He nodded and quickly departed.

"I haven't seen you for a few days," he remarked. "I was beginning to think you were no longer working for the company."

"Actually, today is my last day," she replied

"Oh, really? That's too bad." He looked at her. "You mean, they're not taking you out to lunch on your last day?"

"Oh, no," she said with a nervous chuckle. "If I was a permanent employee, they might. But I'm just a temp. No one cares about temps."

I care, he almost said. "Well, I for one will miss seeing you around the office."

"Actually," she said, giving him a quirky smile, "I was hoping that you and I could continue to see each other."

Dan looked sharply at her, startled by her statement. The

last woman who had given a similar offer had been Amy. It felt very strange to hear it come from another woman.

"We could," he said, more than a little apprehensively. Images of him and Amy on their first date floated through his mind.

"You don't sound too sure of that," Lettice frowned.

"Well, I—" He was interrupted by his sandwich arriving. He thanked the waiter. To Lettice, he said, "It's just that you caught me off guard. I wasn't expecting you to say that."

"Yeah, right!" she exclaimed. "Like no girl has ever said that to you before."

"Actually, it's only happened once," he said. She looked at him quizzically. "I'm recently widowed."

She stared at him for a heartbeat then gasped. "Oh, I'm so sorry! I had no idea! D-Do, do you want me to go? I should just—" She started to get up.

"No, no, please stay," he insisted. "It's all right. She died over a year ago."

"But you're still not over it," she said, still standing. "Over her. Not over her."

"I can't say that I ever will be," he admitted solemnly. "But I've got to get on with my life, don't I? I would like to continue seeing you, Lettice."

"I don't know. Are you sure?"

"Yes, I'm sure."

She smiled and sat back down. "How about tonight, then?"

He grinned. "Okay. Dinner and a movie?"

"Sounds traditional," she replied. "But, okay. Pick me up at seven?"

"Okay," he said, unable to stop grinning. "Which movie do you want to see?"

Lettice shrugged. "Surprise me."

Lettice's hair stuck to the condensation of the car window

as Dan pushed her against it, his mouth pressing hard on hers. "Ow!" she cried, her hand going to her scalp.

"I'm sorry, I'm sorry!" Dan exclaimed immediately. "What did I do?"

"My hair's pulling." She reached back and smoothed it down. "Okay, you can continue now."

They resumed kissing, Dan's hand on Lettice's breast. The condensation on the windows increased, becoming as dense as sheet of ice.

Lettice finally pulled away. "Whew! It's hot in here, isn't it?"

"Yeah," Dan breathed. He gazed into her eyes then laughed nervously. "Shall we just—?"

"I'd love to," she said, her voice low and sultry as she straightened her top. "I've been wanting to see your house, Dan. It sounds like a neat old place."

"Uh, huh," was all Dan could say. His blood felt like it was boiling and he was suddenly very nervous, anxious. His hand shook as he started up the car. He hoped he could drive safely.

He glanced at Lettice and she smiled. His eyes dropped to her cleavage. I just had my hand there, he recalled with a goofy grin. His gaze then dropped to her legs.

"Watch out!" she cried.

Dan swerved to avoid an oncoming vehicle, his breath caught in his throat.

"Watch the road, silly, not me."

"Sorry," he said. "But I'd rather watch you."

"Thank for the compliment, but that's the way to get us both killed." She glanced sidelong at him, smiling promisingly.

They kissed in Dan's driveway, the act urgent. Dan's hand was inside Lettice's blouse, his fingers trying to wend their way under her bra. Lettice had to insist he stop until they got inside, though she, too, was flushed with heat and excitement. Dan reluctantly relented until they got through the front door. He flipped on the light then devoured her lips, making her laugh giddily.

"Aren't you going to show me around?" she asked, trying to catch her breath.

Dan's affection had moved downward. "Sure," he said, his voice muffled by her breasts. He straightened. "Okay." He slipped an arm around her middle and walked her into the living room.

"I sure like that fireplace," she remarked. "It looks nice and cozy. You play the guitar?"

"Barely," he said, wishing he'd remembered to put the instrument away. He hoped she wouldn't ask him to play anything. "Over there is the dining room and beyond that is the kitchen." He turned her toward the stairs. "Watch your step. I need to replace some of the boards. They're rotten."

"Looks like it," she observed.

Dan switched on the hall light. "There's the bathroom, that's the computer-slash- storage room and right here is my bedroom."

"Then this is our destination," she replied with a grin.

She faced him and unbuttoned her blouse, letting the garment slide slowly from her shoulders. Dan's eyes were instantly drawn to her nipples pressing hard against the sheer black material of her bra as she reached back to unfasten it. The straps fell down her upper arms, but she squeezed her arms to her breasts, keeping the garment from falling further. She batted her eyes exaggeratedly at Dan then giggled. He laughed nervously.

"Would you rather do it out here?" he inquired.

"Maybe another time," she said, finally letting the bra fall. She stepped into his arms and kissed him as she unbuttoned his shirt. She then pressed her breasts against his bare flesh, gazing up into his eyes. She drew his shirt the rest of the way from his body and began caressing his back and shoulder blades. She moved her arms to his shoulders, standing as close to him as she could. Pressing down with her arms, she heaved her body up and threw her legs around his middle.

Dan staggered back before steadying himself. "That was unexpected," he declared. He gripped her buttocks and spread his legs slightly in order to balance himself, two of his fingers slipping beneath her panties in the process. She kissed him as he tried to walk sideways into the bedroom.

He sat heavily upon the bed, Lettice still straddling him with her skirt hiked up around her waist.

They kissed extensively, hands exploring every fleshy nook and cranny. Lettice then stood up to remove her skirt and panties. She tugged off Dan's pants as he stared at her, then, before he could do it himself, she leaned forward to yank his underwear from him. She then stood up straight and saluted. Dan glanced from her to his erection and laughed. She giggled.

"Oh, condom," he exclaimed. He opened his drawer and started searching through it.

"It's not necessary," Lettice informed him. "I wear the patch. See?" She extended her posterior and pointed.

"I do," he replied with a grin. "But that only takes care of the pregnancy part."

"You've not been with anyone in over a year and before that, you were pretty monogamous, so I'm not overly concerned about catching anything from you."

"Great," he said. "That's good."

He bit his lip, his eyes still searching the drawer. He suddenly realized he was in a very sticky situation.

"I'd like to use a condom as a purely precautionary measure," he told her, heat flushing his face. How could he tell her that it was for his own peace of mind? He didn't think that she carried any kind of disease, but how could he be sure about that? He didn't really know that much about her, nothing about her sexual history. "Those patches aren't a hundred percent effective, are they?" he asked.

"Pretty much," she said. She had started to come closer but his words made her stop.

Dan found a condom and turned around. She had her back to him, arms crossed. He'd blown it, he realized. His bad luck had reared its ugly head again. The situation could be salvaged, though, he thought.

He had to think fast.

"I'm just so overly concerned of pregnancy, Lettice," he pleaded without letting it sound that way. "A baby is not something I want right now."

"Well, me neither," she said. She looked pointedly over her shoulder at him.

Dan didn't know what to say next. Even if she were no longer mad at him, the mood was still blown. He knew he could get back into it very quickly, but he didn't know if she could. If his previous experience with women were anything to go by, it was highly unlikely.

Lettice dropped her arms and turned around. "I'm sorry, Dan," she said, an apology in her eyes. "It's been a long time since I've been in a relationship, too. I guess I just overreacted. I just wanted this to be perfect. To tell the truth, I've been imagining this night ever since I first saw you."

Dan was still speechless, but he was in the mood again. He wasn't aware she felt that way about him. Of course, now he didn't know if she just wanted to have sex with him and nothing more or if she was expecting more out of the relationship. Hell, he didn't know what he wanted out of the relationship. Or if even a relationship was anything he wanted at all.

Don't panic, he told himself. Just concentrate on tonight. Worry about the future later.

When he still didn't reply, Lettice laughed and stepped forward with her arms outstretched. She embraced and kissed him. "How old is this condom anyway?" she asked, taking the item from his hand. "I don't think they make this brand anymore. Look, it expired five years ago." She and Dan both laughed as she tossed it over her shoulder. "Why don't we lie down for a while and see what develops?"

He smiled and joined her on the bed.

An erratic clacking sound woke Lettice from her fitful slumber. Her eyes opened to look directly into the sleeping face of Dan, his breathing just barely loud enough to be qualified as a snore. She couldn't help but reflect on their night of love with a gleeful, satisfied smile. She reached out and gently squeezed his arm. He didn't stir.

The clacking sound was very loud.

Lettice didn't want to get out of bed. Half her clothes were still in the hallway and it was cold in the house. Yet, she couldn't sleep with that irritating sound.

She spotted Dan's shirt lying on the floor in a beam of moonlight. She sat up and slid her feet out from under the blankets. The carpet was cool, but not cold. She picked up the shirt and donned it, buttoning the middle three buttons only. She started out into the hall.

She didn't want to risk waking Dan by turning on the light, so she walked down the hall in the dark. The sound was coming from the room where Dan had said his computer was. How could he sleep through that? Maybe he was used to it.

Lettice experienced sudden trepidation the instant she reached the door. She didn't understand the reasoning for it, so decided to ignore it. Why should she be suddenly scared to go into this room? It didn't make sense. She was starting to feel rather silly, though still a little anxious. She chuckled softly in spite of herself.

The door was ajar. She pushed it open.

The source of the noise was shutters banging in the wind. She could see them in the moonlight. One blew open as the other blew shut, clacking against the wooden window frame. The sound was very annoying and extremely loud, echoey. She was starting to develop a massive headache. She placed the fingers of one hand against her temple and started forward in the dark.

She reached out to grab the closed shutter while reaching for the open shutter with her other hand. She glimpsed something in the backyard as she drew the shutter toward her. It had looked like a person standing by the old oak tree. A prowler?

Curious, she opened the shutters again and screamed. She ran from the room and screamed and screamed and screamed.

A naked Dan was behind her in less than thirty seconds. "What's wrong?"

She shot into his arms, nearly knocking him into the wall. She sputtered and stammered and Dan couldn't understand a single thing she said until, "The shutters, Dan! The, the... *face!*"

"*What?*" She clung to him tightly, sobbing uncontrollably, hysterically. The shutters banged loudly, nearly drowning the both of them out.

"*That sound!*" Lettice screeched. She tried to bury one ear in the crook of Dan's neck while clamping her hand to the other. "That horrible, *horrible* sound! That *face!*"

"What face?" Dan wanted to know. "Lettice, what are you talking about? What happened?"

She couldn't stop sobbing and shaking. Her skin was ice cold and pale. "The face, oh, the face," she sobbed. "There was a face in the window, Dan. Oh, my God, it was hideous."

"A face in the window?" he repeated. "But this is the second floor."

"I know," she cried, looking him straight in the eye. She was utterly terrified. "But I saw it Dan. As clear as I'm seeing you right now. A horrible, hideous face."

He continued to hold Lettice until she calmed somewhat, while the banging continued. "I have to go close that," he declared finally. "I can't take it any more."

"Dan, don't!" Lettice cried, staying him with her arms. "Don't go in there."

He looked pointedly at her and she let him go. She watched him as he stepped into the room then looked around the hallway. She didn't want to be alone, but she certainly didn't want to go back into that room. She didn't know what to do so she didn't move at all.

Dan reached out and closed the shutters. He secured them with the clasp and gave them another test shove. They didn't budge. He stared at the shutters and, when they didn't fly open again, he left the room. He shut the door and switched on the hall light.

"Okay," he said, facing Lettice. "Exactly what happened?"

She groaned and rushed back into his arms. "Oh, Dan, I don't think I've ever been so scared. It was the most terrifying thing—"

"What? What?" he insisted.

She started to speak then became suddenly self-conscious. "Maybe you should put on some pants," she said, separating from him. "I don't want to associate what happened with your naked body." She began buttoning the shirt she wore the rest of the way.

Dan nodded and returned to the bedroom. He put on his underwear and pants while Lettice lingered in the doorway. When he was done, he went with her down to the kitchen. He microwaved some hot chocolate sat down next to her to her at the kitchen table.

He gave Lettice a large mug of the chocolate and, clutching it tightly, brought it to her lips. "Ow," she said. "This is still a little too hot." She sat the mug down on the table then propped her head in her hand.

"Okay," Dan said. "Are you ready to tell me what happened?"

Lettice drew a shallow breath. "I don't know if you'll believe what I have to say, but I'm pretty sure I saw a ghost, Dan."

"Really? A ghost?"

She nodded. "Haven't you seen it?"

"No."

She sighed, shuddered. "It was a horrible face, Dan. Really horrible."

"Yes." He reached out and touched her hand. She curled her fingers around his.

"It was a woman." She hesitated. "I had seen her in the backyard a second before I closed the shutters. I thought there was a prowler in your yard, so I opened them again—" She clenched her eyes shut and shivered. "She was right there, Dan. Looking at me! God, I wish I could forget it, but I can't. I never will."

"Of course," he said calmly.

She looked sharply at him. "You're just patronizing me."

"No!" he declared. "I believe everything you've said so far."

She looked down at her mug. "That wasn't the worst part. Except for her hair and, and her neck, she had no, no face! No face, Dan. No face at all! There was just a, a void there. I don't know how else to describe it. She gave off such an aura of pure hatred—" She shivered again. "Your house is haunted, Dan. No bones about it." She laughed nervously. "Ha, bones, get it?"

Dan sat back and looked at her as if she had just yanked an anaconda out of her nose. "Are you sure you weren't just dreaming?"

Her shoulders slumped. "God, I knew you didn't believe me."

"No, no. It's not that. I'm just trying to cover all of the bases here. Wouldn't you ask me the same thing?"

She looked at him then away. "I don't know. I have no idea. I only know what I saw and I wish to God I never had. I do know that I was awake, Dan. The shutters woke me up. I was naked when I got out of bed. I put this shirt on, for Christ's sake!" She pulled on the shirt for emphasis.

"Okay, okay." Dan exclaimed. "I believe you."

"Look, I don't believe in ghosts either, all right? But I know that whoever it was I saw could not have been a living person." She took a sip of chocolate. "I feel like I should go now."

"I don't want you to go."

"Well, I can't go back up there."

Dan was quiet for a moment. "Do you want me to take you home, then?"

She looked at him and sighed. She patted his hand. "No, not just yet. I haven't even showered or anything. And I'm starved."

"Let's go out, then," he said. "I hear the Danforth Inn has the greatest pancakes this side of Delaware."

She smiled and laughed through her nose. "Sounds good." She stood up. "Well, let's go get that shower before it gets too late. Look, it's five-thirty already." Dan smiled then hesitated. "Um, the shower's upstairs."

"But I don't have to walk by that room in order to get to it, do I?"

"Nope."

She took a deep breath. "I think I'm okay with that." She smiled.

❦

They dallied in the shower for awhile then got dressed. Lettice had to wear the same clothes from the previous night, but didn't complain. Dan didn't have to, but he wore his same clothes anyway, hoping it wouldn't make her feel any more isolated. She was feeling alone enough already, having been the only one to see a horrifying faceless woman in the house. Dan thought she still didn't quite believe that he believed her. He wasn't sure he really did, either. Above all that, he couldn't help but get a thrill recalling Lettice wearing his shirt and nothing else. That was the main reason he was wearing the shirt again. He couldn't glance down at it without picturing her in it.

After breakfast, Dan asked her what she'd like to do next. She looked at her watch.

"Shit," she muttered. "My friend Lane wanted to play tennis this afternoon. I completely forgot!"

"Understandable." He held and kissed her. "I'll just have to take you home then."

She rested her head against his shoulder. "I'm not really in the mood to play tennis, though," she said with a nervous laugh. "I'd rather spend the day with you."

Dan smoothed his hand up and down her back. "I'd like nothing more, but maybe you'd better stay away from me for a little while. Just a little. You need to get away from what happened last night."

She smiled wanly. "I'm sorry. Was I that much of a dud at breakfast?"

"Oh, no, no," he assured her. "Not at all. You've had a very strange, terrifying experience. I don't expect you to be Miss Sunshine after something like that."

She smiled and kissed him. "Thank God for you, Dan," she

whispered, her voice suddenly tiny. "I don't know what I would have done if you hadn't been there."

"You would have been just fine," he told her, secretly reveling in her compliment. He hadn't felt needed by someone for a long time.

"It's such a life changing experience," she said. "You just have no idea. I mean, you hear about people seeing ghosts, but you never expect to see one yourself. It really makes you think about things differently, you know?"

"Things like what?" he asked. "Life and death and Heaven and Hell?"

"Yeah," she sighed. "Those thoughts occurred to me during breakfast. I mean, what if there isn't a heaven or a hell and we all end up being ghosts, trapped here on earth forever? It's a pretty depressing thought, don't you think?"

"Unless those who become ghosts just don't want to move on," he replied. "Maybe they're just stubborn."

"I don't want to be stuck here forever, wandering around invisible most of the time."

"Me, either."

"Of course, if that ever were to happen, I'd like to be stuck here forever with you." She gave him a kiss.

"What, so we should make a suicide pact or something?"

She laughed. "Oh, and I suppose you have a problem with that?" She laughed again and so did he.

"I think you should keep your date with your friend," he stipulated. "We can see each other later on."

"Okay," she said reluctantly. "But only if you promise."

"I do. I'll call you."

"Not if I call you first."

He returned her to her apartment then returned home. He decided to go for a jog and changed into his sweats. He took the same route he normally did, but since it was a little later in the day than he was used to it felt strange, kind of irritating. It was quite a bit warmer and there were many more people walking about. He had to dodge them, having to slow his speed from time to time. The running helped him relax, however. He kept thinking of Lettice, of her experience with the face in the window. She had certainly seen something and, the more he thought about it, the more he was inclined to believe her. The apparition had certainly terrified her. Thinking about the incident was combative to his relaxing, however, so he shrugged it off. He then thought of what he and Lettice had been doing before the ghostly sighting, but it worked against his relaxing, too, though in a different way. He simply couldn't stop thinking about her.

"Hello, Mr. Smead."

He continued on his way until he realized that he had just been spoken to. He turned to see the old woman with the Irish setter. She was smiling at him.

"I'm sorry, are you speaking to me?" he asked.

She nodded. "Yes, I am, Mr. Smead."

"My name's not Smead," he informed her with a frown. "You must be mistaking me for someone else."

She continued to grin at him while her dog took a huge crap on his neighbor's lawn.   Dan didn't linger further. He turned and jogged quickly away before the woman could fart again.

He decided that it would be best to take a different jogging route in the future.

5.

"Your grandmother is in the hospital again."

"Oh, no."

He had just come in from jogging when the telephone rang. He was sweaty and out of breath and not in the mood for bad news.

"What's wrong this time?"

"She's had a stroke, Dan. She's in a coma." His mother took a deep breath then sighed. "She was doing fine this morning when I talked to her. I was telling her all about you and your move and about Sarah's troubles and I guess after she hung up she had the stroke. The doctors don't think she'll make it this time."

"That's terrible." Dan tried to feel sad for his mom's sake, but in actuality, he didn't feel any emotion whatsoever. He had never met his grandmother. She lived across the country in Washington and had been there for as long as Dan could remember. He'd spoken to her on the phone during the holidays, but he had never had any other contact with her. He hadn't spoken to his grandmother since he'd moved out of his parents' house years ago. It did make him sad that his mother was sad, though.

"How are you doing?" he asked her.

"Oh, fine, I guess," she sighed. "It's raining here again. Is it raining there?"

"Nope," he said. "No rain, no clouds even. I just got back from jogging. It's a little cold, but otherwise it's a pretty nice day."

"So, I guess you've got plans today then."

"Well, kind of. I was going to go out and get some wood for the stairs. I really need to fix them; they've nearly rotted through. The hallway is kind of bad, too, but not urgent. I was, uh," he began then smiled, anticipating his mother's reaction. "I met someone."

"Oh, Danny, you did!" she gushed. "Oh, that is so wonderful. That's such good news. What's her name?"

"Lettice."

"Lettice? That's a pretty name. I don't think I've ever met a Lettice before. She sounds French."

"Yeah, I guess so," he replied. "We haven't discussed genealogy yet. We have another date later this week..."

"Uh-huh. What does she look like?"

"Blonde hair, blue eyes." He shrugged. "She's really beautiful, Ma. And funny."

"Is she younger than you?"

"Yes, Ma, about five years. What difference does that make?"

"On, none at all, I'm just curious. Five years isn't too bad. How serious is it between you two?"

"I only just met her last Monday."

"Have you slept with her?"

"Ma!" he exclaimed. "That's kind of personal."

"Uh-huh. So you haven't then. That's okay, dear. No reason at all to go that fast. Six days isn't that long. How many dates have you had?"

"Just one," he sighed. He was suddenly very exhausted. His mother tended to wear him out. "I'd better let you go now, before this call gets any more expensive."

"O-kay," she said reluctantly. "Good luck, dear, with the house and the girl and everything. I will update you later on your grandmother's condition."

"Okay, Ma. Bye."

He dressed after a long shower and the telephone rang again.

It was Lettice. "Hey, how's it goin'?"

"Uh, great!" he replied happily. "I just got back from my run."

"You run? So do I. We should do it together sometime."

"Yeah, we should," he said. Hopefully in her neighborhood, he thought, thinking of the weird old lady.

"Yeah," she echoed enthusiastically. "Anyway, I'm calling to invite you to dinner. My place, six o'clock."

"Sounds great."

"I hope so," she said. "Otherwise you'll just find out how terrible a cook I am."

"Oh, I don't believe that," he said.

"You better not," she replied laughingly.

Dan laughed. "Oh, by the way, I'm so sorry about what happened last night."

"Oh, stop apologizing already," she insisted. "That sort of thing happens."

"It's just that I was really tired," he went on. "It's been a long, trying week and I guess I just needed the sleep."

"Oh, just stop it and come over. We can always try again, after dinner."

"Is that a promise?" he chuckled, looking at his watch. It was still several hours to six o'clock. "Maybe I should get a nap, just in case."

Lettice laughed. "You do whatever it is you think you need to do. Do you remember the way here?"

"Yeah. I'll be there, six o'clock sharp. Bye."

"Bye."

Lettice's apartment was part of a three-year-old complex in a new part of town. Her apartment wasn't that large, but the money she made as a temporary employee didn't allow for big rent payments.

She answered the door clad in blue jeans and a dark green sweater, her hair tied back. She greeted him with a peck on the cheek and one on the mouth.

Dan smelled a litter box immediately. A blue-point Siamese

lounged lazily on the couch. He stretched and yawned as Dan walked through the door.

"Dan, meet Simon," Lettice introduced. "Simon, Dan."

"Hi, Simon." Dan extended his hand for the cat to sniff. Simon's nose worked for a moment then jutted forward to slide across his fingers. Approval. Dan petted him, Simon's ears twitching. After thirty seconds of petting, Simon suddenly leapt off the couch to rub against Lettice's legs.

"Oh, Sime, I just fed you." She stepped over the feline toward Dan. "Dinner's almost ready." She leaned in to kiss him again. "Just a few more minutes. Make yourself comfortable."

Dan removed his jacket and sat on the couch, suddenly very nervous. He was still embarrassed that he had fallen asleep the previous night, although Lettice seemed fine with it. In the back of his mind, Dan thought she was just being polite and that in reality it had annoyed her. If that was the case, she didn't let it show. She remained in the kitchen for some time, humming to herself.

Dan decided to spend his waiting time surveying her apartment. It was very modest: a few knickknacks and wall hangings. He didn't give them too much attention, however, as he was finding it very difficult to relax.

He found himself gazing at the dining table in the corner of the room. Two places had been set and a tall, unlit burgundy candle had been placed in the center. He suddenly started to wonder if he should be here or not. Amy had been gone barely a year and here he was already in another woman's apartment. He felt like he shouldn't be here, like he shouldn't *ever* be with another woman. He felt like he was committing an unredeemable sin. It wasn't entirely because he had loved Amy and he felt that he was cheating on her somehow, but partly because he hadn't been completely up front with Lettice. He had certainly been tired that night, but that wasn't the whole story.

"What have you got planned for this Friday?" Lettice called from the kitchen.

"Huh, what?" he asked, startled from his thoughts. "Friday?"

She emerged with a large bowl of pasta. "Yeah, Friday. You know, Halloween?" She set the pasta on the table. "Your house would be perfect for a Halloween party," she added with a giggle.

"Very funny," he said with a grin.

"No other strange happenings?"

"Nope. Haven't seen or heard a thing."

Lettice leaned against the back of a chair. "Maybe you should get a psychic to check the place out," she said seriously.

"Maybe." What she said didn't properly register in his brain. He was too busy looking at her, looking at her clingy sweater and tight jeans.

She smiled and returned to the kitchen. "That's what they do in television shows and movies, anyway. Or do you still not believe me?"

"I believe you," he said. "I thought I told you that."

Lettice returned with a bowl of vegetables. She set it down on the table and stared at it. "Oh, drinks!" she exclaimed. "Is champagne okay?" She returned to the kitchen.

"Champagne's fine."

"It might loosen you up a little," she called back with a laugh.

"Actually," Dan began, his mouth suddenly dry. "I wanted to talk to you about that."

She returned with a bottle and two crystal glasses. She looked curiously at him. "You wanted to talk to me about what? No, wait. Let's sit down first."

Dan nodded. He got up and slid her chair out for her. She thanked him and he took the seat next to her. She poured the champagne and they toasted the evening.

Lettice took a sip. "Okay," she said. "What is it you wanted to talk to me about? Help yourself first, though."

He did, heaping his plate full of pasta and veggies. "Mm. This is good."

Lettice grinned and shrugged. "It's just something I threw together."

He smiled slyly, playfully hinting that she didn't care what she fed him. "Oh, I'm so lucky."

"I didn't mean it like that," she laughed. "I was trying to be modest."

He ate a few more bites of pasta and sipped some champagne. He looked up at Lettice to find her gazing at him expectantly.

He set down his fork. "I just wanted to tell you the entire truth about last night."

"Which part of last night? Seeing the ghost?"

"No, no," he said. His face felt hot. "The other part."

"Oh..." she said. Her smile faded somewhat. "What about it?"

"Well, it's true that I was tired, but tiredness wasn't the only reason for my lack of enthusiasm."

"Really." She looked at her plate. "Does it have to do with your wife?"

He paused, surprised. "Well, yeah, actually. It feels like I'm doing something wrong."

"No need to explain further," Lettice said. She reached out to pat his hand. "I had a girlfriend whose husband was killed by a gangbanger's stray bullet. He was just walking down the street, minding his own business and *blam*. Anyway, she had a really rough time there for a while. Then, about a year later, she met this other guy who—"

"My wife was murdered," he blurted, heat coming to his face. "My son, too." He looked down at his plate, suddenly not hungry anymore.

"You had a son?" she gasped. She gazed at him with sincere sympathy. "You never told me about that." She rose from her chair to stand beside him. She pulled his head against her side and wrapped an arm around him. "You poor man. No wonder you had a hard time. Well, difficult is probably the right word there," she added hastily.

"I probably should have mentioned it earlier," he said,

speaking into her stomach. "But I didn't think the time was right."

"You didn't want to chase me away," she finished for him. "I understand your reasoning, but I must tell you that it wouldn't have turned me away from you, not in the least."

"Really?" He looked into her beautiful blue eyes.

She nodded, pulling his head back against her.

"Well," he began, swallowing hard. His mouth was dry again. "I came home one night from work, like I always did. I parked in the garage and walked in through the kitchen. The television was on and so were all of the lights. I knew something was wrong right away. My son, Billy, didn't come running to greet me like he usually did and neither did Amy. She was in between jobs at the time, so she should have been home, waiting for me."

He took a deep breath.

"I walked into the living room and there was Billy. He—" His voice broke, a sob working up in his chest. "There was a butcher's knife..."

Lettice made a sympathetic sound and pressed him tighter to her.

"Amy was in the upstairs bedroom. Her arms and legs had been cut off."

He buried his face in her sweater and wept soundly. Lettice comforted him, stroking his hair and caressing him. When his sobbing subsided, she asked him if he was okay.

He nodded and sniffed then laughed nervously. He was more than a little embarrassed. "Sorry about that."

"Oh, no need to be sorry," she assured him tenderly. "No need to be sorry at all."

He sighed relief and wrapped his arms around her middle. Neither of them spoke for some time.

"Did they ever catch the guy?" she asked.

"Nope. They think it was a random killing. They didn't steal anything. Amy and I had no enemies that we were aware of. It's still unsolved."

"God, that's awful, Dan," she said. He noticed that her eyes were red, as if she too had been crying. "We can take it slow if that make you feel more comfortable. Whatever you want to do is fine with me."

"Actually," he said with a slow grin. "I was looking forward to tonight."

"Well, you certainly recovered fast," she said, returning the grin. "I was looking forward to tonight, too." She slipped away toward her chair. "But at least have some more champagne."

She poured him another glass, hesitated, and then poured herself another. They drank and looked at each other, giggled and dribbled champagne down their chins.

Lettice leapt up. "I'll be right back." She ran her hand up his arm on the way to her bedroom. She also dimmed the lights.

Dan gulped his champagne and wiped his mouth on his sleeve. He was about to stand up when Simon abruptly jumped onto his lap. Simon stretched his neck forward, shoving his nose against Dan's plate. Dan stood up then deposited the cat into the chair.

"Bon apetit, Simon."

6.

"What the hell is he doing over there?"

Damita turned angrily from the window, hating her new neighbor ardently. She had liked it better when no one had lived there. Nothing about it had annoyed her then.

"Mom!" her fourteen-year-old son Andres called from the living room. "Something's burning." His eyes remained focused on the television screen, his fighter kicking the head of his opponent, blood spraying outward.

"There sure is," Damita muttered, peeking through the curtain again. "I'll tell you what's burning: my neighbor in Hell!" She picked up the telephone and called the police. Then she smelled the smoke. "My T-bones!" She ran into the kitchen, yanked open the oven door and pulled out the broiler pan with one bare hand. "Ow! Fuck!"

The meat was charred beyond edibility. The kitchen and dining room were choked with black smoke.

"Goddamn fuckin' sonovabitch!"

"Beg your pardon?"

"Oh, not you!" she said into the phone. "I want you guys to do something about my neighbor."

When she had finished speaking to the police, she went out to her driveway to await their arrival. The loud racket next door continued, all of the lights in the house flashing. It sounded like every pot, pan, glass, bowl, plate, saucer, pitcher, skillet, vase, light bulb, coffeepot and lamp were being thrown around inside the house while at the same time every door, cupboard and drawer were being opened and closed forcefully, repeatedly.

Damita grimaced angrily. "How the hell can one man make so much *fucking noise?* He's got to have other people in there helping him. Fuckin' idiots."

"Mom, what's going on?" Andres asked from the porch. "What are they doing over there?"

"You just now noticed it, did you?" she snapped. "Finally something outside your own little video game world grabbed your attention, did it? That's a first."

Andres hesitated before he asked, "Did you call the police?"

"Yes," she returned angrily. "A long time ago. They should be here by now."

"What?" Andres called. "I can't hear you!"

"Yes!"

Andres flinched and retreated inside.

A blue and white car arrived. The officer on the passenger side got out. "What's going on here?" he asked. His partner, a woman with short blonde hair, emerged from the driver's seat. Both officers gazed at the noisy house.

"That's what I called you about!" Damita barked. "It's about time you got here. That's asshole's been driving me nuts with that shit for hours."

"How long's it been going on?" asked the policewoman with a nod.

"Almost a half an hour."

"Sounds like they're trashing the place," commented the policeman.

He and his partner walked up on the porch and rang the doorbell. The screen door flew open and smacked him in the face.

"Are you all right?" inquired his partner.

"Yeah, yeah," he told her, rubbing his jaw. "Must be a faulty hinge." The main, wooden door had remained shut. He rang the doorbell again. The racket inside ceased.

The cops drew their weapons. The policewoman stood to one side as the policeman tried kicking the door down. The door didn't budge.

"Markowitz, what are you doing?" his partner asked. "That door is solid oak."

"So it is, Neilssen," he said with a grimace. The front door then gently opened, hinges creaking softly.

Markowitz looked to Neilssen who shrugged. "Police!" he shouted into the darkness. To his partner, "Guess I should have announced that before, huh?"

"They probably wouldn't have heard you." She glanced over her shoulder to see Damita standing on the porch steps, trying to look inside the house. Neilssen ignored her and followed Markowitz inside.

They emerged from the house a short time later. "Everything seems to be fine," Markowitz informed Damita. "No one's home."

Damita was aghast. "But all that noise! Are you sure you looked everywhere?"

"There's no one home, Ma'am," Neilssen told her.

"B-But, the noise. The light flashing. You guys saw it."

"Yes," Markowitz said. "It must have been either a television or a radio that went off just when we arrived."

Damita gaped at them, amazed. "Now, how would it do that?"

"A timer, apparently," Neilssen supplied. "I can't explain it otherwise." She and her partner exchanged glances, but said nothing.

"Can't you do anything?" Damita persisted.

"No, Ma'am," said Markowitz. "Let's just forget all about this little episode, shall we?" He and Neilssen returned to the police car.

"But I heard something!" Damita shouted at the car. "I saw it!"

"Go back inside, ma'am."

Damita made an exasperated sound then turned to raise her fist at the house. "I know you're up to something, asshole. And I'm going to find out what it is!"

Lettice's bra fell silently to the floor, her eyes fixed seductively on Dan.

"Simply magnificent," he stated, his voice barely a whisper.

She smiled then shimmied out of her panties. She displayed herself to him with a pirouette. "Well, what are you waiting for?"

"Oh," he said. He removed his underwear and stepped into the embrace of her arms and lips. When she felt something prodding her, she looked pointedly at him.

"I told you I'd make up for last night," he said. He then startled her by sweeping her into his arms. He carried her to the bed and deposited her gently. He then threw himself on the mattress next to her, causing them both to bounce into each other.

"Ow!" Lettice cried when Dan's elbow collided with her breast.

"Oh, sorry!" he exclaimed. "I didn't know your bed was so springy."

"Don't worry about it," she said, drawing his head to hers. She kissed him passionately. She took his hand and brought it to her breast. He caressed her, his hand lingering momentarily before moving between her legs. Lettice gasped then made a soft purring sound.

"Can you feel how ready I am?" she asked.

"Yes."

He moved his fingers against the one external part of her body that was the most sensitive. She gasped then shoved him onto his back. She threw a leg over him and kissed him hard on the mouth, her tongue intertwining with his.

She moved against him, hastening effortless penetration. Each of them groaned pleasurably then began moving as one, slowly, as if they were a heavy flag flapping in a lazy wind.

"Mm," Lettice hummed. "I like it like this."

"Me, too," he breathed.

A slow grin pulled her lips from her teeth. "But I like it fast, too."

Dan smiled back. Gripping her upper thighs, he increased the rhythm. Their motion equaling the motion of a boat caught on a tumultuous wave. The breathing came faster, the blood pumped faster. Dan could only think of the feel of Lettice, inside and out, could only think of keeping her on top of him, enveloping him. His desire was reaching a crescendo and he could feel his climax rising.

Lettice threw her head back then brought her body down on his. She clung to him, pressing her fiery skin to his, her hands hooking under his shoulders as they increased their pelvic motions.

All Dan could hear was her erratic, yet rhythmic hot breath in his ear. He knew she was about to reach orgasm and he was on the verge. If he could time it out right, they could climax simultaneously.

He was aware of his own grunts and groans. The sounds grew louder in his ears. He was louder than Lettice, but he didn't drown her out. He was on the verge. She was on the verge.

Then he slipped.

"Ow!" the lovers cried out as one.

As Lettice withdrew from him, he ejaculated. It shot up her abdomen, belly, breasts and neck. She fell onto her back and cried out. "Ugh!"

"Oh, my God!" Dan cried. "Are you okay?"

"You stabbed me," she cried. She reached down to examine the afflicted area. She winced, sucking in breath. "It hurts!"

"I know, I'm sorry," he said. "I slipped."

Lettice turned her head away and her body started quivering. Dan thought she was crying, but it was laughter he heard an instant later.

"What?" he asked, alarmed.

She turned her face to him. "This whole thing!" she said, laughing again. She reached down and pulled up the corner of the blanket hanging down to the floor, wiped herself with it.

Dan was humiliated. He stared up at the ceiling. "I've screwed everything up."

"No, you haven't," Lettice told him. "You didn't puncture a new hole in me, so everything's fine."

Dan laughed in spite of himself. "Well, that's one good thing, I guess."

She looked askance at him. "What do you mean? It felt good, didn't it?"

"Well, yeah—"

"Then there's more than one good thing about it." She scooted over to him. "That's just one of those things that happens every once in a while. Life isn't perfect."

"Has it happened to you before?" he asked. Thinking better of it, he said, "No, wait. I don't want to know."

She smiled at him, placing her hand on his shoulder. "There's always next time." She squeezed his shoulder. "Man, you're tense. Roll over."

He did as ordered. Lettice straddled the backs of his thighs, her fingers kneading the flesh of his upper back. "You're not suppose to be this tense after sex, you know," she pointed out. "You should be relaxed."

"I know," he sighed. "It's just that—Oh, I don't know. Ah, that feels good!"

"It's just that what?"

Dan hesitated. He wanted to just let her fantastic fingers work their magic and ignore his troublesome thoughts. However, she had asked. "It just seems like too many bad things happen to me."

"What do you mean by too many?" She found a knot on his shoulder blade and started to work it out.

"Ah, ah!" he cried. "Right there, that's it."

"Everyone has bad things happen to them, Dan."

"Ow, ah, I know." He sighed. "It just seems like more bad things happen to me than most people."

"Like what?"

"Well, Amy and Billy, of course," he said. "Those are the two biggest. There are a myriad of other, smaller things that have happened—"

"Are you saying that our sex life is a smaller thing?" she interrupted.

"Uh..."

She laughed. "I'm just teasing. I know what you mean. But you've had some good things happen to you, too. I mean, you're a supervisor in a big company, you make good money, and you were able to buy that house. You met me."

He looked over his shoulder and smiled. "Yes, meeting you was a very good thing," he admitted. "But the only reason I got the supervisory job was because the previous guy was arrested for embezzlement and they needed someone fast. I don't think there was even anyone else on the list. I didn't get it because they think I'm qualified, I got it because they needed someone real bad, whether they were right for the job or not. I just happened to be in the right place at the right time."

"It's still a good thing, though," she said. "You lucked out."

"Maybe," he replied. "I'm not so sure I like the job, though."

"You've only been there a week."

"Yeah, but from what I'm seeing already... I don't know. You ever start having a bad feeling about people for no good reason?"

"Not for no good reason," she said. "There's always a reason. You either just don't know what the reason is or you refuse to recognize it."

"Yeah, I guess," he sighed. "I just think my boss has the potential of being a total jackoff." Lettice chuckled, making him laugh in turn.

"Now, your marriage," she said. "There's another good thing."

"It was a great marriage," he agreed. "For the most part."

Lettice made a clicking sound with her tongue and stopped massaging. "Okay, what happened?"

He looked over his shoulder again and took a breath. "There was a rocky period just after the wedding," he told her. "Before we had Billy, Amy and I nearly divorced."

"Really? Why?"

"Because of my family."

Lettice pressed her body against him, her arms outside of his, squeezing. She waited for him to continue.

"My dad didn't like her because she was originally from California," he explained.

"What?" Lettice asked. "That's stupid. Why?"

"Well, all I know is that he thinks Californians are rich, fat, spoiled and lazy and he hates them all because of it. I don't know where he gets such ludicrous ideas."

"That's pretty ludicrous," she said. "Your father must be a very small man."

Dan paused. "I don't know. I've never seen him naked."

"I didn't mean it like that!" she exclaimed with a laugh.

Dan chuckled. "I need to roll over. This is getting uncomfortable."

He rolled onto his back and Lettice lay on her side, an arm and a leg thrown over him.

"Anyway, there was a big blow up that first Thanksgiving," he continued. "I started yelling at him. He just can't keep his mouth shut, can't stop being so antagonistic. He was looking for a reason to fight." He sighed again. "I don't know. I just couldn't take it anymore. I haven't spoken to him since. And the rest of my family keeps defending him instead of trying to patch things up. They just push me further and further away. Except for my sister. And my mom, half of the time."

Lettice stroked his chest. "Family infighting can be rough."

"Do you have a large family?"

"Not really. Just me and my mom and an aunt. There are a bunch of cousins in Kansas whom I don't know. Have you even tried to talk to your father again?"

"Nope," he said curtly, his lips tight against his teeth. "Not until he apologizes to me. He acts like nothing ever happened and expects me to forget and forgive and act like nothing happened. I don't think so. I get so mad just thinking about it. I hate him so much."

"You don't mean that."

"I really do," he told her. "At least most of the time. I'll be going along with my life, minding my own business, then something will remind me of him and I'll get pissed off all over again."

Lettice paused. "You're a psychiatrist's dream, aren't you?"

Dan had to laugh. "Yeah, I guess I am. But I'm not about to fall into that trap. Ever notice how people who see psychiatrists never seem to get any better? They always end up going to them for the rest of their lives. Besides, with my luck, my psychiatrist would be on the verge of a psychotic episode and my story would be the last straw that broke the camel's back. He'd probably end up on the roof with an AK47 or something. I don't need that kind of crap in my life, thank you very much."

Lettice said nothing. Dan saw her from the corner of his eye, gazing at his face. He turned to her.

"What?"

She paused before answering. "Before today, I had no idea just how much emotional pain you deal with on a day-to-day basis. It's mind boggling."

Dan looked at her then fell back onto the pillow. "Oh, great. Now I've turned you away."

"No, no," Lettice insisted. "Not at all. I like you a lot, Dan, and I can tell you don't go around telling everybody about your problems. You are a very private person and I feel honored that you have poured your heart out to me. I mean that." She took his hand in both of hers and placed it to her breast.

He gazed into her eyes. "You are the best thing that's happened to me in a really long time," he whispered. "You know that?"

Lettice smiled then pulled the rest of his body to her.

7

Dan returned home mid-morning Sunday. A nasty note from his neighbor taped to the door welcomed him. "What the hell are you doing?" was all it read.

He crumpled it up, unable to make sense of it. The woman's crazy, he decided, having no time to think about her. He wanted to get started on replacing the inside stairs.

Clad in jeans and an old work shirt, Dan plodded down to the basement to get his tools. He took measurements of the steps then started making cuts. He put newspaper down in the kitchen and used his band saw to size the replacement steps. It was a little too quiet once he was finished with the saw, so he deposited a Foo Fighters CD in the player then began tearing up the old boards.

Before he tore up the fourth step from the top, he noticed the corner of a yellowed piece of paper sticking up. He completely removed fourth step and retrieved the paper.

Only the exposed corner was yellow and it wasn't just a piece of paper. It was a Christmas card depicting Santa with a bag overflowing with toys and one foot inside a chimney. In the top right hand corner in red, was the date: 1937.

Dan opened the card. "To Mom and Dad," the long, drawn-out handwriting began. "Hope you had a wonderful Xmas without me this year. Things w/me and Harold are simply grand. Winters in So. Dakota are rough, though. So much snow! See you next year – Love, Savannah Smead."

Dan snorted in surprise. Savannah was his grandmother's name. Johnson, however, not Smead. Still, it was an odd coincidence. And where had he heard the name Smead recently? He knew that there was a company called Smead which manufactured envelopes or something, but that wasn't it. Oh, yes. That weird old lady with the dog. She had called him Smead. It was an even stranger, though convoluted, coincidence. And how had that card slipped into this crack? It would have had to fall at a diagonal angle in order to avoid the lip of the third step hanging over it. It wasn't impossible, just highly unlikely. Strange things happened sometimes.

The telephone rang. He paused the Foo Fighters CD and answered. Before he could say hello, his mother said, "Your grandmother was awake a few minutes ago. She was babbling something about a curse and how the house you moved into is haunted and that you should move out immediately." She paused then said, "I think the medication is giving her nightmares."

Dan looked at the card in his hand, momentarily speechless. Speaking of strange, this phone call would certainly qualify! "Haunted?" he finally was able to sputter. "How would she know that?"

"I don't know," his mother sighed. "She's either lost it or—" She sighed again.

"Actually, Ma," Dan began, his mouth extremely dry all of a sudden. He hurried to the kitchen to get a soda, the phone clutched tightly to his ear. "Remember that girl I told you about? Lettice? She told me she saw a faceless woman in an upstairs window the night she stayed over."

"Really?" his mother gasped. "She stayed over one night?" She couldn't hide the concern and disdain in her voice.

"Yes, Ma," he replied wearily. "She stayed over."

She paused. "She's not a druggie, is she?"

"No, Ma," Dan sighed. "Do you think I would date a drug addict?"

"You haven't known her long enough to know if she does drugs or not."

"Ma, I know she's not an addict. Believe me, I can tell." She had succeeded in angering him as she often did. "Ma, I gotta go. I'm right in the middle of something here. I just started remodeling the stairs—"

His mother's words were sharp and short. "Okay, bye." She hung up.

Goddamnit! Dan thought, tossing the phone on the couch. I wanted to tell her about the Christmas card. But no, she has to bring up drugs and piss me off. Lettice a junkie? Give me a break.

He decided to call his sister.

"Okay," Sarah said, throwing her coat on the couch. "What is it you want to show me?"

He shoved the card into her hands. "Look at the names," he told her. "Doesn't it seem strange that the name matches Gramma's?"

"Yeah, Dan, but this woman is named Smead. There were no Smeads in our family last time I checked." She handed the card back.

"No, but some weird old lady called me Mr. Smead."

Sarah shrugged. "So? Coincidence."

"Coincidence," he repeated. "Why, of all names, would she call me that out of the blue? Huh?"

"Maybe she knew the people in the card," Sarah said. "I don't know."

"That's possible," Dan said pensively. "She certainly looks old enough to have known anyone living here back in the thirties. It just sounds weird, you know?" He sat down on the couch, staring at the card. "Of course, she would have been a child back then."

"Sounds to me like you're looking for a plot for that novel of yours," Sarah said with a grin.

"What? Oh, I've already forgotten about that," he told her. "I still want to do it, but I haven't even thought of it. I've been too busy this past week."

"So what are you thinking then?" she asked. "Do you think that Gramma lived a secret life in this house under a different name?"

"No, the woman in the card was in South Dakota. Her parents lived here."

Sarah sighed. "You asked me to come out here from Connecticut for this?"

"Something else happened," he said. "Something strange. Well, for starters, have you talked to Ma today?"

She hadn't. "Well, anyway, I'm seeing someone."

"What, a shrink?"

"No," he replied. "A woman."

Sarah laughed then congratulated him. "Way to go, bro!" She swatted him on the arm. "Why didn't you tell me?"

"I just did," he said, the proceeded with what he wanted to say. "Anyway, she saw a ghost here Friday night."

"What? Really? Where?"

Dan stood up. "I'll show you." She followed him upstairs, avoiding the missing stair before he could warn her. "It was in this room over here."

Sarah looked in, her arms crossed. "She saw it in here?"

"In the window, actually. Behind the computer." He paused as they both looked at the window. "You know, I was having problems with these shutters before that. They kept coming loose and banging in the wind. That's what they were doing when she came in here. They woke her up."

"It's really cold in here, Dan," Sarah said, arms folded. "Whether it's from the ghost or bad heating, I don't know."

"Ghosts make things cold?"

Sarah nodded. "From what I've read, anyway. Dormant spirits tend to come to life when a tenant starts remodeling. They don't seem to like that sort of thing." She shrugged when he stared at her. "You know, I like reading about that stuff."

"I didn't start the stairs until today," he said. "Lettice saw it on Friday."

"Maybe it knew you were going to start," she replied with a shrug. "Have you seen it since?"

"I've never seen it," he said. "Do you think it'll come back?"

"I don't know. I'm not an expert; I've just read a lot about it. They're both fascinating and terrifying to me. If I ever really encountered one I'd freak out like nobody's business! You ever like something yet were terrified of it?" When he didn't reply, she looked away. "It could come back, Dan. Judging by most of the true accounts I've read, they usually make more than one appearance. Hey, do you have the Internet? There might be a record of a haunting in this house somewhere." She sat down at his computer and hit the power button.

"I haven't turned this thing on since I moved," he told her. "I just hooked it up and left it."

"I'll search for you," she said. "You can go back to doing your stairs or whatever."

"Okay," he said. "Can I order us a pizza or something?"

"Sounds good to me," she said then turned her full attention to the computer. She wasn't aware of Dan again until he returned with a plate of pizza for her.

"Thanks," she said. "Got the stairs done already?"

"Not yet. Any luck with the search?"

"Not yet. I kinda gave up, actually. I'm looking at a ghost site. Found one where you can order books on hauntings. There's a possibility your house could be in one of them, but the only way to find out is to buy one of the darn things."

"Hmm. I might have to order a few."

Sarah grinned. "So, suddenly you're interested, too, huh?"

"Well, yeah. If I'm going to be living with a ghost, I guess I better read up on them."

"I guess that makes sense."

"Have you tried looking up 'Smead'?"

"Yes, but all that came up were genealogy sites."

Dan edged in behind her. "Bring those up again. I'd like to look at them."

Sarah obeyed. She brought up the history screen and clicked on one of the sites listed there. The screen started loading when suddenly the Internet connection disconnected.

"What happened?" Sarah exclaimed.

"Must be my call waiting," Dan said, the phone ringing downstairs. "Maybe I should disable it before going on the

Net." He ran down the steps, barely remembering to avoid the missing fourth step. He grabbed for the receiver on the end table, but it wasn't there. He was about to curse when he saw it lying on the couch. He hurriedly picked it up.

"Hi." It was Lettice. "Whatcha doin'? Did ya get started on those steps like you wanted?"

"Yeah," he said, out of breath. He told her about the Christmas card.

"Wow, that is weird," Lettice replied. "Anyway, listen. I got invited to this Halloween party and I was calling to see if you wanted to go."

"I would love to," he said. "Speaking of Halloween, my sister's over—"

Lettice clucked her tongue. "That's not a nice thing to say."

"No, there's a reason I said that. She's really interested in ghostly activity. I told her about what you saw the other night and she's looking stuff up on the Net about it. She thinks there might be a mention of my house on a site somewhere." He walked back up the stairs to the computer room as he spoke. Sarah had exited the room to meet him in the hall.

"Really?" Lettice asked. "That's nice of her. I sure hope someone else has seen that thing. I don't want to be the only one."

He looked at Sarah, who was gesturing wildly. "Actually, I think she'd like to talk to you about it."

"Is she a psychic?"

"Oh, no. It's just a hobby of hers. Here she is."

"Hi, Lettice? This is Dan's sister, Sarah. It's nice to meet you over the phone. Now, can you please tell me about what you saw?"

Dan took Sarah's empty pizza plate back down to the kitchen then walked back upstairs, stepping past Sarah to the computer room. He approached the shuttered window and flung them open. He half expected to see the ghostly face, but it wasn't there. He sighed and looked down to the backyard. He couldn't see much. It was dark and overcast. He could see the denuded oak tree, but not much else. Sarah reentered to the room.

"Really? Wow," Sarah said to Lettice. "Well, that was a great story. Of course, I believe you. It was nice talking to you. Here's my brother."

"Hi," Dan said.

"Sarah's very nice," Lettice told him. "I better let you get back to the Net. I'll call you later in the week about our costumes for the party. Bye."

"Lettice seems very nice, Dan," Sarah said with a wide grin. "I really like her." She sat back down at the computer, the modem's high-pitched boot-up piercing Dan's ears.

"Thanks, Sarah," he said. "I like her quite a bit myself."

"I can tell. Now, you wanted me to look up that Smead thing, right?"

"Yeah, there's something about that name that disturbs me."

"Smead," she repeated, waiting for the screen to load. "Sounds English. I picture tri-corns and blunderbusses and powdered wigs. I picture a guy with a big bulbous red nose named Ichabod... Okay, here we go."

"Oops!" read the screen. "The file you are looking for has been deleted."

"What?" Sarah exclaimed. "I was just there a few minutes ago. Did they take it off the Net in that short amount of time? Let me try it again. Could be a problem with your server."

She tried three more times with the same result.

"Oh, well," Dan said. "I guess that takes care of that. Thanks for trying."

"No problem," Sarah said with a sigh. "Oh, there's something else I want to look up."

"Okay, I'll be down working on the stairs." He yawned and left the room.

She was still researching when Dan returned to the room, tired and ready for bed.

"Do you want me to go?" she asked him, her eyes staying on the screen, hand on the mouse.

"You can keep looking if you want," he said, yawning and stretching. "You can even stay over if you want, I've got an extra room, blankets in the hall cupboard." He yawned again.

"Okay," she said, turning her head only slightly. "See you in the morning, then."

❧

As he drifted off to sleep, Dan could hear Sarah clicking away on the mouse from his room. The sound began to change, becoming louder and sharper. Tap-dancing. More specifically, Dan was tap dancing. He was on stage in front of his family and classmates from high school. In the front row, his dad was scowling disapprovingly. He leaned over to say something to Dan's mother. She nodded and they stood up, turned and started to leave the theater. Sarah stood up and watched them in confusion. She glanced at Dan and shrugged. She then followed her parents down the aisle and out of the theater.

Dan stopped dancing, feeling dejected and worthless. His own family had just walked out on him! He stomped his feet angrily as he walked off stage. He was angrier with his father than anyone. If *he* hadn't come here tonight, his mother and sister would have stayed for the entire performance. He was sure of it. Dan's father always got his way by bullying his mother and Sarah never wanted to rock the boat so she placidly went along with her father's moods. Dan thought his father could have at least pretended he thought his son was a good tap dancer. Everyone else he knew thought he was good. They thought he was fantastic. At least, that's what they told him. Dan would have liked to think that they were sincere, but they could have been just humoring him. They could have just been polite and let him make a fool of himself in front of everybody because he enjoyed tap dancing so much. Perhaps his father was the only person honest enough to let him know how bad he really was.

Dan ripped off his tap shoes and threw them across the room, knocking over a card table stacked with props. The props flew everywhere, some of them breaking. Dan didn't care. He was never going to tap dance again.

His parents and Sarah arrived backstage, obviously anxious to go home.

"Come on, before the traffic gets worse," Dan's father said gruffly.

"I have to change," Dan replied weakly.

"No time for that. Where's your shoes?" He looked and saw the toppled table. "Did you throw a tantrum like a baby?" he demanded. "Poor little baby can't tap dance so he throws a fit?"

He stooped and scooped up the tap shoes as if they were piles of steaming shit, thrusting them into Dan's arms.

"Now, come on, before the parking lot gets jammed. And act like a man for once, not a baby, all right? Do you think you can do that?"

"I thought I was dancing well tonight," Dan replied.

His father looked down his large nose at him. "Tap dancing is for fags. Now, get in the car."

❧

Sarah sighed. Three hours on the Net and she had found nothing on Dan's house. She didn't know what was more aggravating; the fact that she couldn't find anything or that Dan's modem was agonizingly slow. She checked the speed, finding it was 28.8 baud. No wonder, she thought with a groan. Dan wasn't very knowledgeable of computers, so he probably had no idea. I'll have to sign him up for a DSL line this Christmas, she decided. She shivered suddenly, feeling a very cold draft. The lights went out and the computer screen went black. The shutters flew open.

Sarah jumped and nearly fell out of her chair. "Oh, shit, no!" she gasped. She instantly recognized the symptoms. She was about to have the experience she had longed for, yet dreaded.

When the seconds ticked by and there was only silence, she started to feel relieved. No face appeared in the window, no figure manifested itself beside her. The computer screen came back on, rebooting. Just a brief power outage, nothing more. Though the computer was back on, the lights were still out.

Her calm wavering, Sarah uneasily looked around the room then back at the computer screen. She expected to see the faceless ghost gazing eyelessly at her, but it was only the flying windows logo. Windows, shutters... How appropriate. She nearly laughed.

She reached for the mouse and caught movement out of the corner of her eye. A blue mist was drifting in through the window, shapeless and wispy. She smelled something burning, like meat.

"Sssssssssmmmmmeeeeeeeeeeaad..."

Sarah froze, uncertain she had actually heard anything. It had been so faint. Was she imagining it?

"Yoooooouuuuuuu'rrrre Sssssssmmmmmeeeeeeeeaaad."

The mist took a sharp turn and headed toward her. She yelped and sprinted out of the room.

8.

Dan thought he saw a figure standing in the doorway. After blinking once, he saw no one. He blinked again and someone was there. The light switched on.

Sarah was as white as a sheet and trembling.

"What happened?" Dan asked then knew. "You saw something."

Sarah nodded slowly, her face long and pale. She stood as rigid as a pole, her lower lip quivering, her frown lines as deep as canyons.

"The faceless face?" Dan asked.

She shook her head. Her voice was tremulous. "I-I don't know, Dan. It wasn't a face." She ran her hand through her hair, took a shallow breath then relayed her experience to him.

"You're Smead?" Dan repeated. He glanced at his alarm clock. "It's late and you've been on that computer a long time. Are you sure you didn't just fall asleep with ghosts and the Smead name running through your brain?"

"No, I was definitely awake, Dan. I know what I saw. Besides, *you're* the one obsessed with the name, remember?"

"Hmm," he said. "Why would it tell you that you're Smead?"

"I don't know!" she cried. "Why don't you ask that old lady?"

Dan shook his head. "This is getting stranger and stranger."

"You're telling me!" Sarah sniffed. "Maybe you're right after all, about all of the coincidences. I mean, a voice from beyond the grave telling me I'm a *Smead?* I mean, why would it do that if it wasn't true?"

Dan pondered. "Maybe the voice was saying 'yore' Smead. You know, like tales of yore. Maybe it was going to start to tell you the story of Smead."

She cocked her head. "That doesn't make any sense."

"You're right," Dan sighed, lying down again. "I'm still a bit groggy."

"But why would it tell me I'm a Smead? I'm Sarah Briggs, not Sarah Smead." She laughed nervously, still shaken.

"It must be what you said, then," Dan said. "Gramma's real last name is Smead."

"Maybe—" She shook her head. "Even if that were true, it wouldn't change our names any. We're Briggs because of dad. It doesn't make sense, Dan. Wake up!"

"Yes, it does make sense, because we're still descendents of Smeads, no matter what we call ourselves."

Sarah laughed hysterically. "All this conjecture is baseless! You're hinging all of this on a strange lady, a lost Christmas card and a warning from Gramma, who is an incoherent invalid, I might add!"

"What are you talking about, 'baseless'? You're the one who saw the blue mist. Don't you think a voice from beyond knows what it's talking about? You of all people should be able to understand what's going on here!"

"Just because I believe in ghosts doesn't mean that I think Gramma changed her name and never told anyone. I mean, why would she do something like that?"

"That's what I would like to know."

Sarah sighed. She bowed her head and pinched the bridge of her nose. "I'm tired, Dan. I need to get back. It's a long drive."

"It's midnight. Stay here. I've got a spare room down the hall—"

"Oh, yeah, right. Like I'm staying here."

"Why not? There aren't any ghosts in the spare bedroom that I'm aware of."

"Uh, yeah, well, I'm afraid to sleep here at all. Have *you* slept in that room?"

"No." He paused. "Take this room, then. Nothing's happened in here so far."

"Yeah, but you haven't seen anything anywhere in this house. It only shows itself to company."

"Do you really want to risk driving all the way back home while you're this tired? You could cause an accident. Besides, what are the odds of seeing two ghosts in one night?"

"I have no idea, but—" She threw her arms in the air. "Okay! I'll sleep in here. But if I see or hear anything supernatural, I'm outta here!"

"Fair enough." Dan climbed out of bed, wearing only boxers. Sarah averted her gaze as he padded out into the hall to get sheets and blankets for the other bed. "By the way," he said, "I had a dream that I was tap dancing on a stage in front of you and Ma and Dad."

Sarah stepped into the hall. "Tap dancing? *You?*" She chuckled in spite of her agitation.

"I know! I'm no dancer. But that dream was kind of like when I was in that concert in seventh grade. Remember that?"

Sarah leaned against the doorframe of the spare bedroom, watching her brother in his boxers make his bed. "Oh, yeah. The clarinet incident."

"Yeah," he said, smoothing the sheet. "In the dream Dad came backstage, called me a baby and said tap dancing was for fags."

Sarah snorted. "Sounds like him."

"But why would I dream about tap dancing? I hate tap dancing!"

Sarah shrugged. "It's just a dream, Dan. Dreams aren't supposed to make sense." She took a shallow breath. "I guess I'll start getting ready for bed. You got an extra toothbrush around here?"

"I've got a toilet brush, would that work?"

She stuck his tongue out at him.

"Baby."

"Fag."

Dan grinned. "Yeah, there's an unopened one in the medicine cabinet."

"Thanks."

Dan finished making the bed then crawled under the covers. It took him some time to fall asleep again, but he managed. He also dreamt again.

Dan looked down to see two large conical breasts jutting from his chest. He wore a showgirl-type outfit boasting a deep décolletage with feathers festooning the hips and torso. Similar feathers were in his hair. He wore tap shoes.

"What's going on here?" he demanded, his voice feminine, low and husky. A smoker's voice, he thought. He'd kicked the habit years ago in real life.

He stood backstage, watching people mill about, most of them anxious and nervous about going onstage next. None of them paid any attention to Dan. A brunette woman rushed by, glanced at him and kept going.

It suddenly dawned on him that *he* was going on next. The comedian ahead of him had just finished with a big laugh and was throwing kisses at the audience. He took large strides to the backstage area, tugging on the opening of his brown jacket. He looked directly into Dan's eyes. "Knock 'em dead, kid."

Dan was suddenly very nervous.

"Five minutes, Mrs. Smead," a voice intoned.

A young, scrawny man scurried away the second Dan turned to look at him. Everyone seemed afraid of him for some reason. Something definitely wasn't right. It was Dan's big night tonight, his first show! His *own* show! He was going to prove once and for all to those people in his life who taunted him, told him he was a nobody, that he really was a *somebody*. His tap-dancing was damn good and people wanted to pay to see it. The five thousand-seat auditorium was nearly a sell-out.

Dan anxiously walked to stage right and awaited his introduction. He let his arms hang loosely at his sides and moved his feet up and down in anticipation. He was going to knock their socks off.

He continued to wait, not hearing the intro yet. He started trembling and suddenly realized his feet hurt. His tap shoes felt as tight as a vice. It would be worth the pain, though. His current discomfort would disappear the moment he was on stage and people were cheering him, reveling in his tap dancing performance. They would pay to see him again and again. He couldn't wait to get out there and wow 'em.

Then he remembered he was supposed to stand behind the curtain. He walked over to the spot on the floor marked with tape and waited. His hands were cold and clammy and he felt like he had to pee. He tugged at his outfit. It felt too tight about his breasts. His nipples were hard and sensitive.

"Ladies and Gentlemen!" blasted the announcer's voice, startling Dan. "We are pleased to introduce, on this fine stage, the soon to be legendary performer – Audrey Smead!"

Fanfare erupted from the orchestra pit and the curtain went up.

The first person Audrey saw was her husband, sitting in the first row. Her daughter sat next to him, all gussied up in her church clothes, a pink bow in her hair. She looked like a cute little lady. Audrey smiled at them, her entire inner being flooded with self-confidence and a sense of accomplishment. This was her night. The eyes of thousands of people were on her. She planned to make it a night they would never forget.

The curtain continued to rise. Her eyes followed the hem of the curtain as it ascended, all other senses momentarily forgotten. Her grin was as wide at the Pacific Ocean. This was the moment she'd waited her entire life for.

Then her other senses came back.

Spread throughout the five thousand-seat auditorium was perhaps only fifty or sixty people. All of the other seats were devoid of human presence. Empty.

Audrey stood frozen. She glanced fearfully at the orchestra leader. He nodded and raised his baton. The orchestra started to play, but Audrey didn't dance. She couldn't make her feet move. She tried to tell herself to go on with the show, to be a professional, but she couldn't move. Be a professional, Audrey.

Professionals always went on with the show, no matter how bad things went, didn't they? The show was the thing. There was nothing more important than the show. To heck with the people who left.

She opened her mouth and a tremendous sob resounded throughout the auditorium. She turned and ran off stage.

Dan awoke to darkness, anxious and sweaty. *Another* tap dancing dream? What was that all about? And there was the Smead name again. His subconscious seemed awfully obsessed with that name. And why was he a woman? It was greatly disturbing. He couldn't remember ever having dreamt of being a member of the opposite sex before.

It took him a very long while before he finally fell asleep again.

Although he was very tired, he woke up at his normal time to go jogging. He encountered the old lady with the dog again, but was able to avoid her. Sarah was still asleep when he returned. He showered, changed clothes and went to work.

The telephone sounded like an electrical discharge to Sarah when it wakened her. She groaned and rolled over onto her back. The answering machine picked up the call. She heard her mother's voice, tinny on her brother's cheap answering machine, echoing downstairs. She got up and hurried down, clad only in underwear and a T-shirt.

"Mom, Mom. It's me. What is it?"

"Sarah? Your grandmother passed away last night."

"Oh," Sarah said, feeling sadder than she sounded. "That's too bad." She didn't know what else to say about a woman she'd never met in person. "Are you okay, Mom?"

"I'll be all right," she said with a sniff. "Where's Dan?"

"He left for work."

"Oh. Is it that time? I didn't realize. Shouldn't you be at work, too?"

"Mom, I work four-tens, remember? I have Mondays off."

"Oh, that's right. Did Dan tell you about his girlfriend seeing ghosts in that house?"

"Yeah, Mom. I saw one, too."

"You did?"

"Yeah. It even talked to me."

"Really? What did it say?"

"'You're Smead.'"

"Smead?" Her mother fell silent for a moment. "Anyway, I thought you'd like to know about your grandmother. I know you kids never met her, but you would have loved her. She was great. I really wish you and her could have gotten together. It's really sad. I'll be here for a while yet. Will you check in on your father, Sarah? He never calls and never answers when I call him."

"Sure, Mom," Sarah said with a sigh. "Mom..."

"Yes?"

"Did Dan tell you about the Christmas card he found?"

"Yes, he did."

"He thinks Gramma's last name was Smead, not Johnson."

"I know. It's quite ridiculous. I mean, I think I would know if my own mother had changed her name."

"Not if it was a secret," Sarah said.

"Why would it be a secret?"

"I don't know. Why would a ghost talk to me and tell me I'm a Smead?"

"If, in fact, you saw a ghost."

Sarah sighed again. Her mother was testing her patience. "I saw a ghost, Mom. Well, kind of. It was more like a blue haze, but I definitely heard a voice. It was scary."

"I have the family tree at the house," her mother said. "There are no Smeads in it. None whatsoever."

"Okay, Mom, I believe you," Sarah said, dropping the subject. She should have known better to talk to her mother about anything like this. "So, when are you going home?"

"The funeral's Wednesday," she said. "I'll be back Friday."

"Okay, Mom. I'll call Dan and let him know about Gramma. Bye."

Ella rushed into Dan's office the instant he arrived for work. "The network's down," she informed him irritably.

"Again?" he asked, annoyed. "That just happened on Friday."

"I know." With mock disappointment, Ella added, "It's such a bummer we can't work, isn't it?"

"Uh, yeah," he said.

"By the way, Frank wants to talk to you."

"Frank?" Dan asked, alarmed. "What about?"

Ella shrugged. "He didn't say. He wants to see you at eight-thirty."

Dan sighed and fell into his chair as Ella departed. He stretched and yawned then answered the phone.

"Hi, it's me," Sarah said. "Mom just called. Gramma's dead."

Dan let out a long sigh. "That's too bad."

"Yeah, that's what I said."

"How's Ma doing?"

"She said she's doing fine, but she always puts up a brave front. She said she wouldn't be back home until Friday."

"Halloween," Dan said. It reminded him suddenly of the party he was going to attend with Lettice. He found himself looking forward to it. He didn't care about the party itself – he hated dressing up – but the thought of being with Lettice again excited him. The thought of Lettice's naked body in his arms led him to recollect his dream. It disturbed him. He decided to tell Sarah about it.

She guffawed. "You dreamt you were a woman? I think you need therapy. Did you feel yourself up?"

"No," he laughed. "I wish I had, though."

"Then you definitely need a check up." She chuckled. "But there's that Smead name again, huh? Mom swears up and down that there are no Smeads in the family tree. She was quite adamant about it."

"She just doesn't know the secret," Dan replied.

"She doesn't believe there *is* a secret. It sounds like you do, though."

"Do you?"

Sarah paused. "If it weren't for the ghost talking to me, I would say no. But... I'm not sure. Something weird in going on, that's for sure."

"I'll say," Dan replied. "Look, I've got a meeting with the boss. I'll have to let you go. Talk to you later, Sare."

"Okay," she said. "I'll be leaving in an hour or so."

"'Kay. Bye."

"You wanted to see me?"

Frank was a short, balding man with thick curly hair and a ruddy complexion. He gestured to the chair in front of his desk. "Have a seat." He closed the door then fell into his chair with a squeak. "Are you aware of a situation with one of your employees?"

Dan was startled. "A situation? Who? Do you mean Lidia? Oh, yeah. She's having problems with Pam. I asked her to be more tolerant of Pam's personality, that Pam's the way she is and nobody can change that."

Frank nodded. "And do you think your advice solved the problem?"

Dan shrugged. "I haven't heard any further complaints."

Frank leaned back in his chair and looked at Dan. "Pam has been verbally abusive toward Lidia and is saying bad things about her behind her back. Lies."

"I was not aware of this," Dan replied truthfully.

"Lidia tells me she told you about it last week," Frank said coolly. "She came in after you went home Friday and told me that when she tried to talk to you, you just shoved her aside like you didn't want to deal with her. She thinks you don't really care about her, that she's just a peon to you. Her exact words."

Dan was astonished. It took him a few moments to collect his thoughts. "Honestly, Frank, I don't remember her coming to me on Friday for any reason at all."

Frank was silent, rocking gently in his chair. "What do you plan to do about this?" he said finally.

"I guess I'll just have to talk to Pam, find out why she's doing this to Lidia," Dan said. "I'll ask her to stop it."

Frank leaned forward. "*Tell* her to stop it."

Dan nodded. "Yes. Okay."

Frank leaned back again. "Then there's the fact that your department is a little backlogged."

"Yes, I know. We're working on that. We had a couple of people out sick last week and that put us behind even further."

"Perhaps you should see about distributing the workflow better," Frank said. "Don't just let it sit there when people are out sick. Delegate it to someone else. Train them if you have to. Just get the work done."

"Okay," Dan said, feeling like a child being scolded by his father. "I'll tend to that, Frank."

"Hire more help if you need to. Get some temps in here. I'll okay it."

Dan nodded, but didn't say anything else. He waited for Frank to continue. He had no idea there were so many things wrong with his department. Of course, he'd only been there for a week.

"How are you adjusting to your new position?" Frank then inquired, his face opaque. "Is everything going all right for you here?"

Dan looked at him. What was he trying to say? Is he implying that I can't handle my job? Perhaps it was just a subtle hint, Frank's way of telling me to shape up quickly. It certainly sounded like it.

"I'm doing fine," Dan said finally.

"Great," Frank said flatly. "I won't take up any more of your time then."

Dan left his boss's office feeling awful. Not only had he been scolded and warned, he had to look forward to having a talk with Pam. He didn't know Pam, or anyone else in his department given the short time he'd been there, but he was a more than a little intimidated by Pam. Maybe Lidia had spoken to him and he had selectively forgotten about it. He didn't want to deal with Pam. She was very self-centered, pushy, arrogant.

Everything was either her way or no way. Dan decided to put off the talk until the afternoon.

He returned to his office to find Lettice had left a voice mail message. He returned the call. "Hey, what's up?" he asked cheerfully with just the hint of a weary sigh.

"I just called to say hi." She paused. "Is there something wrong?"

"Uh, no. Not really. I have to have a talk with Pam, that's all."

"Oh, her," Lettice replied. "She's the one with the short bleached-blonde hair, right? Stocky? I heard she's a terror. Lucky for me I didn't have to work with her. Good luck with that."

"Gee, thanks," he said wryly with a grin. "Are we still on for Friday?"

"Of course," she exclaimed. "I'm so excited, Dan. I can't wait. What are you going to wear?"

"Oh, I don't know." He had honestly not thought about it. "Why don't you pick a costume out for me?"

"Okay," she said. "One sheet with eyeholes coming up," she giggled. "Of course, mine won't have holes."

"Really? Why's that?"

"Because of the ghost I saw," she replied laughingly. "Did you forget already? Oh, it was a lame joke, I know." She paused. "Are you sure something isn't wrong?"

"Well," he said. "I found out this morning that my Gramma died."

"Oh, Dan, I'm so sorry."

"Thanks, but that's okay. I never really knew her. I talked to her on the phone over the years, but that's about it. I never met her in person."

"Still, she was your grandmother. It's sad."

"Yes," he sighed. "Even more so, since I wanted to ask her a question."

"What did you want to ask her?"

"If she changed her name from Smead to Johnson." He then relayed his dream and Sarah's sighting of the misty ghost.

"Wow," Lettice said. "That's weird. So, your sister finally got to see a ghost, huh? I told her she didn't really want to."

"You were right about that," Dan said with a chuckle. "She was totally freaked out. Not like you were, though."

"Hey, is that a dig?" she asked. "I can't help it that I'm not brave like you are."

"I'm not brave," he cried. "And it wasn't a dig. It was, I was, I just—" He took a deep breath.

Lettice laughed. "Dan, I was just messing with you."

"I know," he said, lying.

"Okay. So, you think your grandmother changed her name from Smead to Johnson, huh?"

"It makes sense, doesn't it? I mean, ghosts telling my sister that she's a Smead... There's got to be something to it. Unless ghosts habitually come back and just screw with the minds of the living."

"Don't forget your weird dreams," she said. Dan was thankful that she made no cracks about his being a woman in one of them. "It could be the ghosts trying to tell you something, though indirectly. I wonder why they would rather visit you in your dreams than in person? Why do they have to scare the women in your life and not you?" She chuckled.

"I couldn't answer that," he replied seriously. He glanced out his office door to see Frank walk by and eye him. He groaned inwardly. "I hate to cut this short, but I need to go have that talk with Pam, now."

"No problem. How about seeing a movie or something tonight? Your treat."

"Tonight? Sure. I'll pick you up around seven."

"What movie do you want to see?"

"You pick. I have no idea what's even out right now."

"Fine," she said with mock irritation. "First I'm picking out a costume for you and now a movie. When will it ever end?"

"Uh, Lettice—"

"I know, I know. I just hate to say goodbye."

"I know, but I really have to go."

"Okay. Goodbye, Dan."

"Goodbye, Lettice."

"I forgot to ask," Lettice said in the car later. "How did your talk with Pam go? Did she give you any trouble?"

He shook his head and chuckled. "Oh, no. Now that she's aware of the situation, she'll be okay. She was quite good about it, actually."

"That's good," she said. "But whether or not she behaves herself is something else, huh?"

"Yes," he sighed. "Thanks for pointing that out."

"I'm sorry," she replied with a smile. He parked in front of her house and looked at her. She asked, "Would you like to come in, or are you in a hurry to get back to that haunted house of yours?"

"I would love to come in," he said then frowned. "But with everything that's going on with my Gramma, I think I should stay home in case my mom calls again. She'll probably want to talk to me in person since she didn't get to before."

Lettice sighed heavily and slumped her shoulders. "Fine. I guess I understand." She smiled and asked, "If you wanted to stay home, why did you go to dinner and a movie with me tonight?"

"Because I wanted to see you again," he said without hesitation. He leaned forward and kissed the corner of her mouth. She grinned and returned the kiss full on the lips.

"Well, okay," she said. "I guess I'll see you Friday then. How about *I* pick *you* up this time? I'll be over right after work to give you your costume."

"Sounds great." He ran his hand up her arm, his eyes fixed on hers. "I don't want you to go."

"Me neither." She moved closer and kissed him. Her fingers went between the buttons of his shirt as her lips caressed his. His hand went to her breast. Condensation started forming on the windows.

Lettice suddenly pushed away. "Whew, are you sure you don't want to come on up?"

"I do," he said, his voice a croak. "But I better not. I should get on home."

"I know." Lettice copped a fake pout. "I have to go four whole days without seeing you again?"

"Sucks, doesn't it?" he asked. "You know, that's about half the time we've known each other."

She smiled and laughed. "Doesn't it seem like things have gone by really fast?"

He shrugged. "No, not really. I feel like I've known you for quite a while. A month, at least."

She chuckled. "I don't know if that's a compliment or not, but I'll take it. What I was really asking is if you think we're moving too fast? Remember, you wanted to take it slow."

He smiled. "I think I've decided to just let it happen, not force it either way."

Her eyes and lips glinted in the diffused moonlight. "Sounds like a good plan." She placed her hand on his cheek. "I've never been four days without you."

Dan sighed, placing his hand on hers. "It's going to be tough."

"I want to remember your face, just in case we never meet again."

"Oh, stop it!" he said with a laugh. He pulled her close and kissed her.

The passion heightened quickly and before either of them knew it, they were making love in the car. Dan remained in the driver's seat, the steering wheel at Lettice's back. The wheel was no discomfort to her until after her climax struck.

"Ow!" Lettice groaned. "The wheel!" She shifted her position in his lap then started laughing.

"What?" he asked, his smile enormous.

"I can't believe we did that!" she exclaimed. "It wasn't even planned or anything."

"Sometimes, that's the best way," he said, smoothing her hair.

"I'll second that." She kissed him. "Oh, my God, I'm naked in your car."

"Not entirely," he said, one hand down the back of her panties. He squeezed her buttock. "There was no time."

"Evidently," she giggled and snuggled against him. She held him for a very long time, neither of them speaking. A car passed, the headlights flashing them.

"You better get going before your mom starts worrying," she whispered.

"I know." He chuckled. "You make it sound as if I still live at home."

"Yeah, it kind of sounded that way, huh?"

Neither of them moved. They held each other for fifteen additional minutes before Lettice complained of a cramp. She climbed out of his lap and put her sweater back on. She looked at the dashboard clock.

"It's almost eleven."

He nodded. She leaned over and kissed him.

"Until Friday, then," he said. "Although, there's nothing saying we have to wait until then before seeing each other again."

"No," she said, grinning broadly. "But, maybe we should take a short break. You know, so the polish doesn't wear off."

"I think you already wore the polish off—"

She swiped at him, laughing loudly. "That's not what I meant."

"Okay," he said. "A four day break. Until Friday, then. Or did I already say that?"

"I think you did, but that's okay." She smiled and nodded then glanced at his lap. "You might want to zip up, you know, in case you get pulled over or something."

He laughed and obeyed. Lettice opened the car door and got out. She blew him a kiss and waved. He waved back. He watched her unlock the door to her apartment then open the door. She stopped in the entrance to blow him another kiss. He blew it back. She waved again then closed the door.

Dan became suddenly contemplative. Things with Lettice were moving along fast and strong. They had just entered a new stage in their relationship, he felt. It was more than just lust. He really cared for her and felt that she really cared for him. He wondered for a second why his cheeks were so sore before realizing he was smiling. He couldn't stop thinking about her. He tried to think of other things, but couldn't. Lettice was all he knew. There simply was nothing else.

Another car's headlights flashed in his eyes and he reluctantly decided it was time to go home.

9.

Dan's mother called every day for the next four days, days that seemed to drag on and on. He talked to Lettice every day, too, the moments with her the only ones where time seemed to accelerate. Otherwise, it was an agonizingly slow week.

Meanwhile, Pam continued to be a problem for Dan even though she had assured him she would behave. The work in his department fell farther behind because he had to train people and the temp he requested never showed up for work. He was more than ready for Lettice's Halloween party when the day finally arrived. He had completely forgotten about bad dreams and ghosts until he realized it was October thirty-first.

Lettice phoned him to say she was going to be late. There was a problem with her costume. It was too tight against her breasts and she had to take it back. That left Dan with some time to kill. The party wasn't for another two and a half hours.

He picked up his guitar, stared at the music sheet in front of him then set the instrument down. He didn't feel like playing. He sucked anyway.

He sat on the couch for a minute then went up to the computer room and sat down. He booted the computer up and gazed at the shuttered window. It looked sinister to him now, considering all the supernatural activity that seemed to revolve around it. He wondered why the ghost always appeared at this window and never any of the others. Perhaps, before becoming a specter, the room had belonged to it.

Dan took a deep breath and brought up his word processing program. He'd wanted to write a book and now was his opportunity. He decided to at least brainstorm and see what he could come up with. It was hard to concentrate, however, when all he could think of was Lettice and her costume being too tight.

He shook his head, trying to dismiss the thought. It was very difficult. Think of a story, he told himself. Think of a story, think of a story, think of a...

He gazed at the screen and suddenly felt very tired. There had been so much going on the past two weeks and it had left him exhausted. His vision started to blacken around the edges. He dozed off.

He was jarred awake before he even knew he was asleep. It wasn't a noise that had prompted him to awaken, but an idea. An idea for a story. Without another thought, his fingers began moving deftly across the keys. He was an expert typist; it was part of his job. The story flowed from his consciousness to the tips of his fingers, the act of typing fading into the background.

It was a balmy summer's day. Rebecca Duncan was on her way back to her father's house, her basket full of eggs, when she ran into John Smead. Rebecca gasped and dropped her basket, breaking some of the eggs.

"Oh, excuse me, Miss!" John Smead exclaimed. "I must apologize. I didn't mean to startle you."

Rebecca crouched down to retrieve the few eggs that hadn't broken, meanwhile trying desperately not to look at John Smead. He was so handsome that he had inadvertently caused her to lose her grip on her basket. She had never before encountered such beauty in a man. He was a gentleman, too, as he helped her to her feet. She glanced at him then looked quickly away.

"I am so terribly sorry," he said when she did not reply. "Allow me to replace your eggs. Please, come to my house so I can give them to you. That is, if it is no imposition."

"It is not," she replied meekly. He took her arm and escorted her to his home.

Along the way she passed a Puritan girl named Dinah Abbot. She gave John her friendliest smile. When she saw Rebecca on his arm, however, her eyes narrowed and her nostrils flared. Her smile vanished.

Rebecca was alarmed by Dinah's vehement countenance. She again dropped her basket of eggs. The remainder of the shells broke, leaving nothing for her to bring home.

John said nothing until Dinah had passed them. "Did she frighten you?" he asked.

Rebecca nodded.

"She has frightened me, as well, on other occasions," John told her. "I try to avoid her and I suggest that you do the same. She is mischief."

Rebecca agreed and proceeded with John Smead to his house. Like most houses in Boston, it was two stories high with a wide swatch of land around it.

Rebecca commented to John Smead about how nice his house was and how proud he and his wife must be to own such a large plot of land.

"My wife died a year ago," John said. "Many are the hours that I wish I could see her face upon the completion of this fine house, but, alas, it is not to be."

"Oh, I am so sorry to hear that," Rebecca exclaimed, honestly affected by his sad tale. Her heart went out to him. "Surely, you have children to help you with chores around the house."

John shook his head. "My dear wife died whilst giving birth to our only son. He did not survive."

Rebecca gasped, feeling like she could cry. There was so much tragedy in this poor, kind man's life. Certainly, he did not deserve all that had befallen him.

John Smead opened the door to his house, stepping aside to let Rebecca enter first. He then bade her to wait a moment while he fetched the eggs for her. He returned with an extra half dozen with the comment, "I have much more than I need."

Rebecca accepted the eggs gratefully, but felt poorly for it. Surely, she could do something in return for this man. He had been so kind to her and had endured so much over the past year. She formulated an idea, but wondered if it was proper. She didn't even know him. Still, she was about to impart her idea to him when she suddenly paused. She decided that it was not proper after all. She thanked him for the eggs, adding, "You have been so kind to me. Thank you." She curtsied, basket in still hand.

"Think nothing of it," John Smead replied kindly. "It was the least I could do."

Rebecca hesitated, not wanting to leave. Coyly, she inquired, "Perhaps I could visit you again, seeing as you are all alone here in this big house."

"I would like nothing more," he replied with an inviting smile.

Rebecca smiled in kind then backed toward the door. She abruptly turned and bolted out through it, cradling her egg basket as she ran. She felt ashamed that she had asked such a direct question. It was so unladylike. Yet, she was overjoyed at the fact that he had seemed happy at the prospect of receiving her again. The only problem was: how to find a suitable excuse to visit him again.

She was so occupied by these thoughts that she nearly walked past Dinah Abbot without seeing her. Dinah stepped in front of her, blocking her path. Rebecca gasped then fell silent as the Abbot girl stared determinedly into her eyes.

"Don't you *ever* go to his house again," she snarled, her voice beast-like.

"Wh-What?" Rebecca asked, frightened

Dinah stepped closer. "If I ever see you walking or talking or *being* with him again, you will know well the pain his wife and son knew when they perished!" Dinah's gaze bore deep into Rebecca a split second more before she turned and walked away as if she and Rebecca had been conversing convivially.

Rebecca ran home.

Dan gave a sharp yelp, suddenly acutely aware of a hand on his shoulder.

"Hey, it's me!" Lettice exclaimed, seeing that she had startled him. "Calm down!"

"Sorry," he gasped, his pulse racing. "You scared me."

He looked up at Lettice to see that, beneath her long black coat, she was clad in a serving wench's costume. The garment laced over her breasts and revealed quite a bit of flesh. Dan found it difficult to remove his eyes from such an intriguing sight. "Nice outfit," he commented with a crooked grin.

"Why, thank you." She shoved her bosom forward and downward, closer to his face. "I wonder why you like it," she said. They both laughed. "Look, I got you a pirate costume. I thought the two would go nicely together. And I think you will look good in it, too. The pants are nice and tight.

"I'll go put it on, then," he said with a chuckle. He got up and kissed her on the mouth as she handed him the costume.

"So," she said, sitting in his chair. "What were you doing on the computer here?"

"I started writing a story," he said, removing his clothes. "I've been wanting to write one for some time now and this story just came to me."

"What's it about?"

"I don't know yet," he confessed. "I just started writing the events as they played out in my head. It takes place in colonial times." He shrugged.

Lettice read a few paragraphs of the story. "You used 'Smead', I see."

"Yeah. It just sort of came out. I guess it's stuck in my head right now."

Lettice looked at her watch. "Hurry and get that costume on. It's getting late."

"Okay." He had only succeeded in taking off his shoes and shirt. He gazed at Lettice again. "That costume—"

Lettice jutted her chest forward again, giggling. "You can't stop staring, can you?"

"I sure can't." He stepped out of his pants. "It really does something to me."

Lettice rose and sidled up to him. "You know. We could always skip the party and have some fun of our own." She placed her hands on his bare shoulders and drew her face to his. They kissed and embraced passionately. Once again, the passion between them heightened quickly and Lettice ended up against the wall with Dan trying desperately to untie her bodice.

Lettice withdrew suddenly. "These laces are for show, silly. You'll ruin the costume. There's a zipper in the back." She removed her coat and reached back to unzip her costume.

The doorbell rang.

Dan groaned. "Stay right there," he instructed Lettice then headed for the door.

"Wait!" she cried, starting forward. "You're almost naked. And quite visibly aroused, I might add."

"You're right," he said, looking embarrassed. "Um..."

"I'll get the door," Lettice said.

She went downstairs and peeked through the curtains at the visitor. She hurried back upstairs, finding Dan standing in the hall clad in his pirate costume. "Very smart," she commented. "You look very good in that. I knew you would."

"Thanks," he said. "Who's at the door?"

"I don't know," she said with a frown, "but she looks mad."

Dan sighed and went downstairs. Just as he suspected, it was his neighbor. "Yes?" he asked, opening the door a fraction.

"I do not appreciate being stared at," Damita blurted rudely, causing spittle to land on Dan's face.

"What are you talking about?" he asked, flinching. His hand went to his cheek.

"That man," she shouted. "He keeps staring at me from your kitchen window. He's very rude and if he doesn't stop it, I'm calling the cops!"

"*I'm* the only man in the kitchen," he said. "And I have *not* been staring at you."

"Not you, asshole, the other man that lives here. I see him in the window almost every night. Do you think I'm blind? He's always wearing that fucking Revolutionary War uniform and he's always staring at me. You can tell him that I said he's some kind of sick, perverted creep."

"Look, lady, I have no idea what—"

Damita squinted her eyes at his pirate outfit. "Is there gonna be a party here tonight? If there is, you better keep it down. I'll call the cops again if I hear noise."

Dan took a deep breath. "Look, there's no one in the kitchen, all right? Why don't you go back home, have another glass of tequila and leave me alone, okay?"

Damita put her hand on her hip and glared at Dan menacingly. "Just because I am Hispanic, does not mean I get drunk on tequila every night. Man, where do you get that racist crap anyway?"

Dan was losing what little patience he had with this woman. Not only was she talking gibberish, she had interrupted foreplay with Lettice. "Look, I just said tequila because obviously you are hallucinating. There is no other man here."

Lettice tugged on Dan's pirate sleeve. "Uh, Dan, maybe she's telling the truth. You know, considering what's been going on here lately?"

"What's been going on?" Damita asked belligerently. "What's she talking about?"

"Ghosts," Lettice answered in a whisper.

"What?"

"Yeah," Dan sighed, realizing that Lettice was probably right. This annoying woman probably had seen a man in the kitchen window after all. "This house is haunted. It was probably a ghost staring at you. Would you like me to ask it to stop?"

Damita gazed incredulously at Dan and Lettice then slowly shook her head. "You assholes. I don't know what's going on here, but I'll get you. Just you wait."

"Okay, I will. Bye!" Dan slammed the door in her face.

Lettice snickered. "You sure weren't very nice to her."

"She's a bitch," Dan remarked sourly. "He's *staring* at me," he mocked exaggeratedly. "Give me a break. Leave me alone.

Besides—" He took Lettice in his arms and tried to kiss her. She pulled away.

"Dan, if that was a ghost, I don't want to stay here," she told him frankly. "I don't want a repeat of that last time." She gasped. "My God! I can't believe I even went back into that room."

"It's safe in *my* room," he said, holding her close from behind.

"Yes," she said, enticed by his affection. Her lips drew closer to his and she was about to kiss him then abruptly pulled away. "How about we go to my place instead?"

Dan sighed then smiled. "Okay. Let me go turn off my computer first."

Lettice followed Dan back upstairs, stipulating she did not want to stay in any room of the house alone. When they reached the computer room, they found that the computer was already off. "Damn!" Dan exclaimed. "I didn't get to save what I wrote. Good thing I remember most of it."

Lettice crouched beside the computer desk. "Look, Dan. It's been unplugged from the surge protector."

"Somebody's playing games," Dan remarked with a smirk.

"The Minuteman?" Lettice inquired, plugging the computer back in. "Or whatever he was? She didn't say if he was British or American, so I suppose he could have been a Redcoat, too."

"Either him or the faceless woman you saw." Dan paused. "Damn, I've got two ghosts in this house now."

"I don't even want to think about her," Lettice said. "I don't like being in this room as it is." She crossed her arms over her chest. "It's cold in here." She picked her black coat up from the floor. "Let's get going to that party, Dan, and forget all about this ghost stuff."

"It will be hard to forget ghosts at a Halloween party," he pointed out.

"Well, you know what I mean," she replied with a quick kiss. "Come on, let's go."

"We'll be late, won't we?"

Lettice shrugged. "We'll be fashionably late, as they say."

"Are you sure you wouldn't rather go back to your place?" he inquired with a lascivious grin.

"Maybe after the party," she replied. "No offense, Dan, but I need to get out of this house." She left the room and started for the stairs. Dan reluctantly followed.

The phone rang. "Let the machine get it," he told Lettice. It was his mother.

"I should answer that," he said apologetically. He hurriedly picked up, cutting off his mother's answering machine message. "Hi, Ma. How was your flight?"

"What? Oh, hi, Dan. There was some turbulence, but I took my pills and I was fine. I just got in, actually. Have you gotten any trick-or-treaters over there yet?"

"No, Ma, I'm not doing that this year. My light's off. Lettice and I are on our way to a party."

"Really? Well, I better let you go then. How is Lettice?"

"She's great, Ma."

"How are things at your new job? I haven't heard you say anything about it."

Dan sighed. He was trying not to get sucked into a conversation with her, yet he couldn't bring himself to lie and say work was great. "Not so good," he replied with a weary glance at Lettice. He told his mother about the situation with Pam and the run-in with his boss.

"Do you like the job, Dan?" his mother asked.

"It's okay, I guess. It pays well and I think I'm fairly good at it."

"Do you still play that guitar of yours?" she inquired, catching him off guard. "Maybe you could start a rock band or something."

"Where did that come from?" he asked with a laugh.

"Well, it's obvious you don't like your job. Maybe you'd rather do something else for a living. You like playing the guitar."

"Yeah, but I'm not really that good," he admitted. "Besides, I'm over thirty now. I'm a little too old to be starting a band."

"You're never too old, dear."

Dan sighed.

"If you aren't good, just practice. That's all you need. I've heard plenty of guitarists that can't play a lick and they make millions of dollars. You should think about it."

Dan looked at Lettice and laughed. "Do you believe it? A man who's making an honest living working in an office and his mother is urging him to throw it away and start a rock band. How often does that happen?"

"I'd like to hear you play guitar some time," she said with a smile. "Or are you too busy writing your book now?"

"Oh, yeah, Ma, I forgot to tell you. I'm writing a book."

"Really?" She sounded genuinely surprised. "You know, getting back to the guitar thing, my aunt once tried show business, back in the fifties. She was in her late thirties."

"I didn't know that," Dan replied. "What did she do?"

"She tried her hand at tap dancing."

Dan emitted a strangled sound, his heart pounding suddenly very loudly in his ears.

"Get it?" his mother asked. "Hand? Tap dancing? Anyway, she bombed horribly, poor thing. More people showed up to see the comedian that opened for her than stayed to see her perform. She ran off the stage and never tap danced again." She paused. "I'm not making a very good case for your going into show business, am I?"

"Audrey Smead," he muttered, barely listening to his mother's words.

"What? No. Well, Audrey, yes. Not Smead... Why do you keep bringing that name up, anyway?"

"Ma, did she, Aunt Audrey, live in Boston?"

"Yes," she replied. "Before she killed herself."

Dan stiffened again. "She killed herself? I didn't know about that."

"No one in the family likes to talk about it," she said. "But since I'm now the only one left besides you and Sarah, I thought I may as well tell you."

"That's—" Dan sighed heavily. He had no idea what to say, but he knew that he didn't want to tell her about his dream. She would call it nonsense anyway and prattle on about something else.

"It was so humiliating for her," she went on. "No one mentioned tap dancing in front of her ever again. Then, after her body was found, nobody wanted to talk about her."

"Where was her body found?"

"Someplace in Boston there, wherever she lived. I don't know. Are you coming here for Thanksgiving? I'm roasting a turkey. You can bring Lettice so I can meet her."

"Uh, sure, Ma," he replied, unable to think about anything other than his Aunt Audrey and tap dancing and dreams and ghosts. "I've really got to go. We're already late."

"Okay, Dan. Good-bye."

Dan stood with the phone in his hand for two seconds before he remembered to hang up. Lettice touched his shoulder.

"What was that all about?" she asked.

"My Aunt Audrey was a tap dancer," he told her. "Here in Boston. She also killed herself here. Somewhere."

"That is very weird," she said. "Sounds to me like the ghost of Aunt Audrey is making you have dreams about her."

"Her name was Audrey Smead," he said. "Not Johnson. My mom said she wasn't a Smead, but she was."

"It could just be a dream, Dan," Lettice said after a moment.

He shook his head. "No, my grandmother's last name was Smead. I'm almost convinced of that now. I just don't understand why she changed her name and kept it a secret from her own daughter." He looked around the room and up at the ceiling. "Aunt Audrey?"

"Dan, don't!" Lettice pleaded, alarmed. "I don't want to do this. Let's go to the party."

Dan nodded and went to the door with her. When he opened it, he discovered Sarah standing on the porch. Tears streamed down her face and there was a bruise on her cheek.

"Oh, my God," Lettice gasped.

"What happened?" Dan asked, alarmed.

Sarah stepped into his arms and started weeping uncontrollably. "He hit me!"

"What?" Dan exclaimed, shocked. He held her rigidly and looked apologetically at Lettice. Would they ever make it to the party?

Sarah sniffed, her hair was plastered to a beet-red face drenched with tears. "He was drunk and he fucking hit me," she sobbed. "I had no idea he was like that, Dan. I swear it! He's been hiding his real personality from me. He's been lying to me."

"That's terrible," Dan said, unsure of what else to say.

She nodded, sniffed and lurched across the room to the sofa where she collapsed. She looked up and noticed Lettice. "Hi," she said with a wan smile. She brought the back of her hand to her nose and sniffed again.

"Hi," Lettice replied with concern. She seated herself next to Sarah. Dan sat in the chair across from them.

"Were you guys going someplace?" Sarah inquired, finally realizing they both wore costumes. "I could come back later— "

"No, stay," Dan urged, looking to Lettice for approval. She didn't protest and looked genuinely concerned. "The party can wait. Is this the first time he's hit you? Has he ever been drunk like this before?"

"Well," Sarah began, shifting uncomfortably on the couch. "We've both been drunk before, together, but always in a group. Today he'd been drinking at home all alone. He just got laid off from his job."

Dan groaned and sat back in his chair. Lettice cast him a look.

"Is that why he hit you?" Lettice asked Sarah.

"No." Sniff. "I can't remember why. It was something stupid. I ran out of the house right after. I didn't know what else to do. I drove and drove and before I knew it I was here." She leaned forward, her elbows on her knees. She heaved a tremendous sigh. "Why do such horrible things keep happening to me?"

"That's one of life's mysteries," Dan replied dourly. "Shit happens."

"What an astute comment," Sarah said with a frown. "But, it's not just me, is it? I thought about it in the car. Bad things keep happening to you and Mom and Dad. Do we all just have bad luck or what?"

Dan took a deep breath. "Well, our mom and dad's relationship isn't the result of bad luck," he reminded her. "They should have split up years ago, but for some reason they stick it out and I have never been able to understand why. That looks like incredibly good luck to me."

"Probably out of fear," Lettice commented. "I mean, if it's okay for me to say so. They probably fear being alone more than being together."

"But wouldn't you rather live alone than with someone you can't stand?" Dan asked.

"Not if you think you'd be even more miserable alone," Lettice replied.

"I don't know if that's it," Dan said. "I think they actually enjoy making each other miserable. I mean, you'd have to meet them, spend some time with them to understand what I mean."

Lettice nodded. "Okay."

"I mean, the odds of them finding someone else that would put up with that crap is probably astronomical."

"It's not just them," Sarah continued, shaking her head. "There are a myriad of bad things that keep happening to us, to our family, that don't seem to happen to other families." She looked up at her brother. "I mean, I see people much happier than us, people with much better lives, people with good things happening to them all the time. Sure, good things happen to us occasionally, but not that often. The bad outweighs the good, in case you haven't noticed. No one in our family has had good luck in abundance. Absolutely no one, Dan."

He shrugged. "It's just the way it goes," he replied. "That's how I look at it."

"But don't you ever wonder why us?"

"Well, yeah. Sometimes. Especially after— "

Sarah looked away from him. She didn't want to think

about the murders. That incident, like the suicide of Aunt Audrey, was not openly discussed within the family. The tension in the room mounted.

"Perhaps you should adopt a positive outlook on life," Lettice offered. "I know, it sounds corny, but it seems to work for people. I mean, I don't really know you, Sarah, but you seem to look at things pretty negatively."

Sarah snorted. "I'm not negative, I'm neutral."

Dan snorted louder. "Bullshit! If that's true, why is Nine Inch Nails one of your all time favorite groups? You should have seen her, Lettice, moping around school with her dyed black hair and black clothes with the pale, white face and blood-red lipstick. Oh, it was the Cure back then, wasn't it? Or was it the Smiths?"

Sarah frowned. "I outgrew that a long time ago, Dan. You know I'm a lot more positive than I was back then."

"Not by much."

She glared at him.

"If you're so positive, why do all of your relationships end in a fight?"

"They don't always," Sarah replied defensively. "And it's not always me that starts the fight." Before Dan could interject, she quickly declared, "I don't fight unless I have a good reason."

There then followed more tense silence before Lettice broke it. "Do you guys believe in God?"

Sarah gave a hissing, dismissive sound. Dan just shrugged.

"Well, I do," Lettice told them, without an ounce of superiority. "And I think it helps me deal with things positively. I'm not saying I'm a religious fanatic," she said hastily. "I don't go to church nor follow any particular religion, but I do have faith, and it's faith that helps keep me going."

"I tried religion once," Sarah said, staring at the floor. "I backed out. It was a scam."

"Yeah, because it was Scientology," Dan clarified. "What did you expect from a religion created by a godawful science fiction writer?"

"As if that makes it any different from all the others," Sarah countered. "All they want is your money and your undying obedience. It's all just a big fucking club where you have to do what they tell you. They're all on huge power trips using faith in God to get them what they want. I find it very difficult to think positively under such constraints. You'd think I'd confessed to mass murder the day I told them I wasn't coming back. I thought they weren't going to let me leave."

Lettice nodded. "I don't agree with organized religion, either. It has major problems I don't think will ever be ironed out. No, I think everybody should have their own belief system. Faith is very personal and you should not let anyone manipulate or take control of it. I make my own rules and adhere to them." She looked over at Dan. "What's so funny?"

"Nothing's funny," Dan replied with a wide grin. "It's just that I agree with every single word you've said."

"Really, Dan?" Lettice asked, gazing at him admiringly.

"Well, up to a point anyway," he added, making her lose her smile a bit. He noticed and shifted uncomfortably in his chair. How did he get into this conversation anyway? If he wasn't careful, he'd offend Lettice and it would be the end of their short relationship. He didn't want to continue, but he was too far into it now.

"I guess you could call me an agnostic," he said, clearing his throat. "I don't know if I believe that there is a god or not. I think Jesus was a man ahead of his time and that he was revered, but I don't think he was the 'Son of God.' I think people transformed him into that because of this reverence and I think the Bible is useful advice mixed with fanciful legend handed down and mistranslated and embellished over time. I don't believe there is any way for man to know if God really exists and I'm not so sure even dying will solve that riddle. What if we just go to another world similar to this one? What if there's nothing? What if we go somewhere so far removed from what we know that's it's completely unimaginable? To me, this is all an unknown and I can't understand how people can be so certain that what people have told them is true. And when people tell others about God and Jesus and Heaven and Hell, a lot of the time they are just using these things to impose their own belief systems on other people. It seems like it's all about power and I don't want to be any part of it."

He took a deep breath, then looked up at Lettice to see she was staring intently at him, hanging on every word. Meanwhile, Sarah was staring off into space, bored out of her mind.

"I-I just don't get it," he finished hurriedly then started gazing at his hands.

There was a pause before Lettice said, "Those are the rules you live by, Dan. I admire that. I don't necessarily agree with them, but I admire them. I think you have a very interesting point of view."

Dan looked up at her. She was smiling. He smiled back.

Sarah stood and changed the subject abruptly. "Anybody besides me starving?" she asked.

"I'm starved," Dan admitted, apparently glad to shift to a topic of lighter conversation.

"Hey, I'll cook for you guys," Lettice said, getting to her feet. "How does that sound?"

"Oh, no, I couldn't let you do that," Dan protested.

"I'll help," Sarah interjected, leading Lettice into the kitchen. "It'll be fun. And we'll get to see what kind of mess he's got going in here."

Lettice giggled and looked back at Dan as she followed Sarah into the kitchen. She smiled and blew him a kiss.

Dan returned the kiss then shook his head. Evidently, the party was off. That meant the tights pinching his crotch were for nothing. He stood to pull the constricting fabric from his body and suddenly had an urge to return upstairs and continue writing his story. He had to start all over again and he wanted to get started before he forgot everything.

He booted his computer and immediately went into his processing program. He centered the word "UNTITLED" at the top of the document and saved it. He then set the program to save the document every five minutes and began retyping what he had written earlier. He saved the story when he was finished then decided to save it to a floppy disk, just in case something happened to the hard drive.

He had rewritten everything he remembered then stared at the screen. There was more to the story, he knew, but nothing was coming to him. Writer's block already? *I was just getting started. It's awfully quiet in here.*

It was also quite chilly and getting colder. The goose bumps on his arms and legs felt like pebbles pressing against his costume.

He suddenly recalled what Sarah and Lettice had said about the ghosts and became suddenly alert. Each time the manifestations had occurred, the temperature had dropped dramatically.

Am I going to see a ghost now? he wondered with a mixture of curiosity and dread. *Do I really want to see one?* Fear crept up his spine and his whole body tingled with terrible anticipation.

Well, if he was going to see one, he wanted to hurry up and get it over with. He couldn't stand sitting here waiting for the supernatural to happen. His anxiety mounted, causing him to leap up and throw the shutters open. He heard a few late trick-or-treaters talking and laughing in the street, but could not see them. It was as cold outside as it was inside.

He realized he was relieved he hadn't seen the faceless ghost in the window. He recalled the terror he had seen in Lettice's eyes and he didn't want to share her experience.

No, in a strange way, he did. He wanted to see the ghost, too, so that he and Lettice could compare and have a little more something in common. *Oh, well,* he thought. *We already have other things in common, like the incident in the car.* Still, he wanted to know what the ghost looked like.

He closed the shutters and secured them. He turned back to the computer and sighed. *I should really go down and help them with dinner,* he told himself. *Lettice is down there and I want to be with her. Why did I come up here anyway? This could have waited.*

Dan continued to sit at the computer, however. He stared

bleakly at the screen for some time before his fingers started flying across the keyboard.

10.

Rebecca avoided John's house for several days, but found it quite unbearable to be away from him. The Devil with what Dinah had said. She was going to visit John, perhaps bring him some bread or biscuits. Whatever she could muster.

Before departing, she made certain her father wasn't watching. She then slipped out and headed for John's house. As she neared it, she saw Dinah approaching, heading straight for John's door.

Rebecca hid behind a large tree by the street and watched her adversary's advance. She was afraid to encounter the woman but was curious as to what she might be up to. What was she doing visiting John? Were they courting? She didn't think so. John didn't seem to have too high of an opinion of Dinah. At least, that was the impression she got. She certainly hoped they weren't courting.

Dinah knocked on the door, an impeccable smile plastered to her face. It was meant to be friendly and polite, but the smile chilled Rebecca to the core of her being, making her insides feel like icicles.

Dinah lifted her hand and Rebecca saw a basket clutched in it, a basket that she was certain hadn't been there a moment ago. Rebecca was positive that when she had seen Dinah approaching her hands had been empty. Where had that basket come from? It looked familiar.

Rebecca looked down to see her basket was gone, her hands empty. She looked on the ground to see where she had dropped it, but it was not there. She looked back up at Dinah. Dinah turned her head and grinned.

Rebecca paled. She ran home, up the stairs to her room. She looked frantically around, not thinking about what she might be looking for. Her mind was racing. How could she have taken the basket? Dinah hadn't been anywhere near her. Not only that, Dinah was giving the bread and pastries to John as if they were from her. How dare she?

Fear turned into anger. Rebecca raced back down the stairs and out of the house. She received curious glances from passersby as she ran as fast as she could to John's house. She rapped sharply on the door then started pounding on it with her fists.

John answered. Upon seeing Rebecca's face, his slight smile vanished.

"That's not her basket," Rebecca cried. "It's mine. Dinah got it from me when I was on my way to visit you. That basket is from *me*, not her."

John looked overwhelmed for a moment then stepped aside. Rebecca went inside, only to end up face to face with Dinah.

"Now, Rebecca," Dinah said in a condescending tone. "That's not entirely the truth now, is it?"

Rebecca glared at Dinah then looked over at an utterly dumbfounded John.

"Dinah told me you had baked them, Rebecca, but that you had given them to her," he said.

"And, seeing as that I had plenty myself," Dinah interjected happily, "I decided that I would share them with John." She smiled at Rebecca, making Rebecca's internal organs ice over.

"I didn't give them to you," Rebecca said quietly, her rage having vanished.

"Then how did I get them, Rebecca?"

"I-I don't know." Rebecca's gaze faltered. She was suddenly very embarrassed in front of John and she couldn't look at him. There was only thing she could do: flee.

She was crying in her bed when her father walked in. "There's a man at the door to see you," he said, his voice questioning.

Rebecca looked at her father with bleary eyes that quickly

cleared. She rushed by him without a word, taking the steps two at a time. When she saw John, however, she became suddenly aloof, keeping her distance from him.

John gazed at her, his expression stern. "I believe there is something you wish to tell me about Dinah."

Rebecca looked up, but could not hold his gaze. She saw her father standing on the stairs, silently demanding an explanation. She had never enjoyed that particular look on his face, for it usually meant he thought there was something seriously wrong with her.

She looked at John, but still did not speak. She was reluctant to say anything about Dinah lest the wretched girl suddenly appear. Finally, after several moments of self-conscious hand-wringing, Rebecca found her voice.

"She took my basket."

"I know she did," John replied. "I do not believe what she told me."

Rebecca boldly stepped forward. "Stay away from her, John," she warned. "She threatened me, told me to never see you again. She told me she was the one responsible for—"

John waited. "Responsible for what, Rebecca?"

Again, Rebecca's gaze failed her. She turned away, the sound of him saying her name both pleasurable and frightening. Her eyes became cemented to the floor.

"Dinah is responsible for—what befell your wife and child."

John looked sour, said nothing for a time. He turned to Rebecca's father who now wore a serious expression.

"That's a serious charge, daughter."

"She told me it was so, Sir," Rebecca replied, wringing her hands rapidly. "This is not a fabrication on my part. I only tell you what Dinah has told me herself."

"I believe your daughter, Mr. Duncan," John declared. "But I find it quite impossible that Dinah could be responsible for what happened to my wife and son. My wife's death was not murder, for she died during childbirth. There is no possible way for that to be Dinah's doing. I believe she was just trying to scare you, Rebecca."

"She told me it was her doing," Rebecca insisted. "I wholeheartedly believe her. She frightens me greatly, Sir. She took my basket without even stepping foot near me."

Both men were shocked into momentary silence. John then asked, "Are you insinuating that Dinah possesses powers beyond this world? That she's a witch?"

Rebecca hadn't thought of calling Dinah a witch, but it did suit her. "I don't know how else to explain what I have witnessed, Sir."

"This is another serious charge, daughter," Rebecca's father said. "The punishment for witchery is death. Are you certain you want to put forth such an accusation?"

"I do not wish to accuse her of any such thing," Rebecca cried, on the verge of tears. "I just want to know why she is treating me so."

"If she is treating you in such a roguish manner and if it is because she is a witch, something must be done." Her father removed his hat from its peg by the door. "I must notify Pastor Ritch at once."

❧

Dan jerked suddenly, a startled scream jolting him. He had been so engrossed in his writing that he had forgotten where he was. The scream didn't register at first and he sat blinking at the screen, catching movement at the edge of his vision.

Lettice stood silent behind him, unmoving, her hands folded in front of her mouth. "Another ghost?" Dan whispered, a chill traveling up and down his spine.

She nodded. "She was standing right next to you, Dan." Her voice was a low whisper. "She was staring at you with her hands outstretched, her palms touching your shoulders. Didn't you feel it?"

"No—" Dan said, startled.

"She vanished as soon as she saw us," Sarah said from the doorway. "She looked surprised."

"I didn't know she was there," Dan exclaimed, alarmed. "I believe that you both saw her. Was it the faceless—?"

Lettice shook her head. "This was a different ghost. She wore fifties-style clothing, slacks, high-collared blouse. She looked sort of mannish."

Dan looked at Sarah. "Sounds like Aunt Audrey," he said. "Don't you think?"

Sarah shrugged. "I don't know. I can't remember ever seeing a picture of her."

"Audrey is the failed tap dancer, right?" Lettice asked.

"Yes," Dan replied. "It might not be her, but your description sure fits. She died in the late fifties, so the clothing style fits, too. And it would make sense that her spirit is here. I strongly suspect she committed suicide in this house."

"Aunt Audrey lived here?" Sarah asked. "Are you sure?"

Dan shrugged. "That's the picture I've pieced together. It all makes sense, doesn't it?"

"Why did she have her hands on you, though?" Lettice asked. "It's like she was—I don't know. Like she was moving your arms while you typed or transferring something," she said.

"Let's see what you've written," Sarah said. "Page up to the top."

Lettice said, "I think I know what you're thinking, Sarah."

"What?" Dan asked, wanting to know.

"You used 'Smead' in the story, Dan," Sarah said. "Why?"

Dan shrugged. "No reason. The name's been stuck in my head for the past few days."

"Where'd you get the idea for the story?"

"The whole thing just came to me. I must be getting inspired by all the old houses in this neighborhood."

Sarah nodded. "What year is it supposed to take place?"

"The late 1600s," he replied. "That's the picture I get in my head, anyway. You know, the time of the witch trials and stuff."

"Hmm," Sarah hummed. "It just came to you, huh?"

"Well, yeah," he said. "It hit me like a rock in the back of the head. I hear that's how it works with writers sometimes. An idea will hit them like a Mack truck and they can't do anything but hurry and write it out."

"Hmm," Sarah said. "It could be that, or Aunt Audrey writing it through you."

"I knew you were going to say that," Lettice said with a frown.

"What?" Dan asked, surprised and more than a little horrified. "Why would she do that?"

"She sent you that dream about being a tap dancer," Sarah said. "And now she's making you write this story. In order to find out why she's doing this, though, I think we should conduct a—"

"Oh, no," Dan said. "I know what you're going to say."

"What?" Lettice asked.

"A séance," Sarah replied succinctly.

"They never work," Dan said. "Not with her, anyway. I've never seen anything happen in all the ones I've attended."

"You've only been to two," Sarah pointed out.

"Yeah, and they both flopped. Nothing strange happened."

"Okay, so we won't do a séance," Sarah sighed. "But the only reason they didn't work was probably because mom and dad's house isn't haunted. A séance would work in this house, though. Most definitely, I think."

"Seems to me that the ghosts are perfectly capable of communicating with us without performing any sort of ritual," said Dan.

"Yeah, I guess." Sarah sighed again. "But why you? I'm the ghost expert here."

"How should I know? You said it yourself: you're the expert."

"Whatever," Sarah said sourly. She turned away from the computer with a look of great disappointment.

"Try writing again," Lettice said, leaning over Dan's shoulder. "Maybe she'll clarify what she's trying to tell you."

Dan looked at her. "Are you sure about that? I thought you wanted nothing to do with the ghosts in this house."

"I don't, but this is too interesting to drop. I want to know what this ghost wants. It seems to be important. Besides, your Aunt Audrey wasn't nearly as scary as the other one."

"Well, okay," Dan decided.

The computer screen instantly went black.

"Shit!" he cried. "This is the second time this has happened. Good thing I had saved it to disk first." He rebooted the computer.

"This happened earlier," Lettice explained to Sarah. "He didn't save it last time, though. We thought maybe the ghost—*a* ghost, was doing it."

"It could just be the computer," Dan said. "Strange things happen to computers all the time. It used to happen a lot at my old job and not even the 'experts' at the company could convincingly explain them. Then again, they could have just been lousy at their job. That's probably more likely, now that I think of it."

Once the reboot had completed, Dan checked his floppy disk to make sure the story file had been saved. The disk was blank.

He cursed. "I know I saved it. I had it on autosave and I manually saved it right after I realized you were both in the room. Oh, wait—let me check the hard drive. Maybe I saved it there by mistake. Nope. It's gone."

"Ghosts," Lettice said with a shiver.

"Witches," Dan said two heartbeats later.

"Huh?" Lettice replied.

"Like in the story. Oh, you didn't read that far, did you?" He relayed the story to her.

"What I don't understand," Sarah said once he was finished, "is why Aunt Audrey would erase the story she just had you type out. Seems to me that if she wanted it written out, she'd want it to be permanent."

"If she's making me write it," Dan interjected. "I could be just making it up, you know."

"Are you making it up?"

"I thought so," he said dubiously. "I thought I was just

typing whatever came to mind. It certainly didn't seem like I was being guided by a ghostly hand."

"There's more than one ghost here," Lettice pointed out. "The one *I* saw, the one *you* saw, the one we saw together."

"All I saw was mist," Sarah said. "It could have been Audrey in a less-than-solid state or it could have been the faceless ghost."

"Or it could have been the Minuteman that the neighbor saw in the window," Dan added.

"No," Sarah said. "This voice was a woman's. Heck, Audrey and the faceless ghost could be one and the same."

"I don't think so," Lettice said. "The one I saw wore very old clothing. I think—You know, I'm not sure now."

"Hmm," Sarah voiced, thinking.

"I just had a thought," Dan piped in. "What if one of the ghosts, say, the faceless one, doesn't want Audrey to tell me the story and it is the faceless ghost that keeps erasing it from my computer?"

"Why?" Sarah wanted to know.

"'Coz she's a witch," Lettice answered. "The faceless one. She's Dinah, I betcha."

"You think the faceless ghost is Dinah?" Dan asked.

"Yes, it makes sense if you think about it. If she was lying about the basket three hundred years ago, she might be averse to letting people know about it now."

"Yeah, but Aunt Audrey isn't from the 1600s," Dan replied. "Why would she be telling me about this Rebecca person and her problems with Dinah?"

"Maybe to warn you about Dinah, about what she's capable of," postulated Sarah. "If she's a witch, it might be in your best interest to know all about her."

"Great," he murmured. "The ghost of a witch haunts my house. Just what I needed!"

"Wasn't there a reason we came up here in the first place?" Lettice asked Sarah.

"Dinner," Sarah exclaimed. "I completely forgot about it. It's probably all cold by now."

"I'll finish this later, then," Dan said, switching off the computer.

He got up and followed the women downstairs. Lettice led the way, Sarah between her and Dan. Dan looked down at the back of Lettice's head, enjoying the bounce and sway of her hair as she descended the steps. Then her hair, along with the rest of her body, was suddenly gone. There were several loud thumps accompanied by the staircase vibrating under his feet. His gaze darted to the foot of the stairs to see Lettice lying there, motionless.

"Oh, my God!" Sarah exclaimed. She hurried down the last three steps and fell hard to her knees beside Lettice. She took her wrist, feeling for a pulse. "She's still alive, at least."

"Of course she is," Dan exclaimed. "She's only knocked herself out for a second, she's not dead." However, he was worried. Memories of his dreams, of stairs soaked in blood, of his son lying in a pool of it—

"I was worried she might have broken her neck," Sarah said through clenched teeth. "It can happen, you know."

Lettice groaned, her head rolling to one side. She opened her eyes, moaned loudly and shut them again. "Wha... 'pen?"

"You fell down the stairs," Dan told her, taking her hand. "You were unconscious there for about thirty seconds."

"My head hurts," Lettice relayed, wincing in pain. "Ah, my ankle, too."

"You might have sprained it," Dan said, looking at the affected body part. The ankle was swollen and red.

"I'll call an ambulance," Sarah said, darting to her feet. "She might have a head injury."

"No, Sarah, I'll be—" Lettice started to sit up, but couldn't. She tried to inhale and only gasped. "I can't breathe," she whispered.

"Her costume's probably too tight," Sarah said urgently, the telephone against her cheek. "You'll have to loosen—Oh, yes, hi! I need an ambulance! A woman fell down the stairs and I think she hit her head. She was unconscious for a little while and her ankle's swollen—"

"Loosen what?" Dan mumbled, momentarily unable to figure out what his sister was trying to tell him. Loosen Lettice's costume? Then it hit him: Loosen her costume so she can breathe. Of course.

Recalling hearing somewhere that moving an accident victim wasn't a good idea, Dan ruled out rolling her over to unzip her from the back. The only option was to untie the laces of her bodice. Since they weren't functional laces, he had to cut them somehow. Scissors. Where were his scissors? He thought he might have put them in a drawer in the kitchen. He ran in, found and retrieved them. Lettice would be breathing in a matter of seconds.

"You're going to be fine," he told her, brandishing the scissors.

"What are you doing with those?" she asked deliriously.

"I've got to cut these laces so you can breathe better."

"Are ya gonna pillage me, Dan?"

"What?" he asked, startled. "Of course not."

"Isn't that what pirates do, pillage and plunder?" she asked with a painful smile, referring to the costume he still wore. "Pirates with scissors—"

Dan hurriedly cut the laces then pulled the fabric outward to make sure her lungs had enough room to expand. "How's that?" he asked her. "Can you breathe easier?"

"Mm-hmm," she voiced. "Did you get a good look at my boobies?"

"Lettice, I'm trying to help you—"

"I'll have to warn you, I'm a pretty lousy lay right now. I hurt all over."

"The ambulance should be here in about fifteen minutes," Sarah said, disconnecting from the call. She looked down at Dan with the scissors and at what he had done to Lettice's costume. "Dan—"

"You told me to loosen her costume, so I did," he replied more than a little defensively. With a frown, he added, "She seems to think I was trying something, too. But I'm not, I'm trying to help." He picked up Lettice's hand and held it.

Her eyes fluttered. "What are you doing?"

"We're waiting for the ambulance," he told her patiently. "It should be here soon."

"No, not you. Her."

Dan turned to face Sarah who was in turn looking at him. Then they both turned their heads to the staircase.

"It's her again," Lettice whispered. "Old No-Face."

"She's here?" Dan asked, his voice a whisper. "I don't see her."

"She's always here," Lettice informed him, sounding weaker by the second. "Always." Her eyes fluttered and closed.

"No, no, come on, stay awake," Dan insisted, squeezing her hand.

Her eyes opened again and oriented on him. Her mouth parted, the lips pulling apart from one another as if made of glue. "Are you crying?"

Dan shook his head. He lowered his head and sniffed, wiping his eyes on his sleeve.

"Old No-Face pushed me, you know," Lettice whispered. "She's laughing at us. It's weird, because she has no face. It's really creepy, Dan. You're lucky you can't see her." Her eyes closed again.

"No!" Dan cried. He first lightly slapped her hand then slapped her face when that elicited no response.

"She's still alive, Dan," Sarah said. "She's breathing. You don't need to keep beating on her. She's just unconscious."

Dan looked to the door. "Where is that ambulance? Shouldn't it be here by now?"

Sarah checked her watch. "It's only been five minutes."

"Is that all?"

Twenty minutes later the ambulance arrived. Dan opened the door just as the paramedics were getting out of the vehicle. "Sorry we're late," one of them said as he approached. "We got lost. Your light was out and we couldn't see the number."

Dan looked at his porch light. It was blazing. "It's been on all night."

The paramedic ignored him. His partner caught up with him and went inside.

II.

Dan stood in the kitchen, the faucet dripping. It was dark and oppressive and he wanted nothing more than to leave immediately. He couldn't, of course. It was the dream again. He had to continue on to the living room. His feet pulled him forward, stepping inside bloody footsteps that led the way.

The television was on. A news clip of a young boy being stabbed by a man in black wearing a hood was being broadcast. The boy was Billy. He lay in a pool of blood in front of the television, the butcher knife jutting from his chest. The crimson ochre of his short life streamed from his mouth, down his chin and down his chest, fueling the ever-growing pool around him.

Dan tried to scream, but his vocal chords seemed to have been ripped from his throat. His mouth contorted soundlessly as he gazed upon his dead son.

It took him a moment to realize that Billy's eyes had opened. He stared blankly at Dan for a moment before the expression turned menacing. His eyes narrowed and he grinned.

"She's upstairs, dad," he whispered hoarsely. He chuckled then fell forward, driving the tip of the butcher knife out his back.

Dan was horrified. Billy's body had only spoken to Dan after he had gone upstairs and could no longer see him. He didn't have time to think on it long, however, for his feet dragged him backward toward the stairs.

His heels thudded against the bottom step, urging him to turn around and ascend. He had no choice but to obey, knowing full well what awaited him. He unwillingly took the first step. Blood squished beneath his shoe.

He expected the bedroom door to burst open and deluge of blood wash over him, but it didn't. It wasn't happening like it had in the last dream. Everything looked normal. Billy was eerily silent.

Dan approached the bedroom door with caution. Something horrible was still going to happen, he just didn't know what. The nightmare was never pleasant or even mediocre. It was what all nightmares were: terrifying no matter what the circumstance.

The door was ajar. No sounds emanated from within. Dan was terrified, all his nerve endings awake and trembling. What was going to happen next? He couldn't stand it anymore. He placed his palm on the door and shoved the door open.

Amy lay in bed, the covers and sheets thrown into a heap on the floor. Only a pillow remained and upon it had been placed Amy's head, her eyes gouged out. Her body was spread out in pieces across the mattress, blood soaking into the springy material.

Next to the bed stood a woman in an old fashioned dress, a bloodied axe in her hand. Where her face should have been, there was nothingness.

A very thin, gray line appeared in the nothingness, pulled upward at the ends as if trying to imitate a smile. The figure took a step forward.

Dan awoke violently, his clothing drenched with sweat. It took him ten heartbeats to realize he was sitting in a chair in a hospital, Lettice sleeping soundly in the bed beside him.

She moaned softly and her eyes opened. "Dan?" she whispered, her voice hoarse. "What—?"

"You had a bad fall," he told her, still unable to completely shake the effects of his nightmare. He was very jittery, on edge. "You broke two ribs and took a severe blow to the head. Oh, and you twisted your ankle, but that's minor in comparison."

"Ow, my head *hurts*," she groaned. "I think I remember what happened now. Was it earlier today?"

"Last night," he said and looked at his watch. "It's three-thirty in the morning now."

"Really?" she inquired. "And you're still here?"

He shrugged. "I couldn't leave you. I wanted to be here when you woke up, just in case you didn't remember how you got here." With a smirk, he added, "I wanted to make sure the bump on your head didn't make you forget me."

"I could never forget you," she said, giving him a tired smile. "You're the guy with the ghosts." She winced in pain as she laughed. "A very painful memory."

"I'm so sorry," he chuckled softly then yawned. "The doctor said you'll be fine, but you'll have to stay here for at least one more day."

Lettice sighed. "Well, no sex this weekend, I guess." She then glanced sidelong at him, grinning mischievously.

He laughed. "I'm surprised you can even think about sex in your condition. Are you in very much pain?"

"A little," she said. "My chest hurts." She gazed at him. "Halloween's over now, isn't it?"

Dan was confused for a second, then looked down at himself and laughed. "You're right. I haven't had a chance to change. Actually, I've become quite used to this outfit. I might have to wear it all the time now."

"Ah, but the rental fee would be astronomical," Lettice quipped. Then, "Dan, do me a favor? Go to my apartment and get me some clothes? I don't want to wear that barmaid outfit out of here tomorrow, especially after you've taken scissors to it."

"Sure," he said. "Sorry about that, but it was an emergency. I'll pay for the costume."

"Oh, don't worry about that now. I just need some clothes."

"Okay, but I don't have a key."

"It should be in my purse."

"Oh, that's back at the house. I think. I'll go fetch it then head out to your place. Anything in particular you want?"

"Oh, just a shirt and pants, whatever," she said. Her eyes

fluttered as if she was getting sleepy. "Don't worry about it right away. Go home, get some sleep. You look like a – dare I say it? – a ghost!"

"Okay." He stood, hesitated, then bent down and kissed her. "I'll be back." He squeezed her hand then started for the door.

"Dan?" she called weakly. "Thank you for staying here all through the night with me. It was very sweet. I don't know anyone else who would have done that."

He smiled, nodded and departed.

He tossed his keys on the coffee table, yawned loudly and headed for the stairs. When he reached the second step, he realized he heard his printer upstairs.

He burst into the room just in time to see the last sheet of paper land in the tray. The printer fell silent. A blinking red light told him to add paper.

Dan's eyes darted to the computer screen. Lines and lines of text were displayed in a very small font. It was the story he'd started about Rebecca.

"What the—?"

He retrieved the pages from the printer and started reading.

"Sir, no!" Rebecca exclaimed, tugging at her father's sleeve. "You mustn't! There's no telling what she will do if she is found out!"

"Daughter, I must!" He glared at her until she let go. He donned his hat, nodded once to John, and stepped through the door.

Rebecca went instantly to John, her eyes fixated upon her father as he walked out of the yard. "I fear for him, John," she whispered.

"If it is true what you say about Dinah, others must also know. She must be brought to face God's justice."

Rebecca said nothing, her fears not allayed.

Her father never came home again. He had never arrived at the church and no one had seen him since he left Rebecca and John. No body was ever found. Rebecca's father seemed to have vanished off the face of God's Earth. Rebecca and John suspected Dinah had something to do with the disappearance, but neither said anything to anyone.

His disappearance left Rebecca alone in the house. John asked her if she would rather live with him, but the community of Boston would be in an uproar if she took him up on the offer. They had to be married before they could live together. So, John proposed to her. Flustered yet pleased, Rebecca accepted. She sold her father's house after the wedding and moved in with John. Dinah was suspiciously absent during this time, but Rebecca and John had not forgotten about her.

The week following the wedding, John fell seriously ill.

Rebecca stayed at John's side and strongly suspected that the illness was Dinah's doing. As the days wore on and John's condition worsened, Rebecca became increasingly angry with Dinah. On the fifth day of John's illness, Rebecca finally left his side and stormed over to Dinah's house, ready for a confrontation.

She rapped hard on the door, but there was no answer. Rebecca kicked the door and screamed, but it remained shut. She cried out in raging anguish then returned to John's bedside, tears streaming down her face.

John recovered after a time and Rebecca was glad that Dinah had not been home that day. Rebecca eventually decided she must have been mistaken, for surely if the sickness had been Dinah's doing, John would never have recovered.

Rebecca saw Dinah from a distance occasionally during the course of the next year, but Dinah never seemed to see her. Rebecca became pregnant and gave birth to a son. Her older sister, Submit, and her husband, Edward, moved to Boston after the baby was born. They stayed with Rebecca and John while awaiting the construction of their own home.

The day after their arrival, Dinah showed up at the door

to welcome the newcomers to town. In actuality, she had seen Edward the previous day and had taken an instant liking to the man. The fact that his wife was pregnant with their second child was no concern of hers.

Rebecca slammed the door in her face.

Submit had a miscarriage that night. Two days later, Submit vanished. Her body was never found.

Rebecca was again both upset and furious, instantly convinced that Dinah had caused the death of the infant and the disappearance of her sister. She relayed to her brother-in-law, Edward, that Dinah was a witch and was to blame for the death of his child and disappearance of his wife. She told him that Dinah was also responsible for the disappearance of her own father and the demise of John's former wife and child.

Edward was shocked and mortified, though did not doubt a single word of the story. His shock quickly turned to anger, however, and he announced he was going to confront Dinah. Rebecca and John warned him against it, but could not convince him to stay away from her. Edward was found dead the next morning. He lay in the street in front of John's house with one of Rebecca's knitting needles jutting from his throat.

The town authorities instantly assumed Rebecca committed the crime. She was summarily arrested and thrown into jail. There followed a trial and Rebecca was accused of witchcraft. John tried to defend her, but the judge ordered him to sit down and be quiet or he, too, would be arrested.

Dinah, acting convincingly, told everyone at the trial that she had seen, with her own two eyes, Rebecca Duncan fly by her window and threaten to cast an evil spell on her. She continued to say Rebecca had told her she had caused the death of John's first wife and child and that Dinah herself would meet the same fate if she didn't stay away from him.

The jury was entirely convinced by the testimony, but it wasn't Dinah's words alone that convicted Rebecca. Three women examined Rebecca's body while the court awaited their findings. One of the women emerged from the examination stating she had personally seen, with her own two eyes, a blue spot the size of a pin's head on Rebecca's shin: a "devil's teat" from which demons suckle.

There ensued such an uproar that Rebecca was instantly condemned. She was thrown back into her cell where she examined her own shin and found no such blue spot. Either the women had lied or Dinah had made them see something that wasn't there. It did not matter; Rebecca would be executed the next day.

She was to be hanged, but the judge had a sudden change of mind and decided that the best way to dispose of a witch was to burn her. A broken neck might not be enough to destroy such a creature, he announced to those assembled. Besides, he was a devoted Christian who held to the long-standing belief that no prisoner of the Lord shall be killed by human hands, and since hanging involved the hands of a man placing a rope about Rebecca's neck, he deemed that particular means of execution unacceptable. The judge didn't consider the lighting of fire by that same man's hand to be in the same category, however.

Rebecca was tied to a post just outside of Boston with the entire town to witness her demise. Without ceremony, the fire was lit and Rebecca's last minutes of life were about to end. When the flames licked her feet, she screamed.

The shrill, heart-wrenching sound chilled the bones of John and he was abruptly overcome with rage. He saw Dinah grinning happily at the impending death of his beloved and his fury heightened. He launched himself at Dinah and grabbed her roughly by the arms. Dinah was too startled to say or do anything as John dragged and flung her face-first into the blaze.

The judge seized John and pulled him away, but the damage to Dinah had been done. Her face was horribly charred and most of her hair had been burned off.

John was thrown in jail for thirty days. After he was released, he took his son and moved away from Boston. Years later, his fully-grown son returned to Boston to build a larger house on the site of the old house that had burned down. He moved his new bride in and they had six children.

Rebecca's ashes are buried in the cemetery nearby.

᷒

Dan put the pages down and leaned back in the chair.

So, Dinah is the faceless ghost. Just like I thought.

He reread the last part of the printout. So this is why Aunt Audrey wanted me to write this. Cemetery, huh?

He leapt from his chair, pages still and hand, and rushed out of the house.

The fact that the Colonial Cemetery was only a few blocks away made him realize that the house he now lived in was at least the third house built on the site. Things were starting to make sense. However, he still didn't know why Dinah was haunting his house and pushing his girlfriend down the stairs. Did it have something to do with John burning her face?

The iron cemetery gate was locked. Dan yanked at it anyhow, testing the strength of the padlock. It didn't budge. He then examined the gate, searching for footholds. He found them and thought that if they were going to go through the trouble of locking the place up, they'd use a gate that wasn't very easy to climb.

He grabbed the wrought ironwork and shoved his foot into a curve. He jammed his other foot into another curve, climbed up and over and fell hard onto the gravel road. A sharp pain in his side, just below his ribs, caused him to cry out sharply. He groaned and slowly got to his feet, scowling at the large rock he'd fallen on.

Darkness still held the day, as it was only four-thirty a.m. There was little illumination coming from the moon as thick cloud cover obscured it, making it difficult to read most of the tombstones. Some were faded or covered in moss, making them even more illegible.

Dan thought of returning for the flashlight in his car, but he didn't want to risk falling and hurting himself even worse than before. He decided to wait until sunrise, which was now only couple of hours away.

He located an old oak and fell asleep underneath it. Some time later, he awoke with a start.

Someone had kicked his foot.

He looked up at a bearded man in blue overalls. "Huh?" he exclaimed groggily. "Oh! I was, uh, just looking for a certain headstone."

The man frowned severely. "Ah. And it was so urgent that you had to climb the fence at night and fall asleep?"

"I was tired," Dan replied. "Look, I know this sounds strange, but I just had to find the tombstone of Rebecca, formerly Duncan, Smead. I forgot about how early in the morning it was and when I got here I couldn't see anything. So, rather than go back for my flashlight, I thought I'd just wait until dawn and—"

Dan stopped talking, suddenly realizing that the man had taken a startled step backward. "R-Rebecca Smead?" the man asked. "The witch?"

"She wasn't a witch!" Dan replied defensively. "She was wrongly accused, by a real witch." He shook his head. "Do you know where her marker is?"

The man gazed at him, his face closed. "It's that way," he said, jutting his thumb. "But I never go near it. I suggest you do likewise."

"Why?"

The man didn't reply. His closed look vanished as he watched Dan get up and brush himself off. When Dan stepped forward, the man backed off. "Uh, thanks," Dan said then walked in the direction of the man's thumb.

He read the tombstones as he walked and found himself standing before a large mausoleum. It didn't have the name Smead, or any name at all, carved into it and had been placed about a hundred years too late. He thought Rebecca's ashes should have been put inside such an impressive edifice as this before he remembered the story had said her ashes had been buried. He bypassed the imposing structure and resumed his search.

He ended up walking by her marker twice before he saw it.

Rebecca Smead's headstone was broken at the base, the upper portion of the stone lying in the grass, half covered by a large bush. Her name was clearly readable.

Upon further inspection, Dan found her marker had fallen forward, not backward. The marker had been carved on both sides and the bush was not on top of her grave as he initially thought. On the other side of the stone, on top of Rebecca's grave, was a huge pile of dog shit.

"What do you care about her, anyway?" the maintenance man asked abruptly.

"I'm, uh, researching my family tree," he said quickly, nervously, not looking at the man.

"Are you a Mormon?" the man asked after a short pause.

"Uh, no," Dan said cautiously. He was suddenly frightened and didn't know why.

"Mormons are into that, you know. They make a livin' out of it." The man paused. "So, you said Rebecca's an ancestor of yours?"

Dan nodded, wanting nothing more in the world than to turn and run to his car.

The maintenance man was silent again then gazed down at the excrement. "Fucking dogs," he muttered. He brought his boot down on the pile, grinding it into Rebecca's grave. He then grinned and snorted.

Dan took the opportunity to walk briskly back to his car.

He was so disconcerted from the events at the cemetery that he found himself driving aimlessly about town, his mind racing. The old woman with the dog kept invading his wildly meandering thoughts. He was certain that the dog poop on the grave had something to do with her and couldn't convince himself it was just a coincidence.

As his car neared his block, Dan saw the old woman with the dog speaking to his annoying neighbor. Both women glared at him as he drove past.

What the hell's going on around here? he wondered. It felt like his flesh was crawling.

He drove past them to his house.

A message from Lettice waited for him. She was ready to come home from the hospital. Dan grabbed her purse and rushed out to her apartment.

Damita watched Dan's car pull out of the driveway. When he was safely out of sight, she hurried from the window and ran to the door. She went into Dan's yard and opened his side yard gate. She slipped into his backyard.

The old lady had told her it would be easy and it was. The old lady had also told Damita the dog that kept crapping in everyone's yard was here. Damita was going to take care of that dog once and for all. She knew that son-of-a-bitch neighbor of hers had been lying to her and he was going to pay for those lies. She spied a shovel leaning up against the shed and picked it up.

She looked around the yard and found no evidence of a dog. The old lady told her that it was most likely an inside dog and that the back door would be unlocked. She was right again. Damita went inside.

"Here, poochie!" she called, making puckering sounds. "C'mon, doggie. Aunt Damita's got something for you!"

"Help!" a voice called distinctly. A woman's voice, overhead, muffled. "Help me!"

"Hello?" called Damita, suddenly wary. "Who's there?"

"Help me, please!" the voice cried desperately. "I'm trapped!"

Damita paused. "Where are you?"

"Upstairs!" the voice told her frantically. "Hurry, please! Before he comes back!"

So he's got a woman tied up in here, Damita thought with a grin. It's worse than I thought. Wait until I tell the news people about this. I'll be a hero.

"I'm coming," Damita called, running through the kitchen to the stairs. She flew up the stairs as fast as her chubby legs would take her, brandishing the shovel like a spear. Her foot landed hard on the middle step and it gave way. The shovel flew from her grasp, clanking dully against the wall. Incredible pain shot up her leg as she laid sprawled forward, jagged pieces of wood stabbing into her ankle.

She cried out, the pain intense, searing. "I'm stuck," she cried out, her voice frantic and piercing. "The stairs were booby-trapped."

The voice was silent.

Damita struggled for a few minutes, but was unable to free herself. Every time she moved, the pain would increase. She was afraid to look at her leg, fearing that it would hurt worse if she saw how bad it was. She imagined a hundred splinters sticking out of her ankle and leg, blood streaming down her foot. Indeed, she could feel something trickling against her skin.

"I can't get loose!" she cried.

A blue mist formed at the top of the stairs. Damita gazed at it, her voice suddenly caught in her throat. The mist quickly dissipated, only to be replaced by a young woman, her face turned to the side. Her clothes were old fashioned, surmounted by a lacy bonnet.

Damita suddenly remembered what her neighbor had said about the house being haunted. She recalled the Revolutionary soldier and became suddenly frightened. She didn't scream, however. Not until the ghost of the young woman turned her face to her.

12

Dan dropped the bag on the floor. "I didn't know what to get, so I just grabbed jeans and a T-shirt. I also put your purse and keys in there."

"Did you remember to pack a bra and panties?" Lettice asked with a smirk. She laughed at his reaction. "That's okay, Dan. I can do without them, as well you know."

"Sorry," he laughed nervously. "I also brought this." He withdrew folded pages from his coat pocket.

"What's that?" she asked as she picked up the clothes bag.

"This was on my printer when I got home." He watched her as she took the bag into the small bathroom. She glanced back at him and closed the door. "It's the rest of the story."

"Okay, Paul Harvey, lay it on me."

"What?"

"The rest of the story. That's what Paul Harvey always says. Never mind. What's it say?"

He read the document to her. She emerged from the bathroom just as he finished.

"Weird," she said, brushing her hair. "It's not even written in your style, so I know you didn't do it. It's concise with no dialogue. A ghost writer, you think?"

Dan chuckled. "Literally. Aunt Audrey, I presume. After reading this, I went out to the cemetery and found Rebecca's grave. It's there, all right. Creepy caretaker there, too. Oh, and I think that old lady with the dog was there recently, too."

"What old lady?"

He relayed his experiences with the woman and her dog, including the most recent sighting where he'd spotted her with his annoying neighbor. "It really creeped me out to see them together, conspiring."

"Huh," Lettice said. "So, that old lady knows something about what's going on. Do you think the neighbor does, too?"

"Nah, she's just an idiot. The old lady probably has something up her sleeve."

Lettice gazed at him, deep in thought. "Old Faceless is Dinah."

"Do you think so?"

She nodded. "Yeah. Her face was burned so badly that she doesn't want anyone to see it. She blanks it out. Makes sense, doesn't it?"

"Yeah, I've already come to the same conclusion. So, the old witch is still hanging around the house. Well, it's not the same house anymore. Can't be; it's not old enough."

"I don't think it has to be the same house in order for a ghost to stay glued to a particular spot," Lettice postulated. "For all we know, that pyre was lit where your house is now. That also makes sense. Angry witch haunts spot where she feels she was most wronged... Poetic, in a way," Lettice added with a frown.

"No, I think the old house was still there when Rebecca was executed." He sighed, ran his hand through his hair. "Just great! Why did it have to be *my* house? I'm trying to get *away* from the past!"

Lettice's face brightened. "Hey, let's go get something to eat. I'm simply *starving!*"

⚘

"You're not headed back to your place, are you?"

"Not right away," Dan said, keeping his eyes on the road.

Lettice looked askance at him. "If you recall, I'm not wearing any underwear."

He mocked swerving off the road then righted the car. He grinned at her. "Yeah, but wouldn't that hurt your ribs?"

"Not if we're careful," she pointed out. "Like if I were on top, or bent over—" She flashed her breasts at him.

"You're going to cause an accident," he chuckled. "But I think you've talked me into it."

"Good." She leaned against him, her hand going to his thigh, moving between his legs. "Are you sure you can wait until we get to my place? Feels like you're ready now!"

"We're almost there," he said, his voice a hiss through his teeth. He was finding it very difficult to concentrate on his driving skills.

"I know," she said, kissing the corner of his mouth. "I'm keeping you prepped."

The door to her apartment burst open, Lettice and Dan passionately, urgently kissing and caressing one another. Lettice slammed the door with her foot and backed Dan up against it, not breaking away from him. She removed his shirt and he removed hers. She gazed at her breasts, gingerly kissing them, mindful of her fractured ribs.

"I'll complete it this time," he promised her.

She put her finger to his lips. "Don't talk about it, just do it!"

Soon they were naked, Lettice walking backward, her body pressed up against Dan's, headed for the couch. She gently nudged him down and straddled his lap.

"Ever done it this way before?" she asked, tossing her hair.

"Would you want to stop if I said yes?"

She giggled and kissed him. "Of course not. I was just wondering."

Dan had no problems completing the act this time. Guilt touched his conscious afterward, as his mind flashed back to Amy, but Lettice was foremost in his mind as he lay with her naked on her bed. She ran her fingers through his chest hair.

"Dan? Have you thought of moving out of that house?"

"I just moved in!" he cried good-humoredly. "But I know what you mean. To tell you the honest truth, I really kind of like it there. I like the house, even though it's creepy."

"I don't like it there," she said. "I mean, to be as equally honest. I only go there because of you. And even then..."

Dan sighed. "Well, then, I guess you'd say no if I were to ask you to move in with me."

"Oh, Dan, I'd love to move in with you, just not into *that house!* You are very special to me and I want to spend more time with you, but that *faceless bitch tried to kill me!*"

Dan blinked at her, popping himself up on his elbows. "What?"

Lettice looked at him pointedly. "She pushed me down the stairs, Dan. I saw her just before I blacked out."

"Well, you didn't mention that bef—" He paused. "Actually, I do remember you saying something odd... I thought it was because you were delirious."

"I might have been, but I still saw her. I can see her clearly in my mind, hovering above the stairs. She had no face, but I could swear she was leering at me, mocking me." She looked away, waiting for him to say something. When he didn't, she thought he might have fallen asleep.

"I don't blame you for not liking it there, then," he said finally.

She threw an arm and leg over him to draw herself closer. "I still want to be with you, though."

He looked into her eyes. "And I want to be with you."

"Just not in that house."

Dan sighed.

"What's the matter?"

"I hate moving!"

Lettice laughed. "I'll help you."

"Where to, though?"

She shrugged, still grinning. She looked meaningfully at him.

"Here?" he asked.

"No, not here!" she declared. "There's not enough room for two, barely enough for one. We'll have to find a different place."

"That might take a little time."

She shrugged again, snuggling up as close as she could. A golden band of afternoon sunlight stretched across them as they slept. Dan didn't return home until Sunday, and only because Lettice had a previous engagement with a friend.

There was a teenage boy sitting on his steps and the gate leading to the back yard was open. Dan frowned. What the hell...?

"Have you seen my mom!" the boy called as Dan exited his vehicle, flashing his mouthful of braces.

"I don't know who your mother is," Dan replied, more than a little annoyed.

The boy stood up and pointed at the house next door. "She hasn't been home since yesterday."

Dan grimaced. "I saw her yesterday morning, talking to an old lady. Haven't seen her since. Thank God."

The boy looked concerned. "Do you think I should call the police?"

Dan shrugged. "Maybe she met a guy last night and stayed over."

The boy shook his head. "No, she usually calls my aunt and has her come over to baby-sit me when that happens."

"Why are you asking *me* where she is, anyway?" Dan said, wishing the boy was with his mother right now, wherever she was. "I'm no friend of hers."

The boy sighed and stomped down the steps past Dan. "Guess I'll go call the cops, then."

"Good idea," Dan said, walking to his door. He hesitated, recalling that his back yard gate was open. Had that stupid woman trespassed and the boy knew it? He decided to investigate.

He walked through the gate, closed it. He looked left to see his back door wasn't completely shut. He instantly supposed she had sneaked inside. That stupid bitch!

He started for the door, but hesitated midway. On impulse, he looked up at the second story windows. He saw no one, living or otherwise. He began to wonder if the neighbor had encountered one of the ghosts and suffered an 'accident', like Lettice had. The stupid neighbor could be in the house right now, hurt or dead. Dan groaned.

Nothing seemed out of ordinary in the kitchen. The living room was also in order, but the stair he had recently repaired was again broken. Just as I suspected, he thought with another groan.

He approached the step cautiously then noticed the shovel in the hallway. Why the heck did she bring *that* in here? Perhaps she had just grabbed it to use as a weapon. A weapon against what, though? Perhaps she'd seen Dinah. Where was the neighbor now?

A thorough search of the house revealed no sign of the neighbor. *If* in fact it had been *her.* He strongly suspected it was. The phone rang.

"Dan, where have you been?" His mother sounded upset and agitated. "Sarah told me about Lettice—"

"That's who I've been with, to answer your question," he replied testily. "I took her home yesterday and spent the whole day with her. I just got home."

"Oh," she replied. "Okay. I was going to ask you if you had any plans for Turkey Day."

"Do I have plans? I always spend it with you and Dad."

"I know, but I thought you might have made plans with Lettice and her family."

"I'll bring her over," he replied. "You know, so you can meet her."

"Oh, we don't want to have it here," she said flatly.

"What?"

"We haven't been to your new house yet, Dan. Your father and I want to come over there. Sarah, too. It sounds like a nice place."

"Dad's okay with this?" Dan asked, incredulous. "He doesn't mind driving all the way out here to Boston?"

"Well, he grumbled a bit," she admitted, "but it might surprise you that it was his idea in the first place."

"Really? That's different." But, why would he grumble about it if it were his idea? Dan thought. Perhaps his mother was fibbing, to cover for him. As usual.

"We're still doing the turkey, though," she told him. "We'll bring it over and heat it up in the microwave."

"What? No!" Dan protested adamantly. "That's not Thanksgiving! You have to cook it traditionally, in the oven. I'll cook it, ma. I've done it before, you know."

"You have? When? We've always had Turkey Day over here."

"It doesn't have to be Thanksgiving for a person to eat turkey, ma. I've made it several times before for..."

His mother made a disgusted sound. "One day a year is all I can take of that bird."

Dan sighed. "Okay, ma. I've got to go now. Talk to you later." He hung up and stared at the phone for a moment. Now he had his parents to deal with for Thanksgiving. Just what he needed! And he wasn't looking forward to Lettice meeting them. Dad was likely to merely grunt at her while watching television and ma would simply fall all over her, trying to please and impress her then get in Sarah's face for not finding a man as nice as Lettice. Sarah might end up hating Thanksgiving more than me, this year, he thought with an amused grin.

Dan returned his attention to the stairs. He contemplated calling the police, but nothing had been stolen. He retrieved the shovel and placed it in the back door alcove before going back outside. He retrieved a plank of wood, a hammer and some nails from the work shed. Luckily, he'd fashioned more steps than he'd needed the other day and needn't now bother with the task of fashioning more. Although, the plank he'd used before must have been really bad quality for it to break so easily.

He went back inside the house and started to fix the step. He crouched down to see bits of blood and denim clinging to the jagged edge of the bad plank. She scratched her leg up pretty good, he thought. Cheap denim to tear so easy, though. She must not have been hurt too bad, or she'd still be here. Either that, or—

According to the story he'd written, Dinah had made more than one person disappear. What could have happened to the neighbor? Would she ever be heard from again? But, if Dinah had gotten rid of the neighbor that way, why was Dan being spared? Or Sarah? Why did she just shove Lettice down the steps instead of getting rid of her? It didn't make any sense.

He ripped the broken stair from its nails and replaced it with the new plank. He jumped up and down on it with all his weight and rocked back and forth. It held. He hopped off and he heard the bang of a shutter.

Dan paused. Was that the neighbor? Or something else? He darted up the steps to the computer room. The light was off. Dim sunlight filtered in through the shutter slats. The inside shutters were closed.

"Dinah!" he hissed. "I know you're here."

The inside shutters remained idle. It could have just been the wind, he told himself. He hesitated then threw the inside shutters wide.

For a split second he thought he spotted something, someone, standing by the oak tree. The phone rang, startling him enough to let out a short yelp. He hurried down the steps, wondering why he didn't have more than one phone. He then recalled that he'd had two but one broke during the move. He needed desperately to get another one.

"Hey, lover, it's me," said Lettice. "What are you up to?"

"Hmm, let's see. First I talked to the neighbor kid whose mom has disappeared, you know, the bitch from Halloween? Then I found the stair I just fixed broken—" He told her everything up to the point he answered the phone.

"You really need to move, Dan," Lettice told him, "before something really bad happens."

Dan yawned. "Well, there's nothing I can do about it tonight. I'm pretty sleepy, Lettice. I haven't gotten much rest with all that's been going on."

Lettice chuckled. "I know what you mean. I'll let you go to sleep, now, but be careful. I don't want anything to happen to you."

"Be careful taking a nap?" he asked with a laugh. "Okay, I'll be extra careful not to fall asleep on a knife."

"Dan, you know what I mean. It's not funny. I want you all in one piece for our next date."

"How about tomorrow night?" he suggested.

"Sounds like a plan. See you then. Bye."

13.

Morning meant Monday and work. Dan didn't really want to go in; he needed to get that book. He decided he would call in sick. It was a risky thing to do since he hadn't had the job very long – he might be written up – but he didn't see any other option at the moment.

He slid out of bed, looked at the clock and stumbled to the bathroom, still clad in the clothes he'd fallen asleep in. He flipped the light switch and nothing happened. He tried it again with the same result.

"Shit," he muttered. The bulb had burned out. He had to urinate so badly he decided to forgo looking for a new bulb until after he went to the bathroom. He stood in front of the toilet in the dark and hoped that the stream hit the bowl.

Water hit water and he sighed. Without flushing, he stumbled back out into the hallway, scratching first his head then his buttock. He froze when he heard footsteps downstairs.

Was it a ghost? It sounded like a spectral activity. No one else was in the house. He turned toward the stairs.

"Grandma? Audrey?" He wanted to call the soldier's name, but he didn't know it. *"Dinah?"*

The shutters banged loudly, violently in response. Dan gritted his teeth and burst into the computer room. He threw the window open and reached out to grab the outside shutters, but they banged against his hands, scraping and bruising them. The shutters were moving too fast.

"Stop it!" he shouted. "God*damn* it, Dinah, knock it off!"

The shutters banged one last time against his hands then

fell off their hinges. They fell to the ground two stories below with a soft thud.

Dan turned and saw her. She was just as Lettice had described. Where her face was supposed to be, there was nothing. It was void, bereft of features. Hair framed the void like brambles framing a worn tombstone. It floated toward him.

Dan backed against the window, his fear escalating. He wanted to look away, but couldn't. He tried to cry out, but no sound escaped him. His eyes widened and his jaw worked aimlessly.

Dinah raised her hands as if to attack then spun completely around. When she was facing him again, Dan could see her face. He gasped in horror. Her ghostly flesh was charred and blackened, one eye socket empty, smoldering with a portion of cheekbone showing through. The lips curled back, revealing blackened stubs of jagged teeth. Her ears were crisp lumps of flesh.

She hissed at him. "Your kin did this to me and there's nothing any of them can do to protect you now."

Dan stared in horror as Dinah reached out to strangle him with her spectral hands. They seemed very solid and real now, capable of doing him great harm. He could smell burning flesh.

Without thinking, he lurched suddenly forward, running straight through her and out of the room. He made it to the top of the stairs and halted, breathing heavily. He felt like he had just swam the Arctic Ocean, he was so cold and clammy. He turned around, feeling Dinah's presence, but didn't see her.

A cough caused him to turn around again. At the foot of the stairs was a familiar face. His neighbor. She looked forlornly up at him.

"So, she got you, too, huh?"

Dan was startled then suddenly very angry. "What...What are you doing here?"

She limped forward to ascend the two bottom steps. "I've been here for a while," she told him, her voice strangely calm, devoid of emotion. "I don't know how long. I tried to talk to you, but you kept ignoring me. You looked different, too, like you were faded or something. You looked kind of like that ghost who sent me here. I know she must have got you, too, because now you can hear me and you're not faded anymore." She paused. "Why is she doing this to us?"

Dan steadied himself on the railing. "Wait, what are you talking about?"

"We're trapped here, wherever here is. We can't leave. I tried it."

Dan ran down the steps, pushing her aside. He yanked open the front door and skidded to a halt. Beyond the door was blackness, nothingness. There was no yard, no sidewalk, no street, no houses across the street, no anything. Just void. Like Dinah's face. He stretched his arm out into the nothingness. The air was ice cold, tingly, a million tiny needles pricking his skin. Pain shot up his arm. He pulled it back, clutched it. His skin had turned blue.

He ran upstairs to the bathroom and shoved his hand under the faucet. He ran hot water on it until his arm became numb and itchy.

"I did the exact same thing."

Dan turned to see Damita in the doorway. He edged past her and went back downstairs. He picked up the phone. There was no dial tone.

"I couldn't get that to work, either."

He glanced at her. "I need to call Lettice."

"There's no calling anyone," said an unfamiliar male voice.

Dan turned to see the Revolutionary War soldier, his tricorner hat askew atop reddish-brown hair pulled back in a ponytail. "We are trapped here forever, I'm afraid." Another man and a woman stepped up behind him. They were dressed in seventeenth century Puritan attire.

"He's right," said the second man. He was quite a bit older than the soldier, his hair a smoky gray. "I'm Ebenezer Duncan. Father of Rebecca."

"I'm Submit Duncan," said the woman with a curtsy. "Rebecca's sister."

Dan gaped at the three ghosts then abruptly turned and walked over to the couch. He seated himself gently and stared blankly ahead at the drawn curtains. He told himself it was time to wake up.

"What is this?" he asked, slowly turning his gaze upon the others. "What's going on here? I must be having a nightmare."

"It's very real," Submit said, resting her hand on top of her white bonnet. "Unfortunately."

"I'm dead?" Dan asked. "I'm a ghost? I know you are." He looked at the soldier.

"No, we are not ghosts," replied the soldier with a shake of his head. "None of us has ever died. We were all banished here by that infernal witch, Dinah. My name is Jesse Smead, a descendent of John Smead who married Rebecca Duncan. Submit's sister."

Dan's gaze moved over to Ebenezer and Submit. "You're from the story. Now I know why your bodies were never found. Now I'll never be found."

No one said anything.

"Wait a second," Dan said. "How could you be banished here? This house wasn't even built until long after you all—" He was going to say "died", but it wasn't the appropriate term.

His three ancestors looked at one another, seemingly confused.

Ebenezer said, "I don't understand. This is the same house as it was when we were banished here."

"Really?" Dan asked. "When was it built?"

"In the eighties," he replied. "The 1680s, that is."

Dan shook his head. "No, this house was built in 1851. I know that for a fact. I have documentation."

There followed confused silence until Submit said, "Perhaps we perceive a different house than you do, sir."

"That would certain explain some things I've witnessed over the years," Ebenezer said. "I've seen folk walk in mid air where there are no stairs and sit in chairs that aren't there. Now I know why." Jesse and Submit nodded agreement.

"But wouldn't you have seen the old house being burned

down?" Dan asked. Nobody had an answer to the question. "Well, you may not be ghosts but I know there are some here. My Aunt Audrey and my grandmother, for instance."

"I've seen them," Jesse said. "But I don't think they're in quite the same place we are. They're somewhere between the real world and here. Or perhaps we're the ones trapped in-between. I don't know."

"I haven't seen them," Ebenezer said. Submit hadn't either.

"Damn," Dan sighed. "Dammit! I don't have time to be stuck here. I need to get that book."

"There's no getting anything from here," Ebenezer told him. "You're stuck here with us. Forever."

"What went wrong, Audrey?"

Audrey turned to face her sister and shrugged. "I didn't think she could still banish people."

Dan's grandmother, Savannah, nodded agreement. "I didn't know, either. Who's that he's talking to down there? I see Jesse and that nosy neighbor woman, but not anybody else. Are there other ghosts here I don't know about?"

"Jesse's not a ghost and neither is the neighbor."

"Really? I thought—well, not the neighbor, I guess. But if they're not ghosts, what are they?"

"Dinah banished them here. Whatever. I don't think we're on the same plane as them. Those people we can't see must be—wait, Savannah, I think I know."

Savannah gazed curiously at her sister then nodded. "Yes, I think I know who they are, too. Audrey, we've got to help them."

"I think that perhaps you are correct."

Lettice waited impatiently for Dan to answer and got his work voicemail for the third time. She hung up in frustration. Maybe he's home sick, poor guy. I hope that's all that's wrong.

She tried his home number and got the answering machine. She left another message then sat staring at her telephone. She needed to get back to work. She had only been calling Dan to tell him that she had landed another temporary job, but now she was worried. Why wasn't he answering? He wasn't ditching her, was he? She didn't think so. He wasn't the type of man to do that to her. Had he gotten into an accident? She remembered that he had said he had very bad luck...

She dialed his work number again, but this time asked to speak with his boss.

"I haven't heard from him and he hasn't come in," replied Frank. "Maybe he heard that we were being bought out and that his department was being eliminated."

"What?"

"It's not my decision. New owners. Try him at home."

Lettice again received no answer at Dan's house. She sighed and dropped the phone in the cradle. She looked up to see her supervisor looking back at her. He sniffed and pushed his glasses up with his thumb.

"Need some help?"

"Oh, no."

The man walked away and she bit her lip. Everything's okay, she told herself. Maybe he found out about the new owners and is out getting a new job right now. Maybe—She called her home number. There were no messages. He hadn't tried to call her.

Lettice tried to get back to work, but she couldn't stop thinking that something was wrong. She decided to call Sarah, found her number in the phone book.

It rang six times before Sarah picked up. Her voice was raspy. "Hello?"

"I'm sorry, did I wake you? This is Lettice."

"Oh, hi. No, I'm home sick. What's up?"

"I can't get hold of Dan. He's not at work and he's not answering his phone at home. I'd go check on him, but I just started this new temp job and I think I'm already in trouble."

"He probably just overslept." Sarah coughed. "If you want, I could drive out there and check on him, wake him up."

"I couldn't ask that. You're sick!"

"Just a head cold," she sniffed. "It's no bother. Besides, if something is wrong—"

"Now I've got you worrying." Lettice sighed. "It's probably nothing, but just to be on the safe side—"

"No prob. I'll have him call you when I get there. I'll kick him out of bed and tell him how worried sick he has you."

"That would be so great. Thank you so very much, Sarah."

"No problem. I'll talk to you later. Bye."

"Bye."

"So what do we do? Just stand around?"

Dan glanced at Damita and said nothing.

"There's nothing we can do," Jesse informed her.

Dan said, "We'll just wait until someone comes by and say we need them to get *The Book*."

Ebenezer shook his head. "No. They rarely ever see us. And even when they do, it's only briefly. We wouldn't have enough time to speak to them."

"They think we're ghosts," Submit said.

"How about writing a note?"

"We do not have the means with which to do so," replied Submit.

"I've got pens and paper by my computer." Dan ran upstairs. He hesitated in front of the door before stepping in. No Dinah. He grabbed a pen and some paper from the printer, wrote down the name of the book and went back downstairs to wave the paper at the others.

"I've got it written right here. Now if anyone comes looking for me, they'll see the note right here." He placed it on the coffee table. "I can't believe that none of you have thought of this before."

"We possess no such articles in our house," Ebenezer told him.

"Oh," Dan said. "That's right, you don't see this house." He then turned to Damita. "You know, you could have warned me about this. Maybe I could have done something."

"I didn't know how to tell you," she insisted. "I didn't think of writing a note."

"Oh, yeah? What exactly were you thinking when you broke into my house?"

Damita's eyes darted back and forth. "I heard screaming upstairs. I grabbed the shovel then the stair broke and I saw... *her*. Then I was here. I could see you but you couldn't see me. I was scared. I didn't know what to do."

"Well, do you believe me about the house now?" he asked angrily. She bowed her head.

A knock at the door pre-empted the follow-up questions Dan had for the woman. He hurriedly opened it.

Sarah took a wary step back as the door had seemingly opened by itself; she couldn't see Dan standing directly in front of her. She looked pale and her eyes were puffy. She stepped into the dark house and turned on the light.

"Dan?"

She walked right by the note on the coffee table.

She ventured into Dan's empty bedroom and jumped when the door suddenly slammed shut.

Dan and the others had also jumped. None of them had touched it.

"*She's* here," Submit murmured.

Dan ran to the stairs. "Sarah! Get out of the house!"

"Dan? Where are you?" Sarah hurried down the stairs and abruptly stopped. The faint form of Dinah appeared at the foot of the steps. Sarah's mouth opened and twitched in horror just before her eyes rolled and she collapsed. She tumbled down the last two steps into a motionless heap.

"Dammit, Audrey, you weren't fast enough."

"Well, I'm sorry, but your grandson was standing in the way. And by the time your granddaughter was in the house, so was *she*."

"We'll just have to try harder next time," Savannah said. "Before my entire family is trapped inside this godforsaken house."

14.

When Sarah awoke, she was lying on the couch. Dan was sitting in a chair across the coffee table from her.

"There you are," she exclaimed. "I've been looking all over for you. Where were you—?" She noticed other people in the room and gazed uneasily at them. Leaning into Dan, she whispered, "What's going on?"

Dan took a deep breath. "Sarah, I'd like you to meet Ebenezer, Submit and Jesse. They're our ancestors."

Sarah returned a still wary eye to them. "Ghosts?"

Jesse stepped forward and tipped his tri-corn. "This is not the place of ghosts. We are as alive as you are."

Sarah blinked. "Huh?"

"We saw you come in," Damita said behind her.

Sarah turned to Dan. "Who's that?"

"The neighbor," he said curtly. "I opened the door to let you in, but you didn't see me. I tried to warn you—"

"I didn't see you," she cried. "I thought that it was odd that the door opened by itself. Why didn't I see you? Dan, What's going on?"

"You saw Dinah. She's the reason you're here. She's the reason all of us are here. And we'll be trapped here forever unless we can get someone to find a book for us." He held up the sheet of paper he'd left on the coffee table. "I was hoping that you would see it when you came in."

She glanced at the paper. "Trapped? What are you talking about?"

Dan went to the door and opened it. "Look."

Sarah looked out at the void and gasped. "What the hell did she do?"

"She banished us."

"Why?"

"Because she hates us," Ebenezer said. "She wants us to be eternally in misery."

"But she's dead. How can a dead person do this?"

"She's a dead witch," Jesse clarified. "Evidently she still possesses power even after death."

"She was very much alive when she banished my father and I," Submit put in.

Sarah looked at her and Ebenezer with dawning realization. "You're from the story, both of you."

Ebenezer and Submit exchanged glances.

"You know, the story that Aunt Audrey had Dan type out."

"They don't know about the story," Dan told her. "Aunt Audrey and Grandma don't exist on this plane."

"They don't?" Sarah asked, frustrated and confused. "Where the hell are we, then?"

❧

Audrey gazed out the front window. "Who's that woman out there talking to the neighbor boy?"

Savannah followed her gaze. "I don't know, but I don't like the looks of her."

The woman stopped talking to the boy and turned to her observers. She grinned, showing her broken blackened teeth.

Savannah gasped. "Oh, my God! I think I know who she is."

"What? Who?"

"'What' is more accurate. That woman is the reason *she* is able to banish people from this plane. That woman is Dinah's conduit."

Audrey sighed and dropped the curtain. "Looks like we've got our work cut out for us."

Savannah nodded and sighed. "Shit."

❧

Andres came home from school and was surprised to see the old lady in front of his house. He saw her every so often and always managed to keep his distance. He did not like her, but did not know why. Usually she seemed to pay him no attention, but she was smiling at him today. It was a very unpleasant smile and he could smell her rank breath from a distance. He tried to run by her to the front door, but she blocked his path.

"How's your mother?" she inquired flatly, her breath thick and smothering. "Is she well?"

Andres didn't look at her. "I don't know how she is." He tried to edge by her, but her dog was blocking him. It panted happily, drool oozing from its tongue.

"Oh, that's right. You wouldn't know, would you?" She glanced over her shoulder at the Dan's house and grinned.

Andres experienced a sudden chill in his stomach and spine as nausea welled up in his throat. He turned away from the woman, but the feelings did not subside.

"You don't know where your mother is, do you?"

Andres could barely speak, all of his energy having left him. He could barely mutter a reply. "No—"

"Would you like to see her?"

"No."

The woman was quiet. Andres looked up to see her rear her head back in muted laughter. He felt like he was going to barf. He heard a car pull up. The old woman turned to look, giving Andres his chance. He still felt weak, but he was able to get away and into the house.

The old lady didn't pursue him.

Lettice got out of the car only to be pinned up against it by a large dog. It barked maniacally, foaming at the mouth.

She held her arms up to fend off its attack, but it tore at her sleeve and her skin, its bark loud and scathing in her ears. She screamed and tried to kick it, but it kept jumping around, dodging her. It clawed at her, scratching her neck and chest and arms. Lettice emitted a louder, piercing scream.

The dog abruptly ceased its attack and ran over to an old woman on the sidewalk. She grinned at Lettice as she reattached the dog's leash. "Go right on in, dear," she said, smiling crookedly. "They're all waiting for you."

Lettice stared at the woman, trying to catch her breath. Her arms felt like they had been scraped bloody and her throat was scratchy from screaming. Blood pounded in her ears. "Your dog just attacked me!"

The woman chuckled. She yanked on the leash and the dog gave a little yip. With one last grin, she turned and walked away with the animal.

Lettice cursed at the woman and ran to Dan's door. There was a note on it.

"Lettice! Whatever you do, don't come in here! I'll explain later. I need you to get a book called *The Book of Curses and Their Remedies, Or How to Defend Oneself Against Witchcraft.* There's probably only one copy, so it will be very hard to find. It's our only hope. We're all counting on you. – Love Dan."

As she finished reading, another note slid from under the door. It was a much longer note, describing what had happened to Dan and Sarah and why the book was so important. Dan's name and Sarah's name had been scrawled at the bottom.

Lettice's hand covered her mouth as she read. She had asked Sarah to come and check on Dan and she, too, had suffered his fate. She felt horrible for both of them, felt somewhat responsible for what happened to Sarah. She had to get that book and get them out of there.

She turned around to come face to face with the old woman again, her belligerent dog snarling beside her.

"What are you waiting for?" the woman screeched. "I told you, they're all waiting."

"I'm not—"

Lettice's reply was cut off by the dog's sudden fit of barking. Without further hesitation, she ran past woman and dog to her car. She slammed the door in the dog's face and hurriedly started her engine.

"We'll be out of here in no time, now," Dan exclaimed.

"She took the note?" Sarah asked.

He clapped his hands together. "Yep. Both of them." He turned to his ancestors. "Hear that? We'll be getting out of here soon."

The three looked back at him, uncertainly.

"You don't look very excited."

"We have been here for a very long time," Submit said.

"Yes," said Ebenezer. "We cannot be happy leaving just as we cannot be happy remaining here."

"Everyone we ever knew is dead," Jesse added. "Everything we ever knew no longer exists. It no longer matters to us if we escape this place."

Dan arched his brow. "If you all want to die, why didn't you just end it all a long time ago?"

"I just want justice," Jesse suddenly, angrily expounded. "I want that witch destroyed!"

"Aye to that!" Ebenezer said. Submit remained silent.

"Glad to hear it," Dan said with a wry grin. "Maybe once we're free of this place, we can do something about her, once and for all."

"Your neighbor's out in the backyard," Sarah said later, returning from the kitchen. "The void is beyond the backyard instead of right outside the door for some reason."

"She shouldn't be out there," warned Ebenezer. "*She* dwells there."

Submit nodded. "She lives in the old oak. Methinks she was buried there."

Although Damita annoyed him greatly, Dan still felt he should see if she was all right. He sighed and headed for the kitchen. Damita walked in through the backdoor as he approached.

"There's no way out." Her voice was high and tremulous, panicky. "I've checked and checked and there's no way out at all."

"Yes, there is," Dan told her. "My girlfriend's going to

get the book and we'll all get out of here. It's only a matter of time."

"What if she doesn't find it?"

"She will."

"How can you be so sure?"

"I trust her. She'll get it."

Damita gazed intensely at him for a moment then lifted her hands and eyes to the ceiling. "Oh, I don't know! I don't know!" She turned away and paced the room, behaving like a caged tiger waiting for its chance at escape. She began wringing her hands and muttering to herself in Spanish.

"She's gone crazy," Dan said, adding, "Not that she had far to go."

Jesse said, "We've seen this happen to people before."

"There have been others?"

Jesse nodded. "They are no longer here, however." His eyes went to the door just as Damita wailed and placed her hand on the knob. No one was close enough to stop her before she opened the door and plunged out into the void.

Dan and Sarah hurried to grab her only to see Damita floating limply two feet in front of them, her lifeless body a frozen mass of icy blue crystals.

The three ancestors turned away from the door, their heads bowed.

15.

Damita's body floated slowly away from the house until it was merely a dot in the distance. Dan sat in the window, watching the dot until it was gone, willing Lettice to return with The Book of Curses.

Sarah stood behind him. "I wonder how long it's been since Lettice was here last."

Dan's voice was low and hollow. "I think it's been a week. It seems like a week."

"Maybe she didn't get the note."

"I know she's got it. It's just a very difficult book to find. There's only one in existence."

"Maybe it was destroyed somewhere along the line." Sarah paused. "I wonder how Mom's taking our disappearance. I wish there was a way we could tell her what happened. Do you think Lettice will tell her?"

"I don't know that they would believe her if she did."

Sarah sighed. "I don't want to end up like them." She glanced at Submit and Jesse who sat on some unseen chairs in the dining area.

Dan followed his sister's glance. "I wonder what it is they see. I mean, I know they see their old house, but I wish I knew what it looked like."

"I think it quite odd that they still see the old house. I wonder what causes that."

"It's probably just part of the curse. What sorts of rules do curses have? I certainly don't know."

Sarah and Dan observed them in silence for several moments. "They seem remarkably sane for people who have been isolated for two and three hundred years," Sarah commented. "I wonder how they pass the time."

"They have something going on between them," Dan said, catching her drift. "Look how they speak to one another, how close they sit. They are sleeping together."

"Great! I suppose that leaves old Eb for me, then. Wouldn't that be considered incest, though?" Sarah asked.

Dan smiled wanly, but did not meet her gaze.

"You miss Lettice."

He nodded sorrowfully just as a note slid under the door. He snatched it up hurriedly and read:

"Dan & Sarah: I'm sorry I didn't leave a note earlier, but I'm having great difficulty finding the book. I looked on the Internet, but no luck. Your mom called looking for you. I think I managed to persuade her not to call the police, but I don't know how long that will last. It's been three days. She's really worried about you two. I'm trying very hard to find the book. I would quit work, but I'm nearly broke as it is. It looks like it's going to take me a long time to find the book, but don't lose hope. Sarah, I'm really sorry. Dan, I really miss you. I love you. –Lettice."

Dan handed the note to Sarah. She read it.

"It's only been three days?"

Lettice drove furiously from Dan's house when she again spotted the old lady approaching. She had no idea what the woman had to do with Dan and Sarah, but it wasn't good. Somehow, the old woman was either wholly or partially responsible.

Meanwhile, Lettice had a lead on the book.

Or so she hoped.

The man she went to see in Delaware appeared to be about seventy years of age. He still had a full head of hair, white and bristly, and a wispy goatee. He answered the door with a lit cigar jutting from between his false teeth. He greeted Lettice and waved her inside. The house smelled like cigar smoke and bird droppings. Finches cohabited within a cage situated by the door. They were currently asleep.

"I'm glad that you could meet with me on such short notice, Mr. Coffeen," Sarah said. "I need to find this book ASAP."

Mr. Coffeen puffed on his cigar and blew smoke out his nose. "Why do you need this book so badly, Miss?"

She flashed a nervous smile, hesitant to tell him just yet. "I would have told you, but didn't want to in an e-mail. Someone in my office might have read it and think I'm nuts."

Mr. Coffeen regarded her curiously. "I suppose that, since this book is involved, it must be a very incredulous story you have to tell. Please, sit down. Care for some coffee, my dear?"

"I would love some, thanks." She removed her coat and sat down on his divan. When he returned with her coffee, she relayed her tale to him.

After she finished, Mr. Coffeen gazed pensively into space. He puffed his cigar, stubbed it out in the palm of his hand. "I have never heard of this happening before, but I think I can find a book that will fix it for you."

Lettice blinked at him. "But I already told you the book I need."

Mr. Coffeen chortled. "My dear, that book is fictitious. It doesn't exist."

Lettice frowned. "Then why would a ghost tell Dan to get it?"

"I don't know." He sat back in his chair. "Perhaps he heard the apparition wrong. Or perhaps the ghost was mistaken. All ghosts were human once, therefore just as fallible." He gazed pointedly at her.

She averted her gaze. "But how do you know it doesn't exist?"

Mr. Coffeen sighed. "My dear—" Lettice clenched her teeth, her nerves grating every time he said those two words. "I'm something of an expert on the subject. I've searched for that particular title you're looking for for thirty-five years. I assure you, it doesn't exist. I would have found it by now, trust me. If it ever existed at all, which I doubt, it is now lost.

Perhaps it was burnt up in a fire or some other such disaster. I don't know. Irregardless," Lettice clenched her jaw again, now irritated by the man's misuse of the English language. "I can find a book that will solve your problem."

Lettice abruptly stood. "That's very nice of you, Mr. Coffeen," she said with forced politeness. "But, if you will please excuse me, I must be leaving now."

❧

The door suddenly burst open. Dan jumped up from the couch in alarm.

The police had arrived.

He and the other banished folk stood by helplessly as the house was searched from top to bottom. Dan had to laugh when he heard one of the cops remark that the house felt creepy to him, like he was being watched.

Sarah grinned at the cop's comment. "That's probably because there are five invisible people standing right in front of you."

When the police were about to leave, the forensics team arrived. Dan shook his head at the sight of them.

"Good luck finding us."

"I wonder if they're checking my place out, too," Sarah said. "God, I could really go for a drink right about now."

"Huh," Dan snorted. "I haven't been thirsty since we've been here. Hungry, either."

"I'm not really thirsty, Dan. I just want to get drunk." She paused. "Hey, I haven't had to go to the bathroom either. I wonder why that is?"

Dan shrugged. "Probably just comes with being banished."

"Maybe," she replied. "I sure am horny, though."

"Thanks for telling me." Dan turned to find his sister gazing at Jesse across the room. He and Submit were sitting quietly on their unseen chairs, lost in their own little world.

Dan sighed and thought of Lettice. Would she ever find the book? How expensive would it be? Could she even afford to buy it? He wished he could see her again. Touch her. Speak directly to her without having to resort to notes.

She will find it, he told himself. Eventually. She just needs some time.

"Dan," Sarah said, touching his arm. "What if mom and dad come in for some reason? We need to warn them."

"I'll write a note."

"What if the detectives see it first?"

"So what if they know? What can they do? At the very least it will let them know that we're not dead. I'll put today's date on it." He paused. "What day *is* it?"

Sarah shrugged.

Dan scribbled out the note and taped it to the outside of the door. The detectives had gone by then, so he waited.

He held vigil in the window.

᰾

"You have probably already noticed that there is no need to eat or drink here." Ebenezer sat in midair, his hands folded in his lap.

"Yes," Dan replied. "What are you sitting on?"

"The stairs. I don't know why we don't need to eat, but I think it's because we're neither dead nor alive. We do require sleep every so often, however. Once every two weeks or so. And, there are other functions that still overcome us." He looked at Sarah.

She gaped at him and gave a startled laugh. "Wh-*What?*"

Ebenezer stood, his feet on the floor. "I have had no one to—love for three centuries. There has only been Submit and Jesse, both of whom I love as children. I have had no woman to share my love with for three hundred years."

Sarah was stunned to momentary silence. "But...I'm your great-great-...however many...great-*granddaughter!*"

Ebenezer began to pace the room. "I am quite aware of that. However, I was thinking that three hundred years is a very long time and that the family line has been mixed with the blood of so many other families that it is quite diluted by the time it gets to you. Any *meeting* that I would have with a descendent that far along the line would no longer be a problem. Do you understand?"

Sarah said nothing. She looked to Dan who shrugged. "I would think that anything going on between any direct ancestor or dependent would be bad," Sarah said finally. "You're a Puritan. I shouldn't have to explain this to you."

Ebenezer lifted his chin. "After you have been here for a while, you will understand. You will want someone and I am the only man available to you." He turned and walked up his invisible staircase.

Sarah snickered nervously. "Do you believe that?"

"I do believe that I heard somewhere that five generations removed no longer counts as incest."

"You're no help."

"Not that it would come up normally."

"Shut up."

♪

Lettice removed Dan's note from the door then wrote one of her own. She still hadn't found the book, but she assured Dan that she hadn't given up yet. She kept a wary eye out for the old woman as she slipped the note under the door. She didn't read Dan's note until she had driven out of his neighborhood. It was the proof she needed.

She knocked on the door and waited. She glanced at the folded note in her hand, tapping her foot nervously. Dan's mother, Miranda, opened the door and Lettice introduced herself. The two women had spoken over the phone, but they had never met in person. Lettice handed Dan's mother the note.

Miranda read it then glared suspiciously at Lettice. "Exactly what is going on here? Is this some sort of prank?"

"Oh, no," Lettice said. "I would never do such a thing. Every word of this note is true. That's Dan's handwriting. Don't you recognize it?"

Miranda frowned severely. "The police say that the woman next door is also missing."

"I know. She's stuck there with them."

"And they were sent there by a witch's ghost?"

"I can take you there and show you," Lettice said. "I can ask Dan to write a note for you."

"But this note says not to go." She looked at it dubiously.

Lettice sighed. "Look, I can't make you believe this, but I swear it's true. Now, I'd love to stay and chat but I've got a book to look for. It was nice meeting you." She turned and walked toward her car.

"Wait!" Lettice stopped and turned around. "What exactly is your interest in my son, anyway?"

Lettice paused then took a deep breath and lifted her chin high. "I'm in love with him. That's all."

Miranda crossed her arms, intensely appraising Lettice. "Does he know this?"

"I-I haven't really been able to tell him yet. I mean, not in any meaningful way."

"Why not?"

"There hasn't been time. Like I said, I'm trying to find this book."

Miranda paused then waved Lettice over. "Come on. Tell me everything again. I'll see if I believe it this time."

❧

The curtains fluttered and drew themselves aside. An old witch and a not nearly-as-old dog were framed perfectly within the window frame. The dog was defecating on the grass as the witch smiled down at it.

"I don't think there is anything more we can do, Audrey," Savannah said. "Especially now that she knows about the book."

Audrey bit her lip. She turned away from the window. "I think we should try to manifest ourselves to Dan and Sarah. Tell them to write a note about the conduit. The incantation won't work with her hanging about."

"I know, but how do we show ourselves other than accidentally? I have not been able to do it so far."

Audrey grinned. "Wait for them to fall asleep."

16

"So this is the house I'm paying the bills on?" Miranda asked.

Lettice stepped up onto the sidewalk to stand beside her. Dan's mother had agreed to take on the bill payments in order to keep the house from being sold. It would be very difficult to do what needed to be done with a third, unknowing party occupying the house. At the moment, only beings ethereal inhabited the place.

Lettice pointed. "Look. There's another note on the door."

Miranda removed the note and read it. She rubbed her chin with her forefinger then handed the note to Lettice. "Does this make any sense to you?"

Lettice read the note hurriedly. "I *knew* it! I knew the old crone had something to do with this."

She stopped suddenly and turned toward the sidewalk. The old witch was without her dog this time as she headed for the house.

Lettice grabbed Miranda's arm. "We have to go now."

"What—?" Miranda felt another hand grab her other arm. Hot, stinky breath assaulted her senses.

"What's it like to be childless?" asked a horrible voice.

Miranda tried to pull away with a little help from Lettice. "What? Let go of me! Who are you?"

"Why, I'm the one who can reunite you with your son." The witch chuckled hoarsely then pushed Miranda into Lettice.

"Ow! Stop it!" As Miranda started to fall, her foot kicked the witch's foot, knocking her off balance. The witch fell backward, thudding hard upon the porch steps. She bounced to the ground, hitting her head on the concrete walkway.

Aghast, Miranda stared at the woman as Lettice hurriedly removed her note from her purse and slid it under the front door. She then took Miranda's arm again. "Come on." She tried to pull her past the witch's body.

Miranda wouldn't budge. "She looks dead."

"She's a witch."

"I killed her."

"Maybe you did, maybe you didn't. We need to get out of here."

Miranda finally relented and allowed Lettice to take her to the car. Lettice slid into the front seat and started the engine.

"Where's that note?" Lettice handed it to her. Miranda read it twice then stared at the signature. "This really was written by him."

"Yes, it was." Lettice kept her eyes on the road.

"What are we going to do?"

"We're going to keep looking for the book."

"No, I mean about the dead woman."

"The dead *witch*," Lettice clarified.

"So what if she's a witch? I still killed her. I've never killed anybody before. Oh, my God!" She covered her face in her hands. "I'll go to the gas chamber."

"No, you won't." Lettice wasn't sure if she believed her own words, but she knew she had to concentrate on getting the book. Nothing else mattered. If Miranda went to jail, maybe something in the book would get her out. Lettice didn't have time to think about things like that now.

At least, with the witch dead, one obstacle was eliminated.

A woman with dark circles around her eyes stepped wearily up the porch steps. Her hair haphazardly kept with berets, her frame thin. She had been very busy the past six weeks, yet still her task was incomplete. She was haggard and tired, discouraged.

The front door swung noiselessly open. She balked. With the witch gone, it was probably safe to enter, but old habits died hard. Perhaps if she had good news she wouldn't have hesitated. She felt tears trickle down her cheeks.

The interior of the house was oppressive, stuffy, the air thick. She switched on the light. Goosebumps elevated up and down her arms. She felt like she had just walked into a tomb. Memories of Dan bolted into her brain and she recalled when she had last seen him. Time traveled backward from there and Halloween returned. She recalled the time she had tumbled down the stairs and Dan had taken care of her until the paramedics had arrived. She recalled the love they had made in his bedroom and afterward the ghosts she had encountered.

This house was a tomb in so many ways. The dead and the undead lurked here, as did dead and undead memories. She hated to think of Dan as 'undead', but what else was he? Did existing on a separate plane mean you no longer lived? Could you appear as a ghost to others, yet still have a beating heart? It was all very confusing and it tore her heart up every time she thought about it. She was so afraid she would never be able to find the book.

A pen and pad floated quickly through the air toward the recliner where it abruptly jumped and stopped. The pen scribbled rapidly across the paper and the paper tore itself from the pad. The page floated toward Lettice.

"What's the matter?" it read.

Lettice sniffed and sat deftly on the dusty sofa. She was relieved to find no resistance, that no unseen being was currently occupying the spot.

"Dan, your parents are going to have to sell the house."

Silence.

"They can't afford to continue paying the bills for this place." She took a deep breath. "They're especially strapped for cash since your mother was arrested for manslaughter. Her lawyer thinks that he can have the judge rule it an accident and get her off, because there are witnesses across the street that testify that she and I were being attacked. I don't know if the jury will believe that, though, since the witch was old and appeared disabled and weak."

The pen wrote again. "The curse is still in effect. My mother will go to jail."

Lettice dropped it and leaned back. Her face contorted. "Oh, Dan! I don't know what to do anymore. I miss you so much."

Another note landed in her lap. "I miss you, too. And I love you."

Lettice gazed at the note as sobs wracked her body. "Oh, Dan, I love you, too. And I won't stop looking for that stupid book until I find it. I'll die trying."

"If you die trying, I'll never see you again."

A hard sob caused her to hiccup. "I won't die. I promise. Oh, if I could just hug you and kiss you!"

A soft touch on her hand made her jump. The pad and pen lie on the coffee table. She stood up and felt gentle pressure along her torso and back. She moved her arms, embracing the apparent nothingness that embraced her. There was no warmth, only a slight resistance. She felt no heartbeat, no breath. It was if she were embracing slightly solid air. She felt another great sob welling up within her.

Movement caught her attention. She glanced over to see the wispy, transparent form of Dan's grandmother standing by the door. She pointed at it.

Lettice was about to ask her what she was doing when she heard footsteps on the sidewalk.

Savannah jutted her finger urgently then pantomimed opening the door.

Lettice understood. "Good-bye, Dan. For now, anyway." She blew him a kiss as she walked out the door.

A man in a dark gray suit that matched his hair and beard stood on the porch steps. Lettice halted outside the door just as it slammed shut, hitting her in the rump. The man grinned a grin that Lettice was all too familiar with.

Her eyes darted to the porch steps. He was blocking them. If she tried to run past, he would surely grab her. Instead, she ran to the left, to the edge of the porch and jumped over the wooden railing. She landed hard on one knee in the driveway, pain shooting up her body to the tips of her fingers. Her knee was scraped and bruised, but she was otherwise unhurt.

She saw the man looking over the railing at her just before she broke for her car. She managed to leap in and close the door before he could reach her. She started the engine and pulled away from the curb. Her car felt sluggish, as if it were rolling through syrup. Or, as if it were being held back. She gunned the engine and it lurched forward, causing her to clash violently against the steering wheel. She inadvertently wheeled up onto the curb before she regained control of the vehicle.

She glanced in the rear view mirror. The man was gone.

Lettice came home to a message on her machine. Mr. Coffeen had located a book. Not *the* book, of course, for he still insisted the tome didn't exist. He assured her, however, that the book he had found held the spell she sought. Lettice decided it was worth a shot.

She was surprised when a younger man answered the door. He looked at her curiously. "May I help you?"

"Um, I'm here to see Mr. Coffeen."

The younger man took a shallow breath. "I assume that you refer to my father. Well, he has suddenly taken ill. Who might I ask is calling?"

"My name is Lettice," she said, suddenly uneasy. "He left me a message on my phone earlier today. He said he'd located a book I've been seeking. I do hope that he's all right."

The man paused. "He's suffered a heart attack. A rather major one, actually. My sister's with him in the hospital right now. I'm Eli, his son. Please, come in. Maybe he left the book in his office with your name on it." He didn't step aside to allow her entry and continued to gaze curiously at her.

He made her nervous. "Look, this is a bad time. Perhaps I should come back—"

"My father's not expected to live. There may never be a good time."

Lettice hung her head sadly. He stepped back and motioned her in. She felt awkward, but she walked in, following Eli to his father's office. A desk faced the window surrounded by shelves overflowing with books. There were additional books either lying on tables or stacked precariously on the floor.

"Do you know what the title of the book is?" Eli asked as he started shuffling through papers and books on the desk.

"No, he didn't mention the name. Actually, it isn't even the book that I originally wanted, but he said that he'd found a book that would work just as well."

Eli glanced at her just as he opened a desk drawer. He withdrew a brown covered hardback with a sticky note on it. "Are you Lettice? This is your book, then."

Lettice picked it up. In the center of the cover was a stylized, gold-leaf sun. "How much is it?"

Eli held up his hand. "Just take it." He shut the drawer, his brow creasing as he read the title on the spine of the book. "Witchcraft? Are you a witch?" He sounded amused.

Lettice would have laughed if circumstances had been different. "Oh, no! I just need to lift a curse."

Eli looked at her as if she were mad. She took the opportunity to quickly thank him and leave.

She glanced down at the golden sun as she drove away, hoping the spell Mr. Coffeen recommended actually worked. Strange that Mr. Coffeen had suffered a sudden heart attack. He had sounded perfectly all right on the phone message. She hoped his condition wasn't too serious.

A sudden explosion shook the street, causing her to veer sharply to the right.

❦

Television news reported that the explosion had been caused by a gas leak, that Eli Coffeen had lit a cigar with deadly results. Lettice knew differently. She was positive that the man at Dan's house had been responsible. She had also come to the realization that he had more than likely been responsible for Eli's father's suffering a sudden heart attack. I have been close to the book, she realized. That warlock – she was certain now that the man was the replacement for the old lady with the dog – has done everything in his power to keep me from getting any closer to it.

Lettice turned the television off and picked up the brown-covered book Eli had given her. *Witchcraft for the Non-Practitioner – Pyburn*. The book wasn't as old has she had expected. It had been published in 1952 and was in excellent condition. The gold on the edge of the pages had not been worn away and the spine was tight and stiff. It was nearly brand new.

One of the Coffeens was dead, the other dying.

Simon leapt into her lap, making her lift the book to keep the animal from climbing into it. She absently stroked the cat twice before returning her attention to the book. She leafed through the pages, in search of the curse-lifting spell.

There were several such spells, including one that supposedly protected a person's home from harmful castings. Lettice deemed it a good spell to try out. She wasn't positive she could even perform a spell, but she needed to find out. After all, if she couldn't, how could she hope to free Dan and Sarah?

The spell required candles and calf's blood. Luckily, Lettice possessed both items. She gathered the candles she kept in a drawer then went to the refrigerator. She withdrew a package of hamburger from the freezer and frowned at it. The blood was frozen. She placed it in the microwave and hit the defrost button. When the hamburger was sufficiently defrosted, she drained the blood into a bowl. As she did so, she realized she didn't know if the blood was actually from a *calf* or not. She hoped it didn't matter.

She walked back into the living room and looked at the carpet. Not a good place to perform the spell. There was no carpet in the kitchen. It was small, but there was enough room.

Lettice circled the candles, lit them then dimmed the lights. She seated herself in the center of the circle and dipped her fingers in the blood with a disgusted grimace. The preparation was in English, but the actual spell was in Latin. She had to guess at the pronunciation as she recited the words, flicking the blood at the three northernmost candles. The flames fizzled and flickered, but did not go out. She turned and flicked blood at the easternmost candle and so on to the southernmost and westernmost candles.

When she had finished casting the spell, she didn't feel any safer than before.

Dan sat on the steps, morosely watching the men and women remove everything from his house. At least, it appeared to the movers that they had removed everything. To Dan's eyes, they only removed the "ghosts" of his belongings. Everything remained just as he had left them, even after the movers had packed up and rolled away. Only vague outlines of his household items remained, as if they were images burned onto an old computer screen.

He departed the stairs and walked to his couch. He was still able to seat himself on the removed item, but found he couldn't pick up the pad and pen he had left on the coffee table. The table and pen had been removed from the premises and only ghostly forms remained. Dan could, however, place his hand on the pad and pen and feel the paper and plastic. He just couldn't grasp either item. He found the situation both fascinating and heartbreaking.

He could no longer communicate with Lettice.

He buried his face in his hands and wept.

A gentle weight on the cushion beside him let him know that he wasn't alone in the room. He wiped his eyes and looked over at his sister.

Sarah gazed forlornly at him. "I was just talking to Eb."

Dan sniffed and cleared his throat.

"You know we're not really alive, right? I mean, we're not breathing and our hearts aren't beating."

"Yes, I noticed that a long time ago."

"Well, according to Eb, none of our bodily fluids are renewed. Saliva, mucous, blood, tears. Once they're gone, they're gone for good."

Dan smiled wanly. "Well, I guess that was my last cry, then. I don't think I'll miss it, to tell you the truth."

"...sperm—"

"What?" He narrowed his eyes at her.

She shifted her weight on the sofa. "Well, Dan, surely you haven't just been sitting around the house all this time without, well, you know. Taking care of yourself."

He was offended and shocked. This was his own sister. It was a subject they had never discussed before and he had never wanted to. "As a matter of fact, if you must know, I haven't," he said.

She looked away, then laughed. "You must be horny as hell, then." She ignored his angry stare and continued. "I don't need to tell you that you'll only be able to come once. After that, well, I guess it'll be like a dry faucet."

"You're disgusting." He turned away then whipped his head back to face her. "You slept with Ebenezer, didn't you?"

She pretended to pick lint from her pants. "I'm not proud of it, but I needed, *wanted* sex, and he was there, so—"

"That's disgusting."

"Actually, it wasn't. I thought it would be, but it was quite excellent. You'd never know he was a Puritan."

"I don't wanna hear it." Dan lurched up from the couch.

"Probably my last complete orgasm."

Dan let out a cry of disgust and left the room. He didn't know he was in the kitchen until he saw the backyard through the backdoor window. He gazed out at the oak tree, at the void beyond. He couldn't go out there. That was *her* area. Not that he wanted to go out there, anyway. Where was Lettice with that book? It seemed like weeks since he'd seen her.

He turned around and was startled by the sudden appearance of Submit. She was standing very close to him and appeared anxious.

"I wouldn't hold out much hope for the return of your lady

friend, Dan," she said, her voice low. "The three of us have been here for a very long time and will be until Judgment Day. That is, if God hasn't forsaken us already. Jesse seems to think that He has."

"Lettice will find the book," Dan assured her. "I'm very confident that she will."

Submit looked down at her hands. "You are upset about your sister and my father, are you not?"

Dan snorted. "It's none of my business. I don't want to know anything about it."

Submit looked away, wringing her hands. "There is not much else to do here, except that." She glanced meaningfully at him.

"Oh, no," Dan said, taking a step back. "Don't even think it!"

"But you have no one else," she cried. "You certainly cannot bed your sister."

"Of course not, but neither do I want anyone else," he protested. "No one except Lettice."

"But you cannot have her. You cannot even touch her. Not in any substantial way, that is. And self-gratification is a sin."

"And sleeping with your ancestors isn't? How does that work?" He turned to leave the room.

"We are too far removed by time for kin to matter in this respect, Dan." She sighed then took a deep breath. "There is only one desire left to us in this place. It is the last remaining link we have to the people that we once were. Without it, we are mere shades of humanity, existing for naught. 'Tis only when we join together that we feel alive."

"Even though you cannot complete the act?"

She nodded grimly. "We have to settle with what we are given."

"But you do this with Jesse. Why do you come to me?"

The front door opened, interrupting anything Submit may have said. A Caucasian woman in a business outfit stepped in followed by a black man and an Asian woman. From the nametag the woman in the suit wore, Dan discerned she was a real estate agent.

The house was being sold.

Other people arrived over the course of the next three weeks, many of them seeming to sense that there was something terribly wrong in the house. Some simply didn't like the house or thought it was too expensive. One woman seemed to look directly at Dan and shiver. The real estate agent told them nothing about the history of the house. Dan wondered if she even knew anything about it.

The house was quiet for three days before another note from Lettice was slipped under the door. She informed Dan that the house had been sold and that the new owners had been fully apprised of the hauntings.

Dan scratched his head. They must have discussed the matter outside the house. He hadn't heard the agent mention a thing about ghosts or curses or anything. What kind of people would purchase the house knowing what had happened, knowing what was still going on inside of it?

Lettice went on to say that she would try to visit if she could avoid the conduit that lurked nearby. Dan's grandmother had told him in a dream, one of the few he had now that he rarely slept, that there was a warlock lurking in the neighborhood he could no longer see.

The new owners moved in. They had two young daughters, eight and six. Dan was somewhat amused at their behavior as they brought in their furniture and belongings. The man didn't seem too terribly frightened, but the woman kept darting her eyes back and forth, as if expecting to witness an apparition at any moment.

They didn't finish the job the first day nor did they stay in the house the first night. They returned the next day with another truckload of stuff. Lettice was with them. She held a pad and pen in her hand.

"Dan, are you here?" she called. "I want to introduce you."

The man and woman stood uneasily beside one another, their girls running about playing some kind of game. The woman tried to hush them, but the children ignored her. The girls giggled piercingly and ran out of the house. The man put his arm around the woman and she relaxed somewhat.

Lettice stood in the middle of the room. "Dan, Sarah. This is Mike and Karell. They are your new housemates. They know all about you and your plight and Karell has agreed to help me locate *The Book*. Oh, and I must tell you, I'm moving into the vacant house next door." She smiled. "Yes, I have a new job, Dan. The pay and benefits are great." She hesitated. "Um, in case you aren't in the room right now or couldn't hear me for some reason, I've written everything I just said down on this piece of paper." She ripped off a page from the pad and placed it on the stairs.

"I love you, Dan," she added with a sniff. She nodded to Mike and Karell then departed.

Dan cried, "I love you, Lettice!" She didn't hear him, of course.

Mike and Karell stood around awkwardly for a few more seconds then commenced moving the rest of their things in.

When Mike returned with a box, Dan followed him down to the basement. Dan realized he hadn't been in the basement since he'd first moved into the house. He watched Mike place the box onto a wooden shelf built into the brick wall, next to a box already on the shelf. Mike paused to look at it then walked right through Dan to the stairs.

The writing on the box looked familiar to Dan. He stepped closer. The writing was his. It was a box of stuff that someone had forgotten to remove. Dan placed his hands on it. He could touch it! He lifted it and brought it to the floor.

Inside were notebooks, pencils, and pens that had once belonged to Amy when she went back to school three years ago. There was an entire box of unused pens, half a package of unsharpened pencils and three unused notebooks. He let out a cry of jubilation. He could still communicate with Lettice.

The first note he wrote, however, was to Mike and Karell. "Do not remove this box," he said. He underlined and signed his name at the bottom.

"Whatcha doin'?"

Dan jumped. "Sarah, you scared the shit out of me." He held up the notebook and the pen in his hand and grinned.

Mike returned with another box. He walked right through Sarah then saw the pen and notebook hovering in the air. His eyes widened and he took two steps back. He nearly dropped the box he was carrying marked "Old Dishes."

The note floated in the air towards him and he read it.

"Okay, okay," he exclaimed, his voice a hoarse whisper. "Whatever you say, Dan." He hurriedly set down the box and ran upstairs.

17.

The box was back on the shelf and Dan sat against the wall beside it, his eyes on the stairs. He felt like he needed to guard the box, make sure no one tried to take it from him. He hadn't left the basement since he'd rediscovered it. He felt he couldn't keep his eyes off the box for a minute. He couldn't trust anyone not to take it from him.

He grew tired after ten days and fell asleep. Screaming and pounding jarred him awake. Streams of sunlight filtered through the high basement window as the sounds of Karell trying to subdue her two girls carried down through the vents. The girls were rambunctious, not wanting to get ready for school.

Sarah sat on the stairs. "I feel like I'm eavesdropping," she whispered. "What spoiled brats they are, huh? They have run of the whole place. We never acted like that when we were kids, did we?"

"I don't know." His voice was wispy, barely audible. "I can't remember. It seems like so long ago."

Sarah sighed, trying to blow a stray strand of hair from her face. She had momentarily forgotten that she possessed no breath. The hair remained in place. "Submit keeps asking me about you, you know."

"So?" he snorted. "I don't care." The kids screamed piercingly and Karell finally lost it and screamed back at them. The kids didn't scream again. "What have you told her?"

"Not much." Sarah leaned her head against the wall. "I told her about Amy."

Dan sat upright. "That's none of her fucking business. You

had no right to tell her about her." He set his hand against his forehead.

Sarah frowned morosely. "Shit, I'm sorry, Dan. It just sort of came out, you know? We were just having a conversation. In case you haven't noticed, there's nothing much to do around here."

Dan grunted and returned to leaning against the cold, brick wall.

"Submit is curious about us," Sarah went on. "I've been telling her about television, cars and NASA... She's completely enthralled. Aren't you the slightest bit curious about Eb and Submit? I sure am. Did you know—?"

"Sarah, I don't really care, okay?"

She shut up and glared at him. "Okay, fine." She got to her feet, gave him one last dirty look then left the basement.

Dan sighed. He wanted to be left alone. He didn't want to deal with anything ever again, not until he got out of this place. He ached to see Lettice again. She was the only reason he didn't just open the front door and step out into the void, ending it all. He couldn't wait until he was reunited with her.

Time had lost its meaning. There was no clock in the basement and Dan had never kept the habit of wearing a watch. Lettice visited him several times, always meeting with him in the basement. She asked him why he was down there all the time. He replied that he liked it there and that the house wasn't his anymore, anyway. He was uncomfortable upstairs, where Mike and Karell and the girls were living their lives. He wasn't a part of it.

Lettice nodded and informed him of her progress in locating the book. She always felt that she was close, but it continued to remain just out of reach. He would ask her the current date and she would tell him. It always amazed him, for it was always much later than he thought. He realized that he had completely missed Christmas and New Year's and Valentine's Day and Memorial Day. All the holidays had passed. Twice. Lettice had now been looking for the book for two years, with no success.

Lettice and Dan embraced. It was the only contact they could manage. They tried to kiss once, but it didn't work. He felt lighter than air to her and she felt the same to him. Dan thought it was only because of their previous intimate contact that they were able to touch each other at all, though he had no solid basis for the theory. Everyone else who wasn't cursed just passed right through him. That is, on those rare occasions anyone should dare venture down into the basement. After each hug, Dan and Lettice would weep, longing to be able to touch one another in a more substantial way. Dan's tears, however, were dry, for his tears were not renewable.

The daughters of Mike and Karell grew up and the seasons changed. So did hair and clothing styles. Television shows debuted and ended. New fads started, old ones faded. The weather changed from bad to worse, from better to wonderful. A new president was elected, a former one passed away. Technology advanced at a rapid pace. Old computers were replaced with newer, faster ones. Old cars were replaced with newer, faster ones. Endangered species became extinct while new species were discovered or created. Children were born, adults perished. The world continued to gradually slow its rotation as it hurled around the sun at an ever-so-slightly decreased rate of speed. The universe slowly expanded.

Dan was aware of nothing but the basement and his box of notebooks and pens.

He slept more than he needed to and sometimes he would dream about the past. Sometimes he would dream that Amy was trapped in the house with him, as well as his mother and some old friends from high school. He would write the dreams down in the notebooks and read them later. It eventually turned into a diary. Dan would document what had happened to him and philosophize about his situation. He then started writing down his life story, everything that had happened in his life up until this point.

He didn't have anything else to do.

⚬⚬⚬

Lettice stood on the stairs, appearing nervous, pensive. He eyes shifted around the room. "Dan, are you down here? Of course you are. You're always down here."

Dan lifted his pen, his signal to her that he was present and paying attention. He couldn't help but be concerned about her apparent apprehensiveness. He hurriedly wrote, "What's wrong?"

Lettice took a deep breath. "Dan, there's no easy way to say this, so I'll just—" She took another, shallow breath as her face started to contort. "Dan, I'm seeing someone else."

The pen fell to the floor.

Lettice jumped at the sound of plastic striking concrete. She stared at the fallen instrument and could not see nor think of anything else for a moment. The only link between her and Dan had been suddenly discarded. What had she been talking about?

Her bottom lip started to quiver uncontrollably. She turned away, cupped her mouth and nose in her hand. The sobs were insistent, but she tried desperately to subdue them. She couldn't lose it now. What she had to say was important.

"He...He doesn't..." She tried to regain her composure. "I haven't told him about you, Dan. I thought it would be for the best." She wiped her eyes and cleared her throat, but her body started to tremble. She was killing him and she knew it. She braced herself against the railing. "I-I'm so sorry, Dan. I've been so...so *lonely*. I didn't go looking for this, it, it just happened."

She didn't know if he was listening, or even still in the room, but she kept talking.

"Dan." Her tears refused to cease and her body wouldn't stop shaking. "I still love you. Nothing will ever change that. It's just that I need someone here. Someone I can touch. Especially with the war and everything." She knew it sounded horrible and heartless as the words spilled from her mouth. She needed to give him some sort of excuse, to diminish what had happened, make it seem insignificant. "I haven't forgotten you, Dan. I haven't stopped looking for *The Book*, either."

The truth was, she hadn't looked for it in months. She'd

been meaning to start looking again, but things kept getting in the way. America was at war and resources were limited. She was afraid it had been destroyed like Mr. Coffeen had said. Besides, she was too preoccupied with her new relationship to look for *The Book*. She could never seem to get back to looking for it, even though she thought of it, and of Dan, often.

"Dan?" she called, tears rolling down her cheeks. "Are you still here?"

Dan's shoulder collapsed against the brick as he slid to the floor. His world had ended. His life was over. There was no reason for him to exist any more. He couldn't look at Lettice. He yearned to, *ached* to, but he couldn't. The love he thought existed between them wasn't as strong as he believed. It was weak. At least on her end of the relationship.

He didn't believe anything she said anymore. He couldn't. It was less painful to deem her untrustworthy now. Less painful, but nothing had ever hurt him more in his life. Nothing except the murder of Amy and Billy.

Dan wept, soundlessly. Dryly.

Lettice wanted to reach out to him, but she had no idea where he was. Was he even still in the room? He could have run up the steps past her and she wouldn't have noticed. Or would she? The steps were narrow. Surely, she would have felt him brush by her.

"I really do still love you, Dan," she said, her voice choked with emotion, "even though you probably don't believe me at this point. I don't blame you. It's true, though. I love you and I want you here. If you were here, now, I would leave him in an instant! I'm just so *alone*, Dan! I can't find the stupid book."

She wanted one of his ethereal hugs desperately, but it was not forthcoming. It was cold in the basement. She felt like a heartless witch. She felt like Dinah. She felt like she had just cursed Dan as Dinah had cursed his ancestors.

"I don't deserve someone like you anyway." She thought that saying so might make the situation better, but it rang hollow in her own ears. She was a bad person trying to evince sympathy from him now, trying to turn things around. It wasn't going to work. Not on Dan.

"I didn't want things to be like this. After all you've been through you don't deserve this, not by a long shot. You can't know how sorry I am, Dan. I promise that I'll keep looking for the book. I promise."

She waited for some kind of response. There was none.

"I promise I'll keep looking for it," she repeated, waiting anxiously. "Please, Dan, write something. Don't let it end like this."

She gazed hopefully at the pen, though she was ready to turn and bolt from the basement. She wanted a response, but she wanted terribly to just leave. She couldn't take the silence.

Then, miraculously, the pen slowly lifted. The notebook followed and the two objects connected. The pen slid slowly across the paper. The message was short. The page tore and upended toward her.

"No you won't."

Lettice started to reply, but her lip was quivering again. "Yes, Dan," she finally managed to whisper. "I will. I promise you."

The pen scribbled, faster this time, sloppier. "You'll forget about me. You'll have children and a life and I'll be lost here forever, forgotten."

"No, no!" she insisted, her heart genuine. "How can I make you believe me? I swear on my life I'll never stop trying to save you."

"Even if you free me, you'll still be with him. There will be no place in your life for me."

"I told you." Her voice was low, determined. "I will leave him instantly. I don't love him nearly as much as I love you, Dan."

She waited for him to write, "I love you, too, Lettice," but the pen and notebook fell to the floor. She felt like she wanted to die.

She hesitated only a moment before her feet became insistent. She bit her lip, glanced to the top of the stairs then back at the basement. She couldn't take it any longer. A great sob choked her as she bolted up the steps.

∽♪∽

Dan looked up in time to see her shoe disappear through the door.

He was truly alone now. Everything he'd ever had was gone. What was keeping him from opening the front door and leaping out into the frozen void? He was never going to be free of this place. Death was the only escape.

He ventured up from the basement for the first time in years. The place looked just as it had been when he'd owned it. Where had all the furniture gone that he had seen the new owners move in? It was strange the way this place worked, he thought, not for the first time. Nothing here made sense.

Karell was in the kitchen talking on a telephone Dan couldn't see. She was startled into silence when she saw the basement door open. It didn't stop her conversation, however. "I just saw another door open, Mike. No, the basement, this time. Yeah, probably Dan. Lettice was just here to talk to him. She seemed upset."

Dan paid her no attention. She was insubstantial to him. He hurried into the living room to stand before the front door. He yanked it open, feeling the frozen iciness waft toward him, beckoning him. Gradually, he sensed that others were there. The two girls showed only the mildest interest at the opening of the door. They gazed in Dan's direction for only a moment before they returned to their coloring books.

"What are you doing?"

Dan looked over his shoulder at his sister. She seemed concerned. He thought he should say something to her, but he couldn't find the words. He stared back out at the darkness, recalling his old neighbor floating dead, frozen, in the void. That would be him soon.

He lowered his head, energy suddenly leaving him. "Sarah, I... I just can't do this anymore." He felt like he was about to cry, but he didn't have the strength. Besides, it hurt to cry without tears. "It's no use."

Sarah gently placed her hand on his shoulder. "What did Lettice tell you down there?"

Dan glanced at her. He had the feeling that she already knew the answer, but that didn't make it any easier. "She's found someone else."

Sarah's mouth moved as if to make a sound like "Oh," but she remained silent. She instead embraced him.

Dan returned his eyes to the void. "She told me that she'd still look for the book, but—what do I have to go back to even if she finally does find it? I mean, I can't just keep going through all this crap, Sarah. I can't keep losing the people I love. I could barely hold it together when Amy and Billy—" He heaved a long, heavy sob. "I just can't do this anymore."

Sarah turned him from the door and held him as he wept. Dan eventually removed himself from her and stepped away from the door. Jesse appeared before him.

"If it is any consolation, we all know how you feel," he said flatly. "I lost my wife in childbirth. It was a child that never knew me because I was banished here before his birth. I watched poor Abigail's face contort with pain. I heard her screams." He looked at the floor.

"You know our story," said Submit. Ebenezer nodded.

"Thank you," Dan said to them all. "I think it helps a little, hearing this. At least I'm not alone here, huh?"

"No, definitely not," said his sister.

"It still sucks, though."

"A lot."

Dan smiled wanly at Sarah. "You're lucky, in a way. You don't have anyone."

"Thanks a lot," she replied with a frown.

"You know what I mean."

She forced a smile. "Going back to the basement now?"

He pondered the notion, glanced at the open door and nodded. "For a little while, I think."

"Do I have to stay by the door to make sure you don't come running up here to throw yourself out there?"

He shook his head slowly. "I don't think so."

She gazed at him. "Mm-hmm. I think I'll park myself on the sofa for a while. You know, in case you change your mind."

Karell walked right between them, dusting the furniture. She and her pre-teen daughters were oblivious to the fact that a life had nearly ended in their midst.

18

For Dan, time no longer possessed meaning. Self-pity had obliterated everything else except the coldness of the dark, dank basement. He wished he'd never been born. Thoughts of running out into the void still occurred to him, but he didn't think Sarah would let him anywhere near the door now. Besides, what if Lettice did find the book and did leave the guy she was seeing? He didn't want to miss that chance. She could still follow through on her promise, whether or not he trusted her anymore.

He dreamt when he finally fell asleep. Amy sat across a park bench from him. Billy sat on a swing, surrounded by other children. He waved cheerily at Dan and Dan waved back.

"Don't worry, Dan," Amy said, placing her hand on his. "You will be rescued."

"I wish that I could believe that," he sighed. "Why couldn't you have been banished with me? You and Billy?"

"We are always with you."

He gazed into her eyes and needn't remember exactly how beautiful she was for that beauty was here with him, now. In fact, she was more beautiful than ever. "You know what I mean."

"Only those who inhabit that house can be banished, Dan. She didn't have the power to reach us in our old house."

"I know that," he said. "Except for the neighbor."

"She was one of the few exceptions, yes," Amy replied with a nod.

Dan took a deep breath, forgetting that breathing for him lately was not normal. Two worlds were colliding in this dream:

his life with Amy and Billy and his life as a banished victim of Dinah's. It started to occur to him that Amy had never known about Dinah or Lettice or any of the events that had happened after her death. How could she have? This was just a dream.

Amy leaned forward and kissed the corner of his mouth. "You will be freed in time, Tickles. I promise you that."

He couldn't help but laugh. He had forgotten about that particular nickname she'd had for him. So easily did time take away what was once so normal, so important. He could feel a great sob welling up within him and fought hard to keep it down.

"After you are freed, you must end Dinah's family line."

Dan whirled around on the bench to see his grandmother sitting behind him. The grandmother he had never met in life was now sitting next to him.

"You must end the curse, Dan," she told him. "End the curse that has plagued our family for so long. Your descendents will never know peace until it is done."

Descendents? He looked back at Billy on the swing then back at Amy. "Don't I have any cousins or anyone else that can do it?"

Savannah shook her head firmly. "There is only you. Isn't that right, Miranda?"

Dan turned to face his mother standing behind Amy. She placed her hand on his dead wife's shoulder. "I'm afraid she's right, Dan. And I'm sorry."

The dream suddenly broke and loud footsteps banged against his eardrums. "Dan?" called a woman's voice. Karell's. "Are you here? I have a note here from Lettice."

He glared at the folded piece of paper in the woman's steady hand. He was still too angry with Lettice to want to read anything from her. If she had found the book, she would come here with it. What was this letter? Another apology?

"I-I think it's important." Karell unfolded the paper and held it up for him to read. On the paper were five simple words:

"Dan, your mother's killed herself."

Karell held the note for a minute then carefully placed it on the floor. She calmly walked back upstairs.

Dan glanced down at the note. "Thanks a lot," he shouted after Karell. "I can't turn it over, you bitch. I have to stare at that goddamn fucking note forever now." He turned his back on it and slumped back into the corner.

He remained in the basement, huddled in the corner for what seemed like years. He never once saw Sarah or the others. Sometimes Mike, Karell, or the kids would come down, but he paid them no attention. There was no point. There was no point in doing anything at all. He merely existed. He wanted to die, but Sarah wouldn't let him. He slept, and the dreams were fragmented and vague. Neither Amy nor any other member of his family came to visit him.

He felt pressure on his shoulder and ignored it. When it persisted, he mumbled, "Go away." He thought it was Sarah, but it was Submit. He glared at her and she said nothing. She sat on the floor behind him and removed her Puritan bonnet.

"This thing gets quite uncomfortable after a couple of hundred years," she said with a grin.

Dan grunted, facing the brick wall. "Then why do you wear it?"

She shrugged. "Habit, I suppose. Though it not be a nun's habit, be it?" she added, laughing suddenly. She abruptly stopped when he didn't appear amused. "You should relax, Dan. You are going to be here for quite a long time. I venture to state that you have been here a few years already."

He shook his head. "No, we are going to be rescued soon."

"Who told you this?"

"My grandmother. She told me in a dream. Actually, my wife Amy told me first."

"Your wife?" Submit asked.

"Yes. She and my son Billy were murdered."

"Yes, Sarah told me," she said. "I am so sorry. The fiend was never apprehended?"

Dan shook his head. "Not that I know of. He broke in, killed my family and took some jewelry and our DVD player. It was part of the curse, though I didn't know it then. Didn't my sister tell you?"

Submit looked away at the mention of Sarah. "I have not been on speaking terms with your sister of late. She and my father have a thing going. He has been utterly enamored of her. She and my father have been upstairs—"

"I don't want to hear about it," Dan cried, covering his ears.

"I'm sorry." She looked at him. "Are you going to avoid us forever?"

Dan didn't reply. He didn't feel like talking. He rarely spoke aloud anymore. It seemed pointless. Why talk about anything? There was no point, no point in doing anything.

"I am so lonely, Dan," Submit whispered urgently. "I haven't been so lonely since meeting Jesse. I thought maybe I could keep you company."

"I know what you want," Dan snapped.

Submit was affronted for only a moment. "I know you do. You should want it, too. There's no point in continuing to resist. It will consume you, Dan. Or have you been content to manipulate yourself?" Her cheeks reddened, her own words embarrassing her.

Dan glanced at her, not wanting to participate in the ridiculous conversation. He remained silent.

"You will give in, Dan," she assured him gently. "It might take ten, twenty, fifty, a hundred years, but you will. You cannot fight it forever. I couldn't. It's the closest I can come to being truly human in this Godforsaken place."

"You've said that before and it doesn't make any more sense now," he replied coldly.

She cast her eyes downward. "You may find your own reasons for giving in, Dan, but give in you will. Granted, there is no lubrication, but the act can still be done. With a little patience."

"So, you just want me to roll on top of you and slake my lust without any regard for you as a person? Is that it?"

Submit took a step back, startled by the force of his words.

"It can't be completely slaked, but it feels nearly like ecstasy for a few moments. It hurts a little at first, but you get used to it. Do you want me to start?" She reached back and began untying her dress.

"No, stop," he protested.

Her hands ceased movement, but did not drop. "I'm not going back upstairs until we have done this, Dan. You have hidden away in this basement for far too long."

"Fine," he said. "Stay here. See if I care." He got up and walked to the opposite corner.

"I have all the time in the world," she told him loudly, frustrated.

"Whatever!" He turned away from her and stared at the brick wall.

Silence ensued. Submit stayed in her corner and Dan in his, tracing the mortar between the bricks with his finger. Eventually, perhaps days later, slumber overcame him and he fell asleep.

⚜

Lettice was lying next to him, her body warm and soft against his, the curve of her buttocks fitting perfectly in the cradle of his groin. His hand moved over her hip and down. She groaned pleasurably. His hand moved to cup her breast, squeezing the nipple between his fingers. He throbbed hotly and stiffly against her backside.

She turned her head to kiss him and their lips locked. She lifted her leg and rested it atop his. He placed himself at the entrance to her vagina and pushed in slowly, gently.

The dream abruptly faded. Dan's eyes blinked open, adjusting to the darkness of the basement. Submit lay across the room, her back to him.

Dan groaned. His dream was a fantasy and would never again be anything more than that. He would never be with Lettice again.

He didn't realize that he was staring at Submit's slumbering form until he'd been at it for some time. He had been thinking of Lettice, of the time they had spent together, of the sex they had enjoyed together. How many years had passed since then? He hadn't slept with a warm, feminine body next to him since being banished. What was keeping him from doing so now? He was no longer attached to Lettice and he might not ever meet another woman... Of course, it wouldn't be the same with Submit. Not only was she not Lettice, but also because the act would be different here. It would hurt, according to Submit. Most assuredly, without moisture, it certainly would. Yet, since Dan hadn't pleasured himself since being banished, he still had some fluids.

No, he couldn't. Submit was his direct ancestor. Maybe he should just pleasure himself, alone. What if Submit woke up and saw him, though? Or Sarah? Or Jesse or Ebenezer? That would be embarrassing. He'd just have to fight his sexual urges and not give in.

Submit rolled over onto her back. Her head lolled to the side and she gazed at him.

Dan turned his eyes to the ceiling. He didn't want to look at her, but couldn't fight the urge. When he returned his eyes to her, she was smiling. She had a very attractive smile. Her eyes seemed to sparkle even in the darkness. He'd never noticed how pretty she was before.

"Submit—" he whispered.

She put her finger to her lips then rolled onto her hands and knees. She crawled over to him and sat back on her heels. She undid her Puritan dress, drew it over her head. She was naked underneath. Her body appeared to glow in the darkness, radiating with womanly magnificence. Dan thought it might be his libido enhancing her body or perhaps an ethereal effect this plane of existence had on human skin. He decided it didn't matter either way, especially when Submit leaned forward to kiss him and help him remove his own clothes.

Once he was sufficiently naked, she rolled on top of him. "Trust me, it's easier for you this way," she whispered in dulcet tones. "Put your finger there. See? Completely dry. It will hurt me a little, but don't worry about that. I'm quite used to it."

He didn't worry. Submit hid her initial pain well. She had done it too many times for two hundred years with Jesse to let it hinder her now. It was difficult and took some time, but he managed to find himself inside her. His hands caressed her body as she rocked gently back and forth against his thighs. After a few minutes, Dan realized they weren't entirely dry; there seemed to be a thin film of moisture on their bodies. Sweat? Not possible, if their bodies didn't retain or renew water. It took him a few moments to figure out that there was a substantial amount of humidity on this plane. It was constantly muggy. He had noticed this some time ago, but had grown used to it. It had bothered him before, but now he was thankful for it.

His wandering mind prolonged the coital act, but once the moisture problem was solved, it didn't take Dan much longer to climax. When it hit, Submit let out a cry of surprise, but didn't stop her pelvic motions. She was employing his semen as extra lubricant. Since Dan had been celibate for years, there was plenty of it. Her vagina squished and popped with every motion until her body was quaking and her thighs were clenching tightly. Her mouth worked soundlessly before a curt, shrill cry escaped her lips. She collapsed on top of him, making low purring sounds. She wasn't breathing heavily and neither was Dan; no breath existed for them here.

Submit looked into his eyes and giggled. "I guess you haven't manipulated yourself since you've been here. I feel honored." She kissed him with her dry lips and started moving on him again. "We shouldn't let the slickness go to waste, should we? We'll never be able to feel it again."

Dan's second climax was painful yet pleasurable. Dry. Submit had been right, it was an odd feeling that he gradually came to enjoy. He would have to enjoy it, or never have sex again.

He and Submit remained in the basement for many months. He didn't want her to leave him and he didn't think he could leave the basement and face Sarah. He had done with Submit what he had chastised his sister for doing with Ebenezer. And with Submit formerly being Jesse's lover. How could he ever go upstairs again?

Dan did finally emerge from the basement one day after Submit had gone to speak with Jesse. He saw them sitting on their invisible chairs, their bodies inches from one another. He left the room and stared out the backdoor window.

A man was digging up the ground around the old oak tree.

BOOK TWO

I.

Kalendra was jarred from her sleep by a sudden rapping at the door. "Time to get up. First day of school!"

She groaned and rolled onto her back. She glanced at her clock, realizing she had forgotten to set the alarm. It had probably been a subconscious decision to leave it off. She wasn't looking forward to today.

"I don't wanna go," she groaned, rolling back to her side. She heard her grandmother's footsteps down the stairs.

Kalendra sighed, staring at the clock. A month ago she had been excited at the prospect of starting college, of getting to know new students who were interested in the same things she was. That was before her grandfather had suddenly died of an aneurysm. No one had expected it. Her grandfather had been fit and trim and healthy and young and appeared indestructible. He hadn't deserved to die.

Kalendra moved in with her grandmother after that. She didn't have a job or any means with which to support herself, so saw no other choice. She had no other living relatives. She had never really known her grandmother, having grown up in a completely different state, but here she was in Boston, ready to attend a college she didn't want to go to. She didn't want to go to college at all.

She eventually forced herself out of bed, stumbling wearily to the mirror. She examined the bags below her vaguely Asian eyes. She had been crying herself to sleep – what little sleep she got – and had lost a lot of weight. Her face looked skeletal to her, her cheeks so sunken that they forced her lips apart, showing the world her clenched teeth. She had to constantly lick her lips to keep them moist. Her nose looked larger, too. She hadn't really noticed how sallow her features were until just this moment. She needed to gain weight, but what difference did it really make? Nevertheless, she showered, dressed and met her grandmother downstairs for breakfast.

She stood by the stove, stirring eggs. "How are you feeling, dear?"

Kalendra sniffed as she shuffled to the table. "'Kay."

"You don't look okay. Did you get enough sleep?"

"Of course not," she snapped, then flatly apologized. "Sorry."

Her grandmother nodded and finished heating the scrambled eggs. She ran a fork through the smooth, flat surface of the eggs and broke them up before serving them to her granddaughter. She sat across from her, picking up a half-eaten piece of toast from a plate.

Kalendra ate in silence a moment, then said, "It's just that," she sighed, "you seem to think that I should stop grieving and act normal, like nothing ever happened. Don't you understand at all what I'm going through?"

Her grandmother lowered her toast. "Yes," she said quietly. "I understand perfectly. That's how I know what I'm talking about. You need to just continue on, no matter how wrong or pointless it seems. There's nothing else you can do."

"But—"

"Just because you stop grieving doesn't mean that you stop remembering. Kalendra, we've talked about this before."

Kalendra stared at her eggs, absently running her fork through them. They tasted strange to her, having been cooked on an old fashioned electric stove. She wasn't used to it.

"Maybe you're right."

"I am," her grandmother said. "I've lost plenty of people in my life, so I know what I'm talking about. I've lost your mother, my husband—"

Kalendra looked up, seeing a faraway sadness in her eyes. She thought she might cry but the expression vanished.

"Hurry up and finish. It's getting late." She got up and left the table.

The first day of college wasn't nearly as traumatic as Kalendra had envisioned. It was really rather pleasant, except for the fact that she ended up with a ton of homework by the end of the day. It would be easy enough to do, but would consume a considerable amount of time. She'd always been told that college would be more work than high school and she had hoped it wasn't true. Unfortunately, however, it was.

The bus ride home was quiet, the vehicle filled mostly with fellow students. Kalendra didn't know any of them so kept to herself. She gazed at her screen, hoping to get some studying in, but she couldn't concentrate. She looked out the window instead, getting acquainted with Boston as best she could. The bus ride was agonizingly slow, stopping every three blocks. She had a long way to go before she got home.

She looked away from the window and noticed a very handsome student reading a calculus book. An actual book, not a hand-held screen like everyone else used. She found herself interested in this man because of the book, wondering why he was reading from such an outmoded invention. Surely his professor didn't hand it out to him. He must have gotten it from a library. The book was old and worn.

The student signaled his stop as the bus entered an old neighborhood. Most of the houses had been built more than two hundred years ago and a good number of them were up for sale. There were two or three newer houses mingling with the old, however, replacing older houses that had burned or been torn down. Kalendra thought the newer homes looked woefully out of place.

She watched the student exit the vehicle. He didn't seem to notice her as he stepped onto the sidewalk. He turned to his right and stopped directly in front of Kalendra's window.

Normally the bus would have pulled from the curb, but a handicapped woman in a levchair was boarding and her vehicle was painfully slow in doing so. Kalendra continued to watch the young man before her.

She couldn't see his face, but he appeared to be looking at the woman in the window of the house in front of him. The woman was clad in an old fashioned blue and white dress with a ruffled collar. She was scowling at the man, evidently very angry with him for some reason. It was the most hateful expression Kalendra had ever witnessed. The woman then vanished.

The bus started to move. Kalendra stared aghast at the now vacant window then returned her attention to the student. He was walking away, seemingly unconcerned.

Kalendra sat back in her seat, shaken. What had she just seen? A hologram, of course. What else could it have been? She chuckled nervously. What did she think it was? A ghost? It was utterly laughable. How could she have been frightened by a hologram? That was why the man seemed unfazed. There was nothing to fear from a collection of computerized dots.

She relaxed and pushed it out of her mind as her stop approached. The bus halted abruptly as a cat darted into the road before continuing.

Kalendra stepped off the bus onto the sidewalk and headed for her grandmother's house. It started to rain as she reached the door.

The hologram popped into her head again as she mounted the steps to her room. Why did I think it was a ghost? I've never even thought of ghosts before, not as being real, anyway. Is it because of my father's death that I'm thinking this way? I do wish I could see him again. Maybe on some subconscious level I'm trying to manifest him in my mind. Of course, father looked nothing like an old woman from another century.

A hologram was the most logical explanation. Why it had seemingly been taunting that man, she had no clue, but what else could it be? If ghosts were real, science would have proven they existed by now. Science had proven that Bigfoot was real; it was actually a type of human subspecies. There was even a scientific name for Bigfoot now. But still not for ghosts.

Kalendra changed clothes and joined her grandmother in the kitchen. She was watching a movie while dinner simmered on the old-fashioned stove she loved to use.

Her grandmother smiled at Kalendra as she walked in. "How was school, dear? Have a good first day?"

"It was a breeze." She sat across the table from her, looking glum.

Her grandmother gazed at her with concern. "What's the matter?"

Kalendra hesitated then took a shallow breath. "Gramma, have you ever seen a ghost?"

"A ghost? Of course not."

Kalendra sighed. "I didn't think so."

"Why did you ask me that?"

Kalendra rested her chin on her hands, her arms folded on the table. "I think I saw one. A woman in an old-time dress taunting this guy who got off the bus. She vanished right before my eyes."

"It must have been a hologram," he grandmother said instantly. She pronounced it "hollow-gram."

"That's what I thought!" Kalendra exhaled, relieved.

She sat back and turned her eyes to the movie as her grandmother returned to the stove. A commercial interrupted the movie to advertise another movie called "Lisandra's Curse." The movie was about a woman cursed by a witch whose ghost keeps appearing to her. It caught Kalendra's attention and she thought it sounded like a really good movie. She didn't notice her grandmother staring at her.

Kalendra turned. "That movie looks good, doesn't it Gramma? I think it would be a cool one to be in."

"I think it's complete nonsense," Lettice said, breaking three celery stalks in half with her bare hands.

2

As Kalendra's first college semester continued, she befriended a girl named Celia who was in her Russian class. They went to see "Lisandra's Curse" together.

"That was so cool," Kalendra exclaimed as she and Celia walked to the bus stop. "It was so real. I could actually feel the magic pulsing through my body. Those movies are getting better and better all the time."

"I especially liked the flying part," Celia said. "Especially when, at the beginning, you fall out of the tower and think you're going to hit the sidewalk. It was so scary at first, then I was zooming up, through the air."

"Yeah, that was really cool," Kalendra agreed. "They should have more movies about witches, don't you think? I could really get into that sort of thing."

"Me, too," said Celia. "They don't teach that stuff at school."

"I know," Kalendra sighed. "They really should, though."

Celia's eyes lit up. "Hey, I know. Let's go to my place and call up a different witch movie and have drinks and caramel corn."

"Sounds great," Kalendra said, "but I'll need to let my Gramma know where I'm gonna be."

"Of course," Celia said. "By the way, my mom's out of town for a couple days, so we'll have the entire house to ourselves." She then thought better of her statement. "I mean—"

Kalendra laughed. "I know what you mean." She patted her on the arm. "It'll be fun."

Kalendra left her grandmother a message via her handheld then went to Celia's. They watched movies, ordered pizza, made caramel corn and cookies until they could no longer even look at anything remotely edible.

"God, I'm stuffed," Kalendra said, lounging heavily on the couch next to Celia. "I feel like I just ate a basketball and a bowling ball." She glanced over at the bowl of chocolate chip peanut butter cookies on the coffee table and reached for another one. She returned her attention to the movie credits. "Boy, these flats are weird, aren't they?" Flat movies are those that can't be interacted with.

Celia nodded, also munching on a cookie. A crumb fell on her chest and she gazed down at it, picking it off. "Yeah, it's like being a voyeur or something, like we're looking in on someone else's life, uninvited." She laughed. "I almost feel like I'm doing something wrong."

Kalendra agreed and got up with a grunt. "I need another soda. How about you?"

"I'm fine," Celia said. When Kalendra returned from the kitchen, she said, "This house is supposed to be haunted, you know."

Kalendra stopped by the couch and stared at her friend. "I didn't tell you this before," she began, "but before I met you, I saw this old lady in your front window. I convinced myself it was a hologram, but now I don't think it was. You're telling me this place is haunted?"

Celia nodded. "Yep, and it sounds like you saw one of the ghosts."

Kalendra was quiet a moment. She set her drink on the coffee table and gazed at it. "Then there was this guy who got off the bus. He stepped off right in front of the house and stared right at the... lady. He looked annoyed, like the lady was bothering him. He didn't seem scared, though."

"Strange," Celia said thoughtfully. "There is supposed to be an old lady ghost here, but neither my mom nor I have seen her. Or any of the other ones this house is supposed to have. We find it very quiet and boring."

"So, I did see a ghost," Kalendra said, taking a deep breath.

She found breathing difficult as she had just taken a big gulp of soda and was about to belch. She made a strange gurgling, squeaking sound which she promptly ignored.

"Yeah, you saw one, all right," Celia said. "Pretty cool, huh?"

Kalendra forced a grin, feeling the hair on her arms prickle. "Yeah, kinda."

"I wasn't even sure that the stories we heard were real," Celia said. "It's nice to know someone I know personally has seen something. I'm glad you told me." Her eyes roamed the room, searching for an unseen spirit.

"What are some of the stories?" Kalendra asked.

"Well, one of the neighbors told my mom something she was told by the woman who used to live here. She'd said there were several ghosts here and then something about witches that no one could really figure out. The neighbor thought she might have been crazy."

Kalendra pondered. "Witches. What a coincidence."

"Seems to be the theme, huh?" Celia asked.

"Hey, I know," Kalendra said abruptly. "Let's have a séance!"

"A what?"

"A séance. You know, so we can try to contact the ghosts."

"I don't know," Celia said pensively. "What about the witches?"

"What about them? Maybe there weren't any to begin with. Like you said, the lady was crazy."

"If she was crazy then there wouldn't be ghosts here, either," Celia reasoned.

"Not necessarily," Kalendra said. "Scared?"

Celia looked sidelong at Kalendra. "Yeah."

Kalendra sighed. "So am I. But it sounds like fun, doesn't it?"

Celia shrugged. "I don't know how to do a séance."

"Well, we'll just have to find out." Kalendra turned to the wall screen and verbally called up a search engine. After a minute of going through a list, she settled on a virtual Ouija board. She opened the program.

"How do you use it?" Celia asked as the screen turned white. The word "OUIJA" appeared top center while the board, a series of letters and numbers, fanned out below. A palette with a circular window at one end was situated at the top of the letters.

"Just concentrate," Kalendra said. "The words will appear at the bottom."

"What words?"

"The words that will spell out what the ghosts are telling us."

"Oh."

Kalendra waited. "So ask a question."

"I don't know what to ask," Celia declared.

Kalendra glared at her. "How about asking if anybody's there?"

"Okay." Celia took a deep breath then cleared her throat. "Is there, um, anyone out there?"

Kalendra and Celia stared at the screen. Nothing happened.

"Maybe if we turn out the lights," Kalendra said, getting up to do so. Once the lights were out, only the light from the Ouija screen illuminated the room.

"Can anyone hear us?" Kalendra asked firmly.

"This is creepy," Celia whispered.

Kalendra shushed her. "Concentrate!"

Celia kept quiet and closed her eyes. When she opened them, the virtual palette was moving rapidly. Letters appeared below the board:

SOME OF US ARE GHOSTS

Kalendra and Celia gaped at the screen, unable to move a muscle.

"Shit!" Celia gasped finally, he skin tingling, every hair on her body rising.

"It works!" Kalendra exclaimed, somewhat delighted. "Wow!"

"Can we stop now?" Celia pleaded then covered her face with a sofa pillow.

"We're just getting started," Kalendra said, glancing at her. "I thought you wanted to do this."

"I did," she replied, dropping the pillow. "But now I don't. This is too scary, Kalendra."

THERE'S NOTHING TO BE AFRAID OF

Celia squealed and covered her face again.

"I'm not afraid," Kalendra said, realizing it was true. She wasn't the least bit frightened by the mysterious words appearing before her.

GOOD

She was a little unnerved, but also excited. A voice from beyond was speaking to her. What could be more exciting than that? She did feel cold though, like a wind was blowing down the back of her shirt and into her pants. Maybe she was a little afraid.

"What's your name?" she asked the Ouija.

DAN

Celia looked at the screen then at Kalendra. "That's not an old lady's name, is it?" she asked, referring to the ghost Kalendra had seen a few days earlier.

I'M NOT AN OLD LADY
I THINK YOU SAW MY GRANDMOTHER
KALENDRA

She gasped and nearly fell off the couch. "You know my name?"

YES
I LEARNED IT FROM LISTENING TO YOU TWO
CELIA

Celia gaped at the words then shivered violently. "This is too creepy."

WE NEED YOUR HELP KALENDRA CELIA

"We?" Kalendra asked. "There are more of you?"

THERE ARE 5 OF US TRAPPED HERE
WE NEED YOUR HELP

The two friends exchanged glances. "I don't think there's anything we can do," Kalendra said. She was beginning to become frightened now.

WE NEED A BOOK

SOMEONE ELSE WAS SUPPOSED TO GET IT BUT SHE'S GONE

IT'S CALLED Curses and Their Remedies, Or How to Defend Oneself against Witchcraft

WE NEED IT TO ESCAPE KALENDRA CELIA

"Escape?" Celia asked, hugging the sofa pillow tightly to her chest. "Escape from where?"

"I think he means that it will help them go to Heaven," Kalendra interpreted.

NO NOT HEAVEN

I AM NOT DEAD

GET OUT OF THE HOUSE

The two girls were confused by the last sentence. They looked at each other then back at the Ouija.

SOMEONE ELSE IS COMING

GET OUT BEFORE HE COMES OR YOU WILL BE TRAPPED TOO

GET THE BOOK

Celia sat up straight, dropping the pillow. "I think I hear something outside," she whispered.

Kalendra listened for the noise then caught movement on the staircase behind Celia. She screamed.

Celia shot to her feet and turned. He mouth opened wide, but no sound issued forth. She was too shocked by the translucent, faceless apparition that was silently gliding down the stairs toward them.

A horrible shrieking erupted from Celia as she darted for the door. She threw it open to see a man with graying hair and a Van Dyke goatee coming up the walk. She slammed the door shut.

"The back," Kalendra cried, racing her for the house's other exit. The ghost was now less than ten feet away from her.

Celia reached the door before Kalendra, nearly ripping it

from its hinges. She ran two steps into the yard and stopped. The faceless ghost was floating before her, hovering near the old oak tree. It rotated and started floating toward her.

Kalendra pulled Celia's arm, directing her toward the side yard gate. She fumbled clumsily with the wooden gate's sliding metal lock then bolted through to the driveway.

Celia raced past her to the car. "Get in!" she screamed, opening the vehicle's left-hand door. She glanced briefly at the front porch to see the man with the Van Dyke turn to look at her. She lurched into the car and slammed the door shut behind her. She nearly banged heads with Kalendra.

"Car: Start!" Celia yelled. She screamed when Van Dyke pounded on her window.

The vehicle floated a foot off the ground as the dim interior lights flickered on.

"Hurry!" Kalendra urged, keeping an eye on the apparition passing through the closed gate toward the car. "Hurry, Celia!"

"Car: Go to—" She turned to Kalendra. "What's your address?" Van Dyke pounded on the window again and peered inside. Celia jumped and squealed. "No time! Car: Go two miles north, now!"

The vehicle immediately floated into the street, headed in the direction specified. It's passengers gazed back at Van Dyke as he trotted toward the car. The faceless spirit seemed to have vanished.

"Car: Faster!" Celia ordered.

The vehicle obeyed, but went no faster than the speed limit. It still managed to outdistance Van Dyke fairly quickly, leaving him behind. At exactly two miles north, the car pulled over and came to a halt.

Kalendra felt like she had held her breath ever since escaping Celia's house. Now she needed it desperately. She sucked in huge lungfuls of air as she looked out the rear window. She could hear Celia gasping beside her.

"I think we ditched him," Kalendra breathed.

"What the hell happened back there?"

"Someone's after us."

"Well, yeah, but why?"

"How am I supposed to know?" Kalendra snapped.

"I don't know, sorry!" Celia returned defensively. "Snap my head off, why don't you?" She placed her hand on her forehead and then on her chest. "God, my heart's beating so fast. I've never been so scared in my life!"

Kalendra's heart was also beating quickly, but her mind was working just as fast. "Dan wants us to get that book for him. Did you notice that right after he mentioned it, he told us to get out? Do you think that was a coincidence? I don't."

Celia looked at her, her eyes wide. She clearly didn't follow Kalendra's logic.

"They – the ghost and the old guy – don't want us to get the book."

"Really?" Celia asked then threw back her head. "God!" She swallowed hard and looked in the rear view mirror. She slumped in her seat. "Kalendra, do you realize that I can't go back home now? Not ever? Not after all that. I've got to call my mom." She leaned forward. "Phone: Celia's mom. No, wait, she's not at work, she's out of town. I'm so scared I forgot. Phone: Cancel." She slumped back in her seat again.

"I don't think we should tell anyone about this," Kalendra said.

"But I have to tell my mom," Celia exclaimed. "Or they'll get her, too."

"Maybe, maybe not."

"What do you mean?"

"Well, she doesn't know about the book," Kalendra explained. "The ghost and the old guy might not try to get her if she doesn't know anything."

Celia gazed at her friend. "I have to tell her, Kal. She'll be wondering why I'm not there anymore."

"Okay," Kalendra agreed. "Maybe we should get this car moving again before one of those things back there catches up to us."

Celia nodded and was about to issue another order to the car when another vehicle pulled up behind them. A man got out and walked to Celia's side. He looked down at Celia then across at Kalendra.

Kalendra's eyes widened. "I know him."

"Is there a problem, ladies?" His voice came through the internal speakers of Celia's car. He then flashed a smile that left both women speechless for a second.

"Everything's fine," Celia said, returning the smile. "We're just talking."

"You look upset," he replied. "Are you sure there's nothing wrong?"

Celia and Kalendra exchanged silent glances.

"I'm sorry," the man said. "It's really none of my business. I just thought you might be in trouble."

"We're fine," Kalendra assured him.

He smiled again. "Well, good night, then." He tilted his head then returned to his vehicle.

Celia looked at Kalendra and they both started giggling like the schoolgirls they were.

"Well, that was interesting," Celia exclaimed giddily.

"That's the guy from the bus I told you about," Kalendra told her. "You know the day I saw the ghost in your window. Not the faceless one, though."

"Dan said that ghost was his grandmother," Celia recalled.

"And he said he wasn't dead," Kalendra said. "Poor guy's in denial."

Celia looked in the rear view mirror. "That man's still back there. What's he doing?"

Kalendra looked, then returned her attention to Celia. "Let's go to my grandmother's. You can stay there for a while until we decide what to do."

Celia sighed. "I have absolutely no idea what I'm going to tell my mom. What's your Gramma's address?"

Kalendra gave the address to her and Celia ordered the car to go there. "Do you have enough money to move out?" Kalendra asked as they walked to the door. "You could use that as an excuse for your mom."

"I don't have a job."

"Then I guess you will have to tell her," Kalendra relented with a sigh.

"Tell whom what?" Lettice asked, standing in the open doorway.

Both girls fell silent.

3

Lettice's brow furrowed. "What's up, girls? Something's happened, hasn't it?"

Celia gazed at her with eyes as wide as her fear. "Somebody's after us." Kalendra butted her in the back with her shoulder. Celia glanced at her then at the ground. "Sorry."

Lettice looked at her granddaughter, her eyes demanding an answer.

"We don't know who it is," Kalendra replied, unable to look her grandmother in the eye. "Some guy. Celia needs to stay here for a while, though. Is that okay?"

"Only if you tell me what's going on." When no answer from Kalendra seemed forthcoming, Lettice returned her attention to Celia.

"We don't really know what's going on," she replied, her voice small and frightened. "He came through the front door and we had to run out the back. He almost got us before we could get in the car."

"You're very lucky. Come in and I'll call the police."

The girls went straight to the kitchen for drinks while Lettice brought up the Internet on the television screen. Kalendra and Celia verbally filled out a police report then drank their sodas in relative silence.

Lettice stood up and extended her hand to Celia. "Hello, I don't believe we've met."

"I'm Celia," she said. "Nice to meet you."

"Call me Lettice. Now, is either one of you going to tell me what really happened or am I going to have to piece it together later, from your nightmares?"

Kalendra and Celia laughed half-heartedly. "I don't know if we can," Kalendra told her.

"Why not?"

Kalendra shrugged and stared at the bubbles in her soda.

"There was a ghost," Celia mumbled. Kalendra shot her a look.

"A ghost?" Lettice asked. "Where? At your house?"

"Yep," Celia replied matter-of-factly. "A woman ghost, without a face."

Lettice gazed hard at her as she slowly settled into her chair.

"What's wrong?" Kalendra asked, concerned.

Lettice whispered, "Dan tried to contact you, didn't he?"

Kalendra stared at her. "Dan? How did you know that?"

Lettice covered her face in her hands and started weeping. Her granddaughter got up to put an arm around her while Celia looked helplessly away.

"I'm sorry," Lettice said, wiping her eyes. "I didn't mean to do that. I should have known something would happen. Ever since you told me Celia lived in that house—"

"Grandma," Kalendra said pointedly. "How do you know about Dan?"

Lettice stood and went to the kitchen window. Outside, a sparrow dipped its beak below the surface of the puddle in the birdbath. "I knew Dan," she said. "Quite well, actually. We were in love. I wish I could say we were engaged to be married, but there hadn't been any time for that. It was about two years before I met your grandfather." She turned away from the window and took a great breath. "What I did to him was unforgivable. I abandoned him."

Kalendra and Celia gazed at her for several heartbeats. "Are you the one who put him where he is?" asked the former.

"Oh, no!" Lettice gasped, almost laughing. "Of course not. How could I do something like that? No. But I promised him I'd never rest until I found a way to set him and the others free and I didn't follow through with that promise. I gave up. I met your grandfather and eventually, I stopped trying to free them."

"You were supposed to get a special book," Kalendra whispered hoarsely. "Weren't you?"

Lettice nodded slowly, gazing at a dust ball on the linoleum floor. She absently reached for the small broom and dustpan she kept behind the kitchen door. "I couldn't find the damn thing," she said, sweeping the dust ball into the pan. "I was told that it didn't even exist and I began to believe it was true. Still, I'd promised I would never give up. I lied to him." She returned the broom and dustpan to their positions behind the door.

"Dan wants us to find it now," said Celia.

Lettice looked at her. "Then he's given up on me. What am I saying? He must have given up years ago." She leaned against the refrigerator. "I had hoped perhaps he had recruited someone else's help over the years, that he had escaped, married someone else, had children. But he is still there. After all these years, no one has ever found the book for him."

"If it even exists," Kalendra pointed out.

"I don't know," Lettice sighed. "It may exist or it may not. Just because I stopped looking doesn't mean it's not out there somewhere."

"He mentioned others. I think you mentioned them, too."

Lettice nodded. "There are four others, all banished with him. One of them is his sister, Sarah, and the other three are his ancestors. I don't know their names."

"This is weird," Kalendra said. "How come you never mentioned any of this before?"

"Why would I?" Lettice replied. "If I'd talked about it, you'd have thought I was nuts."

Kalendra nodded. "How did they get to be where they are?"

"The faceless ghost you saw," Lettice began. "She and that man at the door. They're both witches."

"Witches?" Kalendra asked, glancing at Celia.

Lettice nodded. "The two of them together banished Dan and his sister. No, it wasn't him. There was another witch before him, but she died. Anyway, it's all part of the curse."

"Curse?"

Lettice took a deep breath and told the two young women everything, starting when she had first viewed the ghost in the shuttered window and ending when she had met the man she married.

"This is way too bizarre," Kalendra said, shaking her head.

"I was hoping this had all gone away," Lettice said, hanging her head. "I had hoped to die before I had to tell anyone about this. I should have known it would come back to haunt me. No pun intended." She laughed weakly.

"Do you still love Dan, Gramma?"

Lettice clenched her eyes shut and nodded. "I've never stopped thinking about him, even when I was with your grandfather—" She trailed off. "Stay right there." She exited the kitchen then returned with a book.

Kalendra gazed at the bounded pages, instantly reminded of the man on the bus whom she had seen again earlier in the evening. Was this the book Dan had asked for? Did Gramma have it all along?

"Is that a book of spells?" Celia asked, her eyes wide with fear and awe.

Lettice glanced at her and nodded. "There are spells in here a non-initiate can cast. I have cast many of them myself, often in secrecy while your grandfather was alive. No initiate has come after me in fifty years."

"Initiate?" Celia asked. "Is that what the witches are called?"

Lettice shrugged. "This book called them that and that's what I call them. They might call themselves something else. Wiccan, perhaps, I'm not sure. I think these witches, initiates, are different from Wiccan, but I'm not positive."

"Is that *The Book*?" Kalendra asked.

Lettice shook her head. "I told you, that book has never been found. This is a different book."

"Can I cast a spell?" Celia asked. "I mean, one that can make me go back home without getting attacked?"

Lettice looked at her and a slow grin spread her lips. "Yes you can. First, we need to get some candles—"

Kalendra snorted. "This sounds like a bad movie. Shall I get calf's blood and some eye of newt?"

Lettice shook her head. "No, the candles will be fine."

4.

Kalendra looked up from her handheld to see him boarding the bus. He looked directly at her and smiled. She returned the gesture.

"Fancy meeting you again," he said, walking up to her.

"No need to fancy it, you already have," she replied off-handedly.

"Is this seat taken?" he asked, taking the seat before waiting for her reply.

"It's taken, now," Kalendra said, scooting slightly toward the window. She noticed the book in his hand. "History of New England" was the title.

"Are you a student?" he asked.

She nodded. "Are you?"

"We're all students," he replied cryptically. "Students of life, that is. I work in the Main Library. My name is Ian." He jutted his hand at her.

"Kalendra," she said, gingerly shaking the proffered body part.

"Pretty name," Ian said. "Very pretty. I don't think I've ever heard it before." He looked at her handheld, observing the website she was viewing. "BookNet. You like books, do you?"

"I guess so," she replied. "I'm kind of looking for one in particular."

"Really? Which one?"

She shrugged. "A rare one. I haven't been able to find it yet."

"Is that so?" he said. "I happen to have a fairly large collection of rare books at my home."

"Really?" Kalendra asked, interested.

He grinned and nodded. "It's not as extensive as my uncle's, but it of a goodly size. My uncle's got just about anything no one's ever heard of. Most of them sole surviving editions. He inherited a bunch from a friend of his a while back after some sort of explosion. Some of the books are singed slightly."

Kalendra looked at him a moment then back down at her handheld. She turned it off.

"Maybe you can come by for a visit," Ian suggested. "Maybe what you're looking for is there."

She stared at her hands then shrugged. "Sure. Okay."

"Well, there's no time like the present!" he exclaimed loudly. "My stop's just about here."

Before she could react, Ian was up and out of his seat. He stopped at the door and turned to her, grinning broadly. She smiled hesitantly in return and, after a brief hesitation, followed him off the bus.

Kalendra once again found herself in front of Celia's house. She was afraid she would see a ghost again and indeed thought she saw a flicker of movement in the window, but there was nothing there. Nothing she could see, anyway. She glanced at Ian to find him scowling, just as he had the first time she'd seen him.

"Is something wrong?" she asked.

"Huh?" he said, looking genuinely surprised. "No, why?"

"You had a horrible look on your face just now."

Ian shrugged and smiled. "I didn't realize. I'm sorry. My house is on the next block."

Ian's house appeared to be just about as old as Celia's, but was much larger and recently remodeled. How much could a librarian possibly make? she wondered.

"Nice house," she said, staring at it from the sidewalk.

"My research helps pay for it," Ian replied, as if reading her thoughts. "I make next to nothing working at the library." He unlocked the door. "My uncle also helps me out when I need it. He's rolling in it."

"What does he do?" she asked.

He glanced over his shoulder at her. "Nothing. At least, not as far as I can tell."

The door opened and a dachshund immediately trotted out to greet Ian, barking happily. He pranced about Ian's feet then saw Kalendra and growled softly.

"Oh, stop it," Ian said sternly to the animal. The dachshund ruffed at him then trotted back into the house, toenails clicking on the wooden floorboards. Ian smiled apologetically. "He's not used to strangers," he explained.

Kalendra nodded. Meanwhile, she was greatly impressed with the stained wood the interior of the house was decorated in. Everything was wood, the walls, floor, ceiling and even the furniture. Interspersed in this arboreal graveyard were various items of statuary, paintings and historical items such as armor, weapons and urns.

"What is this place, Hearst Castle?" she asked.

Ian laughed. "Not nearly as grand as that, but I'll take that as a compliment. My library is in the basement," he said, leading the way. "It's kind of cramped down there, so be forewarned. I've got a ton of books."

Kalendra followed him through the basement door. He pulled on a cord, illuminating the stairwell. She pinched her nose shut, overwhelmed by the musty odor wafting up from below. She watched her step carefully as she descended the splintery, wooden steps.

"The card catalog is at the foot of the stairs there," Ian directed as the stairs turned. "Can I get you some tea?"

"Uh, sure," she said, gazing at the wooden bookshelves crammed together. Only the skinniest of persons would ever be able to maneuver these aisles, she thought. If my breasts were any larger, I'd be out of luck.

She perused the titles for a moment then decided it was best to go straight to the card catalog. It was the old-fashioned type, the title written on cards and catalogued according to the Dewey decimal system.

The Book wasn't listed. She informed him of this when he returned with tea.

"That's a shame," he said. "I'm terribly sorry about that."

"Thanks for letting me look," she said. "That was very nice of you."

Ian gazed at her, tapping his finger on his chin. "I bet you my uncle has it. Maybe I could take you there."

"Uh—"

"Or I could just ask him. What's the title of the book you're looking for?"

"Um..." Kalendra hesitated then decided to tell him.

Ian nodded. "He might have it. He has all sorts of books."

"Great."

"May I ask why you're looking for this particular book? Is it for a term paper?"

"No, it's for my grandmother," Kalendra said. "She's been looking for it for years." She suddenly wished she'd never mentioned she was looking for *The Book*. Ian was going to think she was nuts.

"Is that so?" he asked. "Well, what a nice granddaughter you are then."

Kalendra knew it was a glib compliment, but she felt her cheeks warming all the same. Ian was very handsome and a charming gentleman as well. She tried to think of a reason to extend her visit when he suddenly turned and went upstairs. She hesitated only a second before following him back to the living room.

"Have a seat," he said, indicating an antique chair.

She gazed at it speculatively. "I won't ruin it or anything?"

"The cloth and stuffing isn't original," Ian informed her. "Only the wood is authentic. It's a very nice piece, isn't it?"

She agreed and seated herself. "It's Colonial, isn't it?"

"Most of the furniture is," he said. "But it doesn't really fit, does it?"

"What do you mean?"

"The house was built in the 1880s, hardly during the Colonial Period, but it was built in Colonial style. Close enough for me. I could have found one in a different neighborhood, of course, but I wanted to stay near to my uncle. He lives about seven blocks away."

"Really?" Kalendra said, not knowing what else to say. She really enjoyed his company and hung on every word that was imparted from his lips.

Ian's pet dachshund returned to hop up and down at his feet and make whuffing noises.

"Oh, Brutus," Ian said to the animal, "is it time for your walk?" He stood up and looked at Kalendra. "Care to join me? We could take the opportunity to walk to my uncle's house to see if your book is there."

"Okay," Kalendra said, getting to her feet.

Ian grinned. "Fine. I'll go get his leash."

The instant they were out the door, Brutus pulled the leash taught, anxious to get to wherever he thought he was going. Ian rolled his eyes and smiled at Kalendra. "He's always like this. I know just where he's going to go, too."

Brutus veered right as he and the two humans came upon Celia's house. He lifted his leg and commenced to urinate.

"He always has to go here," Ian said. "I don't know why. He must like the smell or something."

Kalendra shrugged and gasped. The old lady was in the window again, frowning severely at her.

"What is it?" Ian asked. "Do you see something?"

The apparition vanished. Kalendra started coughing, shaking her head. "No," she choked. "Something was in my throat." She coughed again. "There, it's gone. I think I may have swallowed a bug." She forced a smile. Ian looked at her curiously, but said nothing.

Ten minutes later, Kalendra stood before a three-story home sporting two immense Grecian pillars rising up to the top floor. She felt as if she were approaching Mount Olympus or, at the very least, some ancient temple.

"Wow," she said, wondering why she never noticed this magnificent home before. Surely it was visible from the street her bus hovered down every day. Maybe it was situated at just the right angle behind the other houses, obscuring it from view. She'd have to make sure and look for it on her next ride home.

"Impressive, isn't it?" Ian asked with a broad grin. "It was built thirty years ago, after the original house burned down. This is the third house on this site since the late 1600s."

"Wow," Kalendra repeated, dizzy from staring up at the pillars. When she lowered her head, pinpricks of light danced before her eyes.

Ian rang the doorbell. There was no answer. "He may be away," Ian told her. "He often is. He's always going to Europe or Africa or somewhere." He removed a key card from his jacket pocket. He waved it in front of a sensor light then stared into a peephole. The door clicked open

"High security," he said to Kalendra with a wink, stepping inside. "I basically have free run of the place." He tugged Brutus inside after him. Kalendra followed, prepared to be impressed.

She was.

It was similar to Ian's house, but on a much grander scale. She had a feeling that many of the antiques in this house were one-of-a-kind items, perhaps completely unknown to the outside world. Her eyes lingered on the stone table with gargoyles on each corner in the entryway as she followed Ian into the living room. She passed by a suit of chain mail armor complete with horned helmet, a Chinese cherry wood and jade trunk, a sculpture of a naked Grecian woman between two cherubs and a gold and ivory chessboard. There were many other items cluttering the spaces in between, too many for her to take in at once. The interior of the place was far too overwhelming.

"The library is this way," Ian said, Brutus running up the flight of stairs ahead of them. Ian had released him from his leash. Ian opened the double doors at the end of the hallway, revealing a huge room featuring rows and rows and rows of books, with more antiques interspersed amongst them.

"This place is unbelievable," Kalendra cried, once again completely overwhelmed.

"Almost everything my uncle owns is rare, including the

books. They take up almost the entire floor. The card catalog is over here."

Kalendra approached the relatively new wooden cabinet and opened a drawer as Ian wandered amongst the shelves. Brutus's nails clattered against the tiled floor nearby. "Your uncle could open his own public library," Kalendra commented.

"Yes, but he never would," came Ian's voice from afar. "He's a very private person. I would consider myself to be the closest person to him and even I don't know very much about him."

"Really?" Kalendra asked, opening another drawer. "It's not here," she sighed.

"Are you sure?" Ian asked, appearing from behind a shelf.

"Yeah." She sighed again.

"Hmm." Ian walked to a shelf situated against the wall and removed a book. He turned the book around and reshelved it spine first. There followed a grinding sound as a row of shelves swiveled to reveal a hidden room.

"Quite pedestrian, but effective," Ian said, heading into the room behind Brutus. "This is his secret library. I discovered it a couple of years ago by accident. He doesn't know I know about it."

The hidden room smelled like a mixture of sweet pipe tobacco and mildew. Kalendra stifled a cough as she perused the shelves. Most of the books she encountered dealt with the subjects of witchcraft and demonology. One book in particular made her shudder: *Recipe for Man*, subtitled, *A Guide to Proper Preparation of Human Meat for Consumption*. Her stomach lurched as she hastily replaced the book on the shelf.

"There's no card catalog for these books, I'm afraid," Ian said. "So I guess it's browsing time."

Kalendra nodded, having already started. She found that although the books were very old, most of them were in excellent condition. Some of the bindings were blank, without titles, forcing Kalendra to withdraw the volumes and open them to find out what they were.

Brutus scurried happily past her, his tongue hanging loosely from his mouth. She couldn't help but smile. *Oh, to be a carefree animal without the worries of banished ancestors trapped by faceless witch ghosts!*

"Interesting," she muttered, coming upon a stack of scrolls at the end of a row. They appeared ancient, yet spectacularly preserved.

Ian looked over his shoulder at her utterance. "The scrolls? Truly amazing, aren't they? There are between two and three thousand years old, written entirely in ancient Greek. I can't read a word of it."

Brutus ran by again, barking gleefully. He rammed Kalendra's leg with his head and kept going.

"Hey!" she cried with a giggle.

"Brutus, what's gotten into you?" Ian asked, though didn't take his eyes of the shelves.

Kalendra went back to her browsing, but returned her attention to the dachshund when he barked yet again. She found him staring up at a framed map above a nearby shelf. Brutus barked again, hopping up to place his feet against the books on the bottom row of the shelf.

"Brutus!" Ian shouted, hurrying over to scoop his dog up. "What's your problem? Do you see a spider? He gets excited around spiders," he explained. "I don't see one, though. Maybe it crawled away. All gone," he said to Brutus. "No more spi—"

Brutus leapt from Ian's arms onto the top shelf, shoving books aside. Ian yelled at the dog again, appalled that he had knocked over such priceless volumes when Brutus jumped up again, knocking the map from the wall. Behind it was a safe. Brutus sat down on the shelf and stared up at it. Arching his doggie brow, he looked over his shoulder at Ian.

"Come down from there," Ian said gently, reaching to retrieve his pet.

"It's almost like he knew it was there," Kalendra whispered.

"Yes, very curious," Ian said, sounding unnerved. He replaced the map over the safe and Brutus barked again, trying to wriggle free from his master's grasp.

Ian restrained him. "What are you doing?" he demanded.

Brutus didn't reply. Ian's attention was then grabbed by a sudden gasp from Kalendra.

The combination lock on the safe was turning by itself, back and forth, until the combination was complete. The door swung slowly open.

Ian's eyes widened as he stepped back and Kalendra stepped forward. She pulled a stepstool to the shelf and stood on the tips of her toes, pulling the safe door all the way open. Inside was a black book. She withdrew it and gazed at the cover.

"This is it!" she declared. *The Book*!

"It is?" Ian asked, shocked. "Really? How in the world—" Ian gazed at Brutus with intense confusion. He scratched his head.

Kalendra also looked to Brutus as she thought about Dan and the others that were trapped inside Celia's house. "I think we had some help getting this," she murmured.

"I don't think you should take it," Ian said, sounding frightened. "If it's important enough for my uncle to put in a safe, I think he'd be very upset if it were missing."

"Do you think he checks the safe everyday to make sure it's still there?" Kalendra countered. "This room is supposed to be secret. I don't think he'd be worried about someone stealing it."

"Okay," Ian said then paused. "But if he wasn't worried about it being stolen, why lock it up inside a secret room?"

Kalendra shrugged. "Probably just to make it just that much more difficult to find."

Brutus yipped and scurried over to an overcrowded shelf. He bit down on a black-bound book and pulled it to the floor.

"I think our problem has been solved," Kalendra said, smiling slyly at Ian as she walked over to retrieve the book. She put it in the safe, closed it and placed the map back over it. "You're uncle won't miss it, after all," she said.

Ian gazed at Brutus with mixed awe and respect. "My dog usually isn't this smart."

Kalendra shrugged and grinned. "If you'll excuse me, Ian, I must be going."

He didn't try to stop her, as he was too busy staring in wonder at his pet.

"How did you do that?" Audrey asked.

Savannah grinned broadly. "I'm not sure, but it worked magnificently, didn't it?" She laughed and clapped her hands. "It was right where we thought it was, too."

"So, she has *The Book*?"

Savannah nodded. "And I think she knows who helped her, too."

"Does she know whose house she's in?"

"She might," Savannah said doubtfully.

Audrey looked at her, a crooked grin on her face. "So. How does it feel to be a dachsy?"

"Very strange," Savannah said then laughed. "I'm glad to be back."

"I just hope you don't go jumping into every creature that walks by the house now," Audrey said.

Savannah could only laugh.

5.

Kalendra's heart pounded incessantly in her ears as she walked through the door of her grandmother's house. Everything was starting to make a little more sense and it terrified her. She felt like she was a hair's breadth from losing control of her senses and wanted to just run amok down the street, screaming and laughing. The afternoon with Ian had been one of the strangest in her life.

She had just come back from a warlock's house where a dachshund had just helped her locate a book that some people thought had been lost for centuries. She couldn't believe that it hadn't been just a bizarre dream induced by eating too much spicy food.

She was just glad the warlock hadn't been home. He would have known immediately what her intentions were, especially if Ian had told him what book she was looking for. She then thought perhaps he was aware of her, but that perhaps her grandmother had somehow cast a protective spell on her to keep him from harming her.

Or perhaps Dan had protected her somehow. She was positive he had something to do with getting Brutus to open the safe. Or perhaps it was one of the others trapped with him. Whoever it was, they weren't solid like normal people. That safe dial looked like it turned by itself.

Kalendra recalled Ian and had to chuckle. The poor man had no idea who his uncle was, no idea what was going on around him. She decided she wouldn't see him again. Not after this. Even if he wasn't a warlock himself, she didn't want to take any more chances. Besides, she didn't trust him not to tell the warlock what happened. The warlock would be furious when he found out *The Book* was gone. Kalendra hoped she had some time to perform a protection spell like the one her grandmother had taught her. That is, if she didn't already have one protecting her.

Lettice walked into the living room, her eyes going immediately to *The Book*.

"You have it," she whispered.

Kalendra nodded. "It was at the warlock's house."

Lettice gazed at her in alarm then calmed. "Of course. It's the most logical place for it to be. It was probably at his mother's before that. How did you find out where he lives?"

"I met his nephew," she explained. "He, the warlock, doesn't live far from Celia's house, only a few blocks. That's how he gets there so fast."

Lettice nodded curtly. "You have to go there and free Dan now."

Kalendra nodded then hesitated. "Don't you want to go?"

Lettice turned away. "I don't want him to see me like this. Old and wrinkled." She sighed, nearly sobbed. "He hates me, anyway. Because I abandoned him."

Kalendra thought about that, not knowing what to say. "Gramma?" She waited for Lettice to look at her before she continued. "What are we going to do with him once he's freed? Is he going to stay here? Are all of them going to stay here?"

Lettice bowed her head, examined her nails. She grimaced. "I suppose I should face him before he comes here. He deserves that much."

Kalendra waited.

Lettice sniffed and raised her chin high. "Let's go, Kalendra, before I lose my nerve."

Dan recognized the two voices instantly, though one sounded a little different than he remembered. He walked up from the basement and through the kitchen. He stopped in the doorway and gazed at the two women. Submit walked up behind him, still readjusting her clothing. He didn't pay her any attention.

"Lettice," he whispered.

The full weight of his time spent in banishment fell upon him as he gazed upon Lettice's weathered face. She was old, while he didn't look a day older. He was mildly surprised to realize that he found her beautiful nevertheless. She had always been a beautiful person, inside and out. White hair, age spots and wrinkles didn't diminish her beauty in the least.

Only the fact she had abandoned him did.

Sarah walked down the stairs, watching the two visitors speaking with Celia and her mother. Dan glanced at her and she walked over to him. "We truly have been here a long time," she sighed. "Not as long as you, of course," she said to Submit who nodded incrementally. Sarah then turned to look at Ebenezer as he descended the stairs and joined her, taking her hand.

"I am not so certain I wish to be freed," Ebenezer said stiffly.

"I know that I do not," Submit said, taking Dan's hand from behind.

He turned to her, suddenly aware of her presence. "I understand why," he told her. "This world will be completely alien to you. It will be to me, too, though obviously not to the same extent. Still, you must admit that being out there will be better than being in here. We can finally—" His face reddened.

"Finish," Submit completed for him, smiling broadly. "I would like that, very much." She embraced him then gazed at Lettice standing two feet away.

"Where's Jesse?" Sarah asked.

Dan removed himself from Submit and looked at the stairs, expecting to see Jesse sitting on them as he often did. Instead, he saw a white swirling shape coalescing, accompanied by an increasingly high-pitched whine.

"*She* is not happy," Ebenezer commented wryly.

"Her curse is about to be undone," Submit said, grinning at Dan.

"I wonder how they finally located *The Book*," Dan said,

returning his attention to Lettice and Kalendra as they leafed through it. "I wonder why it took so long."

"It must have been in a very hard-to-find place," Sarah said.

Dinah finally took a definite shape, her face no longer a black void of nothingness. She revealed her face to them, the blackened, charred disfigurement it had become at the hand of John Smead. The distorted mouth opened, emitting a high-pitched wail that seemed to exist in every molecule of the house. The three women in the world of the living didn't appear to hear it.

"Why is nothing happening to them?" Dan asked loudly, his hands over his ears trying to block out the shriek. His grandmother appeared before him, her form vague and transparent.

"The warlock is not at home," she informed him. "The women have a spell protecting them. They are safe. For now."

"How—" Dan started to ask just as he felt a heavy blow against the back of his skull.

He awoke minutes later with the witch's shriek still ringing in his aching head. Lettice was standing over him, tears streaking her face. He stared at her a moment then sat up.

"I'm so sorry, Dan," she said, her voice barely a whisper. "So sorry."

He stood up shakily and took her into his embrace. Her body was much thinner, her bones frailer. She was fifty years older than the last time he'd held her in his arms. "I'm sorry, too," he whispered.

"But you've got nothing to be sorry for," she cried, stepping back from him. "I betrayed you! I'd promised I'd never stop looking for the book and I lied! I'm so sorry for that!"

"I forgive you," he said, choking back the tears. He'd not planned on forgiving her, but suddenly realized it was no use holding on to the anger. Besides, she seemed genuinely sorry for what she'd failed to do. "I don't blame you for getting on with your life. You were entitled to that. But, what made you start looking for the book again?"

"I wasn't looking," she said, sniffing and wiping away her tears. "My granddaughter found it. You contacted her, remember?"

Dan looked at Kalendra who was keeping her distance, gazing in awe at the events unfolding before her. She stepped back when his eyes fixed on hers. He returned his attention to Lettice.

She forced a grin. "Her granddad was Japanese and her father was Russian."

He forced a smile. "Nice to meet you," he said, unsure of how to act. It was strange, seeing his former love's granddaughter standing before him, physically not much younger than he was.

Kalendra smiled nervously and introduced herself as if they hadn't already met via the Virtual Ouija. "This is my friend Celia."

"I know who you are," Dan replied. "Both of you. Especially Celia, since I see her almost every day."

Celia's face crimsoned and she lowered her gaze. "You haven't been watching me, have you?"

"There wasn't much to do where we were," he told her, saying nothing more. Celia's blush darkened further.

Dan felt a little embarrassed, too. He looked down and noticed the others had also been freed. Submit, Ebenezer and Sarah all lay on the floor as if they were sleeping. Dan's head still hurt and he was a bit groggy. He felt like he'd been knocked unconscious. "That freeing spell sure hurt," Dan said with a nervous chuckle, rubbing the back of his neck. "I hope they wake up okay."

"They should be fine," Kalendra assured him. "But we need to cast another spell on you guys. A protection spell."

"Wait," Dan said. "One of us is missing. Where's Jesse?"

"We should leave," Celia said urgently, glancing at the staircase.

"The warlock isn't home," Kalendra told her.

Dan glanced at Kalendra then hurried up the stairs. Jesse lay on the floor of the main bedroom. His eyes opened as Dan walked into the room.

"We've been freed," Dan told him. "Get up. We have to get out of the house." Jesse didn't respond as he followed Dan downstairs. The others were slowly awakening when they returned. Submit, Ebenezer and Sarah all looked around dazedly as Lettice, Kalendra and Celia lit candles and placed them all about the living and dining area.

"Do you remember the spell by heart, Grandma?" Kalendra asked Lettice, looking concerned as she lit the wick of a fat, red candle.

"Spell?" Sarah asked, looking alarmed. "What kind of spell are you talking about?"

"A protection spell," Lettice replied. "It's one of the few spells average people can cast. It was how I stayed safe all these years."

"One spell will work for all of us?" Dan enquired.

"Yes," Kalendra said, lighting the final candle.

"How well does this spell protect us?" Sarah wanted to know. "I can't imagine that a powerful warlock, with a little help form a ghost witch, can't overpower something cast by an amateur. No offense."

"None taken," said Lettice. "The spell only protects against small, hurtful spells. If the warlock wants to get at us, he'll have to try really hard."

"That doesn't make me feel very safe," Sarah muttered, glancing at Dan and the others.

"It's better than nothing," said Dan with a shrug.

"Okay, then," said Lettice, sitting cross-legged on the floor. "Let's begin."

After the protection spell was cast, it was time to leave the house. Dan was the first to approach the door. He hesitated, recalling the frozen void that had taken the life of his neighbor so many years ago. He paused for two heartbeats before opening the door.

He expected to see the void, frozen bodies floating in midair. He expected to find out he had been tricked, that this entire episode had been a set up to get him to open the door. Someone would then push him, take care of him once and for all. But there was no void. There was only the front yard, the street and the house across the street. He nearly whooped for joy to see things had returned to normal. He had thought this day would never come. He was finally going to leave this godforsaken house and, hopefully, he would never have to return.

"Wow," said Sarah standing behind him. "The neighborhood has hardly changed at all, has it? Except for that strange car with no wheels parked at the curb, I would think only a few months had passed since we were banished."

"I'm still expecting something bad to happen," he replied. "Like I'm dreaming this whole thing. It wouldn't be the first time."

"I know what you mean."

He took a tentative step forward onto the porch. The old boards creaked beneath his weight. He took two less hesitant steps then turned to see Submit and Ebenezer standing behind Sarah.

Ebenezer glanced at Dan then took Submit's hand, walking with her through the door. He gazed in amazement at the old houses across the street. "Everything is so different," he said. "I'd listened to your stories of your era, Dan, but I'd never accurately imagined them. These houses are old, though, aren't they? They look old, yet they look new, unlike anything I'd ever seen. Very peculiar."

"It is very peculiar," said his daughter, her eyes fixed on the car. She then looked at Dan and smiled quizzically. She craned her neck to look back at Jesse who stood in the doorway looking extremely unhappy.

"I do not wish to leave," he informed her. "I do not belong out there."

"Jesse," Submit said softly. "We did not belong in there, either."

"Yes," he replied. "We should have died centuries ago."

Submit sighed. "This is nothing we have not discussed countless times. We are alive and free. You should be happy."

"I hate to interrupt," Kalendra said, cutting off Jesse's

reply, "but we really need to get out of here in case the warlock decides to put in an appearance. The six of you can go on this trip and the car will come back for me."

"You guys go," Dan said, looking to Lettice. "You and I should talk."

Kalendra glanced at her grandmother who nodded consent. Kalendra led the others to the car, Submit dragging Jesse out of the house.

❧

"I can't go in there," Jesse protested as he neared the vehicle. Ebenezer also hesitated, gazing uncertainly at the strange vehicle.

"It's just a car, Eb," Sarah told him. "It's much different that what I'm used to, but there's nothing to be afraid of."

"You've told me about cars on numerous occasions," he replied. "And what stands out in my mind the most is how dangerous they were."

"They can be dangerous," she admitted, knowing she'd just lost the battle.

"Not so much," Kalendra said, coming to Sarah's rescue. "These days they're as safe as can be. They have a built in resistance field that's enabled whenever they come too close to another object. That makes it almost impossible for it to hit anything."

"Almost?" Ebenezer inquired, raising a brow.

"A car will hit something only if it's malfunctioning. Of course, in off road areas, people still drive the old fashioned kind with wheels, but they're banned from cities and freeways."

"Cool," Sarah said, turning to look inside the car. "I don't see a steering wheel. Or do you not need those anymore."

"Only old cars have that," Kalendra said with a grin. "The onboard computer will take you where you want to go. Boy, do I sound like a commercial or what?"

"Is it electric?" Sarah asked. "Surely all the gasoline has run out by now."

Kalendra shook her head. "It's magnetic. It runs on two

magnets set in a vacuum in the back. Something like that. I don't know the specifics."

Sarah whistled. "Unbelievable. Science fiction becomes science fact."

"We really need to hurry," Kalendra said, ushering everyone in. She sat in the front with Ebenezer and Sarah while Submit and Jesse sat in the back.

"I don't like it in here," Jesse howled, hitting and kicking the door. "It feels like I have been buried inside a coffin. I want out!"

"Car," Kalendra exclaimed, Jesse's tone frightening her. "Open roof." The sunroof slid open, letting in sun and air. Jesse, Submit and Ebenezer all jumped, terrified.

"Witch's work!" Jesse hissed.

"Oh, be quiet," snapped Sarah. "It's technology, not witchcraft."

"Well, if that scares you guys," Kalendra began, "then you really won't like this." She gave the car directions and the vehicle started to rise off the ground. The two ancestors in the back held on to each other, restraining their breath while Ebenezer gripped Sarah's hand tightly.

Sarah herself was more than a little tense. She wasn't used to cars rising off the ground. When it halted a foot above the street, she relaxed. "We'll be fine," she told Ebenezer, squeezing his hand reassuringly.

"I do not like this world," Jesse declared tremulously, his rump rising from his seat. "I do not belong here."

"Hush," Submit insisted, taking his arm. "Nothing bad is going to happen to us. *I* think it's wonderful. A great adventure. Smoother riding than a horse."

"Do you people even have horses here?" Jesse inquired forcefully. "If so, let me out and I'll follow you on one."

"We still have horses," Kalendra replied nervously, her voice quivering and slightly high-pitched. Jesse seemed so unstable, so unpredictable. And not in an interesting way, either. She thought he was scary. "Just not around here," she added, waiting for him to erupt into another frighteningly loud tirade.

Instead, there was silence, except for the barely audible hum of the car.

Kalendra still felt very awkward, very uncomfortable. She felt like a baby-sitter for time-travelers. Who would have known people from the past would behave like such children? And they were all so much older than she was. It was very bizarre. At least until she realized they were just people like anyone else. So what if two of them had been alive for four hundred and fifty years? They were still people.

She couldn't imagine what it must have been like, trapped in a house like that. She wanted desperately to ask them about it, but decided it was probably the last thing they wanted to talk about right now. Still, the silence was driving her crazy. It seemed to her like they were communicating on some level she didn't have access to, that they were talking about her in a place she couldn't access. Had they developed telepathy while they'd been banished? Lately, she'd witnessed stranger things than that.

"So," Kalendra began, wanting desperately to break the silence, yet having nothing important to say. "You guys had to wear the same clothes the whole time."

"Yes," Sarah said after a moment. "Although, I did switch clothes with Eb a couple of times." She looked at him and he smiled.

Kalendra felt embarrassed asking such a dumb question and didn't say another word until the car came to a halt before her grandmother's house. "Well, we're here, everybody."

"Good, let me out," Jesse said. "Now!"

Kalendra hurriedly voiced the command that opened the back door and Jesse sprinted from the vehicle, heading several yards down the sidewalk before he stopped, confused. Submit tried coaxing him back, but he would not take a step until Kalendra had commanded the car to return to Celia's house to pick up Lettice and Dan. With the vehicle gone, Jesse visibly relaxed.

Kalendra ushered her visitors inside while thinking about her grandmother. What were she and Dan doing right now? She hoped they weren't kissing, though it would be a perfectly natural thing for two long-lost lovers to do. It was just a gross image to picture her grandmother doing anything remotely sexual. Especially since she was so old and Dan was so young and handsome. Surely they couldn't continue their relationship now, could they? How would she explain that to people?

She showed her guests inside and all but Sarah stopped in the entryway to gape at the living room. The ancestors had never seen a television or a stereo and they were simultaneously awed and frightened.

Submit, however, was obviously impressed with one particular device. "I've been told about these," she said, tentatively touching the television screen. "This is a television. Dan's told me about them. And that's a computer."

"Actually, that's another television," Kalendra corrected. "Computers and televisions became one unit a long time ago. Dan wouldn't have known about that. As I'm sure he didn't know you can be in a television instead of just watching it. I mean, not actually inside it. Oh, I can't explain what I mean."

Submit blinked at her. "I do not understand."

Sarah did, however. "Virtual Reality, right?" she asked.

"I've never heard of that," Kalendra said. "But I guess that could be it though. Hey, are you guys hungry?"

Everyone nodded in the affirmative. She smiled nervously and headed to the kitchen, her guests at her heels. She stopped and glanced nervously at them, feeling like she was being mobbed.

Sarah smiled at her and said, "I'm sorry. Don't mind us. We just haven't eaten for literally ages. We were unable to eat while we were trapped."

"Really? Why?"

Sarah shrugged. "We don't know. That's how things worked there. We couldn't do much of anything at all, really."

"Just the one thing," Submit interjected with a titter. Ebenezer shushed her.

"So, what would you guys like to eat?" Kalendra asked, going to the nearest cupboard. "Let's see, we have soups, pastas, chips, rice, curry, spaghetti."

"The only thing I understood was soup," Submit said with a slight grin. "Those other items sound exotic. Except for the chips, though. Chips of what?"

"Potato, tortilla, banana—" Kalendra replied. "But that's no meal. Hey, I know what you guys can have and I think you'll really like it. Pelmeni."

"Pelmeni?" asked Sarah first. "What's that?"

"Russian ravioli." She went to the refrigerator and paused. "Oh. Do you guys know what ravioli is?"

"I think only I do," Sarah answered. "You'll have to show them."

"I'm so hungry I'd eat just about anything," Ebenezer said.

"Me, too," said Submit, staring as Kalendra opened the fridge. "Is that food in there?" she asked.

"Yes," Kalendra said. "You didn't have refrigerators in your day, did you? We keep things cold in them."

"Really?" asked Eb. "Then nothing can ever go bad?"

"Oh, it can still go bad," Kalendra explained. "If you leave it in there long enough. It depends on what it is, too. Some of the artificial stuff can keep for months, even years."

"I guess I never told you about fridges," Sarah commented. "Strange, after all those years, the subject never came up."

"Is that a soda?" Submit inquired, pointing. "Dan told me about those. Little bubbles, right? Like on the picture there."

"Yes." Kalendra chuckled and handed each of them one. Jesse refused his.

Sarah opened hers, drank a little, and then sat at the dining room table with a sigh. "Frankly, Kalendra, I'm a little disappointed. I thought things would be further advanced than they are. I mean, the magnetic car is cool and so is the Virtual Reality television, but I thought there would be, I don't know, just more."

Kalendra shrugged. "I'm sorry. I don't know what to say. What did you expect?"

"Are you guys still exploring space? Have we put men on other planets yet?"

"Actually, yes," Kalendra said. "There's a crew going off to Titan or Triton or something. I don't really follow space news. We went to Mars a few decades ago."

"No starship hyper drives or anything like that?"

"Only in the movies."

"Damn."

Submit and Eb waited for Sarah to finish talking for neither of them knew how to open their cans of soda. They saw Sarah pull the tab, but neither of them could do it. Sarah had to pull theirs for them.

"Don't drink from it," Sarah said instantly. "There's no telling what was spilled or sprayed on the top of it." She looked to Kalendra for clarification and smiled when she nodded.

Kalendra fetched them plastic glasses to pour their sodas into then had to try to explain what plastic was.

᭡

As the others drank and Kalendra readied the Pelmeni, Submit asked Jesse, "Are you sure you don't want something to drink? It's been three hundred and fifty years!"

"I do not wish to drink or eat anything this world has to offer," he sternly replied. When Submit stepped closer, he added quietly, "I wish things to go back to the way they were. The way things were before Dan."

"You know we can't," Submit whispered, putting her hand on his arm. "Besides, you were the one that allowed it."

Jesse took a deep breath. "I know. And I've regretted it ever since."

Submit rubbed his arm gently. "Dan's got Lettice back, now. He's never stopped loving her."

"Yes, but she is an old woman now. No matter how much they love each other, I do not believe they will remain together long."

"So, by that logic, *I* would be too old for you."

Jesse looked at her. "That is not the same. You understand my meaning."

"I'm just teasing," she said. She was about to say more when the front door opened, the sound grabbing everyone's attention. "That's probably Dan now. Maybe we'll know what's going on. Meanwhile, I want another soda."

☙

Lettice entered the kitchen with her eyes swollen and red-rimmed, black bags beneath them. She forced a smile when she saw the others. "Has my granddaughter gotten you all familiar with the mid-twenty-first century?"

"She has been very nice," Sarah answered. "Where's Dan?"

The hallway toilet flushed one second before Dan appeared, his eyes in the same condition as Lettice's. He looked at her but kept his distance. He turned to Kalendra. "So, you're the one who found *The Book*. Thank you so very much. I don't know how we can ever repay you."

"You're welcome," Kalendra replied, feeling heat rush to her cheeks. "I couldn't just leave you guys in there. Besides, I just kind of lucked out. It's almost like the book found me."

"Why do you even care?" asked Jesse.

Submit held his arm. "Don't be difficult," she told him, squeezing him hard.

Jesse's face turned white. "Don't tell me what to do, you Puritan whore." He ran from the room. Submit stood frozen for a microsecond then ran after him.

"You son of a bitch," Dan muttered and ran after Submit. He caught up with her and Jesse in the living room. "How dare you say that to her. What's your fucking problem?"

Jesse tried to open the front door, but Dan slammed it shut by shoving his hand against it. "It's her fault," he shouted, taking two steps back, nearly knocking over a table lamp.

"What's her fault?" Dan pressed, keeping his voice level.

Jesse hesitated. "I didn't mean anything by it," he said to Submit, his face reddening. "I just wanted to know why anyone would care enough about us to want to free us. Especially after all these centuries."

"Because I wanted to save you," Kalendra replied, having just entered the room. "Isn't that good enough reason for you?"

"But why?"

"I'll tell you why," Lettice said, wiping her eyes. "Because she's a very brave girl and if you don't behave, Jesse, I'll see if I can't contact the witch and make her put you back there all by yourself. How would you like that, you ungrateful sack of shit?"

Jesse stared at her aghast then turned away. He walked slowly to a chair in the corner, his back to the room.

"I'm sorry," Sarah said, breaking the resulting silence, "but weren't we going to eat something?"

"Oh!" Kalendra cried, thankful for the change of subject. "It should be almost done by now. Let me go check."

6.

Kalendra retired to her room shortly after dinner. She had school in the morning and the day's events had left her drained emotionally and physically. She didn't feel right about leaving the guests with her grandmother, but ultimately decided Lettice could handle it. She chuckled as she recalled her calling Jesse a sack of shit. She'd never heard her grandmother talk like that before.

She slept and dreamt the warlock came in through her window. She was jolted awake, covered in a film of sweat.

We're not safe here, she realized. The warlock could find them here. They couldn't stay very much longer. She'd have to take Dan and the others someplace safe. If such a place even existed. She knew the warlock would employ very strong magic in order to break the protection spell. He could destroy them all for stealing his property.

Kalendra couldn't get back to sleep. The house was too quiet. Then she heard soft mutterings downstairs in the living room. She thought it sounded like Submit and Jesse. She didn't care for Jesse. What a spoiled brat he was for being almost four hundred. And what about that fit he threw last night? She decided he might be more than just selfish. He might be a little crazy as well.

A tremendous sigh that sounded like thunder in the quiet house escaped her lips. She was responsible for the well being of Dan and company. She had freed them and now she had to protect them. Her life had been altered considerably, and for people she didn't even know. She wondered why she'd done it and then realized the answer. She'd done it for her grandmother.

No matter how much she told herself it was the right thing to do, that a great injustice had been done to those people, it was her grandmother that had driven her to rescue her long lost love and his family.

She didn't realize she'd dozed off until the repeated ringing of the doorbell wrenched her from her slumber. She threw on her robe and hurried downstairs. Sarah stood with the door open, a shaken Celia standing before her.

"The witch got my mom!" she cried, seeing Kalendra come down the stairs. She sobbed suddenly and ran into her best friend's arms. "Sh-She puh-pushed her down the stairs and I think h-her neck is buh-broken!"

Lettice stood behind them on the stairs in her nightdress. "She's been known to do that from time to time," she said, her visage grim.

"I thought you were going to get out of the house," Kalendra said pointedly to her friend.

"I was waiting for my mom," Celia answered, wiping tears from her eyes. "She didn't get back until late. I fell asleep on the couch and didn't hear her come in. I woke up when I heard her walking around upstairs. She was walking down the stairs when suddenly she went flying to the bottom. I saw the witch behind her. My mom's all twisted funny and I think she's dead."

"Did you call an ambulance?" Lettice asked calmly.

Celia shook her head. "There was no time for that. I had to get out of the house as fast as I could. I planned on calling when I got here."

"Do it," Kalendra said, releasing her friend. "Hurry." She and Lettice followed her to the web cam in the living room.

"I think it's too late," Celia whimpered as she called emergency assistance.

"What is going on out here?" Submit asked, walking into the room with Jesse in tow. Both looked disheveled, clothes rumpled, hair askew.

"Should we go back to the house?" asked Dan, also entering the room. "Isn't there a spell in that book that will get rid of that witch once and for all?"

"I don't know," Kalendra answered. "I'll go get it."

"No, I'll get it," said Lettice. "I've hidden it in a safe place." She went upstairs and returned moments later with *The Book*. She handed it to Kalendra.

"If we can't find anything in it that's helpful to us," Dan said, "I think we should relocate."

"I've been thinking the same thing," Kalendra said. "But let's see." She opened *The Book Of Curses*.

"You guys should all get new clothes," Lettice suggested as Kalendra, Dan and Celia gazed at the pages of the book. "That is, if we have to get out of here. Well, either way, actually. People will give you funny looks dressed like that."

"Thank God!" Sarah sighed. "I'm so frickin' sick of wearing these clothes!"

Dan stood up. "We should go check on Celia's mother. You can bring *The Book* and look through it in the car."

Kalendra stood up, but no one else moved.

"The rest of us will stay here, I guess," Sarah said, smiling apologetically.

"I'm not going back!" exclaimed Submit.

Kalendra looked to Celia. "Don't you want to check on your mother?"

"I do," she said, wringing her hands, something Kalendra had never seen her do before. "But it's too scary back there."

Kalendra touched her friend's arm. "That's okay. I understand. But if we don't come back soon, come and get us. Please?"

"One of us will," Lettice said, hugging and kissing her granddaughter. "But you better not make us have to do that. You be careful. And, Dan, the same goes for you, all right?"

Dan smiled wanly and nodded. He and Kalendra got into the car. Kalendra had just told the vehicle to go when Celia came running out.

"I've decided I need to go," she exclaimed, getting in. "Sitting and waiting for you guys is more frightening than going back there." She paused. "I think. Yes, I know it is."

Kalendra nodded and bade the vehicle to proceed. It quickly lifted off the ground and headed toward its destination.

"If this car responds to vocal commands," Dan said, "what are all these buttons for? In case you're deaf or can't speak English or something?"

"Correct," Kalendra said. "Or if the voice command breaks down. It rarely does, but sometimes it happens."

"That makes sense," he said. "Let me see that book." He took it from Kalendra and began to thumb hastily through the pages. When he didn't find anything right away, he cried out in agitation, "Goddamn it! There has to be something in here that will get rid of her." He slammed the book in frustration.

"Here, let me see it." Kalendra retrieved the tome from him and turned the pages carefully.

"We should burn the whole goddamn thing down," Dan muttered, gazing out the window. "That should take care of her. Of course, if someone else built there again she could come back."

"Here's something," Kalendra said then frowned. "Oh, you have to know where she's buried first, though."

"Let me see," Dan said, snatching the book back from her. "Aha! Dig up the bones, grind them and burn them. Seems simple enough."

"That's simple enough if you know where the bones are," Kalendra said, gently retrieving the book.

"I know where they are," Dan said.

The ambulance was already at the house, red, blue and white lights blinking in random patterns, a police car parked next to it on the curb. Celia's mother came out of the house on a stretcher, floating toward the rescue vehicle.

Celia ran up to the stretcher. "Is she okay?" she asked the nearest paramedic.

The paramedic looked at Celia. "Are you her daughter?" Celia nodded. "Her neck is broken, but she'll be fine. The police want to talk to you." The woman pointed to where the police were standing.

Celia watched her mother disappear into the ambulance

then turned to face the law enforcement officials. Dan and Kalendra walked past her to the backyard.

"What are you doing?" Kalendra asked Dan.

"Come on," he urged, opening the tall wooden gate. "Hurry, while no one's looking."

Kalendra looked cautiously behind her then followed him, closing the gate.

Dan looked at the sky. "It's a clear night," he muttered. "I was expecting a storm to start brewing, like in the movies. There's always a storm in the movies, ever notice that? It starts raining as the characters start to dig and they get all muddy and the dirt's falling back into the hole and they slip and fall in or something." He shrugged and walked to the oak tree.

"Is this where she's buried?" Kalendra asked, her voice a whisper.

Dan nodded. He glanced at her as he started for the shed. The door was locked. He stopped and looked around the yard, finding what he was looking for propped up against the fence. He returned to the oak with it and handed *The Book* to Kalendra. He shoved the instrument into the ground with his foot.

"She's going to try to stop us," Kalendra said after a few moments, as she watched him dig. She shivered, feeling the hair rise on her bare arms and neck.

"We've got the protection spell," he replied. "I don't think she can get rid of it without the warlock's help."

"What if the warlock comes back?"

"Hit him on the head with *The Book*," Dan snapped. "Hell, I don't know! Just keep a look out, will you?"

The ambulance siren started and its lights began to move. Seconds later, the lights and siren were gone. It was quiet and dark, except for the sound of metal sliding against dirt and rocks and Dan's occasional grunt. Kalendra then heard footsteps behind her and whirled to face them. It was Celia.

"They're gone," she whispered, her eyes on Dan. "Do you need some light?" She went to the shed and retrieved the key from under the mat. She returned with a flashlight and shined it on the hole in the ground.

"What did you tell the cops?" Kalendra asked her friend.

Celia sighed. "That she fell. What else am I going to say? I'm sure not going to mention the ghost. They'll think I'm nuts."

Dan stopped digging to stare up at the house. "You've had the shutters removed. I just noticed."

"There used to be shutters?" Celia asked.

"Yes," Dan said and resumed digging. When Kalendra gasped a moment later, he looked up. "That's my grandmother," he said. She stood facing them from the second story, her finger pointing down. When he looked around the yard and back up at her, she shook her head and pointed more forcefully.

"What?" Dan asked her. "I don't understand. What are you pointing at?"

"I think she's telling you to dig on the other side of the tree," whispered Kalendra, more than a bit unnerved by the interactive specter. "I think. I don't know."

Dan's grandmother nodded and pointed again. "All right. All right," he muttered, climbing out of his hole to start a new one. He paused a moment to wipe the sweat and dirt from his face.

"Need some help?" Kalendra inquired.

"We'd save some time if I had some," Dan replied. "I've already wasted quite a bit of time already digging in the wrong spot."

"There's another shovel in the shed," Celia said and promptly fetched it. She traded it to Kalendra for *The Book*.

Kalendra took the shovel and then dropped it, screaming. A moth had tangled itself in her bangs. She batted it away then stooped to retrieve the shovel. "Sorry," she said. "Where should I start?"

"Right over there," Dan directed with the shovel. "If we're lucky, one of us will hit it before the warlock returns."

Kalendra nodded and set to the task. Her hands hurt her almost immediately. She wasn't used to manual labor. Blisters were already forming on her hands. She stopped to rub them together, wincing in pain.

"I've got blisters, too," Dan told her. "But we've got to keep digging."

"Of course," she said and resumed. Her hands hurt, burned fiercely, but she didn't complain and kept digging.

Dan hit wood before she did. "It's either the head or foot of the coffin," he said. "I can't tell which." His hole was deeper than Kalendra's and there was more than a foot of dirt between the two.

"Shit," Dan cursed. "This is going to take forever. And I don't even know which way the coffin is facing. Which direction should I dig next?"

"You can rest if you want," Kalendra said. "I'll keep digging."

"No, no, I'm not stopping," he said, examining the three holes. "I think we may be headed in the right direction after all. You keep digging. I'll start on this middle part."

Dan and Kalendra dug side by side until Kalendra's hole started to cave in because she had dug the bottom wider than the top. She hopped out and Dan finished the job, eventually exposing the entire coffin lid.

He stared down at it, out of breath. "Guess I should open it, huh?"

"I don't want to," Kalendra said with a shiver, suddenly very cold.

Something hit her hard in the back of the head.

The blow didn't knock her completely unconscious, but everything went black. She was vaguely aware of falling and of wood smacking against her back. She heard a scream, then lost consciousness.

An indeterminate amount of time later, she was aware of something pulling her, carrying her. She smelled and tasted dirt. Then the carrying sensation stopped. Her head started to throb.

"She's alive," she heard a distant voice say. It was Dan's.

"We should get her out of here," said Celia.

"I need to get the bones first," Dan said. "Lock the other

shovel in the shed so *she* can't get it again." A pause. "Well, she might be able to, but hopefully she won't."

Kalendra heard nothing else for some time, except a distant creaking sound. Her head started to pound like a hammer and she felt nauseous. The pain forced her eyes open. She stared up at a starry sky, the moon in the center. She still tasted dirt and a little blood. She attempted to move her hand to wipe the dirt from her mouth, but her arm felt too heavy.

"Are you okay, Kal?" asked Celia.

"I think so—" She tried to sit up, but couldn't.

"You got hit with your shovel. I'll give you one guess who did it."

"Gee, I can't imagine," she groaned.

Celia took a shallow breath. "Then she pushed you into the grave and started to bury you. Dan, too. She knocked him in after you. You were almost buried alive together."

"How'd you stop her?" Kalendra asked, trying again to sit up.

"I didn't," Celia said. "She just went away. I don't know why. Dan wasn't knocked out very long and he pulled you out. I helped a little."

"I've got them," Dan said, walking away from the hole. He'd removed his shirt and wrapped Dinah's bones in it. "Let's get out of here."

They returned to the car and headed back to Kalendra's house. When the car stopped at a light, another car pulled up beside them. The vehicle's sole passenger glanced briefly at Kalendra then quickly back again.

"My God," the man exclaimed, his voice audible through the car's speaker. "What happened to you?"

Kalendra turned away, not wanting to speak to him. "Go away, Ian," she said. "You're the last person I want to see right now!"

"My uncle called me," he said, ignoring her words. "He's coming back. I was on my way to tell you. We should probably put that book back before—"

His sentence was cut short by the changing of the traffic light and the cars moving forward.

"That's the warlock's nephew?" Dan asked Kalendra as Ian's vehicle remained beside theirs. "Either he's a good actor or he hasn't got a clue he's a warlock."

"I think he's acting," Kalendra remarked.

Two muddy women and one muddy, bare-chested man carrying a shirtful of bones emerged from the car and entered the house.

When Lettice gasped at the dirt being tracked in, Dan blurted, "No time for that. Have you got anything I can grind these bones with?"

"Are those—?"

"Yes," Dan replied impatiently. "Have you got a wood-chipper? Or don't people use those anymore?"

"There's a bone grinder in the basement," Lettice told him. "My husband and I used to breed dogs. We'd grind down animal bones to put in their food. They loved it."

"Let's go," he said, making brown footsteps across the living room rug. Kalendra and Celia followed.

"What happened?" Lettice asked, leading the way. "Did you fall into the hole?"

"The ghost witch tried to bury them," Celia exclaimed.

Lettice wasn't fazed. "You both need a shower. Celia, Kalendra can lend you some of her clothes."

"Make sure you take quick ones," said Dan. "Remember, the warlock's on his way back."

A knock at the door got everyone's attention except Dan's as he headed down the basement steps. Lettice answered the door to see Ian standing before her. "Who are you?" she asked.

Ian pointed past her to Kalendra. "She knows me." He stepped forward, edging his way past Lettice. "Hi."

"Go away, Ian," Kalendra insisted, keeping her distance. "I have no time for you right now."

"Why?" he asked then looked to Celia. "Hey, that's *The Book*! I need that." He stepped toward her.

"Please leave," Lettice told him, holding the door open.

Dan returned without Dinah's bones. "That's the warlock's nephew," he said, peering at him. "You have no idea what's going on, do you?"

"Warlock?" he asked, astonished. "Who's a warlock?"

Dan ignored the question. "When is your uncle coming back?"

"In a few hours," Ian said with a shrug. "That's why I need that book back."

"We don't have much time, then," Dan said, turning to leave. Lettice followed.

"I'm getting a shower," said Kalendra, heading upstairs to the bathroom. She didn't want to talk to him or even see him. She didn't trust him for a second. Anyone related to that wretched warlock and that witch Dinah could only be bad news.

She slid her muddy jeans and T-shirt off then realized she hadn't thanked Dan for saving her life. She had nearly been buried alive. She would have to thank him as soon as she was finished cleaning up.

She made the shower quick and dressed in a new pair of jeans and a gray T-shirt, putting her hair up in a wet ponytail. Celia was waiting outside the bathroom and stepped inside the instant Kalendra stepped out.

"I'll hurry," Celia whispered and closed the door.

Kalendra went to bring in some clean clothes for her friend then returned downstairs to see Ian sitting on the couch. What was he still doing here? From below, she could hear the sound of the bone grinder.

"Hi, Kalendra," he said, smiling and holding up his hand. "You look nice today. I'm being filled in on what's going on."

Kalendra slowly realized that Sarah and Ebenezer were sitting across from Ian on the loveseat. Submit and Jesse were nowhere to be seen. She assumed her grandmother was with Dan.

"Fascinating stuff," Ian continued. "I had absolutely no idea my uncle was a warlock. It makes sense, though. It explains why he has all those strange books in his secret library."

Kalendra didn't smile or reply. She walked through the living room to the basement door. An instant before she reached it, she heard two thuds followed by a silencing of the grinder. She hurriedly opened the door.

Dan crouched at the foot of the steps, Lettice's body lying immobile beside him. He looked up at Kalendra. "Dinah strikes again," he grimaced and stood up. He gazed down at Lettice and wiped his eyes.

Kalendra felt weak and queasy. She stomped down the steps and stooped to take her grandmother's pulse. There wasn't one. "What happened?" she demanded, her lip quivering.

"Dinah was here," he said. "We both saw her. She appeared suddenly in the corner where those loose bricks are. One hit Lettice before she knew it was coming."

"A brick?" Kalendra asked, her eyes going to the corner. "What are bricks doing there?"

Dan shrugged and cleared his throat. "I guess she was building a wall or something at one time. They look kind of old and crumbly." He took a shallow breath. "We were talking and this brick flies across the room to hit her in the head." He looked away. "Is that guy still here?"

Kalendra nodded, unable to take her eyes from her deceased grandmother. "He's still here," she whispered. Ian was a million miles away as far as she was concerned or cared. She looked up at Dan, tears welling up in her eyes. She noticed through her mournful haze that there was no brick near Lettice's head, nor was there any blood. It was like her grandmother had just died with no cause. She then happened to look between the stairs and saw the brick on the floor. Her grip tightened on the railing.

"Ian's no harm to us," Dan said, turning back to the worktable where the bone grinder was. He stopped and turned. "Where's that other spell book? You know, the brown one? We should take that book with us when we go, along with *The Book*. As soon as I get done grinding the bones, that is. I still have the skull and the pelvis to take care of. I may have to smash or saw them to get them to fit, though."

Kalendra sobbed softly, barely hearing the loud grinder as Dan switched it back on. She couldn't believe her grandmother was dead. She was heartbroken. Lettice had been a mother to her for most of her life. It was an inconsolable loss. She was also sad for Dan, sad that, after all these years, he had to see her die right in front of him.

She looked up at him, wondering what he was feeling. Great sadness, surely, but he was hiding it well. She'd heard some people dealt with grief by ignoring it, by keeping themselves occupied doing something else so they don't think about their feelings. Dan was obviously one of those people. He looked unconcerned about the death of his former lover as he inserted another bone into the mouth of the grinder.

Celia gasped from the top of the steps and nearly fell down them in her haste to be at her friend's side. "Omigod, Kal! What happened?"

Kalendra looked up, barely hearing Celia over the noise of the grinder. She stood up and embraced her.

Dan switched off the grinder and wiped his forehead. "To be on the safe side," he began, "gather up all throwable instruments, take them upstairs and close the door. Until the warlock comes, all she can do is throw things. Once I'm done here, she won't even be able to do that." He grinned tiredly.

"What about—?" Celia began, glancing at Lettice's body. "We can't just leave her, can we?"

Dan followed her gaze, turned away and sniffed. "Call an ambulance, but not until just before we go. There's nothing we can do for her. She's in a better place, now."

Celia looked to Kalendra who nodded absently and began collecting any throwable items. Dan grabbed the nearby hammer before she could get to it, however, and began smashing Dinah's skull and pelvis.

He dumped the pieces of the skull and pelvis into the grinder and turned to see Ian standing at the top of the stairs.

"What happened?" Ian inquired, coming no closer.

"She's dead," Dan said, his voice sounding hollow in his ears. He noticed Celia and Kalendra had already left with the objects they'd collected.

"So, you're just going to let her lie there?"

"We'll call an ambulance before we leave."

"We should leave right now," Ian suggested.

Dan's brow rose. "We? Are you coming with us?"

"I should think you'd want me to," Ian replied. "I can help you."

"Is that why?" Dan asked. "I would think you'd be coming along because of Kalendra."

Ian looked startled then frowned. "I don't think she likes me. Not since she suspected I'm a warlock. And," he paused, tilting his head, "I'm not so certain she's wrong."

"Really?" Dan inquired, intrigued. "You don't know for sure?"

"I'm pretty sure," Ian said hesitantly. "Everyone can't read minds, can they?"

"You can do that?"

"Sometimes. If I concentrate really hard. I could never read my uncle's mind, though."

"What am I thinking right now?"

Ian chuckled nervously. "I can't concentrate right now, I'm too anxious. Besides, I can't seem to do it all the time. The conditions have to be right."

"Hmm. Is there anything else you can do?"

Ian shrugged. "Maybe. Sometimes things happen that seem like a coincidence, but I'm not so sure they are. Like running into Kalendra a lot, for instance. And like the time when I was in grade school and I had a teacher I didn't like. I wished him dead and he died the next day from a stroke. That could have been a coincidence, too. He was old and unhealthy."

"Can you cast spells or anything?"

"I don't know. I've never tried it. I suppose I could, but I don't know if it's possible without some kind of training first."

"We'll figure it out on the way," Dan said. "I mean, if Kalendra and Lettice were able to cast a spell, I think you should be able to." He glanced down at his deceased former lover and took a shallow breath. "I-I need to finish with the bones here. We can go after that."

"Don't you need to burn them afterward?" Ian asked. "Or do you have to make coffee with them?" He chuckled at his own joke. "Old witch bone coffee, just like mom used to make."

Dan didn't laugh. He turned on the grinder and the bones were powder a minute later. He dumped the powder into the aluminum container and stepped over Lettice's body to get to the stairs.

Kalendra was curled up in a chair in the living room, her eyes puffy and sad. She looked warily at Dan as he approached.

"Anyone got a match?" he asked.

Kalendra turned her eyes away, silent. She nodded toward the fireplace. Dan looked, but didn't see.

"It's this thing," Celia said, getting up from the couch to remove a small plastic stick from the mantle. "Just hit this little button at the base and breathe on the other end to light it."

"Mm, burning plastic," he said. "What will they think of next?"

"I don't think it's plastic," Celia said to his back as he headed outside.

Dan didn't notice Sarah behind him until he had set the aluminum container on the grass. When he did notice her, he ignored her.

"How do you feel?" she asked. "Kalendra and Celia told me what happened."

"Like shit," he replied grimly. "But I'll feel a whole heck of a lot better once I burn this bitch to nothing."

"So, you really think burning the bones will lift the curse?"

He glared at her. "It has to."

"Maybe the warlock's the only one who can lift it," Sarah remarked. "Or maybe only *she* could."

"But they won't, so why even waste time thinking about it. The only thing I can do is destroy them and hope that takes care of it." He pushed the match's button and brought it to an inch from his lips.

"Are you sure you're okay about Lettice?"

He lowered the match quickly as it lit. "The Lettice I knew died fifty years ago. The dead woman in the basement is a stranger." The match extinguished. He raised it and puffed on it. Nothing happened.

"Maybe you have to breathe harder," Sarah said just as a flame sparked to life.

Dan crouched next to the canister just as Sarah suddenly shrieked. He looked up to see Lettice shove his sister to the ground and come toward him. Dan hurriedly picked up the container and held the match over it.

"Don't come any closer, Dinah!" he shouted, yelling so loud that his ears twinged with pain. "This bone powder is very dry and will burn really fast!"

Lettice's body hesitated only a moment before taking more steps toward him. She extended her arms, her hands like claws.

"Have it your way."

Dan dropped the match into the container and Lettice screamed. She swiped at him and he backed away, still holding the container as its contents burned. Her mouth contorted wildly, replacing the very air with a resonant, all-encompassing howl.

The container became hot and Dan dropped it, the burning powder shooting out to cover Lettice's feet. Her dress caught fire and the shrieking increased. The body still came at Dan, swiping its claws at him until the flames covered it. It fell abruptly to the ground and burned quickly.

Soon, there was nothing left but ash and bone smoldering atop a blackened patch of grass.

7

Dan staggered back against an elm, his head and heart pounding. He glanced up to see the entire household staring at him from the porch. All except for Sarah, who remained unconscious, having hit her head on a brick stepping stone.

"She's gone," Dan breathed, chest heaving. He looked back at the burnt remains in the moonlight. He reared back his head and hollered, "*She's finally, fucking gone!*" He laughed wearily and stumbled from the tree, wiping his forehead on his bare arm. He looked down to see Sarah move as she regained consciousness. "Okay," he said to her. "We can go now."

"But where are we going?" asked Submit, still standing with the others. "I was hoping to get some new clothes!"

"Come on," Kalendra said hoarsely, waving Submit inside. "I think I can find something that will fit you."

"Please hurry, girls!" Ian shouted after them. "We haven't much time."

"What about the rest of us?" asked Jesse, looking lost without Submit. "I am not particularly fond of the clothing men wear here, but I am very weary of wearing this uniform."

"I am in agreement with him," Ebenezer said. "I would like new clothing, as well."

"I'll buy you some," Ian declared good-naturedly. "I've got a bit of cash stashed away, no problem." He caught Celia's eye and grinned. She grinned back.

Dan headed for the back door, his pants and skin grimy with dirt and soot and sweat. He was also still shirtless. "So, are we all going to fit in one car?"

"You're not getting in my car all muddy like that!" Celia exclaimed then wrinkled her nose. "You're pretty stinky, too."

He smiled. "I'll take a quick shower then. Give me five minutes." He hurried into the house.

Dan stripped off his shoes, pants and underwear, stepped into the shower and faced a black octagonal ball set high into the wall. There were no hot and cold knobs or one single hot and cold dial. To his right were two dispensers, one marked "soap" the other "shampoo". There didn't appear to be anything to push or press in order to get the soap or shampoo, however.

Naked and dirty and frustrated, Dan let out a great cry. "How do you work this goddamn thing?" When no help was forthcoming, he muttered, "Screw it. I haven't got time for this." He stepped out of the shower, bent down to gather his dirty pants and looked up to see Kalendra standing in the doorway.

She made a startled sound and averted her gaze. "Are you just going to stand there like that?"

"Sorry," he said, wrapping his filthy pants around his waist. "I forgot for a second that people could see me."

"I came up to explain the shower to you," she said, keeping her gaze away from him. "It's voice-activated."

"Just like the car," he said with a nod. "Good. Thanks."

She nodded and closed the door. He stepped inside the shower stall and took a deep breath. "Shower: On." The water issued forth, the temperature moderate. He wanted it a little hotter, however. "Um... Shower: Hotter." It worked. He retrieved soap from the dispenser the same way and was soon enjoying his first scrubbing in fifty years. It felt fantastic.

He then remembered he needed to hurry and quickly finished up. He hated having to put on his dirty clothes again, but had no choice. He dressed and headed for the stairs. Kalendra stood at the foot, leaning against the wall, facing away from him.

"Everyone's in the car," she told him, her eyes not meeting his. "I wish I could have supplied you with a new, clean pair of pants, but I don't have any clothes for men here. Nor do we have any shirts your size."

"That's okay," he said, looking down at his mud-encrusted trousers. "These pants have lasted me over fifty years, they can hold out a little longer." He briefly wondered what she thought when she'd seen him without clothing then decided it didn't matter. He didn't have time to think about that right now.

Kalendra turned to him as he started to descend the stairs. She looked agitated, her hands shoved into her pockets. "Dan," she began, shrugging a little. "Do you feel *anything* for my grandmother? Any sort of sadness at all?"

Dan was startled by the question. When he thought about it, he did start to feel very sad. However, the sadness was misdirected. He felt sad for Kalendra's sake.

"I am very sorry about what happened," he replied, "but I shed my tears for Lettice long before you were even conceived. The woman I knew died decades ago, as far as I'm concerned. It's sad that she is finally, truly gone, but I don't know if you can understand this, but time has a way of killing feelings sometimes. I'm very sad that you lost your grandmother, Kalendra, but I didn't hold out any hope that we would be lovers again. I am sad, but not in the way you expect me to be."

"I think I understand," she said after a moment, unsmiling. "I've never been in your situation, so I can only try to imagine what it must have been like. It must have really hurt you when she told you she'd married my grandfather."

"It did," he said unemotionally. "It no longer does."

She looked up at him. A slightly sad smile spread her lips. "I never did thank you for saving my life. You know, back at the grave." She paused awkwardly. "Thank you."

"Don't worry about it," he said. "I did what I had to. Besides, you rescued me first, remember? Now we're even."

"Okay," she replied, her smile broader now. "We're even."

Dan smiled and walked past her to the door. He stopped with his hand on the handle when she told him she was frightened.

"Where are we even going, Dan?" she asked. "What are we supposed to do now?"

"We're going somewhere," Dan began. "Somewhere safe where we can figure out what to do next. Hopefully, that warlock won't follow us there."

"Do you think he will?"

Dan paused then nodded.

Kalendra gazed at him a moment then turned her eyes to the door. "I guess we should go."

Dan nodded and opened the door for her and walked her to the car. He was stunned to see Submit wearing a silvery-blue dress that stopped mid-thigh. The décolletage of the garment was deep and hugged her breasts and hips tightly. He hardly recognized her. That certainly was not proper Puritan attire. Of course, Submit was no proper Puritan.

Jesse stood near Submit and Sarah, still clad in his Minutemen uniform. Dan was still angry with him. The two of them had never gotten along, especially when Dan and Submit were sleeping together. It had set a bad precedent.

He yawned forcefully. He needed sleep.

"Okay, everyone," Kalendra announced. "Pile in!"

"I'm not getting back inside that contraption!" Jesse protested.

"Well, you have to," Kalendra told him as patiently as she could. "Because we're leaving."

"Hey, let's go out West!" Submit exclaimed excitedly. "Dan, I remember you telling me about all the fantastic cities that sprang up in the past few centuries. I'd love to see them."

"Sounds like as good a place as any," Dan replied without emotion.

Kalendra commented to him with an amused grin, "I didn't know Puritans said 'Hey!'"

"She picked it up from Sarah and me," he explained. "At least, Submit did and Eb did. Jesse not so much. He mostly kept to himself."

Kalendra, Sarah and Ebenezer sat in the front while Ian

and Celia climbed into the back seat. Submit was about to join them, but said, "I don't think we're all going to fit in here."

"Four of us can go in my car," Ian said, getting out. "That way it doesn't get left here. Who knows when we'll be back."

"If ever," muttered Sarah sullenly from the front seat.

"I'll go in your car," Celia said, glancing at Kalendra.

Kalendra smiled. "Go ahead. I don't mind."

Celia smiled back and joined Ian's group. Submit coaxed Jesse toward Ian's vehicle, but cast a furtive look at Dan before they left.

Dan ignored her. "Okay, let's hurry up and get out of here!"

He got into the backseat of Kalendra's car. Kalendra removed herself from the front and sat in the back with him, not wanting to separate Sarah and Eb. Dan didn't notice her at first, however, as he gazed out the window, his eyes fixed on Submit, who was illuminated by the light of the two cars.

He found himself longing after her once again, but knew it was over. He would never again know her body, never in the normal way men who aren't banished by spectral witches know women. He recalled the times he'd spent with her and became immediately aroused. He tried to remember what it was like to have sex in the normal way and found he couldn't. It was like a forgotten dream he couldn't quite recapture.

He heard Kalendra give the car a voice command and turned to look at her. She smiled at him and he turned back to look out the window.

"That's your dress Submit's wearing, huh?" he asked distractedly.

"Yes," she replied. "It's a couple of years out of date, but I didn't think it mattered to her. Besides, she really liked it. I only wore it once, to the prom."

Dan turned back to Kalendra, looked at her, imagined her wearing the dress. "It's a nice piece of fabric," he commented.

"Thanks," she replied uncomfortably.

"Is there a radio?" Sarah asked suddenly, looking at the

control panel. "Or is radio obsolete now? CD player? MP3 player?"

"We still have radio," Kalendra told her with a grin. "Car: Radio: On."

Music with a very fast, seemingly random beat blared inside the vehicle, causing everyone to flinch and reach for their ears. "Volume: Two!" Kalendra cried, the noise decreasing immediately.

"You call that music?" Ebenezer said once the volume was low enough that they could hear each other.

"C'mon," Sarah said, elbowing him. "You've heard similar stuff back at the house. The kids there used to play it, remember?"

"Yes, and I asked the same thing then, too," he replied. "Never could understand where it was coming from, either. I know you tried to explain radio and stereos and CDs to me, but I still can't imagine such things."

Sarah turned in her seat to face Kalendra. "He likes guitars, you know. Loud and screechy, like punk or heavy metal. Funny, huh? I mean, him being from the 1690s and all."

"It's surprising," Kalendra replied diplomatically.

"The electric guitar has a very interesting and intriguing sound," Ebenezer said.. "I would never have heard it if I hadn't been banished. Of course, like I just mentioned, I couldn't see the source of the music. That's because the interior of the house looked the same to my daughter and me as it did when we lived there. We could see, however, the current inhabitants of the house and hear any sounds they made. They would walk through walls or up invisible steps and things like that, but we could see them. I wish I knew what a guitar looked like. Sarah drew a picture of one once, but her drawing isn't exactly life-like."

"Thanks a lot," Sarah exclaimed.

"I can't imagine what you guys must have gone through. I guess the living were the ghosts from your point of view, huh?"

"Dan plays guitar," Sarah said, trying to get her brother in on the conversation.

"I only did it as a hobby," he replied, still gazing distractedly out the window even though he could no longer see Submit. "I was never very serious about it." He shrugged and offered nothing else to the conversation.

Sarah looked away from him and shrugged. "Got any twentieth century music?" she asked Kalendra.

"Which decade?" Kalendra asked. "Or would you like a mix of all of them?"

"How about some seventeenth century music," Ebenezer asked with a grin. "It has been a very long time since I have heard any. I have nearly forgotten what it sounds like."

"Okay," Sarah relented. "Have it your way."

Kalendra called up the requested music and Ebenezer smiled, gazing into the night beyond the windshield glass. Sarah cuddled beside him, interlaced her fingers with his and enjoyed the music.

Dan found the music slightly irritating, but kept silent. Eventually, he dozed off only to awake some time later with Kalendra's head heavy on his shoulder. She snored softly, the sound barely audible beneath the music of lutes and pipes and drums. The sun was starting to rise.

Ian's car moved off the freeway. Kalendra's car didn't follow.

Dan nudged Kalendra awake. She sat up and blinked, her eyes widening then closing. "Ian's car just pulled off the freeway," he told her. "Shouldn't our car have followed?"

"Yes," she cried, suddenly alarmed. "Where'd he go?"

Dan pointed to the off ramp now far behind them. Kalendra commanded the car to exit the freeway and backtrack to where Ian's car had gone.

"Can't you just tell this car to follow Ian's car?" Dan asked.

Kalendra shook her head. "Only law enforcement people can do that."

"Oh," Dan said. "I guess that makes sense. Given the stalker factor, huh? Good idea."

"Are you sure Ian went this way?" Kalendra asked minutes later.

"Yes," Dan said. "Look, there's a clothing store. Maybe he went there."

Kalendra yawned and stretched. "That's right. We were going to go shopping."

Ian and company waited for Kalendra's car to appear as they sat parked in the lot. The doors to the stationary vehicle opened as they approached. Sarah and Ebenezer awoke the instant Kalendra's car came to a halt.

"Let's get you people some new clothes," Ian exclaimed, the first person to get out. "All on me. I'm buying."

"Where are we?" Sarah asked groggily, stretching as her car door opened.

"Yurd Clothiers," Dan told her.

"No, I mean the city."

"Philadelphia, I think."

"Is that all?" She groaned and got out of the car.

"Should we all really go in, looking like this?" Dan asked Ian, drawing attention to his dirty pants. "I mean, I look bad enough, but the rest of us—" He gestured to Ebenezer and Jesse still clad in their period clothing.

"I suppose I could just go in and pick up some pants and shirt and underwear," Ian said. "I don't know anyone's size, though I don't suppose you know yours, do you, Jess?"

"The size of my what?" Jesse asked, sounding somehow confounded and angry at the same time.

"I'll go with you," Celia exclaimed. "I'm good at guessing sizes."

"Okay," Ian said with a grin. "I guess you guys can stay here then."

"Fine with me," Dan said. None of the others objected.

"I just thought of something," Sarah said a few minutes after Ian and Celia had left. "Once we get the clothes, where will we change?"

"We'll go to a rest stop somewhere," Kalendra replied. "I should have taken Ian up on his offer; I haven't bought any new clothes in weeks."

Dan yawned and crawled back into the car. He awakened

an hour later to see Ian and Celia returning. Celia walked a considerable distance from Ian, looking as if she were afraid of him. Dan watched Celia walk up to Kalendra who was just outside his window. He yawned and opened the door.

"What's wrong?" Kalendra asked her once Ian was out of earshot.

"We had a problem with the store clerk," she said quietly, casting a wary glance at Ian, "who happened to be a cyborg and Ian bent his elbow back."

"What?" Kalendra asked before she understood. "Are you saying Ian's a cyborg, too?"

"Only a cyborg would have the strength to bend another cyborg's elbow," Celia whispered. "The store cyborg had a metal arm, too. Ian bent it straight back like it was nothing. At least we were treated well after that," she added.

Ian walked over and Kalendra and Celia both stepped back. "Okay, okay!" he cried suddenly. "I know I should have told you, but you were already afraid of me because I'm a warlock. I didn't want you to be even more scared of me because of my electronic arm. I don't really understand why people are frightened of cyborgs, though. We're people, too, except we can do some things average people can't."

"There was that cyborg mass murder a few years ago, in case you forgot," Celia pointed out. "You know, the guy that went around twisting everyone's heads around?"

"Oh, I remember," Ian said with a frown. "That was the fault of the doctors who worked on him. They should have known he had a history of mental problems. They should have never given him such a strong arm and such fast moving legs. You can't hold that against me, now, can you?"

"Why do you have a fake arm, anyway?" Celia asked, keeping Kalendra between the two of them.

"I was born deformed," Ian told her patiently. "I had an abnormal arm, leg and jaw. When I was old enough, my uncle had them replace my deformities with electronics. My parents died when I was fifteen and my uncle pretty much took care of me from then on. When he was home, anyway."

"So, the warlock's like a father to you?" Kalendra asked suspiciously.

Ian shrugged. "Not really. He's my uncle. He provided everything I needed growing up, but I didn't see him much. I had the run of the house to myself, though. I had a nanny until I was fifteen."

"Why are you helping us against him after he's done so much for you?" she asked. "Why would you turn on him all of a sudden?"

"Because I believe you about his true nature," he replied promptly. "My uncle is a warlock and I very well may be one, as well. He never told me about this and if he's hurting people with his powers. I cannot abide by it. Now that I know who and what he really is—" He faltered for a moment. "Look, don't tell the others about the cyborg thing, okay? They might be even more frightened, you know, them being from the past and all." His eyes darted to Dan in the car, as if just realizing he was there.

Dan wasn't so sure he believed in Ian's proclaimed motivation for helping them, but didn't doubt for a second the man wanted to help. Surely, it was because of the girls that he was helping them. A cyborg that could cast spells would be very beneficial to them if they ever had to face the warlock again.

"Were your parents rich?" Kalendra asked him.

He shrugged. "I guess so. They always had money. We were never poor."

"Do you think they got it the same way your uncle did?"

"What, through witchcraft?" He seemed shocked. "You know, it's perfectly plausible. I never thought about it before, but it makes perfect sense." He wandered back to his car, deep in thought.

"Okay, people!" shouted Dan from the backseat. "Let's get this show on the road before we start attracting attention." He indicated the other cars that were arriving, their passengers staring at the Puritan man and the Revolutionary soldier.

Kalendra asked Celia, "Do you want to switch cars with me? I mean, if you'd really rather not take Ian."

Celia shook her head. "I'm okay now. I don't think I'm afraid of him anymore. Actually," she added with a giggle, "I think I like him."

"Why?" Kalendra asked, appalled.

Her friend shrugged. "He's mysterious and handsome." She shrugged again. "And he sounds like he's had a sad life, whether he knew it or not. Poor guy."

Kalendra shrugged. "I find him creepy and arrogant and highly suspect."

"What do you care?" Celia suddenly snapped. "You have Dan, why can't I have Ian?"

This outburst startled Kalendra and she looked around to see if anyone else heard. Dan was nearby, but appeared oblivious. Kalendra whispered, "What are you talking about? Neither of us have anybody and what makes you think I like Dan?"

"By the way you act around him," she replied. "You seem... I don't know. Different somehow."

"Come on, come on," Dan said, snapping his fingers at Kalendra and Celia impatiently.

Kalendra glared at him. "Maybe I do like him," she murmured. "But I'm mad at him right now."

"Yeah, he's kind of being a jerk with that finger snapping thing."

"No, it's not that," she replied. "It's just that... Well, I'll tell you about it later."

She bowed her head and climbed into her car, sitting as far apart from Dan as she could and still share the back seat with him.

The cars headed for the nearest rest stop. Ian had bought clothes for everyone, but Kalendra didn't know what he'd gotten her until she and Celia were inside the rest stop's bathroom. She took them from the bag and scowled.

"A *skirt?*"

"I picked it out," Celia said with a broad grin. "I thought Dan might like it."

"What?" asked Sarah, stepping from a stall wearing a yellow summer dress with white open-toed shoes. "Are you talking about my brother?"

Celia balked a moment then exclaimed, "That dress looks fantastic on you!"

Sarah smiled. "Thanks. I was worried that the current fashions might be deplorable, but I really like this dress. It almost looks like something from the 1960s."

"I suppose it does," Celia said doubtfully. "I'm not too familiar with the sixties."

Sarah turned to Kalendra, still grinning. "That's a cute skirt, but that top looks a little skimpy."

"I know," Kalendra cried. "I almost might as well be naked."

"I don't think Dan will mind," Celia said.

"Dan?" Sarah inquired, flashing a smile. "Yes, I think he would like it. You would look stunning in that outfit, Kal. Stunningly beautiful and sexy."

"It's trashy," Kalendra countered.

"He'll love it," said Sarah.

"Maybe I don't want him to love it!" Kalendra cried. "Did either of you think of that?"

Celia shrugged. "Put your dirty clothes back on, then."

"They're not that dirty," she sniffed. "I put them on clean before we left. I don't even need a change of clothes right now." She pondered a moment. "Maybe I'll put this outfit on if or when I'm not mad at him anymore."

"Why are you mad at him?" Sarah asked. "If I may be so bold to ask."

Kalendra hesitated then sighed. She felt like she needed to talk to someone about her feelings. She didn't mind telling Celia, her best friend, but spilling her guts to Sarah, a veritable stranger who was also Dan's sister, wasn't a comfortable notion. Although, maybe Sarah could provide some insight into why

Dan behaved the way he did. They had just spent the last fifty years in close confines.

"I just don't think," Kalendra said, closing her eyes and taking a deep breath, "that Dan was upset enough when my grandmother died. I mean, she was killed right in front of him and he didn't even cry out or shed a single tear. Is that any way for a man to act after the love of his life has been killed?"

Sarah put her hand on Kalendra's arm. "I'm not so sure Lettice was the love of his life," she said gently. "Dan got over her decades ago. He felt betrayed after she'd promised to never stop searching for *The Book,* to never stop loving him, but instead found someone else and left him, left all of us, banished in that house. I know it wasn't an intentional betrayal, but she hurt him beyond our comprehension. It broke something inside of him. I think, had we not been trapped in that house, he might have never loved anyone again until he died."

"He fell in love with Submit," Kalendra said with a frown.

"No," Sarah said, shaking her head. "Not love. They just had sex. At least, what passed for sex in our situation. I think Submit may have loved him for a while, but after being freed, he's no longer a unique, new thing. Other things are new and she's always liked Jesse a lot. I think she's fallen into the role as his protector. She cares for him a lot more than she cares for Dan now. Dan can take care of himself."

"Great," Kalendra snorted. "He used another woman for sex for fifty years. That makes him so attractive."

"There wasn't much to do there," Sarah explained. "Sex and talk. That's all we did. And watch the people who lived in the house. Sometimes they'd see us and freak, but usually not. I remember one time Eb and me were having sex right in front of this one couple—"

"Okay!" Kalendra cried, covering her ears. "I don't need to hear about it."

"Yeah, but you don't know what sex was like there," Sarah continued. "You could never finish, you know? Our bodily fluids dried up really quickly and there were no lubricants—"

"I think it's time to go," Kalendra said and hastily exited the rest stop bathroom.

8.

It was quiet in Kalendra's car, except for the music playing softly and the occasional words Ebenezer and Sarah whispered to one another.

Dan gazed at them as he languished in the back seat, still thinking it odd to see his sister and the old Puritan in different clothing. It seemed as if they were totally different people now. He certainly felt like a different person. The clothes he wore felt strange and hung uncomfortably from his frame. He had grown accustomed to the same shirt and pants for fifty years.

The cars reached Cincinnati before nightfall and Ian picked up the bill for hotel rooms, booking two to a room. Dan and Kalendra ended up sharing.

Dan felt awkward and tense as he walked into the room. Kalendra kept her distance and did not speak to him. "I'll call down for a cot to sleep on," he told her. "You can have the bed."

"Thanks," she said, her voice hoarse and raspy. She collapsed onto the bed, bouncing once.

Someone knocked on the door and Dan answered. "Just checking to see if everything's all right," Ian said.

"It is," Dan said, a little irritated. "We just left you. We've barely been here two minutes."

"Oh, sorry," he said. "Didn't realize. Seemed longer."

"I was going to call up a cot."

"Really? Oh, good. I guess. Well, I'll not bother you further. Have a good night." He started to leave then stopped. "Oh, what time tomorrow do you think we should we leave? I was thinking sevenish."

"Sounds good," Dan said. "Good night." He closed the door and turned to Kalendra to see her looking at a listing posted on the wall next to two small chambers. "What are you doing?"

"These are old movie booths," she told him, her eyes fixated on the list. "They stopped making them about ten years ago. You don't need them anymore with the new movies that are out." She smiled in fond remembrance and pointed offhandedly. "I remember these from when I was a kid. They were neat then, but they seem super lame now."

"I remember televisions that had antennae and knobs on them from when I was a kid," Dan said. "And my grandma had an old television from the late fifties with a remote control that had a cord attached."

"Wow," Kalendra said. "That sounds ancient." She then looked at him. "This world is really strange to you, isn't it?"

"Not so much," he said. "Well, maybe. Kind of. It's only just now starting to hit me. I was too busy to notice at first."

Kalendra kept her back to him, her arms folded tightly. "It's almost like you were in a time machine, isn't it? I mean you haven't changed, but everything else has."

"You could look at it that way," he replied. "But time travelers only take seconds to arrive at their destination. It took me fifty years."

"What did you guys do there?" Kalendra asked, sitting on the edge of the bed. "Sarah said you guys talked a lot."

He nodded. "We did. We also watched the living go about their daily lives. They rarely saw or heard us, but it was fun when they did. They'd usually get scared, though. Sometimes they would move out right away and sometimes they would realize we weren't that bad and decide to stick around. Not everyone was afraid, which surprised me. To them we were all just ghosts. I think there were seven different owners while we were there. Maybe eight. I can't remember."

"My grandmother hurt you," she said, suddenly gazing intently at him.

He looked sharply at her. "Yes. She did."

"She betrayed you."

He chuckled. "You'd be a good television interviewer. Yes, she did. I forgave her eventually, though I wasn't able to tell her until you freed us." He frowned severely. "I thought I already explained this to you. I'm sorry you lost your grandmother, but the woman I knew died fifty years ago. I feel sadness for you, but not for myself. Not anymore. Besides, it's part of the curse. It all is. Lettice's death was just the last act of the curse right before I killed it by grinding up and burning Dinah's bones. It-it was..." He faltered a moment, realizing his cheeks were hot. "It was my fault what happened to Lettice. If I'd never gotten involved with her, she would still be alive. I owed it to her to destroy the curse, as much as I owed it to what's left of my family."

He turned away and sniffed, wiping his eyes on his arm. He realized he was crying and didn't want Kalendra to see. He'd thought he was beyond tears, but couldn't hold them back anymore. Though he tried to contain it, a great sob escaped him. He felt fingertips on his arm just as the phone beeped. Sarah's face appeared above it.

"Hey, Dan," she exclaimed happily. "Have you checked out the movie booths yet? They're awesome. This phone's cool, too. Hi, Kal!"

"I think I'll pass," Dan said, turning away. "You and Eb have fun though."

"Oh, I will," Sarah said with an evil twinkle in her eye. "Eb's a little scared, though. He's not used to movies of any kind, you know, but I think I can talk him into it. Anyway, I'll talk to you later and you two behave yourselves. Bye." Her face winked out.

"Your sister seems happy," Kalendra. "Aren't she and Eb related? I mean, aren't you all?"

Dan sniffed and nodded. "Yes, but when the relationship is so far removed, does it really matter? I mean, third and fourth cousins are allowed to marry. At least, they used to be able to."

"They still can," she said, smiling. "You and your sister look a lot alike, which isn't surprising, but you and that Revolutionary guy look a little alike, too. He's a jerk though, not like you."

Dan chuckled. "Yes, he is a pain in the ass. But he and

Submit love each other, so he can't be all that bad. Strange, fifty years living with a guy and I really don't know him. We never talked much."

"It's all very strange," Kalendra said, shaking her head. "A few days ago I was leading a relatively normal life, going to school and making friends and now look what's going on. Here I am, on the run from a warlock with five fugitives from previous centuries. I could never have dreamed anything like this in a million years."

"You saved us," Dan said simply.

"Yes," Kalendra returned modestly. "And I'd do it again, too. It was wrong what happened to you. Besides, I wanted -"

"Wanted what?"

She turned away. "I wanted my grandmother to be happy."

Dan eventually broke the silence that ensued. "Well, maybe we should get some sleep. Oh, damn, I forgot to order that cot." He went to the phone and, with a little instruction from Kalendra on how to operate the device, placed the request.

Dan awoke in the night with a powerful urge to urinate. It was the first time he'd had to pee in over fifty years. After stumbling sleepily into the bathroom, he filled a cup with water from the sink and downed it.

He staggered out of the bathroom to hear Kalendra snoring softly in her sleep. He glanced at the bed to see her fidgeting beneath the blankets, her feet thrashing. Abruptly, she stopped moving. A red stain spread out across the covers, hastily drenching them.

Dan hurried over and pulled the blankets from the bed. Lying on the mattress was his wife from many years ago, her body sliced in half, head removed and staring blankly at him. Dan tried to scream but couldn't make a sound.

"He's coming, Dan," Amy's lifeless lips informed him, her head jostling slightly upon the pillow. "He knows where you are. Save yourself and the others. Don't -"

Dan bolted upright, sweating, his pulse racing. He thought

he might have finally cried out, but didn't know if he'd screamed in the dream or in reality. His pants were wet.

"Shit!" he cried.

"Huh? What?" Kalendra murmured sleepily, rolling onto her back.

"Go back to sleep." Dan got up and darted for the bathroom. He slammed then locked the door. He removed his pants and underwear and jumped in the shower.

Kalendra knocked twice on the door. "Is everything okay?" she asked loudly.

"Everything's just fucking great!" he shouted, scrubbing his groin and thighs vigorously. He then retrieved his trousers and underwear and rinsed them out in the shower, ringing out the yellow liquid that drained at his feet. He got out of the shower, laid his clothes out on the counter then activated the heat lamp. He noted a voice-activated hair drier inside a wall indentation and verbally activated it, pointing the nozzle at his underwear.

Then he realized that in all likelihood, there was a wet spot on the cot, as well. Had Kalendra seen it? He was suddenly very embarrassed. She probably did see it, but he thought it was better to act like nothing happened, he decided. He certainly wasn't going to ask her.

It took quite some time before his clothes were dry, but they eventually were and he put them back on. He exited the bathroom to see Kalendra sitting on the bed, facing him. "All yours," he said with an awkward grin. He looked to the cot and saw the blatant evidence of his nocturnal enuresis.

"I won't tell anyone," she said suddenly, startling him. "I know, it's embarrassing, but these things happen. Especially to people who haven't been able to urinate for over fifty years." She walked past him to the bathroom. "I'll try not to take too long." She closed the door.

Dan sat on the bed, thoroughly ashamed. What she said was right and he was glad she understood, but it was still incredibly embarrassing. He believed her when she said she wouldn't tell anyone. It made him wonder if the other four had experienced similar humiliations since being set free from the house.

Suddenly, he smiled. Kalendra and I have a secret together. How interesting.

When he suddenly realized she was taking a shower, he became acutely aware of another bodily function he hadn't been able to properly perform for fifty years. He'd thought of sex briefly in the car, had been able to suppress it, but now he was incredibly horny. And the thought of Kalendra naked in the shower was almost too much to bear. He'd found her attractive immediately after first seeing her, but had little time to think about her since leaving the house. Now he was thinking about her naked in the shower and was trying to fight the urge to creep up to the bathroom door and take a peek. It was a fight he quickly lost.

The door was shut, but not locked. He opened the door as quietly as he could and peered in. He couldn't see much through the steam at first, but then slowly began to make out Kalendra's vague form behind the opaque glass of the shower door. He could only guess at what he was seeing, her image greatly distorted by the steamy glass.

So much for that, he thought, but couldn't stop staring. He meant for his body to turn away and let Kalendra be, but his body wouldn't obey. His eyes told him that he could see the outline of her breasts and the shadow between her legs, but the images were still very vague.

"Shower off," Kalendra said, sending Dan running back to the bed. He rushed by it to the movie booths to feign interest in the listing on the wall.

Kalendra didn't exit the bathroom immediately, of course. She had to take time to dry off and dress. Dan continued to stare blankly at the list until she emerged.

"Where'd I put my shoes?" she asked, heading for the bed. "Oh, there they are."

Dan glanced over his shoulder at her as she bent to pick up her shoes. Her hair was wet and she wore different clothes. She was now clad in a very short skirt and a top that barely covered her chest. Dan's jaw nearly dropped and he turned not so quickly away.

"You like?" she asked, catching his glance. "Celia picked this out for me back at the store. You don't think it's too revealing, do you?"

Dan swallowed then turned around to face her. He looked her over quickly, trying to act nonchalant and failing. "Not at all. It's, uh, it's very nice." He glanced at the digital clock on the wall above the phone. "We should probably get going."

She nodded and exited through the door as he held it open. "What a gentleman," she commented with a smile.

They were the first to arrive, but Ebenezer and Sarah appeared shortly afterward, hand in hand.

"Where is everyone?" Sarah asked. "Well, I know where Celia and Ian are. Did you guys hear them last night? I thought the windows would shatter and the ceiling would fall in."

"I didn't hear anything," Kalendra said, shocked for a moment. Then she giggled. "Good for them."

Soon the other half of the group arrived and everyone piled into the two cars. Kalendra got in with Dan in the front seat of her vehicle with Sarah and Ebenezer in the back.

Dan glanced over at Kalendra as she got in, finding it difficult to avert his gaze as she settled in beside him, smiling broadly. He didn't even ponder the fact that she had suddenly changed in her attitude toward him. His mind was clouded with sex and he couldn't seem to clear it. He wasn't going to force anything, though. He'd learned that lesson long ago. Besides, it didn't seem right to lust after her. She was Lettice's *granddaughter.* The cars headed out onto the road and Ian's face appeared on the windshield glass. Dan jumped, unaware that the vehicles had this capability.

"Our destination today is Chicago," Ian declared gleefully. "At least, the car says we should be able to make it that far today. Unless it's malfunctioning, it should be correct. Anyway, follow me."

"I've never been to Chicago," Kalendra exclaimed happily.

"I wonder what it's like there. Though, I'm sure we won't stick around long."

"I've never even heard of Shi-cog-oh," Ebenezer said, making everyone laugh. "What's so funny?" he asked, looking confused.

Dan stole glimpse after glimpse of Kalendra's legs and cleavage and when she eventually caught him he turned away, embarrassed.

He turned his gaze toward Ian's car, at the backs of Submit and Jesse's heads. He concentrated on Submit, recalling the time he'd spent with her, recalling their conversation, their touches. Images of Submit flowed into images of Lettice, of his life and his relationship with her before the banishment. He had hoped it would have continued for a very long time, perhaps with a marriage fitting in somewhere. Of course, that was never going to happen.

Ultimately, his thoughts led back to Amy and Billy, of the dreams he used to have. Those bloody, horrible awful dreams.

His entire body straightened. *The dream! I had one last night, right before I awoke in a pool of piss. Amy's bloody body had been in the hotel room bed, warning me not to do something. What was she trying to tell me? Don't... Don't* what? *Don't wet the bed? Don't stare at Kalendra? What?*

He gritted his teeth in aggravation. He couldn't remember Amy saying anything about Kalendra specifically, but she had told him that Lettice was okay, so maybe now she had been telling him that Kalendra wasn't. Then again, Amy had been wrong about Lettice. He was so confused.

Sarah tapped him on the shoulder, startling him. He looked over his shoulder at her and she pointed firmly at Kalendra.

"What?" he mouthed, shrugging.

"Talk to her," his sister mouthed back.

"Why?" he whispered. Sarah put a finger to her lips and kept quiet.

Dan faced forward, trying to think of something to say. Evidently, Sarah thought it important for him to get to know Kalendra. Why it should matter to her, he had no idea, but he supposed he ought to at least talk to the girl. Especially since they'd saved each other's lives. He cleared his throat.

"I don't really know much about you," he began awkwardly, not used to striking up conversations with new people. "And since this is a long trip, perhaps we should get to know each other." He paused. "So, um, what were you doing before all this stuff started?" Kalendra smiled at him, folding her hands in her lap as if ready to give a recital. "Well, Dan, I was going to school full time." Her eyes darted to one side. "Well, that's pretty much it. I didn't have a job or anything. It was a pretty boring life I had, I guess."

"Oh, I don't think school's boring," he replied stiltedly. "What were some of the subjects you were studying?"

She shrugged. "This and that. Nothing too terribly exciting. I really liked my Japanese and Russian classes and I was even thinking of becoming a foreign language teacher. But, I don't know now. I wanted to be a vet at one point, too, but I can't stand to see animals suffer. More than likely, I would have ended up in a dead-end office job." She chuckled, then sighed.

"I'm quite familiar with that scenario," Dan replied. "I had just made it to middle management right before I was banished. I think I was this close to being fired, though. My boss didn't like me."

"That's too bad," she said with sincerity. "What are you going to do when this is all over with?"

"I don't know," he admitted. "I haven't given it any thought."

"I don't know what I'm going to do, either," she said.

"Maybe we should concentrate on getting through this before worrying about what happens after."

"Do you think we'll be safe, Dan?" she asked suddenly, placing her hand on his arm, her eyes searching his. "Do you think we can keep the warlock away?"

"I don't know," he replied honestly, "but I don't think—"

He was interrupted by the car suddenly surging forward, quickly dodging and swerving around other cars while staying close behind Ian's. Abruptly, both vehicles returned to normal speed. Ian's face appeared in the windshield.

"Hey, guys, guess what? I'm a warlock."

"Let me guess, you did that?" Dan asked, his heart pounding.

Celia's face appeared beside Ian's. "He's been practicing that ever since yesterday. That was his first successful attempt. Wasn't it impressive? He's trying to do other stuff, too. If he can get a good handle on his powers, he will be a very powerful weapon against the warlock."

"Well, that's great," Kalendra said, sounding doubtful. Everyone in the vehicle shared her apprehension except Dan. After what Sarah told him about Ian and Celia last night, he was certain Ian would do just about anything for her and her friends.

"Don't worry, guys," Ian said, sensing their mood. "I'm completely on your side. Nothing at all to worry about."

"Then keep making us go faster," Dan cried. "We'll get more distance that way."

"Yes, that's true," Ian said. "But it may attract his attention. I'm not sure if he can detect the powers of a nearby warlock or not, but I don't want to risk it right now. I've got both the books here and I'm going to study them and see if I can't figure something out. Talk to you guys later." His face and Celia's both winked out.

"I still don't like that guy," Kalendra remarked. "No matter what he says or does, I don't trust him."

"Oh, he's fine," Dan assured her. "He's a bit overbearing, but other than that he's okay. Besides, he wouldn't do anything to hurt Celia."

"I tend to agree with Dan," Sarah interjected. "Especially after what I heard last night." She glanced at Eb and they both laughed.

Kalendra looked from them to Dan then smiled wanly. "All right. If you guys trust him, so do I."

9.

Ian stopped the cars in front of an old hotel in Chicago. It was a big block structure built of white brick. A holographic sign, the words swirling in the air then stabilizing every few seconds, boasted,

OLD VICTORIAN ROOMS!
TWO STAY FOR THE PRICE OF ONE
CHEAP!

"Doesn't this look like a neat place to stay, guys?" Ian said as everyone else got out of the cars. "The price is certainly right." No one complained.

"I assume you and I will be sharing a room again," Kalendra said to Dan as they entered the hotel. "Especially since everyone else is a couple."

"I assume you are correct," was his reply.

Ian booked the rooms and paid while a fifty-five year old bellboy entered the lobby. He looked around, confused. "You folks have baggage?"

"We're traveling light today," Dan told him with a smile. The bellhop looked dismayed then went to Sarah and Ebenezer who also carried no bags. The man looked even more confused and a little bit angry. Dan and Kalendra chuckled.

"This is a nice old place," Kalendra remarked, heading for the old-fashioned elevator.

"Yeah, and it's even older than I am," Dan quipped, making her laugh.

The iron lattice elevator door slid aside and the elevator attendant looked up at them from her stool. "Floor?"

"Yes, there is one, isn't there?" Kalendra retorted, making

Dan guffaw. The attendant glared at them. "Fourth floor," Kalendra said quickly, sheepishly sliding into the car with Dan.

"Wow," she said after stepping into the hotel room. It looked straight out of the nineteenth century, complete with overstuffed Victorian chairs and a sofa, a brick fireplace, thick velvet curtains and elegant rugs. A door to the right opened into the bedroom, which boasted a huge four-poster bed. A door to the left opened into the bathroom. "I feel like I just stepped back in time two hundred years," Kalendra added. "This is so cool."

"People still say 'cool'?" Dan asked with a grin. "It is a nice place. Looks authentic, too."

Kalendra nodded quickly and hurried into the bathroom while Dan remained in the sitting area. "There's a olden-style toilet in here," she called, her voice echoing slightly. "You know, the kind with the tank overhead. Just like in the movies. Oh, and the sink and shower have faucets. It's really weird."

"My kind of bathroom," Dan replied. "Do you think you can 'handle' it?"

Kalendra popped back into the main room. "Was that supposed to be a pun?"

"Yeah," Dan said with a sigh. "Sorry about that."

"That's okay," she said, her smile returning. She looked up at the wall, noticing the gas lighting fixtures. They didn't appear to be in working condition, for tall, Victorian-style lamps illuminated the rooms. "At least they don't use gas or whatever they used to use. Candles, maybe."

"No, they had gas," Dan corrected then noticed she was giggling. "Don't people still have gas these days?"

Kalendra snickered. "Oh, yes! Some people have an endless supply." She laughed and Dan laughed and then there was silence.

"I think it's raining," Dan said. He walked into the bedroom and looked out between the drapes. "It's darker than it should be at six-thirty, don't you think?"

"Yes," Kalendra said, peering over his shoulder. "I just hope it's not a lightning storm. I hate lightning storms.

"This is the Midwest, too," Dan added, "where they have lots of tornadoes."

"I don't even want to think about that."

After a few more seconds of gazing outside, Dan let the curtain drop and turned to Kalendra. "Hungry? I'm starved."

"Me, too," she exclaimed. "Let's call room service."

The only modern piece of equipment in the room was the small vidpanel in the main room. Kalendra informed Dan that it was old-fashioned, for it wasn't operated by voice-command. She brought up the menu on the small screen then her and Dan made their selections. Twenty minutes later, a serving cart was at their door, courtesy of the fifty-five year old bellboy. Dan thanked the man then wondered if he should give the man a tip.

"Put it on Ian's tab," Kalendra said, taking her order from the cart. "He's paying for it all anyway."

"What's a good tip these days?" Dan asked.

"Oh, do I have to do everything?" Kalendra replied with a mirthful grin then tipped the bellhop. The man looked at the tip, smiled broadly then bowed before departing.

"Must have been a good tip," Dan remarked as he seated himself at the table. "Of course, thirty dollars would have been fantastic back in my day."

They began to eat in silence then stopped to look uneasily at one another. "Does it feel weird in here to you all of a sudden?" Kalendra asked. "It feels like all of the hair on my neck and arms is standing up."

"Probably an electrical storm," Dan replied, tilting his head toward the window.

The lights went out.

Kalendra gasped just as lighting flashed. She squealed and thunder pealed. Dan looked first to the window then back at Kalendra. She'd disappeared.

"Where'd you go?"

"Down here!" she cried in anguish.

He looked under the table. "What are you doing down there?"

"I don't do thunder!" Her voice was almost a wail.

Lightning flashed again and he felt a tight grip on his pant leg. "Come out from under there," he said, scooting his chair back from the table.

"I can't!" she cried, her voice strangled with fear. "I'm too scared!"

"Nothing's going to hurt you," he said soothingly, drawing her out. "It's just thunder."

"I know," she whimpered, clinging to him, burying her face in his shoulder. "But I'm scared. I can't help it."

Thunder boomed again, frightening Kalendra so badly that she unthinkingly tried to leap into Dan's arms, inadvertently propelling him backward. With her legs wrapped around his middle, she pushed him into a powerless lamp, knocking it and an end table to the floor. The lamp bounced off the edge of the table as it flipped up and shattered into a hundred pieces. Dan ended up on the floor with his back against the table, the pieces of the lamp spread out next to him, and Kalendra facing him in his lap.

"Ow!" she cried, still clinging to him, her body pressed tightly to his as she sobbed. "Oh, I'm so sorry, Dan. Are you all right?

"My ass hurts," he mumbled then turned his head to see the fragments of the lamp in the near darkness. "At least I didn't fall on that." He then lifted his palm and saw it was bleeding, oozing down his arm. "Well, at least most of me didn't."

Lighting flashed again and Kalendra nearly bored her head through Dan's shoulder while emitting a high-pitched squeal punctuated by large sobs. Her entire body shook with fear as her hands pulled relentlessly on his shirt. "I really hate storms, Dan! Hate them!"

"That's okay," he said, patting her on the back as he held her. "I'm here. Nothing's going to happen to you."

Her body was cold and clammy, but Dan felt very warm in her embrace. He was very aware of her legs straddling him, her breasts pressed against his chest. He had become aroused, but Kalendra was too distraught to notice. Lightning and thunder continued to flash and crash, causing her to jump and cry out each time, but eventually the phenomena faded into the distance and Kalendra's shaking sobs faded with it.

"Thank God," she muttered into his neck, his collar damp with her tears.

Sudden light filled the room. The gaslights had come to life, casting their dim light halfway across the room. Dan and Kalendra both gazed up at them.

"They must have some sort of control box in the lobby that activates these lights as a backup to the electric ones," Dan surmised. "Either that, or, like so many other things these days, it's voice activated. From the lobby."

"Maybe," Kalendra said then looked from the lights to his eyes.

Dan gazed back, entranced and embarrassed by his arousal. Uh-oh, he thought. She's just noticed.

"I gotta pee," she said, hurrying to the bathroom.

Dan remained on the floor, his arousal rapidly vanishing. He sighed and got up to correct the table and pick up lamp pieces. He heard the toilet flush as he started putting the pieces into a nearby trashcan.

"That was a nice lamp," Kalendra commented, standing behind him. "I wonder how much it cost."

"I hope they don't charge us for it," Dan said, not looking at her as he continued to clean up. "It was an accident. Of course, if they do charge, it'll be on Ian's bill." He heard her chuckle.

When he was finished, he stood up and turned to her. She threw her arms in the air. "Well, I guess we better get to bed. We've got to be back out on the road in the morning."

Dan nodded. "I'll sleep on the couch here. Good night."

Kalendra cracked a smile. "Good night, Dan. Thanks for being there through the storm. I really appreciate it." She kissed him on the cheek then closed the bedroom door behind her.

Dan sighed and sat on the couch, staring at the cold fireplace. Should I go in there? he asked himself. Did she just subtly invite me to join her? He wasn't sure, but it seemed like she had let her kiss linger a bit before withdrawing. He hadn't had to read a girl's signals in over fifty years. He was greatly out of practice, if indeed he had ever been in practice. He had misread signs plenty of times during his life.

He stretched out on the couch and barely closed his eyes when he heard the return of crashing thunder.

"Dan!"

"Coming!" He leapt to his feet and dashed into the bedroom. He threw open the door to see Kalendra shivering beneath the covers, nothing but her knuckles visible. She peeked out when she heard him come in.

"I don't want to be left alone if this is going to keep happening!" she cried, sobbing fiercely.

"You don't have to," Dan said. He kicked off his shoes and crawled under the blankets with her. He was still dressed, but Kalendra had stripped to her bra and panties. She clung to him the instant he joined her, pressing her entire shaking, frightened body to his.

Not this again, he thought, wrapping one arm around her. He felt her tears soak his shirt. "It's okay," he murmured, trying to calm her. "It's okay." He was becoming more aroused than before, while thinking how inappropriate his reaction was. What kind of monster am I? The poor girl is scared to death and all I can think about is sex? He felt horribly ashamed and unsuccessfully tried to ignore his feelings.

When she drew her head up to look at him, her eyes spurting tears, his heart went out to her and his lustful feelings subsided somewhat. He felt tears starting to swell in his own eyes.

"It's only thunder," he told her again, finding it suddenly unbearable to see her cry.

"Yes, you keep saying that," she sniffed. "But..." Her lip quivered and she sobbed, burying her face back into his chest. "My dad—" She faltered and Dan waited patiently for her to continue.

She took a shallow breath. "When I was ten, my dad was on a shuttle, returning from Mars. He and some other people had just dropped off some equipment there, you know, for the terraforming they did."

She sniffed and whimpered, her voice becoming shakier.

"The systems failed on the way back and they lost life support. They had no power and the shuttle burned up in the atmosphere. What was left of the shuttle crashed in a ball of fire into the Amazon River."

She paused, shivering silently as if recalling the tragic event.

"Anyway, it was storming here that night. Thunder, lightning. My mom and I were watching the news when we saw the crash. We held each other all night, crying until we fell asleep. And when I woke up, my mom was dead," she said, sobbing. "She had died in her sleep from grief. I've been afraid of storms ever since."

"I don't blame you," he replied after a few heartbeats had passed. Without even thinking, he started to tell her about his life with Amy and Billy and how they had been senselessly murdered. "I didn't know it then, but it was the curse at work."

Kalendra sniffed, her face streaked with tears. "Am I cursed, too?"

Dan didn't reply. He pressed her head back to his chest and held her, comforting her with his embrace. The only sounds for quite some time were the beating of two hearts.

"The thunder's stopped," Kalendra whispered, her eyes toward the window.

"Yes," he replied. "I noticed." Then he was kissing her, not knowing if he had instigated it or if she had.

Kalendra withdrew, her lips still parted. "That was—nice," she whispered.

Dan was about to say something, but was suddenly distracted by her bra strap. It had slid halfway down her arm and he stared at it. Her bra didn't look any different than the bras of his time. But what did I expect? he thought. Something with anti-gravity, perhaps? For all he knew, that's exactly what she wore. The high-tech Wonder Bra.

Kalendra looked suddenly self-conscious, embarrassed. "Is something wrong?"

"No," he smiled, returning his eyes to hers. "Everything's just great."

She smiled back then placed a tentative hand on his cheek, her fingers extending to his hair. "Dan, are we going to become lovers now?"

Dan chuckled.

"What's so funny?"

"I've never been asked that question before," he admitted with a lopsided grin. "And I'm not sure I know how to answer it."

Kalendra's hand caressed his face, ran her fingers through his hair. "Things must have been quite different fifty years ago," she said. "I don't quite know how things were in your day, but nowadays people don't engage in sex unless they plan on having long-term relationships. Of course, there are always some who don't follow that etiquette, but they are looked down upon. Those are the people who spread disease."

"Huh," he said. "I'm surprised. It seems appropriate somehow. Victorian ideas in a Victorian hotel. Although, I don't think it's such a bad thing. They sound like rules I can abide by." He rolled over and slid out of bed.

"Where are you going?" Kalendra asked, alarmed.

He stood up and grinned. "We can't 'become lovers' if I'm fully clothed! Well, we could, technically, but—" He started removing his shirt.

"Wait, stop!" Kalendra cried, sticking her hand up.

"Why? What's wrong?"

She slid out of bed and stood before him, bra straps sliding fetchingly down each arm. With a playful grin, she said, "I want to help you."

"Okay," he said, dropping his arms.

She unbuttoned his shirt with some difficulty then slid it from his body. "This reminds me of when you saved me from the grave," she whispered. She placed her hand against his chest the slowly slid her fingers through the coarse hair there. "You carried me in these arms." She lifted his right arm and traced a blood vein up his arm to his shoulder with her finger. "I can never thank you enough for that."

"I was just holding you in my arms a moment ago," he said, awestricken because she seemed so awestruck with him. "Back when we became lovers, remember?"

She smiled and tilted her head up to look deep into his eyes. "I should have you know, this will be my first time. And the first time must be special, mustn't it?"

"Yes," he said, lowering his lips to hers. He pulled her to him, her skin tingling against his. The contact sent sensations throughout his system, arousing every millimeter of his body. As the kiss started to end, Kalendra began undoing his trousers.

She gazed at his member then took it in hand, giving it a squeeze. He gasped. She smiled then began removing her bra and panties. She then returned to his arms, pressing her body to his. Hands, fingers, lips, touching, kissing, searching.

"We need a towel," Kalendra said when Dan started backing her toward the bed.

"What for?" he asked, his mind elsewhere.

She smiled playfully at him again, a smile that he enjoyed immensely, a smile he wished she'd give him all the time. "Because this is my first time, silly."

It took him a moment to realize what she was talking about. "Oh, yeah," he said and waited for her to return from the bathroom with a towel to spread across the blankets.

She lay down on the towel on her side, smiling at him. He stepped to the foot of the bed and she rolled onto her back.

"You are so beautiful," he whispered, reaching out to caress her legs, moving up to her thighs. He dipped his head, touching his lips to her pubis. She gasped then giggled.

"What are you doing?"

"Do you like that?"

"Umm... I think I do. Do it again and let me see."

He did so, this time inserting his tongue. She gasped again, arched her back. He moved up her body to kiss her breasts, her nipples then her neck and mouth. He lay on top of her, his arms clasped to her sides. He gazed into her lustful eyes a moment then kissed her again. When she could wait no longer, she guided him into her. With one quick motion, she wrapped her legs around the backs of his and pushed him all the way in. She let out a brief cry of pain as her hymen was breached, then sighed as the pain turned into pleasure.

"Are you okay?" Dan breathed, smiling.

"Yes," she replied, giving him another kiss. "I'm wonderful."

"That you are."

Dan started moving against and within her and she matched his rhythm. The rhythm changed, became quicker, harder and it wasn't long before the room was filled with ecstatic cries as Dan and Kalendra climaxed at nearly the same moment. They lay entwined in a dazed afterglow, silently reveling in the pleasure they had given and received, still unable to take their eyes of one another. It was as if nothing up to the point of their lovemaking had ever happened. There was now and had only ever had been this moment. They fell asleep clasping each other, gazing and smiling at one another until their lids grew too heavy.

Dan fell asleep first and began to dream. The Victorian bedroom faded, the gaslights dimmed. He felt Kalendra's heartbeat and her light breathing, and then silence.

10.

Kalendra remained awake, content, sated, happy. In love. It had been the most unbelievable, fantastic night. Even with the thunder and lighting thrown into the equation, the evening had equaled no other. She realized she had fallen in love with Dan the moment he had saved her from Dinah's grave. It may have even begun a little before that, but she couldn't be quite sure. There had been so much going on. It was so strange to think that the person who had first spoken to her via the cheesy Virtual Ouija board would become her lover, the love of her life. Of course, compared to the other strange stuff that had happened to her since then, it was relatively normal.

She watched Dan dozing next to her, one arm resting protectively over her, the hand gently resting on her shoulder. It was a little heavy, but she didn't mind. She couldn't help but think that if it hadn't been for the curse, she'd never have met him. Or perhaps he would have married her grandmother and things would have been very different. He'd look eighty now and Kalendra wouldn't be the woman she was today. And though the curse had enabled them to meet, it never would have let them be together afterward. If Dan hadn't burned Dinah's bones – thus alleviating the curse – most likely something awful would have befallen him. She shuddered to think about it.

She stopped mid-shudder and looked to her left. She thought she had detected movement out of the corner of her eye. She almost sat up, but that meant removing Dan's arm and she felt too safe beneath it. She couldn't hear anything except the rain splattering softly against the window coupled with Dan's breathing.

Must have been a reflection from outside, she decided. A passing car's headlights. She settled back down to sleep beneath Dan's arm and had barely dozed off when she heard a sudden scratching. She caught her breath, her skin prickling all over her body. Dan was snoring softly beside her.

There was a flash of light, making her jump. The thunder was very far away, barely audible. She realized it didn't frighten her that much, not like it had before. She looked at Dan's slumbering face and smiled. She closed her eyes and turned onto her side under his arm, facing away from him. There was more distant thunder and she cuddled closer to him, only slightly disturbed by the sound.

She awakened suddenly, bolting upright, her breathing and heartbeat rapid. Dan had rolled onto his back, still snoring. Kalendra heard the scratching again.

"What is that?" she whispered, her voice barely audible even to her own ears.

It sounded like an animal scratching on the door, a cat or small dog. She debated whether or not she should get up and see what it was. She was afraid the warlock had found them and was trying to trick her into opening the door. If so, Dan should be awake.

She gently shook him, but he kept snoring. She shook him some more and whispered his name, but he rolled over, his back to her, still sleeping. He wouldn't wake up. Kalendra became increasingly afraid. She was cold, too, without his arm on her. She reached for his shirt and put it on as she sat on the edge of the bed. The scratching stopped.

She didn't move as she contemplated her next course of action. She was just about to lie back down when a calico cat darted past her into the bathroom. She gave a startled cry then relaxed. It's just a cat. But how did it get in here? She decided it must have already been in the room, perhaps sleeping under the bed or in the closet. The cat was probably just a pet of the hotel, roaming the rooms as it liked. Kalendra was relieved that she'd found the source of the scratching. It hadn't been the warlock after all.

"Hey, kitty," she called to it, venturing toward the gas-lit bathroom. The electric lights were still not operating and there appeared to be no control for the gas lamps anywhere on the walls. "Nice kitty!"

She didn't see the cat until she peered behind the bathroom door. The cat stood on the sink, it's back paws in the basin, its front paws on the rim. Both of its tails swished agitatedly over where its head should have been as the body turned toward Kalendra.

With a scream, Kalendra leapt back and slammed the bathroom door shut.

"What?" Dan groaned, jolted awake.

Kalendra threw herself under the covers and clung to Dan. She was too scared to speak or even scream again.

"What's wrong?" Dan asked. "I don't hear any thunder."

"No, it's—" she began just as the scratching sounded again. "That!" she cried, burying her head into his shoulder. "There's a monster in there."

"What?" Dan asked and started to get out of bed.

A ball of red light the size of a golf ball shot through the bedroom door, passing directly in front of the bathroom door. The calico cat leapt through the closed door and batted at the red light. The ball eluded the cat and shot back through the bedroom door. The cat chased it.

"This place is haunted," Dan whispered, suddenly frightened.

"Haunted by what?" Kalendra demanded.

Dan was used to his grandmother's ghost. Even Dinah's faceless spirit had become less scary to him. But the headless, two-tailed cat and the angry, red ball of light made no sense to him.

"Maybe the cat was born with two tails," he said. "And it was killed by decapitation. The red ball, though—I don't know."

Kalendra gasped. "Do you think it could be the warlock?"

"It could be," he agreed. "I don't know, but maybe we should tell everyone to get out of here anyway."

The two of them dressed hurriedly and Dan threw the bedroom door open. He half expected to see the calico and the red light in the main room, but it was empty. He took Kalendra's hand and hurried her out into the hallway. He hurried to the elevator then changed his mind. It would take too long; the elevator was very slow. He pulled Kalendra to the stairs, looked up and stopped.

"Oh, my God."

"What?" Kalendra asked, following his gaze.

Overhead, the staircase continued up and up and up, seemingly into infinity. Dan looked down to see the stairs ended at a brick wall a few feet from where they were standing. The only way to go was up.

"He's got us," Dan whispered, still gazing in wonder at the infinite climb before them.

"Are we trapped?" Kalendra asked, frightened.

"I don't know, but judging from past experiences, I'd have to say it's a strong possibility. Do you know what floors the others are on?"

She didn't. There was one other room on the same floor as theirs, but when they knocked there was no answer.

"Guess we start climbing," Dan said, starting back toward the stairs.

"What about the elevator?" Kalendra asked, walking toward it. She stopped. "It's gone." There was only a wall where the elevator had been. The gaslights sputtered as if to go out, but flickered back to life.

She followed Dan to the stairs leading up and again came to a halt. On the bottom step was the headless calico, tails swishing. It started to purr eerily, echoing throughout the hallway. It took Dan only a moment to realize the purr matched his own heartbeat.

"Go away," he shouted, moving as if to kick the animal. It responded by leaping at his face, claws extended, only to vanish before reaching him. Dan gasped, took a few involuntary steps backward, and then steadied himself. He regained Kalendra's hand and walked her briskly up the steps.

As they reached the next floor, a shriek caused them both to pause. Celia burst from the door nearest them, clad only in a man's shirt.

"What's going on?" called a voice from behind the door across the hall. Sarah opened the door and stepped out.

"I saw a headless cat," Celia exclaimed, pale as a sheet. "With two tails!"

"We've seen it, too," Kalendra said, taking a shallow breath. "A couple times."

Ian emerged from behind Celia, wearing only his pants. "It's gone," he told her then noticed the others. "Did she tell you about the—?"

Dan nodded and motioned Ian toward the stairs. "Look up."

Sarah followed behind Ian and gasped. "Holy fuck! What the hell is that shit?"

"It must be my uncle's work," Ian sighed. "He's found us."

"Well, let's not hang around here any longer. Eb, we're leaving!" Sarah started down the stairs and stopped.

"Can't go that way," Dan told her when she cursed at the brick wall. "He's blocked us. There's no elevator anymore, either. The only way to go is up."

"Shit, he's really got us, then," Sarah said, bowing her head and shaking it. "Well, let me go wake Eb up and—"

A man's scream sounded from within Sarah and Eb's room, quickly followed by Eb running into the hall clad only in his underwear while pulling on a shirt.

"There's a—"

"We know," chimed Dan and the others in unison. "We've seen it."

"Get some pants on, hon," Sarah said to him. "We're going to get out of here."

"If we can," Kalendra said softly.

"What floor are Submit and Jesse on?" Ian asked. "Are they above or below us?"

"I think they were on the top floor," Sarah said, jutting her thumb at the ceiling. "Whichever one *that* is. I hope it's not way up there."

"Only one way to find out," said Dan, hurrying up the stairs.

🙎

Submit slid her naked body into the bathtub. She positioned herself between Jesse's legs and leaned back with a pleasurable sigh. Jesse's arms wrapped around her and he kissed her.

"I had forgotten what baths feel like," Submit purred, snuggling back against Jesse. "Of course, being a Puritan, I've never had a bath quite like this one."

Jesse's hands went to her breasts. Even though they'd just finished making love, Jesse was still aroused. The warm water and the warm female body against him made every inch of his body tingle with lust. Yet, something bothered him, pushed thoughts of sex from his mind.

"We've never talked about it," he suddenly blurted.

"Talked about what?" Submit asked, her eyes closed. She opened them and turned her head to gaze at him. She waited.

"You know."

Submit gazed at him then sighed. "I didn't want to waste any time talking about something that means nothing."

"You two fornicated for over fifty years," he snapped. "I don't call that nothing!"

"Well, you and I have slept together for over two hundred years," she countered, pulling away from him slightly. "That should tell you something."

Jesse's gaze lowered. "It does," he admitted then pulled her back against him. "I guess I am just not completely assured that you don't have feelings for him still."

"I still do have some feelings for Dan," she said. "But they aren't anywhere near as strong as the feelings I have for you."

Jesse let go of her and sat motionless.

Submit crossed her arms and glared at him. "May I remind

you that it was your idea in the first place? We both felt sorry for him. Remember?"

"What?" he asked, his voice barely audible.

"You remember!" Submit cried. "We—"

She noticed movement in the corner of her eye and turned to see a small ball of light hovering in the middle of the room. She sat forward just as the calico leapt through the shut door. The ball bobbed and weaved, once again escaping the clutches of the headless feline. The calico didn't give up the chase and jumped after it, right back through the door.

Submit and Jesse both leaped up from the tub at the same instant, colliding and sending each other back down upon the porcelain, water spouting in every direction.

Submit cried out in pain as she fell against the faucet. "Ow, Jesse! You bruised my bosom. Look!"

"Sorry," Jesse said, a look of pain on his face as he lay sprawled back in the tub water. "But I think we should get out of here. I smell witchcraft."

Submit had to agree. She and Jesse hurriedly dried off and dressed. Two minutes later they were out in the hallway.

Jesse went to the stairs and gazed upward. "Definitely witchcraft," he whispered then looked down the stairs to see the brick wall.

"I thought we were on the top floor," Submit said, greatly alarmed and frightened by the infinite stairwell above.

"We were," Jesse said. "But I don't think this is the same building we arrived at earlier in the evening."

"I just hope we aren't trapped," said Submit. "Not again."

Jesse felt something rubbing against his leg. He looked down to see the calico as it started to purr, the sound matching the beat of his heart. The creature then leapt up the stairs, its disembodied purr echoing after it.

"I see the elevator is gone," Submit observed.

"The what?" Jesse asked, perplexed. "Oh, the box we came up in." He shuddered at the thought of it. "Well, there's only stairs now. Good, old-fashioned stairs. Too bad we can only go up, though."

They ascended five flights to find every floor was identical to the last. Until they reached the sixth floor. To the right was a large room. One of the double doors was open, a dull light flickering on the surface of the polished wood. At the end of the hall, a foot from the door, a breeze ruffled the curtains of an open window. The window slammed shut.

"Someone's trying to scare us," Submit whispered.

"It's going to take more than a headless cat and a slamming window to scare me," Jesse declared and headed straight for the open door.

"Maybe there's an exit this way," Submit commented, keeping close to Jesse.

The immediate room was dark, a dull light from an adjacent area illuminating tables and chairs that appeared to be set up for dinner. Atop each table sat an unlit candle in a glass bowl. Jesse walked boldly into the room.

"Be careful," Submit whispered, halting in the doorway. She felt a breeze on her back and jumped around to see the window was open again. She slinked into the dining room, her back tight against the wall.

Jesse walked across the room to the source of the light. A candle sat on a low table in a hallway area at the opposite end of the dining room. On the left was a closed door and to the right was an unlit corridor.

The closer Jesse got to the candle, the heavier the surrounding air became. He wondered if he were walking through invisible syrup as he made his way to the table. The heavy atmosphere was very humid, yet also very cold. The candle flame flickered as if from a breeze or a breath. Jesse felt no such movement of air.

He neared the closed door to the left, but he could barely lift his feet off the ground or even slide them forward. It was as if he were encountering an invisible barrier, an unseen, wet, woolen blanket.

He stopped trying to walk and looked down at the candle. It burned as if nothing was wrong while Jesse found it difficult to breathe. The air was oppressive. He damned the candle as witchcraft; nothing could stay alight under such conditions.

He turned and noticed a portrait hanging over the candle. It was a portrait of woman, the face vague, almost comical. It changed color before Jesse's eyes, became darker in hue. It looked like the portrait was burning, yet there was no flame. When the burning was complete, the portrait had become that of an aged, bearded man. The eyes glared menacingly down at Jesse. The door to the left started to creak open.

Jesse decided it was time to leave.

He started to run, but the atmosphere was too thick. He had barely moved before the door burst open with a great force that lifted him into the air. He was propelled across the room, flung over dining tables, face down. He was vaguely aware of candles lighting and shadowy people seated at the tables beneath him as he flew by. Young couples clinked glasses and laughed and children with grandparents talked and smiled as the former Revolutionary soldier whizzed over their heads.

He was too startled to cry out and remained silent as an unseen force pushed down on his legs until he was in an upright position. He was aware of the mirror in front of him only a split second before he smashed into it face first.

Every time Dan and Kalendra climbed a floor, the brick wall would appear behind them, blocking them from going down.

"I'm tired," Kalendra moaned, forcing herself up the last two steps to the next floor. "Let's rest for a second."

"Okay," Dan agreed then heard a woman's violent weeping from above. He and Kalendra exchanged wary glances. Neither of them moved until something about the woman's cry clicked in Dan's mind. He shot to his feet and ran up the stairs.

He found Submit in the dining area, clinging to a body, crying into its shirt. He felt Kalendra slide in beside him and heard her gasp. She clung to him, hiding her face behind his arm.

Submit didn't seem to notice them. She cried out Jesse's name over and over, wailing uncontrollably. A giant shard of mirror jutted from between Jesse's eyes.

"What the hell happened?" asked Dan.

"There are spirits here," Ian said, dim candlelight flickering across his face. "Unfriendly ones. Can't you feel it? It's very oppressive in here. Stifling. I suggest we get out of here."

Sarah nodded and went to Submit. She touched the weeping Puritan's shoulder, but Submit shrugged her away.

"No!" she shrieked.

Sarah looked to Ebenezer for help. He stepped forward. "Daughter, please," he began gently. "There is nothing we can do for him now. He's in a better place."

Submit looked angrily at him, but said nothing. She unsteadily got to her feet and then fell into her father's arms.

"Oh, Papa," she cried, clinging to him. "He didn't deserve to die like this."

"None of us do," he replied softly, walking her slowly to the door.

"Are we just going to leave him?" Celia asked.

"What can we do?" Ian asked. "Drag him up the stairs with us? He's gone. This place isn't real. There's no place to take him. I—" He shrugged.

Celia gazed at him with concern, but let the matter drop.

The open window slammed forcefully as Kalendra passed by. She gave out a cry and inadvertently glanced out into the darkness. A giant animal's skull attached to an elongated skeletal body with tremendous bony wings walked across a barren landscape a great distance below. A variety of other hideous creatures milled about with it, but were to small and far away for her to comprehend in such a short period of time. Dan closed the curtains after she looked away. She let out a sigh and thanked him.

With each level of the supernatural hotel the group gained, the atmosphere became heavier and darker. Gas lamps became fewer and there were no hall windows. They could barely see the other members of the group unless there were standing right next to them.

"This is getting scarier and scarier," Celia whispered to no one in particular. "I feel like something's trying to shove me through the floor. I can barely move my feet anymore. Maybe I'm just exhausted."

"There is a great evil here," Submit muttered, keeping close to Dan.

"That's the understatement of the century," Dan quipped.

"Time for a break," Sarah gasped, falling to the floor into a sitting position. The others joined her, sitting in the nearly pitch-black hallway.

"This is pointless," Ebenezer complained. "Going up all these stairs isn't getting us anywhere."

"I think you are right," Ian said with a sigh. "I wish I could figure out what to do to get us out of here. Unfortunately, I don't know a spell that will do the trick—"

His sentence was punctuated by a faint sound coming from behind a decrepit door at the end of the hall. It came again, sounding like moans and whispers followed by clunking and thumping sounds.

Ian got up. "We should keep going," he suggested.

The others got up slowly as a terrible odor wafted from the old door.

"Ugh!" Celia cried. "Smells like a zoo full of dead animals!"

The door burst open as if reacting to a violent gust of silent wind. A figure emerged from the darkness beyond. It shuffled toward the group, tilting its armless torso back and forth with each step. The hand sewn to its bare stomach flexed its fingers into a claw. Behind the figure was a naked woman, her intestines spilled from her slit abdomen, wrapped around her waist and torso. Clasping her hand was a child with one eye dangling on his cheek and one arm that was twisted and stretched, hanging loosely to his knees.

Behind these three specters came the crack of a whip. A pale woman with long black hair clad in a dark blue Victorian gown emerged, her face contorted and angry.

"Bad, bad slaves," she screeched, her whip striking the backs of all three ghosts before her. "Bad slaves deserve severe punishment!" She whipped them again then turned to smile evilly at Ian. Ian clasped the *Book of Curses* tightly under his arm. "Those who are not slaves sometimes need to be punished, too."

Everyone in the group, except for Ian, backed away. Ian stood his ground. "You must be Madame Lalaurie," he replied to the apparition. "Infamous torturer and murderer of New Orleans slaves. I have read several stories about your hideous crimes against humanity."

Madame Lalaurie grinned maniacally and snapped her whip while hovering closer.

Ian extended one hand toward her and fixed his gaze. He began a low chant that seemed to rise up and swirl about the hallway. Lalaurie stopped moving and her face went slack. The instant Ian stopped chanting, Lalaurie stopped existing. The tortured slaves disappeared with her.

"Wow," Celia exclaimed, hurrying as fast as she could through the syrupy air to be at Ian's side. "You really did it. You got rid of an evil ghost."

"I'm afraid that particular spell only takes care of one ghost," he said. "Or, as in this case, one ghost and any other ghosts that may be attached to it. I don't know if I can use it more than once a day. And it still stinks in here."

"I think we should keep going," Dan suggested from the third step.

"Why?" Ebenezer asked. "Things are just getting worse the further up we go."

"You want to stay here?" Dan asked, his brow raised. "Do you want to see if there's a way out where those ghosts came through? Be my guest." He turned and started up the stairs, tugging Kalendra after him.

Before they reached the next floor, Kalendra heard bumping and scraping sounds, as if someone were moving heavy furniture. A tiny, white insect buzzed about her face and she swatted at it. The bug buzzed frantically away then landed on her nose. The tiny human skull squashed upon the body of a white fly grinned eyelessly at her. She screamed and jerked her head back, one foot slipping from the step in the process. Dan kept her from falling, however, pulled her up to the next step. When they reached the top, they both halted.

At the end of the hallway, curtains bowed out from an open window. Dim light from an unseen source filtered in, grimly illuminating the immediate area. From beyond the window came the distant sound of crying animals and the faint flapping of very large wings. Every ten seconds there was a loud, low thud.

Kalendra recalled the winged monster she had seen and her fear mounted. She hurried Dan to the next flight of stairs and stopped. There were no more stairs to climb.

"This is it," Dan muttered, gazing at the blank wall

where the next staircase should have been. "Must be close to showdown time."

The thumping outside became louder.

Ian walked up the steps behind them, his head bowed as he thumbed through *The Book Of Curses*. An intense coldness enveloped him, freezing his back and neck. He lurched forward then turned around. A specter had emerged from the wall, visible only from the waist up. Ian tried the spell he'd cast on Madame Lalaurie and the ghost vanished.

"I can do it more than once a day after all," he muttered.

Celia had backed down the steps the instant she saw the apparition; it had appeared to float directly into Ian. "That was freaky," she exclaimed, a bit reluctant to continue.

"This is it gang," Dan said as everyone finished tromping up the steps. "As you can see, no more stairs. This is the end of the road."

The sole door in the hallway opened and slammed shut repeatedly as the window did the same. The sound was very loud, louder than any normal door or window should be. The slammings matched the beat of everyone's individual heart: door, window, door, window... *bang BANG! bang BANG! bang BANG!*

"You're going to have to do much better than that, Uncle Ivan," Ian shouted. "You're not scaring any of us."

The door and window both ceased operation at the same moment and the air in the hallway became lighter. The gas lamps shone brighter, their flames long and crisp. All supernatural activity seemed to have abated for the moment.

"Looks like we have only one way to go," Dan said after a long silence. He indicated the slamming door with a tilt of his head.

"There's the window," Sarah said, walking over to it.

"Don't," Kalendra cried, running over to stop her. "Don't look out there."

"Why not?" Sarah asked as she turned her gaze to the glass.

She gasped and stood gaping out the window for a moment before she was able to tear herself away. "Okay, okay!" she exclaimed, shaken. "I believe you."

Ffffffffft!

A knife whizzed past Ebenezer's head, narrowly missing his ear as he had stepped forward at the same instant. More sharp instruments started flying through the walls, herding everyone toward the door. Dan was the farthest away so was he the last one through. The door slammed shut behind him. But the door didn't deter the assaulting knives. The metallic, sharp, murderous instruments continued flying after the fleeing group of soft, fleshy humans.

"Hurry, run!" Dan urged Kalendra and Submit in front of him

A large, blunt object sailed past the knives and hit Dan in the back. The impact sent him sprawling forward to land on his elbows and knees. The floorboards gave way beneath him, depositing him onto a heap of debris.

Dan moved his arm when he regained consciousness. He felt something cold and hard. He lifted his appendage to see a three-inch nail penetrating the skin near his armpit. His breath caught as he realized his heart had escaped being skewered by scant inches. With a grimace, he removed the offending object. Blood gushed from the wound.

He partially blocked the flow with his hand and sat up, causing the loose pile of boards beneath him to shift and scrape him. A bare window nearby allowed a minimal amount of light into the darkened room. Dan looked up through the hole in the ceiling he had fallen through. The item that had struck him was no place to be seen.

"Hey, guys," he called, hoping they were still within earshot. "Hello? Guys? I need some help down here."

Silence.

"Kalendra? Submit?"

Nothing.

Dan detected movement in the corner of his eye: the swirl of a skirt or dress. He turned his head but saw no one. He looked back up at the hole then at the boards surrounding him on three sides. He started thinking he could pile up the boards and climb back up through the hole.

He detected movement once again and turned his head quickly. On the other side of the room a large group of people began to slowly appear. Men, women and children, all in full color but transparent. They stared silently at him.

Dan didn't find the presence of the spirits threatening or frightening. They seemed curious, perhaps even friendly. "Can I help you?" he asked them.

The hair on the back of his neck stood on end as he spoke. Something was behind him. The eyes of the ghosts before him were looking at whatever it was, a look of fear appearing on their fading faces.

Dan slowly turned his head. The giant skeletal being was outside the window, staring at him. He gave out a yelp as something brushed against his leg. He jerked away and the boards shifted, making him tumble backward. A nail scraped his cheek from chin to ear.

The headless, double-tailed calico jumped on his chest. The creature possessed no eyes but it seemed to stare at him as its tails waved and twitched. It started to purr.

Dan could move only his head. He looked back to the window to see the skull had gone. He heard large wings flapping slowly in the distance.

That thing out there is the warlock, he suddenly realized. He's keeping us in here. There's no escape. Just like before.

The calico curled up on Dan's lap as if to sleep, its purring becoming erratic. It leapt into the air abruptly, its powerful back legs shoving hard against Dan's ribs.

Dan sat up, rubbing his side. That hurt. He looked around for the creature then noticed a ball of mist hovering in the air. It was about the size of a basketball and shadows passed over its surface, like dark clouds across the face of a white planet. The crowd of apparitions had vanished. The calico leapt after the mist as it shot across the room and through a wall. The cat was in hot pursuit.

Dan walked over to the wall, his hand still gripping his bleeding upper arm, blood also oozing from his cheek wound. He placed his hands on the dry, peeling wallpaper, almost instantly locating a thin ridge underneath. The ridge traveled down to the floor in a straight line.

A hidden door.

He grabbed a board from the pile and used the protruding nail to scratch at the wallpaper and plaster until a knobless door was revealed. He dropped the board and shouldered the door open.

The adjoining room was small yet contained even more loose boards than the other one. The ceiling had completely caved in except for two beams. It was pitch black with no windows. There was no ball of mist, no headless calico.

Instead, there was one ghost. Only the upper half of the image was visible as it hovered over the pile of boards, looking forlornly down at the floor.

"Jesse," Dan muttered.

The apparition didn't appear to notice. It vanished.

Dan walked around the boards and found Submit, unmoving. He crouched beside her and felt for a pulse. He found one, but it was very weak. Her left arm was broken. The calico sat on a board nearby, tails waving gracefully.

"What do you want?" he asked it angrily. "Are you waiting for something?"

When the calico began to purr again, Dan picked Submit up in his arms. He heard a board fall to the floor just as felt something warm and sticky on his hands.

"Oh, 'Mit," he sighed. A nail similar to the one that Dan had managed to elude had skewered the woman he'd been banished with for over fifty years. He fought back the great sob working up within his chest. She was losing blood rapidly and who knew what organs had been damaged. He needed to get her to a hospital, quick.

The calico rushed past Dan and stopped before a doorway on the other side of the room. It leapt up and vanished through the door.

As Dan stepped forward, the door opened and Ebenezer stepped through, his face pale in the darkness. Dan gasped.

Ebenezer crossed his arms and shook his head. He pointed to the wall behind Dan then vanished.

Dan didn't move, shocked into the realization that Ebenezer had joined Jesse. The hotel's supernatural denizens had killed them both. Dan suddenly became very angry, envisioning himself strangling the warlock to death. He started toward the door then realized Eb had just been warning him away from it. He turned and carried Submit toward the wall.

He had barely taken a step when the line of apparitions reappeared. The temperature in the room had dropped dramatically. One of the ghosts stepped forward: Dan's mother.

"This way," she said clearly, pointing to where Ebenezer had pointed. "Stop following the cat, Dan." She and the other ghosts vanished.

Dan stepped up to the wall and gazed at it in confusion. Unlike the previous room, there was no wallpaper, nor any plaster. This room was unfinished; there were only dry, rotten planks. There was no visible sign of a door.

Yet, when Dan reached out, his fingers met with no resistance. The wall was an illusion. He carried Submit through it.

The calico leapt at his face, knocking him backward. He dropped Submit in the process and gave a strangled cry. The cat's two tails were wrapped tightly about his neck as its claws raked his flesh. He was suffocating. He started to black out.

Abruptly, the cat was gone. A figure stood over Dan, the calico in its grasp. The headless creature struggled and started to change. The creature became something hideously indescribable, a being with scales and feathers and angular limbs. Abruptly, it dissolved into thin air.

"Are you all right?" Dan's savior asked.

"Yes," Dan rasped, rubbing his throat. "Thanks, Ian."

"Don't thank me," he said. "Thank the doctors who

installed my artificial arm. How'd you guess what I was? Did Celia tell you?"

Dan shrugged. "I don't know how I knew. Where is Celia and everyone else?"

"I don't know," Ian said. "I was separated from them a little while ago."

Dan looked around. "Where's Submit?"

"I brought her through."

"Through what?"

"I was able to open a portal back to the real hotel. I couldn't maintain it, though. My uncle has this place constantly growing and changing. I think he's somehow reproducing other houses and buildings, tacking them on to this one. It's far beyond my ability, however he's doing it."

Dan didn't care about that. "Can the rest of us get through the portal?"

Ian shook his head grimly. "The hotel melded with the portal, eliminating it altogether."

"Okay, can you open another one?"

"Um, yes, but it greatly depletes my energy. I'm really tired right now. I was hoping to locate everyone before I tried opening another one."

"My mother pointed me in this direction," Dan said. "She must have known you were here. Submit is hurt."

"I healed her. She'll be fine now."

"You healed her," Dan said, unable to hide a grin. "Man, I knew I let you come along with us for some reason. Ian helped him to his feet. "I'm not in the same room. Did you pull me into a different one?"

"Nope," Ian said. "You were in this one when I found you."

"Strange," Dan said. "But, compared to everything else here, it's almost normal. Oh, by the way," he began sadly. "I've encountered the ghosts of Jesse and Ebenezer."

"Really?" Ian asked, sounding shocked.

Dan nodded. "Eb was shaking his head and warning me

away from a door. He pointed me this way, away from the cat. My mom told me to stop following it."

"The cat is Uncle Ivan's familiar," Ian explained. "Or, rather, it was. Most likely it was created from the souls of a mixture of animals and shaped into the creature we saw."

Dan shuddered. "I like cats, but not that one."

Ian grinned and started walking. Dan followed him. They walked from darkened room to darkened room, all of them identical.

"My uncle Ivan is calling spirits from all areas of the earth to help get *The Book* from us," Ian explained. "Not all of them are evil, but enough are to wreak havoc for us. Obviously, some of them are more than happy to kill us." He paused then sighed. "I can banish them all, but that would drain all of my energy, perhaps even kill me. I don't think I can open a portal if that happens, but if that witch Dinah could perform magic as a ghost—"

"Is there any way I could learn the banishing spell?" Dan asked.

"I'm not sure," Ian replied. "I know some protective spells can be cast by normal people, but I really don't know that much about it. I suppose you could try."

Dan accepted *The Book* from Ian. "It's too dark to read. Couldn't you just tell me how to cast it?"

"Well, if I recite the words, I will be casting the spell, whether there are ghosts present or not."

"Really?" Dan asked with a sigh. "There must be a way. What if you said the words backwards?"

"Then I would more than likely be conjuring a ghost."

"Okay. How about this: say the words out of order, like every other one, and then go back and fill in the missing ones? I would just have to remember what goes where."

"I don't know what would happen if I tried that," Ian informed him. "I don't think it's wise to be fooling around with spells like that."

"You're probably right," Dan sighed again. "Oh, I know.

How about if you just tell me one word of the spell, like, every five minutes or something?"

Ian shook his head. "I would still be casting it."

"What if you said other stuff between the words?" Dan persisted.

Ian lowered his head and let out a long breath. "Dan, look. I know you're trying to help, but I just don't know enough about casting to be comfortable with your suggestions. They may cause more harm than good. I just don't know."

Dan didn't reply. He was disappointed, but understood Ian's concerns. He realized he was a little bit jealous of Ian's powers. He wished he could cast spells as easily as Ian, not just the 'normal people' spells. He wanted so much to take control of the situation and end it. He wanted to get on with his life, whatever there was left of it. Would Kalendra be part of it? He hadn't thought about it and didn't have time to right now.

Dan followed Ian into the next room and squinted. The gas lamps in this room were blazing. Ian halted.

"We've gotten off track somehow," he said.

"We have?" Dan asked, confused.

"Yes. The dark rooms lead the way out."

Dan gazed at him. "How do you know that?"

"Somebody told me."

"Why would the warlock give us a way out?"

"He wouldn't," Ian replied. "But the ghosts would."

"They're helping us?"

"The ones that don't want to be here are. Your mother, for example. You know she's here. My father's here, too." He nodded to the man standing in the doorway ahead.

"Go back," said Ian's father, a tall, frail man with scant hair. His body seemed to float above the air, his feet invisible. "The way is back there."

"But we can't leave yet," Dan said to Ian. "We have to find everybody first. Well, everybody who's left, anyway."

Ian's father nodded then vanished.

"Come on, then," Ian said, once again leading the way.

Beyond the door was the staircase, leading up.

"Not this again," Dan groaned.

A knock sounded on the door across the hall from them. The door slammed open and Madame Lalaurie emerged, prodding the ghosts of Jesse and Ebenezer with an elongated sword. Jesse's eyes had been sewed shut and Ebenezer's arms and legs had been disjointed, pointing in agonizingly odd directions. His ears and nose were gone.

"Uncle Ivan is manufacturing false spirits now," Ian whispered to Dan.

"He is? How do you know?"

Ian paused. "I guess I don't. I just have this feeling he is." He looked to the stairs. "We have to go up."

The stairs only went up one floor. The hallway was dark, as if the shadows were made of smoke. There was the distinct odor of burning wood in the air.

Ian opened a door and gaslight spilled out into the hall. Beyond was a small kitchen with a table and chairs. Constant knocking and clunking sounds filled the room, accompanied by the shrill pinging of glass. Drawers opened and utensils flew out, headed straight for Ian.

Ian grabbed a flying knife in mid-air with his artificial hand, the point of the blade drawing a spot of blood on his neck. A fork flung itself at him a split second later, imbedding itself in his forehead.

The knife and *The Book* fell to the floor as Ian staggered, trying to remove the fork with his strong hand. The handle snapped. He fell sideways, toppling the table and two chairs.

Dan had ducked out of the room the instant he saw things flying. He waited for Ian for a very long minute before everything inside the kitchen quieted down. He poked his head in. "Ian?"

He saw *The Book* on the floor next to Ian's feet. A smoky shape hovered over it.

"No!" Dan cried, lurching forward.

A tremendous *crack!* sounded somewhere outside followed by booming thumps and the sounds of boards being snapped apart. It sounded to Dan like something was coming, something big destroying a huge chunk of the hotel in order to get to him.

Dan tackled *The Book*, at the same time feeling an immense cold envelope him. It was not the sort of cold one experienced in a meat locker; this cold was spine tingling, a cold with an attachment of fear and panic. He fought the urge to just turn and run and held the book in his arms, clinging it to his chest. He felt nauseous and wanted to scream. He *was* screaming, he realized. He just couldn't hear himself over the noise of the oncoming beast.

Abruptly, everything ceased except Dan's screaming. His fear took nearly a minute to subside and he was left breathing heavily, his jaw and throat sore. His heartbeat sounded like pile drivers in his ears.

He looked down at *The Book,* thinking he should do something with it but had no thoughts beyond that.

A figure appeared beside him and the book opened in his hands. A finger pointed at a page. "There."

"Thanks, Ma," he said and commenced to read the ghost dispelling spell. He memorized it then looked up to see the image of a man clad in garb from the 1880s. A scar ran across his nose and he had one bulging eye.

"You will die," he screeched.

Dan recited the spell and the apparition vanished. Dan then stumbled backward, suddenly dizzy and disoriented. He steadied himself against a chair. "Hey, wait a second," he said. "I thought normal people couldn't cast that spell. It even says so right here."

"Many people are unaware of their own capabilities," his mother replied though she wasn't visible. Dan caught a shimmering in the air before him, however, and followed it out into the hallway.

"Mom?" he began. "Are you saying what I think you're saying?"

Light laughter filled the air. "Dan, you are descended from an Arch Druid. Your father descended from him. He lived hundreds of years ago. Your father also had abilities he wasn't aware of. Too bad he didn't find out about them before he died. Things would have been a lot more exciting between us."

"How do you know this?"

The shimmering started to take form, becoming first a vague shape, the outline of a mouth and eyes barely discernible. "There are some things a person doesn't learn until after they're dead." Her vague form wavered. "You must go back into the kitchen, Dan. Your friends and Sarah are looking for you."

"Ma!" he cried just as she vanished.

Dan turned to face the kitchen and suddenly wanted nothing to do with it. The fear he'd experienced in that room had matched nothing he'd felt before. He felt sick with panic just thinking about going back.

The movement of curtains in the hall caught his attention. The curtains billowed though the window was shut. The face of the skeletal creature looked in, glaring malevolently at Dan.

Dan darted quickly into the kitchen.

12.

The gas lamps had gone out and Ian's body was gone and only a pool of dark liquid remained. Dan didn't experience any fear at the moment. All appeared quiet and deserted.

There was a closed door on his right. As he approached, he heard a whistling sound, like wind blowing through a crack. He yanked the door open.

Wind blew back his hair, hot and searing, burning his eyes. He stepped back and shielded his face with his arm until the gust passed. A giant chunk of the hotel had been destroyed.

Stretching out hundreds of yards was a great expanse where hotel rooms and hallways used to be. The hotel had grown to monstrous proportions, seemingly taking up several city blocks and rising higher than most skyscrapers. Dan looked down, but could see only dust and debris floating up from unseen depths. Overhead broiled black and crimson clouds, a tongue of red lighting flashing, accompanied by thunder that sounded like a great gurgling growl. More gusts of hot wind shot up from the darkness below, ruffling Dan's hair and clothes. A hot cinder landed on his shoulder. He quickly brushed it away. It left a small black spot.

Hundreds of yards away, the hotel was still intact. A door was open with a light on inside.

Kalendra is over there, he realized. And Celia and Sarah. How am I going to get across to them?

Uncle Ivan had separated Dan from the others. He was only now realizing the sounds he'd heard earlier were the sounds of the warlock destroying the whole central section of the building. The warlock was keeping him away from the people who he could help with his newfound spell casting abilities.

Divide and conquer, Dan thought. That's what the asshole was doing. He stopped the instant I grabbed *The Book*. It's a source of great power, obviously. That's why he couldn't get at us directly before. He had to call upon the help of other ghostly beings to take care of us. It all made sense to him now. Uncle Ivan could do nothing to him as long as he had *The Book*. His companions, however, were not with him...

He opened *The Book*. "Damn it!" he cried. "I can't see anything in this infernal darkness!"

An ethereal light appeared, hovering directly above the pages. It reminded him of the headless calico, but the beast was nowhere to be seen. He then remembered that Ian had taken care of the familiar earlier. Where was Ian now? Had Uncle Ivan transported him across the gap? Were the girls with him?

"Dan," rasped a voice behind him.

Dan turned to see Ian stooped over, holding his intestines. His abdomen had been ripped open. Blood drooled from his mouth, dripped from his chin, as he shuffled weakly forward.

"Heal me," he gasped and collapsed, slipping in his own blood.

"I don't know how," Dan cried, gazing down at him in horror.

"The book," Ian gurgled. "Use...the book. Spell...there. Hurry!"

Dan took a shallow breath and opened *The Book*, the ethereal light still illuminating the pages for him. Behind him he heard the pounding of Uncle Ivan's huge wings. He slammed the door.

Locating the healing spell, he crouched beside Ian and recited it. Ian's wound healed immediately, his intestines pulling themselves back inside with an elongated *ssssslllurrrrp!* The slit closed up. Ian remained motionless for a few seconds before opening his eyes.

"Go!" he croaked, the blood gone from his chin. "Go save the women. I'm too weak—"

"Wait," he said, a spell in the book having caught his eye. "I can send you across to them." He cast the sending spell and Ian vanished. Dan felt incredibly dizzy and fell back on his rump. He couldn't get up for almost two minutes. The two spells had taken a lot out of him.

The pages of *The Book* began to turn by an unseen hand. When they stopped, Dan looked down at another spell. "Float across," said his mother. "It takes less energy than sending. Hurry."

"Float across?" he asked dubiously. The warlock was out there.

The gaslights in the kitchen flickered back on. Bad things always happen when the lights come on, Dan realized. He quickly got to his feet and opened the door. Lighting flashed directly in front of him, the bolt as wide as he was and the color of blood. In the distance, he saw Uncle Ivan, his giant wings beating incessantly toward him. Behind him in the kitchen, silverware rattled in the drawers. Recalling the fork in Ian's forehead, Dan quickly recited the floating spell. A meat hook flew past him and fell to the darkness below.

Uncle Ivan charged him rapidly. Dan managed to sail by the creature's open maw by inches to land safely on the other side of the hotel. He slammed the door behind him.

He had initially thought the room across the gap was lit, but the source of the light came from behind a closed door. The illumination was brilliant, as if several searchlights on the other side were pointed at it.

Ian lay on the floor, groaning.

Dan looked around to find himself in a sitting room, akin to the main area of the room he and Kalendra had booked. Only Ian was here. Where was Kalendra? And everyone else? His mother had told him they were here.

"Are you okay?" he asked Ian.

"I should ask you that," Ian said, pointing at Dan's arm.

Dan moved his arm and craned his neck to see a fork jutting from his flesh. "I don't even feel that," he exclaimed incredulously. He pulled it out and winced, blood flowing freely down his arm. Choosing not to weaken himself further, he decided not to cast the healing spell on himself.

"Let me," Ian said, getting to his feet. "Let me heal you as you have healed me."

Dan shrugged, but intense pain was starting to grip him. The instant Ian finished the spell, Dan felt better and Ian had collapsed on the couch, exhausted.

Murmurs emanated from the next room accompanied by the sounds of footsteps and the moving of objects. Shadows could be seen under the door, moving back and forth as if several people were engaged in some activity. Dan wished it was Kalendra and Sarah and Celia, but he knew it wasn't. Unless he wanted to go back across the gap and face Uncle Ivan, there was no other way out of the room.

He opened *The Book* and the ball of light reappeared, shining down on the ghost banishing spell. Meanwhile, the murmurs became louder, the words almost distinct, but not quite. The voices were male. The sounds of footsteps increased, as did the sounds of objects moving. Something heavy dragged across the floor. Chairs scooted. A door squeaked quickly open then slammed shut. A man groaned, as if in pain.

"We've got to go that way," Dan said dubiously.

"Go," Ian told him. "I'll be okay here. Take care of them in there. Clear the path."

Dan nodded and caught a flash of fabric at the edge of his vision, the hem of a dress. It swooshed up and down, vanishing by the closed door.

"All right," Dan muttered through clenched teeth. "Here I go."

He gripped the ice-cold doorknob and wrenched the door open.

Men in white coats stood over prone men in blue and gray uniforms. Blood was splattered everywhere, on clothing, furniture, walls, floor, ceiling. A man in white drenched with red snapped a man's broken leg into place and the man screamed. Behind him, another man was sawing off an arm as the victim's jaw worked against a rolled up shirt, his face a grotesque grimace of pain.

The man with the saw abruptly halted his task to look directly at Dan. Dan took an involuntary step back and noticed everyone in the room was gazing intently at him, even though the sounds of a Civil War-era surgeon's ward continued.

The 'doctor' with the saw lifted his bloody instrument and pointed it at Dan. "You!" he rasped, his voice loud and reverberating. *"You!"*

Dan's limbs were rendered immobile. He couldn't think, couldn't remember the banishing spell. He was scared to death. He wanted to turn and flee, but his legs wouldn't obey.

A soldier with a severed leg lifted his removed limb and brandished it like a club. He stood perfectly balanced on one leg, taking short hops in Dan's direction as blood dripped from his stump.

Other men started toward Dan, carrying various severed limbs or sharp implements. All men were very solid, very real. Dan felt they could do him very serious harm. A scalpel sailed by his face, imbedding itself in the doorframe.

The Book nearly fell from his grasp, but he held on to. Suddenly, he recalled the banishing spell.

The ghosts vanished, but the lights remained lit.

"Run!" Ian rasped, lurching into the room past Dan.

Dan followed, the pain in his arm suddenly starting to throb. He and Ian were nearly to the door when the ghosts reappeared. There was a gunshot followed by several more. Dan and Ian hurried through the door and slammed it behind them.

Breathing heavily, they hurried away from the door, should any bullets or other objects come through.

The room they now found themselves in was a walk-in closet, crammed full of old dress jackets and evening gowns. On each side of the closet, above the clothing, was a lit gas lamp.

Dan stopped to catch his breath, clasping *The Book* with

one hand. "I don't hear anything behind us," he gasped. "I think they're gone. Man, I have to rest."

"We have to keep going," Ian insisted. "This room is not safe. We must go out the other side before—"

A woman faded into view, her back to them. She had long, brown hair and wore a green velvet gown. She didn't move. She seemed to be staring at the opposite door.

"Go away!" Dan cried, feeling nauseous and light-headed. He couldn't seem to catch his breath. "I'm sick of all this crap! Leave us alone!"

The apparition turned slowly, as if rotating upon a pedestal. Dan cried out in alarm. Ian was too shocked to make a sound.

Kalendra. She smiled sadly at Dan then vanished. The gaslights winked out.

"They got her," Dan whispered, suddenly feeling hopeless. "They fucking *got* her."

What was the point of this exercise? he silently demanded, wanting something to hit. With Kalendra gone, why bother trying to escape? Why not just give Uncle Ivan his book and end it all right now? Without Kalendra, what was the point of living? He didn't want to live anymore. He was tired of losing every woman he'd ever loved. He wanted to curl up into a ball and wait for the inevitable. He didn't care if he got out of the hotel alive now; he had nothing waiting for him outside.

"Come on," Ian urged. "It's safe now." He grabbed Dan by the wounded arm and pulled him to the door.

"I don't care anymore," Dan whimpered as he was whisked forward. "I don't care if your stupid uncle gets *The Book*. Just let him kill me now and get it over with."

Just as Ian reached for the doorknob, it moved out of reach.

Dan's sister Sarah stood on the other side, knob in hand. "I thought I heard you guys in here," she said with a crooked smile. "What's going on? I heard yelling."

"I just saw Kalendra's ghost," Dan muttered, his eyes on the floor.

"Um, I don't think so," Sarah replied, glancing over her

shoulder. "She's out in the hall. At least, she was two minutes ago."

Dan looked sharply at his sister then bolted past her, toward the location she had specified. Once he reached it, however, he was alone. "Where is she?" he demanded, his voice echoing in the darkness. "I don't see her. Kalendra? Where are you?"

"She was here a second ago, I swear it," said Sarah, walking to meet him. "And I swear there was a hall here, too."

The hall was now a spacious ballroom, complete with chandeliers and red velvet drapery. It was utterly dark.

"Then it was her ghost," Dan moaned. He needed to sit down and did so, on the hardwood floor.

"My uncle is keeping us from staying together so we can't escape," Ian told Dan and Sarah as he approached.

"No, he's keeping us from staying together by *killing* us," Dan retorted angrily, his face red in the blackness. "Celia's probably dead, too. There's just the three of us left, now."

Sarah shook her head. "Nope, Kalendra's not dead, Dan. I just know it." She paused. "What do you mean we're the only three left?"

Dan glanced toward where he'd heard Ian's voice and saw him, his eyes having adjusted to the dark. Ian looked away.

"I saw Eb's ghost, sis," Dan said in a gentle, sad tone. "He directed me away from danger then disappeared."

Sarah looked disbelievingly at her brother and then turned away, her hand going to her face.

"Submit is okay, though," Ian said, hoping to lighten the mood. "I sent her back to the real world."

"You can do that?" Sarah asked, tears streaming down her cheeks. "Why don't you do that for all of us?"

"It's too draining for me," he explained. "I don't have the strength to cast it again right now. Dan can cast it, but I recommend he do it only once. After we find Kalendra and Celia."

Sarah turned to her brother. "You can cast it?"

Dan sighed and smiled wanly. "Mom told me we're Druids on Dad's side of the family."

Sarah laughed and sniffed and wiped her eyes on her sleeve. "Somehow, that doesn't surprise me. Nothing does anymore." She lowered her gaze. "Dan, did you really see Eb?"

Dan nodded sadly. "I saw him clearly. I saw Kalendra clearly, too."

"It could have been a trick," Sarah countered. "The warlock could be trying a new way to get at us, destroy our morale."

"I'm not so sure," Ian put in. "The ghosts were definitely real."

"Wait a second," Dan said. "I just thought of something. When the lights are out, nothing bad really happens. When the lights are on, all hell breaks loose. The lights were on when I saw Kalendra. Not when I saw Eb, though, unfortunately," he added with a frown.   "Then the ghost of Kalendra could have been fake," Ian said. "I was wondering where that green dress came from."

"She would be wearing what she died in, wouldn't she?" Dan asked, his hopes rising. "Kalendra could still be alive."

"Ghosts can wear whatever they want," Ian pointed out. "She could have had a favorite green dress none of us knew about."

"Well, that sounds probable, but I don't think so," Dan said with renewed resolve. "The lights were on when I saw Kalendra. It's gotta be a trick."

"Dan," Sarah said, appearing deep in thought. "If Dad's side of the family are Druids, does that mean all of their descendents are Druids, too? I mean, do we all have powers we don't know about?"

"Mom told me *I* did," Dan replied. "And she said dad did, too, though he didn't know it."

"Then that means *I* can cast spells, too. The three of us together should be able to defeat one warlock." She paused. "Shouldn't we?"

"Possibly," a dubious Ian replied.

"If we all attack together, I think we could," Sarah said.

Dan looked at his sister. "You don't believe that Eb is gone, do you?"

She shook her head and reached out. "Give me that book."

Immediately, the chandeliers lit. The one hanging over Ian came loose and fell, striking him on the back of the head, knocking him on his face. Crystalline glass shattered, sliding like ice across the wooden ballroom floor. Ian didn't move.

Dan crouched beside him. "I think he's dead," he said. "I don't feel a pulse."

He turned his neck sharply at the sound of horse hooves galloping across polished wooden planks. The sound echoed loudly throughout the ballroom as the mounted soldier slowly became visible. He possessed a saber that hung loosely from his belt, but did not possess a head. Rider and horse started directly for Dan and Sarah.

"Run!" Dan cried, leaping for the nearest exit. He found himself in the dark hallway again, Sarah breathing heavily beside him. She had slammed the door to the ballroom shut. All was quiet.

13.

"That was close," Sarah said just before the gaslights came on.
She and Dan hurried across the hall and through the door.
The room beyond was dark. Sarah leaned against the door and
thumbed through The Book. "We need to find a way to stop all
this crap."

The Book suddenly slammed shut and, despite her best
efforts, wouldn't open. She tried and tried to pry the pages
apart, but she may as well have been trying to pry open a single
block of wood

"I can't open it," she cried in frustration.

Her mother appeared, only visible from the neck up. "You
are not a Druid, Sarah."

"Mom!" Sarah gasped.

"I have kept a secret from you all these years, Sarah,"
mother said then paused. "Your father isn't who you think." She
paused again, her eyes darting to the side then down. "I had an
affair. No one knew about it, including your—my husband. You
are my illicit lover's daughter. Therefore, you are not descended
from Druids and you can't cast any of the spells in that book."

"Mom!" Sarah gasped again. "An affair?" She was shocked
and disappointed at the same time.

The disembodied head of Mom bobbed a little. "Luckily,
your father resembled my husband enough that nothing about
your features really stood out as being too different from the
rest of the family. It also worked out that you resembled me
more than him. No suspicions were ever aroused." She appeared
wistful as she spoke.

Abruptly, her eyes turned to Dan. "You're the only one

who can cast the spell that will end all of this. We can try to lead you out, but we are constantly thwarted. You might not make it out of here."

"We?"

Ghostly faces appeared around Sarah and Dan, including the face of Aunt Audrey, other family members and friends from the past. One of the faces belonged to Ebenezer.

Sarah gasped. "Eb, no!"

Ebenezer nodded gravely. "It was far past my time, dearest Sarah. I should have passed on centuries ago. Please tell Submit farewell for me."

Sarah nodded, unable to hold back the tears. "But now you're a ghost! Trapped here forever."

He shook his head. "Once you are safe, I will move on. All of us will."

Another face floated nearby. "Tell Submit farewell for me, also. Tell her I love her, and Dan," he added. "I do not hate you. We were all trapped together in unusual circumstances. I hope you can forgive me for any negative feelings I may have caused you. I forgive you." Jesse's face vanished.

"He forgives *me?*" Dan blurted. "I didn't do anything."

"Kalendra and Celia are near," his mother informed him. "You will find them soon. Oh, and Dan? I apologize for being such an annoyance to you when I was alive. I had no idea what sort of mother I was. I apologize profusely for even causing you any discomfort."

"Oh, Ma, don't say that," he replied, feeling ashamed. "Sure, you bugged me from time to time, but that's what mothers do."

She smiled. "Good luck, son. You, too, Sarah." Her face vanished.

Sarah erupted into tears and Dan comforted her, taking *The Book* from her. "I'm really sorry, Sis," he said. "Sorry for everything."

"It's not your fault!" she cried. "It's not your fault I'm not who I thought I was! Not your fault the only man I ever truly loved—" A tremendous sob prevented her from finishing her sentence.

Dan held his weeping sister, feeling the floorboards vibrate. The familiar booming of the warlock's wings reverberated throughout the building, making Dan suddenly intensely angry.

"Leave us alone!" he screamed at the grinning animal skull in the window. "We have done nothing to deserve any of this. Just because one of our distant ancestors burned the face of your ancestor doesn't mean we should be treated this way. We have lives, too, you know. We don't deserve this."

Uncle Ivan continued to stare at Dan with its empty eye sockets and Dan suddenly realized that what he'd just said was a lie. He had done something to anger the warlock. He had destroyed Dinah's bones.

"Anything we may have done," he added in an even tone, "was only to protect ourselves from you. If you let us go, we will never bother you again."

The warlock stared at him for a long moment then opened its great maw to emit a high-pitched shriek.

"You bastard!" Sarah screamed. She took off her shoe and threw it at the window. The glass shattered. The warlock shrieked again as a powerful, hot wind burst through the now open window.

"Nice going," Dan shouted and ran with Sarah out of the room only to find themselves back in the hallway. Celia was there.

"Omigod, you guys, what happened?" she asked, frightened and alarmed.

"He is there," Dan replied. "Where's Kalendra?"

"We got separated," Celia replied anxiously. "She fell through the floor back there. I was looking for a way down, but—"

"We just came from that room," Sarah exclaimed, her face streaked with tears, her eyes red-rimmed.

"Yeah," Dan said, "but in case you haven't noticed, the rooms change a lot. We need to find the one Kalendra's in and if we stay together, we should be okay. The warlock seems to be thwarted by *The Book*. We should be okay as long as we have it."

Dan led Sarah and Celia into the room. It was dark and humid and was yet another room that greatly resembled the room Dan and Kalendra had shared back before the hotel started to metamorphose. A broken lamp lay on the floor in the exact spot Dan had left it. He thought of Kalendra knocking him down onto it and ached for her. Movement startled him, but it was only Sarah. She put her hand on his shoulder.

"This was our room," he whispered. "Kalendra?" he called. "Are you in here?"

No answer. Dan turned toward the bedroom door and opened it. Beneath the covers on the bed was a lump in the shape of a woman. The lights were off.

"Kalendra," he murmured.

The lump under the blankets moved. Kalendra's head poked out. "Dan?" she asked sleepily, rubbing her eyes. "What's going on? I thought you were still in bed."

Dan walked swiftly to her and sat on the edge of the bed, feeling for her hand underneath the covers. "Oh, Kalendra. I thought you might be dead."

She gaped at him. "Why would you think that? I've only been sleeping." She laughed then became serious, sensing his mood. "What's going on? Did something happen?"

Dan blinked back at her. He was unable to comprehend that what she was saying was true. "You were here the whole time?" he asked. "Just sleeping?" He looked over to Sarah and Celia but they weren't there. The door was closed. "Then it wasn't really you?"

Kalendra cocked her head to the side and regarded him curiously. "You're really upset, aren't you?" She caressed his arm and shoulder. "What a terrible dream you must have had."

He looked down at himself to see that he was wearing only his underwear. Had it been a dream after all? It had certainly seemed real. It would sure be a relief if it had all been a long, horrible dream. It also meant that Jesse and Ebenezer and Ian were all still alive. He couldn't help but grin then proceed to tell her everything. He remembered it all, in vivid detail. By the time he was done, he realized he was under the covers with her.

"You poor thing," she said with a mock pout, taking his hand to put to her naked breast. She kissed him and ran her hand down the length of his arm. She stopped when she felt *The Book* tucked under it.

"Huh," he said, looking at it. "I thought Ian still had this. Odd."

"Yeah, you don't need that for what we're about to do," Kalendra said, pressing her body to his. "Why don't you just put that down, hmm?" She stuck her tongue in his ear.

Dan continued to stare at it, trying to figure out why he'd been sleeping with it. The last time he'd been awake seemed so long ago. Had he been looking at it when he fell asleep? Had Ian brought it by? He honestly couldn't remember.

"Are you listening to me, Dan?" Kalendra asked. "You can put the book away. You'll need both of your hands free for what we're about to do." She gently tried to pry his fingers from around *The Book's* spine and Dan reflexively yanked it away, holding it from her grasp.

"Kalendra," he asked, looking sternly into her eyes. "I have no problem putting it down, but you seem overly concerned about it."

She laughed and her eyes sparkled. "Dan, I'm not *concerned*. I just want you to put the book down so we can make love. Is that such a strange request? Don't you trust me?" She leaned her lips forward as if to kiss him again, but he reared back.

"Trust you?" he asked. "What does me putting this book down have to do with me trusting you?"

Her eyes became forlorn, worried. "Dan, that must have been a really awful dream you had. You're not acting like yourself. You need to relax and I know just the thing. Roll over for a back rub." She pushed him with her hands.

"Wait, stop," he said. "Stop it! I don't want a back rub!"

"Come on, Dan, it'll help you relax. Just drop that book and roll over—"

He scurried out of bed and backed away. "Get away from me!"

"Dan!" Kalendra cried. "What's wrong with you? I thought you loved me!"

"I never said that," he said then started chanting the spell he had memorized.

"*NOOOOOOOO!*" Kalendra screamed just before she vanished.

The thumping of the warlock's wings returned, the shadow of the beast imprinted on the drapes. The drapes parted to reveal the horrific skull face.

Dan turned and ran from the bedroom, only to see the Civil War-era hospital again. He slammed the door shut and the skull shrieked. Dan yanked open the bathroom door and encountered a darkened dining room. The fact that there were no gaslights burning meant nothing now; he could no longer trust the darkness. The last episode with "Kalendra" had shattered that illusion. He ran through the room, knocking over chairs and drinking glasses.

Something moved in the darkness ahead.

"Dan!"

Dan changed direction, pushing over a table, dumping its contents on the advancing figure. He kicked over two chairs to block the figure's path and frantically looked for another exit.

"Dan, it's Ian!"

"No, you're not," Dan said, shoving more furniture aside as he hurried across the room. "You're dead. Just like Kalendra."

"I'm not dead," Ian replied. "I was just unconscious."

"No!" Dan shouted hurrying toward the exit.

"Well, if you think I'm a ghost, cast the spell!"

"I will not," Dan said, out of breath. He turned toward Ian, but didn't look at him. "You're just trying to wear me out, keep me casting spells until I have no energy left over to cast the portal spell."

As he spoke the last word, he backed into a chair, toppling

with it to the floor. A very strong hand reached down to help him up. He yanked his hand back.

"Get away from me."

"Dan, stop it," Ian demanded. "It really is me. Ian!" Ian slapped him with his artificial hand.

Dan felt like his neck would snap. His head rang and the room was even darker than before. Little white spots shot across his vision and lingered in the periphery. Slowly, his vision cleared and he gazed at Ian's face.

"It can't be you," he whispered. "You're dead. I felt your pulse."

"You probably felt the wrong arm," Ian replied with a lopsided grin. "There would be no pulse in this one."

Dan nodded weakly then sobbed. "Kalendra is dead."

"I don't think so," Ian said, pulling Dan toward the exit. "Let's go get her and the girls and get the hell out of here." He opened the door and Dan balked.

"I can't go in there," he cried in anguish.

The room was the kitchen from his first house; the house he'd shared with his wife Amy and his son Billy. Memories of the murders came crashing down on him like water from a dam. His feet froze to the floor and not even Ian with his electronic arm could budge him.

"We haven't got much time," Ian said through gritted teeth. "We must find the girls and get out of here."

A child's scream made the hair on Dan's body stand up. He felt a chill in his bowels that radiated outward, followed by an internal, spreading warmth. The thought that he might have pissed his pants didn't occur to him.

He didn't want to continue, but knew he must. One foot moved slowly in front of the other until he was in the kitchen. As in the dreams, and as in parts of the hotel, he felt like he was walking in syrup. He could only shuffle his feet, could not lift them.

He exited the kitchen and walked to the living room. Rounding the corner, he could see the television, its image stilled, a low hum emanating from it. He knew what he was about to see.

"Please, not this time," he whispered, willing it to be so. "Please, let him be okay this time. Please! I can't bear it. Not again! Not after all this time—"

His fear mounted as the pool of blood came into view. All he needed was see Billy's motionless bloody foot to start screaming and screaming until it felt like his throat would split open and burst into flames.

He finally was able to turn away, but what lay before him was just as terrifying. He turned toward the staircase.

Dan ascended the carpeted steps slowly, the blood that swiftly beaded down the walls squishing beneath his shoes, flowing over the tops of them. It felt like he was walking on raw meat that had been pounded into a fine pulpy hamburger.

The door to the bedroom was also dripping with crimson ichor. Part of him thought it ridiculous there was so much. It seemed like a farfetched horror movie, the blood gratuitous, unneeded.

His hand slipped on the knob, but he was able to draw it open. Inside, Amy lay motionless in bed. He noticed nothing unusual until he stepped closer. Her body had been cut in half at the stomach, the two halves then squished back together.

Dan looked up to see the skeletal creature that was Uncle Ivan standing on the other side of the bed, blood dripping from his bony claws and teeth. Dan stared hard at the warlock and gritted his teeth. "Get out of my house!"

The skull's jaw unhinged and emitted a high-pitched shriek. A strong gust of air blew Dan back against the door, slamming it shut.

"Your kind must die!" Uncle Ivan screamed, the voice full of hatred. The sound was like an inferno swallowing an entire metropolis, the shrieks of the burning inhabitants swirling around him like a hot whirlwind of agony. Uncle Ivan flapped his gigantic wings and flew slowly toward Dan.

Everything that led up to this point became suddenly clear

to Dan as he watched the malevolent being head toward him. *His kind.*

Druids.

What his mother told him reentered his brain like a ricocheting bullet. He was a descendant of the ancient Druids. This creature, this warlock, was the descendent of the enemy of the Druids, the descendent of beings that stood for everything the Druids were against. The curse had nothing to do with Dinah's burnt face at all. The ancestors of Dinah were trying to utterly wipe all traces of the Druids off the face of the Earth, no matter what the cost. It was the single compulsion that drove their entire existence.

There's only one problem with that, Dan realized. If all the Druids were destroyed, there would be no reason for the warlock's kind to exist. They would cease to be. *The Book of Curses* had had nothing at all to do with his safety.

As far as Dan knew, he was the only Druid left.

He laughed weakly, sputtering. Every bone and fiber and organ in his body screamed with pain after striking the door. "You can't kill me," he breathed, eyes locked onto the empty cavernous sockets of Uncle Ivan's skull. "You will kill yourself if you kill me."

The warlock shrieked again, but did not come any closer.

"Well? Are you going to do it?" Dan asked, struggling to get to his feet, his back sliding up the surface of the door. "You gonna commit suicide, you rotten, murderous, wife-killing, son-stabbing piece of *shit?*"

A split second after Dan spoke there was a blinding flash. A myriad of colors followed in quick succession before everything went black.

Consciousness slowly returned. Dan lay sprawled on the floor of an empty hotel room, a band of sunlight across his face. His eyes flickered open as someone called his name.

"Kalendra!" he whispered, getting up hurriedly to get to the door.

She whirled around when she heard him. "Dan!" she cried and threw herself into his arms.

"Omigod, Kalendra," he gasped, holding her tight. "Omigod! I thought I'd lost you!"

"I know," she sniffed, her tears dampening his shoulder. "Sarah told me. I know who it was you saw, Dan, but it wasn't me—"

"You did it, brother," Sarah exclaimed, running up to them. Ian and Celia followed at a slower pace behind her. "You finally got us the fuck out of that hell hole. You're such a Druid!" She joined in on the hug.

Dan laughed and sniffed his tears. "I really didn't do anything except challenge him," he said. "I called his bluff. Thank God it worked!"

"He's still around," Ian commented. "But I don't think he'll be bothering you again. Not for a while."

"Hey, I just realized," Dan said. "Ian, you're one of my enemies, too!"

Ian laughed then sobered. "What are you talking about?"

Dan grinned. "Nothing."

"Is Submit around here someplace?" asked Sarah. "Ian, I thought you said you sent her through that portal thing of yours."

"She's probably in her room," he said. "Or maybe—" He went to the window at the end of the hall and hesitated only a moment before parting the curtains. Three stories below stood Submit. She looked up and waved at Ian.

"Dan," Kalendra whispered, pulling him away from the others. "I was trying to tell you something earlier."

"What is it?" he asked, concerned.

"That person you saw, the one you thought was me—" She took a shallow breath. "Well, that was my sister. She wasn't my twin, but everyone thought she was. She was killed in a freak car explosion when she was seventeen. She was not a nice person, Dan, not at all. We fought all the time and she would steal my stuff and ruin it. She even slandered me in front of my first boyfriend, just because she didn't want me to have him." She paused to expel a shallow breath. "I'm not at all surprised that she ended up here, working for the warlock. She died in a green dress."

Dan laughed. "An evil twin, huh? How cliché. Well, I guess she won't be bothering us again, will she?"

"I hope not," Kalendra replied with a grin. "So, what do we do now? Should we go back to Boston?"

"And live next door to the warlock? I don't think so. We should talk it over with the others first, but I think we should continue west. Start a new life in a place that doesn't remind us of our old one. Perhaps Arizona."

"Why Arizona?" she asked.

He shrugged. "I've always wanted to see the Grand Canyon. I hear it's breathtaking."

Kalendra laughed. "After what we've been through, I don't think I want to experience anything breathtaking again!"

Dan laughed. "We could just sit around and watch television instead..."

"Now you're talking."

Nov 3, 1997—Oct 26, 2001

38517957R00188

Made in the USA
Middletown, DE
09 March 2019